THE
HYPERSPACE
TRAP

Professionally Published Books by Christopher G. Nuttall

Angel in the Whirlwind

The Oncoming Storm

Falcone Strike

Cursed Command

Desperate Fire

ELSEWHEN PRESS

The Royal Sorceress

The Royal Sorceress (Book I)

The Great Game (Book II)

Necropolis (Book III)

Sons of Liberty (Book IV)

Bookworm

Bookworm

Bookworm II: The Very Ugly Duckling

Bookworm III: The Best Laid Plans

Bookworm IV: Full Circle

Inverse Shadows

Sufficiently Advanced Technology

Stand-Alone

A Life Less Ordinary

The Mind's Eye

TWILIGHT TIMES BOOKS

Schooled in Magic

Schooled in Magic (Book I)

Lessons in Etiquette (Book II)

Study in Slaughter (Book III)

Work Experience (Book IV)

The School of Hard Knocks (Book V)

Love's Labor's Won (Book VI)

Trial By Fire (Book VII)

Wedding Hells (Book VIII)

Infinite Regress (Book IX)

Past Tense (Book X)

The Sergeant's Apprentice (Book XI)

Fists of Justice (Book XII)

The Decline and Fall of the Galactic Empire

Barbarians at the Gates (Book I)

The Shadow of Cincinnatus (Book II)

The Barbarian Bride (Book III)

HENCHMEN PRESS

First Strike

THE
HYPERSPACE
TRAP

CHRISTOPHER G.
NUTTALL

Published by 47North, Seattle

www.apub.com

Amazon, the Amazon logo, and 47North are trademarks of Amazon.com, Inc., or its affiliates.

ISBN-13: 9781503949096
ISBN-10: 1503949095

Cover design by Mike Heath | Magnus Creative

Printed in the United States of America

AUTHOR'S NOTE

The Hyperspace Trap is set in the Angel in the Whirlwind universe—and takes place after *Desperate Fire*—but is designed to be completely stand-alone. Kat Falcone and her comrades will return in the next story arc.

PROLOGUE

It was hard, so hard, to think.

The drain was all-consuming, tearing at his mind as if *they* wanted to pluck his thoughts from his brain-sac. Tash could barely extend his eyes, let alone rise and crawl forward on his tentacles. The deck felt odd beneath him, as if on the verge of coming apart. His eyesight was flickering and flaring, fading in and out of existence. He had to focus on each motion just to move . . . his body was betraying him. *They* were draining him too.

Focus, he told himself. His claws and tentacles lashed the deck, frantically, as he struggled to get to his feet. It should have hurt, but it didn't. His tentacles were numb. *Get to Engineering.*

His mind blurred, just for a second. Or was it longer? He didn't know. Perhaps he was dead and in the seven hells, or perhaps he'd died . . . perhaps they'd *all* died. Maybe the others had suffered enough to be released from their sins, to go onwards . . . he wanted to believe it, even though he knew it was nonsense. He was a rationalist. The seven hells didn't exist. *They* existed. He knew *they* existed, but they were not demons. They were . . .

He stumbled over a body and nearly fell. For a moment, he thought the body had reached out to grab him before realizing that his tentacles were spasming. Shame gripped him as he stumbled backward, an embarrassment that tore at his soul. He hadn't lost control of himself like that since he'd been a child, dozens of solar cycles ago. Oddly, the shame gave him an opportunity to focus his mind.

He had to go on.

The body lay there, mocking him. An egg-layer, drained of life. Her tentacles were splayed out, suggesting utter hopelessness. Tash forced himself to look away and crawl onwards despite the looming sense that it was futile. The ship had been trapped long enough for him to lose all hope that they would escape. *They* were watching. He could hear them mocking him as he crawled . . .

. . . or was it his imagination? It was hard to be sure.

Time blurred as he moved down the long corridor. The ship was silent, the emergency alarms gone. He'd darted along the corridors until he knew them as well as he knew his own nest, but now they'd taken on a nightmarish aspect, as if he were walking through a dream. The lights rose to blinding levels, then faded until they were so dim he could barely see. Bodies were everywhere, lying where they'd fallen. The entire crew could be dead.

It felt like years before he finally made it to the engineering compartment, decades before he forced the hatch open and crawled inside. Other bodies lay on the deck, unmoving. Tash flinched, despite himself, as his eyes found the engineer. The egg-bearer had been strong in life, respected and feared by the crew. Now his body seemed shrunken, his tentacles spread out in silent supplication. It hadn't saved him from *them*.

Tash's mind ached. He thought he heard someone *howling*. The sound tore at him as he moved over to the nearest console and pressed his tentacles against the reader. There was a long pause, just long enough for him to start fearing that the power was too far gone for the neural link to engage, and then the system opened up to him. A status report blinked into his mind, confirming his worst fears. There were no other survivors. He was alone.

The howling grew louder, mocking him. His thoughts threatened to fragment, either into *their* domain or utter madness. Or both . . . he couldn't tell if *they* were real or nothing more than a figment of his imagination. Others had heard *them*, hadn't they? He couldn't swear to it. The madness that had gripped the crew, as soon as they found themselves in this cursed place, made it impossible to trust his own mind. He had no idea why he'd survived.

He forced his mind into the computers. They opened, recognizing his authority as the last surviving crewman. It would have been a heady thought—command at his age—if the situation hadn't been so serious. Tash knew it would not be long before he too was dead.

The computers felt sluggish, the neural link popping up constant warnings. A power glitch while his mind was within the computers might kill him, or worse. Tash ignored his fears as he surveyed the command network, tracking the power drain. It was growing worse. The computers, thrown back on their own resources, were trying to compensate, but the maneuver wasn't helping. *They* were draining the ship dry.

That's what they wanted, he told himself. His thoughts were starting to fade. He blanked out, then awoke. *They wanted the power.*

He probed the network, locating the antimatter storage pods. They glimmered in his mind like poisonous jewels, a harsh reminder that their power came with a price. If the containment fields failed, the entire ship would be vaporized. *They* would be pleased. He forced his mind onwards, isolating the storage pods from the rest of the power grid. It might just be enough to safeguard their cargo from *them*. There was certainly no evidence that *they* could just reach out and *take* the antimatter.

The howling grew even louder. Tash flicked his tentacles in satisfaction, disengaging his mind from the computers and slumping to the deck. *They* were angry. His vision was starting to blur again, the world fading to darkness . . . this time, he doubted he'd recover. His entire body felt sluggish, unable to move. He would join the rest of his comrades in death, but . . . but at least he'd spited *them*. His mind remained his own. *They* couldn't touch him. Whatever *they* were, *they* couldn't touch him . . .

. . . and then the darkness reached out and swallowed him.

CHAPTER ONE

"Well," Captain Paul VanGundy said, "that was a good dinner."

"The cooks are practicing," Commander Jeanette Haverford said. "They'll be passing anything that's less than perfect to us, once we get under way."

"Compared to marine rations," Security Chief Raymond Slater offered dryly, "this is heaven."

Paul smiled in genuine amusement. The three of them sat together in his stateroom, finishing a dinner that had been put together by *Supreme*'s cooks. Paul couldn't have named half the dishes at the table before he'd left the Royal Tyre Navy and signed up with the Cavendish Corporation, but he had to admit they were very good. The dinner hadn't been something he could have afforded off duty. Going to a ten-star restaurant cost as much as he made in a month.

They made an odd trio, he thought as he surveyed his two subordinates. Jeanette radiated calm authority, her short brown hair framing a dark face that betrayed no hint of vulnerability. Her clothes were designed to diminish her form, hiding the shape of her body behind a tailored blue uniform. Beside her, Raymond Slater looked very much like the spark plug he'd been before leaving the Marine Corps. His rugged face had a certain unkempt charm—he'd been ordered to have his scars removed when he'd signed up with the corporation—but he'd never win any beauty awards. Instead, he looked like a man no one would want to mess with. *That*, Paul knew, was a very good thing.

Paul himself looked older than his sixty years. Older men commonly had themselves rejuvenated until they looked to be in their midtwenties, but the corporation's image experts had insisted that Paul had to look wise and dignified. They'd designed him a look—graying hair, gray beard, blue eyes, strong jaw—and convinced his superiors that he should wear it. Paul had a feeling he'd been lucky to keep his muscle tone. The captain of a cruise liner couldn't go around looking like a bodybuilder, let alone someone who had their muscles touched up every month in a bodyshop.

Blasted image experts, he thought sourly. It wasn't something he'd had to endure in the military. They'd been far more concerned with beating back the Theocracy and carrying the war to Ahura Mazda. *They'll put style over substance any day.*

He cleared his throat. "We'll probably be glad to get ration bars when we're under way," he said. "Right now, we have different problems."

"Yes, sir," Jeanette said.

Paul tapped a switch. A holographic image of *Supreme* materialized in front of them, hovering over the table. As always, the giant cruise liner, a kilometer from prow to stern, took his breath away. The vessel had none of the crude bluntness that characterized military starships, none of the brutal efficiency he recalled from the navy. Instead, there was an understated elegance that made him smile. *Supreme* was no warship. She was practically a work of art.

He leaned forward, drinking in her lines. The starship was a flattened cylinder, studded with giant portholes . . . practically *windows*. Two green blisters, each one easily larger than a naval destroyer, marked the upper gardens; a third blister, blue instead of green, marked the swimming pool. The bridge, a blister on top of the massive starship, made him smile. It looked good, but he knew it was horrendously vulnerable. A military starship could *not* have such a vital installation in an exposed position.

"We've all written our final reports," he said slowly. He felt nervous, even though he was damned if he'd admit it to anyone. "Is there anything you *didn't* bother to mention?"

"I believe I listed all of my concerns," Jeanette said. "The crew is well trained, but far too many of them are inexperienced. I'd prefer to swap some of them out with more experienced crewers."

"HQ says there aren't many experienced personnel to spare," Paul said. He ground his teeth in frustration. The military drawdown was well under way, despite the chaos pervading the Ahura Mazda Sector. There was no reason the corporation couldn't hire a few hundred experienced spacers. "We're getting some newcomers, but . . ."

He shrugged expressively. A cruise liner was not a military starship. He had to keep reminding himself of that. There were just too many differences in everything from purpose to training for him to rest comfortably. The months he'd spent learning the ropes had convinced him that all newcomers required training before they could take up posts on a cruise liner. Perversely, someone who hadn't been in the military had less to unlearn.

And most of the hosting staff don't need military experience, he thought. *They're civilians through and through.*

Jeanette pointed at the hologram. "I've got the crew working their way through a series of drills with all the usual actors, sir," she said. "However . . . there's a difference between training and reality. Most of our junior crewers will still be on probation until the end of the voyage."

"Some of them didn't quite take the training seriously," Slater rumbled. "It wasn't real."

Paul nodded. He'd graduated from the naval academy at Piker's Peak—and Slater had passed through boot camp—but Jeanette and the other crewmen had gone through their own intensive training course.

The operations crew were as well trained as many of their naval counterparts, while the host crews had gone through a whole series of simulations and exercises. Indeed, they had endured a surprising amount of cross-training. He could put half the host crew to work on operations if necessary.

He'd been astonished, upon being given access to the corporation's files, to discover just how much trouble civilian crews had to handle. Passengers—some of whom were extremely wealthy and powerful—just didn't know how to behave. The crew had to cope with everything from drunken fights to outright misbehavior, behavior that would have earned a military officer a spell in the brig followed by a dishonorable discharge. He'd watched some of the exercises and come away with a new sense of appreciation for his crew. It took a strong person to remain calm in the face of massive provocation.

"They'll lose that attitude soon enough," Paul predicted. The trainers might not have been able to chew out recruits—he'd never met anyone who could outshout a drill instructor—but they had other ways to deal with wayward students. "Real life will see to that."

"Yes, sir," Jeanette said. She held out a datachip. "Overall, our reaction times to everything from medical emergency to shipboard crisis are well within acceptable parameters. I've ensured that all cross-trained personnel are ready to switch jobs at a moment's notice, just in case we need them."

"Quite right," Paul said. The Royal Navy had taught him that disaster could strike at any moment. *Supreme* might not have had to worry about going into battle, but she did have her own challenges. "Are there any staffing problems I should keep in mind?"

"I don't believe there's anything significant," Jeanette said. Her lips twisted. "Some of our guests *will* be bringing their own bodyguards and servants, of course. They may need some additional training of their own."

Paul kept his face expressionless. "Make sure they get it," he said. "And make sure we have a record of their training. We may need to put them to use somewhere else."

Slater snorted. "Their employers will hate that, sir."

"If we need to borrow their servants, we'll be past caring," Paul countered. *Supreme* had over two hundred crewmen with medical training. A crisis they couldn't handle would pose a severe threat to the entire ship. "Check their firearms licenses too, just in case."

"Yes, sir," Slater said.

Paul looked up at the display for a long moment. "Do you see any security threats?"

Slater took a moment to gather his thoughts. "Internally, no. The basic vetting process didn't turn up any red flags. A handful of yellow flags—a few passengers were marked down for bad behavior on earlier cruises—but nothing else. I don't see any reason to worry about our passengers."

"One of them could be an impostor," Jeanette commented.

"Perhaps." Slater snorted again. "We'll be running basic security checks, of course."

"Of course," Paul agreed.

He kept his thoughts to himself. The corporation ran security checks on everyone, from its senior officers and starship crews to third-class passengers. He'd glimpsed enough of the vetting process when he was being hired to know that it was almost as comprehensive as anything demanded by the government's intelligence services. Passengers who might be a problem would be required to spend the trip in a stasis pod, if they were allowed to board at all. Far more likely, they would simply be denied passage. Lower-grade passenger starships were plying the spacelanes, after all.

"I've also run my security teams through a series of exercises," Slater continued. "If necessary, we can isolate compartments or entire decks and then clear them by force. We'll be as gentle as possible, of course, but by that point we might be far beyond any *gentle* solution. At worst, we can dump knockout gas into any compartment and then pick up the sleeping beauties."

"Which will probably get us all fired," Jeanette said. "Out the nearest airlock . . ."

"Probably," Slater said. "I should remind you, at this point, that we do not have comprehensive surveillance of the entire ship."

"The passengers would pitch a fit," Jeanette commented.

"Yes," Paul said.

He shook his head in wry amusement. *Supreme* wasn't just a passenger ship. Travel on her was an *experience*. She had everything from a casino to a brothel, just to make sure that her passengers traveled in luxury. Even the third-class passengers, the ones who'd be crammed into tiny cabins on the lower decks, would have access to the entertainments. The thought of being recorded, even for security purposes, would horrify them. They'd be worried about blackmail or worse.

"I am aware of the issues," Slater said stiffly. "It is also my duty to make you aware of the implications. We may not be able to react to a crisis until it is already out of hand."

"I know," Paul said.

Slater didn't look mollified. "A number of our passengers are also prime targets for kidnap," he added. "While I have no reason to suspect internal trouble, I have to warn you that there *is* a prospect of being intercepted. I'd be much happier if we had an escort."

"So would I," Paul admitted. *Supreme* wasn't defenseless, but she was no warship. A destroyer could take her out if a captain had the nerve to close with the target. "I believe that Corporate is still trying to organize one."

"There have been no reports of pirate activity," Jeanette added. "We're not going to fly through the Ahura Mazda Sector."

"A good thing too," Slater said. He looked at Paul. "Captain, I strongly advise you to ensure that we stay well away from any hyperspace storms. Who knows what they're hiding?"

"We will," Paul said. Pirates were a threat. The Royal Navy had driven them out of Commonwealth space before the war, but they'd been on the rise when the navy's attention had been diverted. It might take some time for the navy to resume its patrol routes and drive the pirates back out. "If nothing else, we can probably outrun any pirate ship."

"I wouldn't take that for granted," Slater said. "Robert Cavendish alone is worth a stupid amount of money."

Paul fought hard to keep his face expressionless. Robert Cavendish was one of the richest men on Tyre, perhaps the richest. Only the king and a handful of other aristocrats came close. He should have been a duke, and would have been if he hadn't been more interested in building his empire. *And* he was Paul's ultimate boss. It was a recipe for trouble.

"True," Jeanette agreed. She shot Paul a sympathetic look. "Doesn't he have his own personal yacht?"

"I imagine so," Paul said. Cavendish was rich enough to own and operate a starship the size of a superdreadnought. Hell, he didn't really need one. A smaller ship could offer as much comfort as a full-sized liner without having to employ over a thousand crewmen. "But there's nothing to be gained by debating it."

"No, sir," Slater agreed. "I suspect there is more to this cruise than simply traveling from place to place."

Jeanette gave him an odd look. "What makes you say that?"

"I read the passenger manifest," Slater said. "It isn't just Robert Cavendish. It's his close family and a number of cronies and hangers-on. *And* a number of smaller businessmen and nobility, enough to occupy an entire deck. I suspect they're preparing a private planning session in between spending most of their time in the casino."

"Joy," Paul said. He rubbed his forehead. Slater was right. *Supreme* would be a magnet for pirates, insurgents, and everyone else with an axe to grind. He'd even raised the issue with Corporate, only to be told to shut up and soldier. Reading between the lines, he'd come to the conclusion that Corporate wasn't happy either. "Keep a close eye on the situation."

"Yes, sir," Slater said.

He took control of the display, adjusting the hologram to show off the weapons emplacements. Paul couldn't help feeling that *Supreme*, for all of her elegance, looked faintly ridiculous. Her design was just too inefficient. But then a full-sized superdreadnought wouldn't win any beauty awards. All that mattered was smashing her enemies as quickly as possible before they smashed her.

"The weaponry crews are still drilling on the latest tactical simulations," Slater said. "I believe we could hold our own long enough to escape a pirate ship. A regular military ship, however, would eat us for breakfast. Far better to avoid contact."

"And we will," Paul said. "They'll have some problems intercepting us."

"Unless they're trailing us at a safe distance," Slater said. He flipped the display to show a star chart. "And they *do* know where we're going."

Paul exchanged glances with Jeanette. He had some leeway—he could alter course, once they were in hyperspace—but he had to take *Supreme* to her listed destinations. He couldn't refuse to go to a particular world unless he had a *very* good reason. Corporate would be very annoyed with him, even if he could prove the world was under siege. If there was one thing corporations and the military had in common, there was always someone flying a desk who thought he knew better than the man on the spot.

"If we can get an escort, we'll be safe," he said firmly. "And if we can't, we'll fly an evasive course. No one is expecting us to arrive on a precise date."

Jeanette smiled. "How lucky for us."

"Quite," Paul agreed.

He glanced from Jeanette to Slater. "Are there any other matters that need to be addressed?"

Jeanette smiled mischievously. "Mr. Cavendish and his family will be expecting a formal welcome, sir," she said. "You'll have to dress up for it."

Paul tried not to groan. The regular uniform was bad enough—whoever had designed their attire clearly didn't have to wear them—but the dress uniforms were worse. His outfit was covered in so much gold braid that he looked like an admiral from a comic opera navy, while the midshipmen and stewards resembled military captains and commanders. He'd never been able to shake the feeling that people were laughing at him behind his back whenever he wore the dress uniform.

"Select a handful of junior officers and stewards to join the reception," he said. The order was mean of him, but he might as well spread the misery around. Besides, he'd never met Robert Cavendish. The man might take offense if only a couple of people greeted him. "How many others do I have to meet and greet?"

Jeanette made a show of consulting her terminal, as if she didn't already have the information locked away in her mind. "There are three other passengers of sufficient status to warrant a personal greeting from you," she said. "It would also build goodwill if you were to spend some time in each of the lounges."

"I'm sure it would," Paul said. He told himself not to take it too personally. Kissing hands and buttocks—hopefully metaphorically—was part of his job now. Besides, he *did* have a good crew. Jeanette could handle anything that might reasonably be expected to happen while they were in orbit. "Is there anything else?"

"Mr. Cavendish might demand your personal attention, sir," Slater said. "We had a number of high-ranking guests on *Capricorn*.

They seemed to believe that Captain Hammond was their personal attendant."

"And he *does* pay the bills," Paul said. "Do we have anything on his previous conduct?"

"No," Jeanette said. She met his eyes. "In his case, sir, that might be meaningless."

Paul nodded stiffly. The host crews kept files on their guests, files that were shared with other host crews. He'd heard they were even shared between corporations, although it was technically against corporate guidelines. An unpleasant passenger would discover that his reputation had preceded him.

And a good passenger would have the same experience, he mused. It wasn't something he wanted to discourage. *But in a better way.*

"It might," he agreed.

He pressed his hands together, tiredly. It was probably a good sign. He'd seen some of the files. A number of people, powerful people, had been marked as everything from being lousy tippers to having wandering hands. Robert Cavendish wouldn't have been spared.

"I think we can hope for the best," he said. "Are there any other matters?"

"We may run out of special ultra-expensive Scotch," Jeanette said. Logistics was her responsibility. "The shipment from Nova Scotia was delayed apparently."

Paul smiled. "Let's hope that's the worst problem we face," he said. "They'll have to drink *expensive* Scotch instead."

"Disaster," Slater said, deadpan. "The end of the world."

"I'm sure some of them will feel that way," Jeanette agreed.

CHAPTER TWO

"Wake up, you lazy bastard," a female voice said. "You're late!"

Junior Steward Matt Evans sat upright, confused. Where *was* he? He'd been out late last night on Downunder Station, barely managing to catch the departing shuttle back to *Supreme*. His head felt as though someone had opened his skull and crammed it with cotton. Several minutes passed before he remembered that he'd made it back to the ship and his bunk before collapsing into blessed sleep. He'd been lucky. A few minutes longer in the pleasure bars would probably have cost him his career.

"Fuck," he muttered. "What *time* is it?"

"Oh-eight-thirty," Carla France said. She was stripping off her night-clothes as she spoke. "The others are already on their way to breakfast."

"Fuck," Matt said again. He'd stuffed a handful of ration bars in his locker, a precaution he'd learned from one of the old hands, but they tasted of cardboard. Not that it really mattered, he told himself as he reached for his water bottle. There was no time to go for a proper breakfast before he was expected on duty. He would just have to make do. "I need a shower."

"And a shave," Carla told him bluntly. "What were you *drinking* last night?"

Matt couldn't remember. The stewards had been granted leave following an endless series of emergency drills, which had started to blur together in his mind, and he'd spent the day in the pleasure bars. Wine, women, and song . . . more of the wine than anything else, if his pounding head could be trusted. Carla passed him a sober-up without comment. Matt took the tab and pressed it against his neck, wishing she'd thought to wake him earlier. But he'd only have felt worse.

Carla turned and headed for the washroom. Matt watched her go, silently admiring her nude body. Like him, she'd been to the bodyshop. Corporate insisted on a specific image for its stewards, and neither of them was in any position to object. Carla was twenty-two, the same age as Matt, but her long brown hair, heart-shaped face, and hourglass figure made her look nineteen. Matt felt his cock stir and flushed, embarrassed. Corporate also had very strict rules against stewards winding up in bed together, which had been drilled into him after he'd signed up for the job.

Down boy, he told himself. He wasn't used to casual nudity. His homeworld had been a place where men and women were expected to cover themselves from head to toe. The old hands, those who had sailed on *Supreme* and other interstellar cruise liners, had sworn the younger hands would get used to it, but Matt found that hard to believe. It wasn't easy to separate the tall tales from the bullshit. One of the very old hands had claimed, with a straight face, that he'd had a threesome with two very rich girls on *Queen of Space*. Matt hadn't believed a word, although he did have to admit the story sounded more convincing than the incident with the female swimming team . . .

He stood and opened his locker, silently blessing his superior for insisting that he have everything sorted out before he left the ship. The ration bars were where he'd left them, their brightly colored wrappings silently mocking him. Rumor had it that decent-tasting ration bars existed, but he'd never met them. He unwrapped one and ate it slowly, taking a sip of water with each bite to help it go down. The bar tasted worse than cardboard.

Carla stepped out of the washroom. Matt caught a glimpse of her breasts and looked away, hastily. He didn't have time to get distracted. He kept his eyes on the unoccupied bunks as Carla moved past him, then hurried into the washroom himself. It was a tiny compartment, barely large enough for a single man. He'd been told that the space had been deliberately kept small to limit the chances for hanky-panky, but he suspected a more reasonable explanation was that the corporation wanted to save money. Outfitting Gold Deck alone had probably cost more than the GPP of a stage-two colony world.

The corporation has money to burn, he told himself as he stepped into the shower and turned on the water. Thankfully the cruise liner didn't have to ration water. He'd been told that military starships *did* ration water, although he didn't believe it. There was no reason why water couldn't be recycled or, if worse came to worst, harvested from a passing comet. *They can afford a few minor luxuries.*

He wanted to spend longer in the shower, but he knew he didn't have the time. The drying field tickled over his skin as soon as he turned off the water, flicking droplets all over the compartment. Matt couldn't recall who was on cleaning duty this week—the stewards were expected to keep their own compartments as neat and tidy as they could—but he hoped it wasn't him. He'd been too busy over the last few weeks to keep track of the rota.

"Hurry," Carla snapped from outside. She banged the washroom door. "You do *not* want to be late."

Matt nodded and stepped out of the compartment, as naked as the day he was born. Carla paid no attention to him, for which he was grateful. She was already dressed and applying makeup, as if she needed it. He reached for his uniform and donned it, slowly and carefully. Senior Steward Dominic Falcon wouldn't be pleased if his shirt wasn't tucked in and his jacket brushed clean.

"Don't forget your cap," Carla reminded him. "We're on greeting duty this morning, remember?"

"Yeah," Matt said. He reached for his cap and placed it on his head. "Just give me a moment to check myself."

He inspected himself in the mirror, feeling faintly out of place in his own body. The bodyshop hadn't changed *that* much, but they'd done enough to make him feel as though a stranger was looking back at him. His short blond hair, blue eyes, smooth face, and muscular body were, according to the focus groups, just right for a young male steward. Matt wasn't so sure—the body was a little *too* perfect—but Corporate wasn't interested in his opinions. If the passengers wanted to be surrounded by beautiful people, male and female, the corporation would ensure that was what they got.

The white uniform clung to him, practically glowing under the light. He had enough gold braid to pass for a military officer or member of the command crew, even though he was a mere steward. He had little prospect of climbing any further than senior steward, he'd been warned. Matt didn't mind too much, if he were honest. A few years on *Supreme* would be enough to set him up for life, particularly if he saved his wages or made sure to get a good reference from the corporation. There wasn't *that* much demand for trained stewards outside the cruise liners, but he could take his skills to a hotel on Tyre if he wished.

"Looking good," Carla said. She inspected him. "You've got muscles on your muscles."

Matt did his best to ignore her. Whoever had designed the uniforms was a sadist. Comfort had been sacrificed for sex appeal. Neither of them was walking around naked, but they didn't have to. A person with a little imagination could easily fill in the blanks.

We're lucky we're all reasonably handsome, he told himself. *And we get to keep the look afterwards, if we like it.*

He smiled. Toying with truth, the old sweats had claimed that Corporate had wanted to make sure all the male stewards were as ugly as sin, just so they couldn't compete with the passengers when it came to attracting female attention. Or male attention, if the passengers swung that way. Matt was tempted to believe them. Corporate had inflicted other indignities on its stewards and the rest of the crew. At times he felt that his wages weren't worth having to bow and scrape in front of people who obviously didn't give a damn.

"You too," he said as he reached for his wristcom and put it on. The device bleeped a moment later as it interfaced with his implants, then linked automatically to the shipboard datanet. He'd been warned, in no uncertain terms, not to leave his quarters without it. The wristcom wasn't just for communicating; it gave him access to much of the ship. "Shall we go?"

Carla nodded and opened the hatch. Matt took one last look at the compartment—their superiors might decide to inspect the space at any moment—and then followed her down the starship's bare corridor. The passengers . . . the guests, he reminded himself . . . never saw this part of the ship, unsurprisingly. Corporate had decided to save money by ensuring that crew passageways were left barren. The only decor was the corporate logo, visible on every hatch. Matt rolled his eyes in amused disbelief. There was no reason to believe that anyone had forgotten just who had designed and built the giant ship. Matt didn't think there was anything, from the fittings in the staterooms to the gifts in the shop, that hadn't come from the Cavendish Corporation.

A hatch hissed open in front of them, revealing the briefing room. Senior Steward Dominic Falcon was standing at the front, looking down at a datapad. He'd been luckier than his younger subordinates, Matt thought. The bodyshops had given him a more dignified appearance— gray hair, kindly eyes, commanding face—even though they had also made him look remarkably frail. Falcon couldn't be much older than Matt himself, but he looked as if a strong gust of wind would blow him over. He'd been sailing on cruise liners for the last decade.

Matt followed Carla over to join the other stewards, nodding politely to a few of his friends and bunkmates. He hadn't found much time to get to know his new crewmates as they'd spent the last two months either drilling or sleeping, but none seemed to be bad apples. Besides, they'd all been warned to keep their disagreements to themselves. No one would give a damn if a steward spent some time in the brig and then was unceremoniously dismissed when the starship reached the next port of call.

There was little chatter. Matt surveyed the chamber, feeling a chill running down his spine. The stewards didn't look precisely identical—that would have been too creepy, even for Corporate—but they all had the same general appearance. Boyish good looks for the men, blatant sex appeal for the women. Focus groups insisted that they looked attractive to everyone, whatever their orientation. The old sweats hadn't said much about that, on the record, but off the record, the new stewards had had quite a few warnings. It was astonishing what some guests wanted, apparently. And very few of the guests were used to hearing anyone say no.

Even the third-class passengers spent more on this cruise than I can earn in a year, Matt reminded himself. *Corporate considers them more important than me.*

Falcon cleared his throat as soon as the last couple of stewards hurried into the compartment. Matt allowed himself a sigh of relief. Traditionally, the unwanted jobs went to the latecomers . . . even though they'd *technically* arrived on time. The last thing he wanted was to get noticed. Meet-and-greet duty was bad, but there were worse tasks.

"Three minor updates," Falcon said. He scowled at the newcomers as if they were personally to blame. "First, two of the casino staffers failed to return to the ship. They have not yet been located, but I've been informed that I may have to provide two replacements. This is not a good thing."

Matt kept his face expressionless. The casino staff were technically separate from the rest of the crew for reasons he was sure made sense to someone in Corporate, but they'd had some cross-training. He didn't envy whoever was picked to work in the casino. The tips were high, but so was the prospect of an unlucky gambler turning violent. He wasn't looking forward to having to remove an unruly guest. The exercises had clearly indicated that he could do everything right and *still* get blamed. Corporate would sooner dismiss a steward, hopefully with a decent severance package, than fight a lawsuit in the courts. The bad publicity would override any sense of obligation to their employees.

"Second, the remaining cabins have been sold and the updated guest manifest has been uploaded," Falcon continued. "Take a moment to inspect it. If you have any concerns, please feel free to mention them to me. As always, all reports will be treated in strict confidence."

A flicker of disquiet seemed to echo through the compartment. Matt wasn't surprised. This was his first cruise, but he'd heard the rumors. In theory, reports were private; in practice, the process didn't always work that way. A prospective guest who'd been blacklisted or put on a watch list might sue, particularly if no evidence beyond rumor was presented that he'd been reported for anything. Matt didn't think that Falcon would set out to betray his subordinates—the man was fussy, but decent—yet he also knew that Corporate might not give the senior steward any choice.

"Third, the roster for Gold, Silver, and Bronze Decks has been updated," Falcon added. Two dozen wristcoms bleeped in unison as the roster was downloaded into their tiny brains. "If you have any problems, make sure you let me know by the end of gamma shift. I'll publish the final roster tomorrow."

Matt nodded. Only a brave steward would ask to be transferred. He rather doubted anyone would, unless it was their last voyage. Falcon had had to balance a whole list of priorities when putting the roster together. The best interests of the stewards were right at the bottom. He made a mental note to check the roster as soon as he could, although he knew his diligence hardly mattered. Whatever came his way . . . well, he'd have to suck it up. He wasn't wealthy enough to afford his own cabin on a cruise liner.

Falcon spoke briefly, assigning duty slots. The latecomers found themselves heading to the casino, not entirely to Matt's surprise. Others were assigned to supervise cleaning crews and inspect cabins, make-work as much as anything else. Matt forced himself to memorize who went where, just in case he needed to find any of his crewmates in a hurry. Stewards weren't encouraged to socialize outside their own little circles.

"Steve, Danielle, Matt, Carla . . . you're still assigned to meet-and-greet," Falcon finished. "It will be the captain in charge, not I. Reread your protocol briefings; then report to the main shuttlebay for 0930. Do *not* fuck up."

Matt swallowed. "Yes, sir."

The others didn't look any happier, he thought, which didn't bode well. Carla and Steve had served on other liners before transferring to *Supreme*. They'd presumably gone through the duty already. He exchanged a worried glance with Danielle, who was as green as Matt himself, and then looked down at his wristcom. He'd already reviewed the protocol, but he would make sure to do so again before reporting to the shuttlebay. Fucking up in front of the captain might just get him a one-way ticket out of an unsecured airlock. VanGundy had practically boundless authority on his ship.

Although Corporate would probably be pissed if he upset the guests, Matt thought as Falcon continued to rattle off assignments. *That would get him fired . . .*

He pushed the thought aside. Falcon had raised his voice.

"The next few days are going to be chaotic," the senior steward informed them. "Those of you who have been on other liners will know this already, but it will be worse here. You'll find yourselves worked to the bone. Please rest assured that things *will* settle down—a little—once we open the vortex and get under way. We'll have time to catch up then."

And go over everything we did wrong, Matt thought. The exercises had been bad. Falcon and the other supervisors, all the way up to the XO herself, had made sure everything that could go wrong *did* go wrong. *Some of us might even be marked down for doing our duty at the wrong time.*

"Report to your assigned stations," Falcon concluded. "And make sure you have a moment to check the duty roster."

Carla snagged Matt as he headed for the hatch. "You did read the alert note, didn't you?"

"Of course," Matt said. Steve and Danielle fell in beside them. "Prostrate ourselves in front of them, never taking our heads off the deck until they walk past—"

Steve elbowed him. "These aren't regular guests," he said. "They're our great . . . uh . . . *something* bosses. A hair out of place could get us in real trouble."

"They might tip well," Carla added. "But . . . better to be very careful."

Matt groaned. "Should I try to take a sick day?"

"Only if you want to spend the next few days in Sickbay," Steve said. "Dr. Mackey isn't kind to malingerers."

"You'd have to take something poisonous to make it convincing," Carla added. "You really don't want a demerit on your record now." She made an unconvincing sickly face. "But we're nothing more than ants to them," she said. "I doubt they'll pay any real attention to us."

"Oh," Matt said, "I hope you're right."

CHAPTER THREE

"You can't keep hiding here forever, My Lady," Marie said. "We're on our approach to *Supreme* now."

Angela Cavendish knew Marie was right, but she tried to ignore her anyway. The family yacht was tiny compared to *Supreme*, yet it was still large enough to provide dozens of nooks and crannies she could use as hiding places . . . if, of course, the person hunting for her didn't have access to the ship's datanet. Her governess didn't have to waste her time searching all three decks. Marie had probably just asked one of the crew. The tiny compartment Angela had found wasn't enough to hide her from the onboard security systems.

"It's good enough," she said. She leaned into the miniature space, wondering if her governess would try to drag her out. "Father doesn't need me along, does he?"

"He expects you to disembark with him, My Lady," Marie said briskly. As always, she sounded commanding. She could *afford* to sound commanding. Angela didn't pay her wages. "And I have orders to prepare you."

"Consider them countermanded," Angela said. "Just leave me alone."

"That's not an option, My Lady," Marie said. Her respectful tone didn't disguise her irritation. "Your mother is expecting you too."

Angela rolled her eyes. "I'm sure she won't mind if I'm late," she lied. "Go back and tell her that you couldn't find me."

Marie's face darkened. "She will know that to be a lie, My Lady," she said primly. "I will not tell her anything of the sort."

"Hah," Angela said. It wasn't Marie's fault that Angela's mother wanted her. Angela *knew* it wasn't Marie's fault. And yet she wanted to blame the older woman anyway. The governess had been a permanent presence in her life, silently watching in cold disapproval since Angela had turned nine. She had no doubt that Marie spied on her for her parents. The woman didn't have a choice. "Mother is too busy telling the servants what to do."

"Come with me, My Lady," Marie said. "Please."

Angela sighed. Marie wouldn't lay a finger on her. She was sure of that. But she *would* go and tattle to Angela's parents, neither of whom would be pleased. Her mother would be upset Angela was daring to think for herself, while her father would be annoyed that Angela was defying him. There were times, too many times, when Angela thought her father had made a mistake in marrying her mother. The age gap between them made it hard for him to empathize with his wife, let alone his daughter.

And he thinks I should do as I am told, she thought.

She stood and inched carefully out of the compartment, feeling the deck quivering under her bare feet. Marie eyed Angela disapprovingly until she slipped her feet into her sandals. Then the governess turned and walked down the corridor. Angela followed, nodding politely to a pair of crewmen. They both pretended not to see her. She wasn't too surprised, not really. Her father was their ultimate boss. A word from him could have them both begging in the gutter.

I should have gone into the navy, she thought.

She had considered it, years ago. There was no shortage of aristocrats who'd gone into the navy. One of them, Kat Falcone, had practically won the war by herself. But Angela's father had vetoed it the single time she'd mentioned the possibility. His influence would have been more than enough to keep her out of the service if she'd abandoned her family and tried to sign up anyway. And besides, she couldn't leave her sister at her mother's mercy. The poor girl was famous, and their mother had never stopped trying to take advantage of the spotlight.

Marie sniffed as they reached Angela's mother's stateroom. A pair of maids stood outside, their faces so artfully expressionless that Angela knew they were pissed. She didn't blame them either. Her mother was a trial and a half. The maids, with duties consisting of everything from hairdressing to cleaning up, were paid well over the going rate, but her mother had problems keeping servants for long. Marie was probably the longest-serving person in her employ.

The hatch hissed open. Angela stood upright and walked forward, feeling like a convict going to her execution. The stateroom was vast yet crammed with boxes and bags. Her mother had brought everything she simply couldn't live without, apparently. Angela rather thought she'd brought her entire wardrobe for the journey. Cold logic insisted that such a feat was impossible—her mother would require a bulk freighter to carry her full collection of couture garments—but it was hard to believe otherwise.

"Angela," her mother said, "where have you been?"

Angela sucked in her breath. Halle Cavendish was looming over Nancy Cavendish, carefully brushing Nancy's hair. Judging by the expression on the twelve-year-old girl's face, she was enjoying the moment about as much as an unexpected math exam. The look she shot her sister—*Get me out of here!*—made that clear.

"I was busy," Angela said sullenly. Her mother was busy. Perhaps she'd let it rest at that. And maybe pigs would fly. "What can I do for you?"

"Get undressed and change into a dress," her mother ordered. "Marie can do your hair once you're ready."

"I don't have to wear a dress," Angela insisted. She jabbed a finger at her shirt. "This is more than enough."

Her mother gave her a sharp look. "You are *not* going to a weekend retreat where you're alone with your family," she said. "This is a cruise liner *heaving* with the great and the good."

Angela bit down on a sarcastic remark about never being alone when she was with her family. Her mother wouldn't see the funny side. Besides, Nancy was starting to fidget under her mother's ministrations. By the time Halle was finished, her youngest child would look like an inhuman china doll. Angela had come to suspect a long time ago that their mother saw her daughters more as animated dolls than living beings with wills of their own.

"Fine," she said shortly. If nothing else, she'd distract her mother from Nancy. "I'll get into my glad rags. And I'll take them off as soon as we're in our cabins."

She strode into the next compartment, silently urging Marie to remain behind. The governess didn't, of course. Angela promised herself, again, that she'd sack Marie as soon as she inherited her father's corporation. The few moments when Marie had actually been helpful didn't make up for the near-complete lack of privacy or the grim awareness that Angela's parents would be made aware of any misdeeds as soon as she committed them.

"I'll get your dress ready," Marie said. "Do you want a quick shower?"

The nasty part of Angela's mind was tempted to answer yes. It would waste time, time they didn't have. Her mother could hardly object if her eldest daughter did as she was told, could she? But the gesture would also annoy her father, and her father had too many other problems to worry about. He might ground her until she grew into her majority.

Although three months in a stateroom would be enough, Angela thought moodily. The servants would do what her father told them. If he grounded her, they'd enforce his wishes. *And I can't stay in the cabin for a day without going mad.*

She stripped off her shirt and shorts, then inspected herself in the mirror. The genetic engineering spliced into her family's DNA had done wonders, as always. She was physically perfect: long strawberry-blonde hair spilling down her back, bright blue eyes, a pale and utterly unblemished face . . . the bodyshops could turn anyone into a goddess if the subject had the money, but Angela had never set foot in a bodyshop in her life. She'd had long blonde hair before Kat Falcone made it fashionable. The other modifications seemed almost unnecessary. And yet she knew they might be more vital, in the long run, than anything purely cosmetic.

Marie fussed around her, holding up a long emerald dress that looked like something out of a fairy tale. Angela groaned, inwardly, but made no attempt to resist as her governess draped the garment over her body. She'd actually *enjoyed* the fashions during the war, when high society had done its level best to indicate that it too was suffering. The dresses might have been made from expensive materials, but they'd been simple . . . now, she had a frock with too many frills to feel comfortable. And the bodice made her look and feel ridiculous.

"You look divine, My Lady," Marie said.

"Bah," Angela said. Marie was paid to lie.

She tensed as Marie fixed her hair, tying it back into a long ponytail that hung down to the small of her back. The governess seemed to think that Angela was nothing more than a doll too, just like her mother. Angela gritted her teeth as her hair was pulled, a handful of individual locks plucked out and discarded. Long hair was a nuisance, she'd come to realize, but she couldn't have it cut. Her mother would march her straight down to the family's private bodyshop and have her tresses regrown instantly.

She'd probably consider it an excuse to visit for herself, Angela thought nastily. *She already spends too long in the bodyshops as it is.*

"Good enough, for the moment," Marie said. She held a mirror up behind Angela's head. "It will do."

Angela glared, knowing that Marie would see the expression in the mirror. "When I am an adult, all *my* parties will be held without a dress code."

Marie looked unimpressed. "And how will you know who to talk to, who to ignore, and who to cut dead?"

"I won't," Angela said. "That's the point."

She sighed as Marie continued to fuss around her. The Cavendish family gave at least one ball every month, but she'd never liked them. Her father and a few of his business partners—or cronies—sneaked off as soon as they decently could, while her mother and the other society madams gathered in small clusters to look down on the rest of the crowd. Angela had been able to slip off too when she'd been a child, but now . . . the only good thing about accompanying her parents on the cruise was that she wouldn't be expected to help host parties. Unless her parents still managed to have a party anyway . . .

The hatch opened. Her mother stepped into the compartment. "Are you ready?"

"Yes, My Lady," Marie said.

Angela looked at her mother, who gazed back at her evenly. Halle Cavendish could easily pass for Angela's sister rather than her mother. Angela had often wondered if her mother had simply cloned herself, even though it would have destroyed her marriage. The aristocracy took bloodlines seriously. Mothers were expected to carry their children to term rather than use an exowomb, but it was hard for Angela to see anything of her father in her features. Perhaps Robert Cavendish had used the bodyshops too when he was younger. Or perhaps Angela had inherited his brains rather than his looks. She loved her mother, most of the time, but Halle Cavendish wasn't the brightest bulb on the tree.

"Good," her mother said finally. A low quiver ran through the spacecraft. "Your father will be pleased."

Angela rolled her eyes again, even though she knew it made her look petulant. Her father wouldn't give a damn what she wore. He was more interested in steering the family corporation through the postwar economic slump than anything else. *Anyone* could have a beautiful and charming daughter—the bodyshops and finishing schools would see to that—but very few men possessed his wealth and power. The ducal title had been passed to his younger brother, but the lack of noble appellation was meaningless. Robert Cavendish could buy half the aristocrats in the House of Lords, and everyone knew it.

"I'm sure, Mum," she said. "When can we get this over with?"

Her mother's expression tightened. She should be called *Mother*, not *Mum*. Mum was distinctly lower-class. Angela wondered if her mother would choose to make a fuss even though they didn't have time. Somehow, marrying well, very well, hadn't been enough to make Halle Cavendish comfortable. She responded sharply to any challenge to her position, real or imagined.

"We will be docking in two minutes," her mother said. "And then we will disembark."

She turned and marched out of the compartment. Angela followed, feeling tired. Nancy stood by the door, wearing a green dress of her own. Angela met her younger sister's eyes, feeling a flicker of pity. Once she had bitterly resented Nancy's fame—Nancy hadn't done anything to *deserve* to be famous—but no longer. They had too many reasons to stick together.

"Very good," their mother said. "Two peas in a pod."

Nancy shot Angela a mischievous look as soon as their mother looked away. Angela winked back at her. There would be opportunities for fun on *Supreme*, she was sure, even though they'd have to be careful. The cruise liner was a controlled environment, just like the estate. Exciting, but also boring. None of the riffraff would be allowed to board. And yet . . . there were adventure decks, elaborate swimming pools, casinos, and plenty of other things to do. Marie wouldn't be able to watch her constantly. She could sneak away if she tried. Perhaps she could find a crewman who would show her the engine rooms and other isolated sections of the ship.

And I'll have to make sure that Nancy gets a chance to slip away too, she told herself. *She deserves some freedom.*

The hatch hissed open. Halle hurried out, carefully not glancing at the three manservants waiting outside. They would start unloading as soon as the ship docked, transferring their luggage to *Supreme*. Angela had wondered why they couldn't keep the yacht with them, but she'd kept that question to herself, not wanting to give her father ideas. Going on the cruise was bad enough, but being stuck on the yacht for three months would be far worse. The bulkheads would start to feel oppressive within the week.

A dull thump echoed through the ship. They'd docked.

"We'll be the first ones on the ship," Nancy said. She walked next to Angela, her voice very quiet. "Won't we?"

Their mother glanced back at them. "That is as it should be," she said. "We do *own* the ship."

You don't *own the ship*, Angela thought nastily.

It was bitchy, but she didn't care. Their mother wasn't exactly a commoner, but she wasn't particularly wealthy or well connected. Her family must have offered something *really* valuable to convince the Cavendish clan that she'd be a good match for Robert. Angela would inherit the family wealth, not her mother.

Or would she? Her father had given her a trust fund, de rigueur among the aristocracy, but he hadn't ensured she had the proper training to manage one of the family businesses, let alone inherit the ducal title. Angela didn't really expect to inherit *that*, but she did expect something more than a trust fund.

Father refuses to discuss it with me, she thought as they reached the outer hatch. The gravity quivered, reminding her that the spacecraft had landed inside another, far vaster vessel, one easily large enough to pass for a carrier. It was bigger than the family mansion back on Tyre. *Maybe I just haven't reached my majority yet.*

The hatch was already open. Her father stood there, wearing a simple black suit, studying his wristwatch meaningfully. Beside him, a handful of his cronies gathered. Angela did her best to ignore them. They flattered her, when they bothered to take notice of her. She'd never met people quite so insincere in their praise and had no idea why her father tolerated them. Some of his cronies were clever, in their own way; others were just milksops and imbeciles with titles.

At least they'll keep him busy, she thought. If nothing else, the more brainless among the group would probably cause problems her father would have to solve. *And out of my hair.*

She took a breath, tasting the scent of a new-build starship. Someone had perfumed the air with the scent of green forests and pinecones, but it wasn't enough to hide the *real* smell. They were lucky that *Supreme* was new. The last liner she'd boarded had smelled of too many humans in too close proximity. She'd grown used to the scent within a day due to her genetic heritage, but her mother had bitched for days.

"You'll go straight to your cabin," her father said. His voice was firm. She had never dared to argue with that tone, not openly. "No detours along the way."

That was fine with her. Besides, he hadn't said anything about not leaving her cabin afterwards. Semantics, perhaps . . . it was all she had.

All she'd have to do was get rid of Marie long enough to escape, if she could.

"Yes, Father," she said.

Robert turned and strode through the hatch, his feet clanging on the stairway. Angela stepped out of the yacht behind her parents and saw the small welcoming committee wearing so much gold braid they practically glowed under the deck lamps. No doubt they were lining up to kiss her father's ass as much as possible . . .

She groaned. It was going to be a long, long day.

CHAPTER FOUR

Under ordinary circumstances, Captain Paul VanGundy would never have dreamed of allowing another starship, even a much smaller one, to land inside his ship like an oversized shuttlecraft. The force fields surrounding the main shuttlebay could contain the blast if a shuttle-craft happened to explode, but he doubted they could stand up to an entire *starship* exploding. And yet, Corporate had insisted. If Robert Cavendish wanted to land his space yacht inside the shuttlebay, he was to be allowed to do so.

He kept his face under tight control as the yacht slowly lowered itself to the deck, the tractor beams ready to catch the ship if the anti-gravs lost control. The craft was impressive, he admitted sourly. The designer had taken a corporate jet design and scaled it up, sacrificing efficiency for elegance. Almost a shame, he thought, that the utterly unnecessary wings hadn't been a little larger. If the yacht hadn't been able to fit into the shuttlebay, it could have docked at one of the airlocks like a normal logistics ship.

And the wings wouldn't keep her from falling out of the sky if the power failed, he thought morbidly. *She wouldn't be able to enter a planetary atmosphere without antigravs.*

The thought made him smile as the deck vibrated under his boots. In theory, *Supreme* could land on a planetary surface; in practice, getting the cruise liner back into space would be practically impossible. She was just too big. The scientists had talked about an expanding series of antigravity platforms, but such musings seemed pointless. Robert Cavendish's yacht was perhaps the largest thing that could realistically land on a planetary surface and take off again. Paul dreaded to think just how much she cost. Even full-sized military logistics shuttles were smaller.

He took one last look at the welcoming committee. Everyone was dressed to the nines, from the command crew to the stewards. The younger staffers looked nervous, although they were doing their best to hide it. Chances were they'd never meet anyone more important than Robert Cavendish and his family in their entire careers. King Hadrian wouldn't travel on a private cruise liner, and neither would many others at the ducal level. Paul silently hoped his younger officers would avoid any glaring mistakes during the voyage. He would defend them, if necessary, but Corporate might overrule him . . . if someone with enough influence brought pressure to bear on his superiors. It wasn't something he cared for . . .

You're not in the military now, buttercup, he told himself. *Suck it up.*

The hatch started to hiss open. A pair of deckhands hastily attached a mobile staircase to the yacht, then scurried away. Paul stood to attention, silently cursing his stiff uniform as Robert Cavendish appeared at the top of the stairs. He looked older than Paul had expected, even though he'd known that Cavendish was in his seventies. Vanity didn't seem to be one of his vices, Paul decided. He could have had his age frozen at twenty-five, or whatever the current fashion was, but he didn't seem to have bothered.

Cavendish was a tall man, walking as though the only thing keeping him upright was sheer determination. His face was lined, suggesting great age; it was hard to believe, somehow, that the younger woman next to him was his wife. Paul knew, of course, that marriages among the aristocracy were arranged, but he still found it odd that *anyone* had considered such a marriage acceptable. Not that it mattered. Halle Cavendish would have been of legal age when the contract was signed.

And she's in her forties, Paul reminded himself. The file had made that clear. Halle Cavendish was mother to two children. *She only looks twenty-five.*

The two girls definitely looked their age, he decided. Angela Cavendish was nineteen, according to her file, but the ill-hidden petulance on her face made her look younger. Nancy, the *famous* Nancy, was just growing into her teens. Due to their resemblance, it would have been easy to believe that the two girls were twins if they hadn't been seven years apart. But then, Nancy's embryo could easily have been placed in stasis. Nancy, thankfully, didn't look as sulky as her older sister or some of the other kids he'd seen on long voyages. He hoped that would last the entire trip.

"Mr. Cavendish, sir," Paul said. He saluted, smartly. The protocol briefing had stated that *Robert* Cavendish didn't have a title, but given his wealth, that was essentially meaningless. "Welcome onboard."

"Thank you, Captain," Cavendish said. He had an aristocratic accent, but one that sounded oddly dulled. Paul suspected that Cavendish spent as little time as possible with the other aristocrats. Everyone knew the best and most motivated engineers came from the commons. "It is a pleasure to come aboard."

Paul nodded. "Please allow me to introduce a selection of my crew," he said. "Commander Jeanette Haverford . . ."

He went through the entire roster, although he had the feeling that Cavendish wasn't paying close attention. Paul wasn't too surprised. Cavendish's implants would have a complete list of crew, both operational and hospitality. He'd have no trouble looking up a crewmember if he wanted to know a name or issue a report to someone's superiors. Indeed, Paul had the feeling that Cavendish was already bored.

Corporate had insisted on the formal welcome, but they might have made a mistake.

Not that they will admit it, Paul thought.

"I thank you," Cavendish said as soon as Paul had finished. "Please have your officers escort my daughters to their staterooms."

Paul concealed his annoyance with an effort. He was the starship's captain, damn it. No one should speak to him as though he were a glorified errand boy. But he was only captain as long as his superiors allowed it. A word from Cavendish could see his career destroyed.

"Certainly, sir," he said. "Steward Evans, Steward France, escort Miss Cavendish and Miss Cavendish to their staterooms."

The stewards bowed hastily. "Yes, sir."

———

Matt hadn't found it easy to remain calm as the yacht lowered itself to the deck. He was no expert, but he was fairly sure that landing an entire space yacht in a shuttlebay was amazingly risky. He'd been given no end of lectures on avoiding risk, on not being a hero . . . after all, he hadn't joined the military. Any display of risk-taking would probably result in immediate dismissal, not promotion. And yet Robert Cavendish had been allowed to land his yacht in the shuttlebay. An unpardonable risk.

Cavendish hadn't impressed Matt when he'd made his slow way down the stairs. He hadn't crawled his way up from nothing, unlike some of Matt's heroes. Matt had reviewed his file and discovered that Cavendish had inherited his power and position . . . and would have had the title too if he'd wanted it. Success was easy, Matt felt, if one started with such an advantage. The wife hadn't struck him as very decent either. There hadn't been much on her in the files, but Carla had insisted that, reading between the lines, she was a social climber. Marrying Robert Cavendish had catapulted her right up into the rarefied heights of high society.

But her daughter . . . Matt had to force himself not to stare as *she* came into view. Angela Cavendish was gorgeous, gorgeous in a way one couldn't get from the bodyshops. She was beautiful, but it was more than *just* beauty. The slightly petulant expression on her face didn't detract from her sheer *presence*. She drew him in and caught him. It was all he could do to keep his eyes off her.

His mouth felt dry. It was hard, very hard, to acknowledge the captain's command.

"Yes, sir," he said. He looked at Angela, fighting to keep his expression under control. "Please, will you come with us?"

Angela seemed oddly amused. "Of course," she said. Even her voice was mesmerizing. "It will be our pleasure."

Matt felt nothing but relief as they walked out of the shuttlebay. He had no idea what Captain VanGundy, Robert Cavendish, and his escorts had to say to one another. He didn't care. His heart beat like a drum. He was silently glad Angela was behind him as they moved onwards, up towards Gold Deck. He would have stared if she'd been beside him.

"We have some luggage," Nancy said. "Will it be brought to us?"

"Yes, My Lady," Matt said. He could have kicked himself for practically forgetting Nancy Cavendish. She was famous . . . but she wasn't her older sister. "The staff will transport your belongings to your quarters."

After they search them, he added silently.

He had to smile at the absurd thought. Robert Cavendish wouldn't be planning to hijack *Supreme*. He practically owned the ship. Matt couldn't imagine any of his family trying to smuggle weapons onboard, but that meant nothing. His training had included a brief description of all the tricks smugglers had used, from stowing weapons in diplomatic pouches to convincing innocent civilians to carry sealed packets for them. Cavendish's family would make ideal unknowing mules. Who'd dare to look too closely at *their* bags?

Several answers occurred to him. He pushed them aside, sharply. Saying any of them out loud would be the end of his career.

"This is Gold Deck," he said as they reached a hatch, covered with the corporate logo in gold. "You cannot pass through this hatch without permission."

Angela spoke from behind him. "Is there a way to get permission?"

Matt blinked at the question. "If you purchased a stateroom on Gold Deck, you have automatic permission to visit the public areas of this section," he said. The hatch opened silently. "If you didn't, you require permission from someone who did."

"Or be a member of the crew," Nancy said. She stepped past Matt and into Gold Deck. "Or be a dab hand at fiddling with computers."

Matt had the uneasy sense he was being teased. "The datanet is very secure, My Lady," he assured them. "Only the captain has the codes necessary to rewrite the system."

"Nancy, behave," Angela said, sounding more amused than angry. "You can chat in our staterooms."

She turned her smile on Matt. "Which way?"

Matt had to look away. "This way, My Lady," he said. "They're right at the front."

He led the way down the corridor, wondering just how rich the two young women actually were. He wasn't sure their wealth could be actually measured without resorting to imaginary numbers, but it was evident. Gold Deck was staggeringly luxurious by any realistic standard, yet neither Angela nor Nancy seemed impressed. They ignored the sheer finery. Their eyes passed over paintings and statues worth more than what the entire crew earned in a year.

The aureate staterooms opened up in front of him. He stepped to one side, inviting the two women to walk into the compartment. Their antechamber was nearly ten times as spacious as his sleeping compartment, yet it was only the beginning. The stateroom included five large bedrooms for the family—he wondered wryly if Robert Cavendish and his wife slept apart—a private kitchen, a giant entertainment room, and sleeping quarters for the servants. A small army could have shared the stateroom without being too uncomfortable.

Nancy opened a door, not a hatch, and peered into one of the bedrooms. A moment later her face twisted with rage. "They think I'm a child!"

Her older sister laughed, not unkindly. "You *are* a child."

"I'm *twelve*," Nancy insisted. "I'm not a baby!"

Matt followed her gaze. The bedroom was pink, bright pink. A small pile of presents lay on the bed, orbited by balloons. A giant teddy bear, larger than Nancy herself, sat on the armchair. He had no doubt who was meant to have the pink bedroom. Nancy's name was clearly written on the door.

Angela giggled. "How old does Mother think you are again?"

Carla cleared her throat. "My Lady, we *can* have the color changed—"

"Please," Nancy said. She looked as though someone had tossed her a lifeline. "Something else, *anything* else . . ."

"Yellow with pink polka dots," Angela said. She smiled brilliantly. "Or green with—"

"Shut up," Nancy said.

Matt was torn between amusement and an odd kind of envy. He couldn't imagine just how much money had been lavished on the suite. Nancy's presents alone had probably cost a fortune. And yet they could get them changed easily. Their lives had to be so easy. Money made everything easy.

He quenched the thought. If the old sweats were telling the truth, Angela and Nancy wouldn't be the worst guests he'd encounter. He should count himself lucky.

Angela glanced into *her* bedroom. "There's a hatch on the far side," she said. "Where does that lead?"

"Out into the corridor," Matt recalled. The stateroom was secure, but the designers had insisted on multiple points of exit. "Just push your finger against the scanner to leave."

"Oh," Angela said. "I can leave without going through the antechamber?"

"Yes, My Lady," Matt assured her. "You won't be able to get back in without a special codekey, but you can leave."

"Good," Angela said. "Can I also lock my door?"

Matt wondered, absently, if he should be concerned. Angela seemed a little *too* interested in the subject. But then, if he were a beautiful young woman, he'd want to be sure the door could be locked from the inside too. Not everyone willingly shared a compartment with members of the opposite sex.

"Of course, My Lady," he said. He led the way into the room, then pointed at the small processor on the desk. "You can access the room's permissions through there and add or remove people from the list. Anyone not on the list will be denied access. Alarms will sound if they enter without permission."

"I see," Angela said.

She looked around the room, her expression twisting. Matt tried to see the giant bedroom as she must have seen it, a tiny little box in a tiny little stateroom. He'd heard that aristocratic mansions had entire wings devoted to each member of the family, from children barely old enough to eat solid food to older relatives who had nowhere else to go. He shook his head in disbelief. The bedroom was too large for comfort . . . three or four people could have shared the bed easily. Angela had no reason to be displeased as far as he could tell. The only minor problem was that no pile of presents had been placed on the bed.

A girl like that probably has her own trust fund, he thought. *She could buy me out of pocket change.*

"Your telltales are here," he said, leading the way back into the antechamber. The silver bands were waiting on the tray, where housekeeping had left them. "Put them on your wrists; then make sure you wear them whenever you go out of the stateroom."

Angela looked displeased. "What happens if we *don't* wear them?"

"Doors and hatches won't open," Carla said. Her voice was polite but firm. "Some sections will be closed to you."

"And in case of emergency, we won't be able to find you," Matt added. "Don't let anyone else use your telltale."

"Yeah," Angela said. She looked . . . downhearted, just for a second. Matt wondered what he'd said to make her feel bad. "Thank you."

Her tone was clearly dismissive. Matt bowed, suddenly unsure if he should wait for a tip. He wouldn't have hesitated with an older guest, but . . . he shook his head, taking one last look at Angela. Even downhearted, she was stunning. He hoped he'd have the chance to see her again, during the voyage. He was fairly sure he would.

"Thank you, My Lady," he said.

Carla followed him as he walked through the hatch and down the corridor. Gold Deck felt eerie, almost empty. It would fill up, he knew, but for the moment, the passages just felt weird. He and Carla might be the only crewmen for hundreds of meters . . .

She elbowed him as they stepped through one of the concealed hatches and into the crew corridor. "I saw you staring at her."

Matt flushed, brightly. "It wasn't that bad . . ."

"You were practically *drooling*," Carla teased. "They'll have to change the carpet because you slobbered all over it."

"I didn't," Matt protested. "I wasn't *staring*."

"You were," Carla said. "Can I give you a word of advice?"

Matt nodded. Technically, they held the same rank, but she had more experience. He knew he should listen to whatever she had to say.

"That girl will have a trust fund with enough money to buy a mid-sized starship," Carla said. "She's also the heir to a father with enough money to buy an entire planet. She is *not* in your league and never will be. Don't even think about trying to bed her."

Matt glared at her. Cold logic told him that Carla was right, but cold logic was . . . cold. "And what if she asks me into bed?"

Carla looked pained. "Because that is *so* likely to happen," she said. She jabbed a finger into his chest. "Keep it in your pants."

"Oh," Matt said.

"I'm sure you'll get it in hand soon enough," Carla added. Matt took a moment to work out what she meant, whereupon he blushed furiously. "Until then, *focus*. We have work to do."

CHAPTER FIVE

"That boy was staring at you," Nancy said.

"Shut up," Angela growled. She wasn't in the mood for childishness. Marie hadn't been allowed to disembark with the family—the governess wasn't *family*—but it wouldn't be long before she arrived. "Get into your room and stay there."

Her sister ignored the order. "He *was* staring at you," she said. "His eyes were following you everywhere."

"Which is a little refreshing, isn't it?" Angela stalked over to her door. The suite was so well designed that she could almost believe she was in one of the family's penthouse apartments rather than onboard a massive starship. The parents apparently had the big star-gazing windows. "At least he's honest about it."

She walked through the door and slammed it behind her, resulting in a very satisfying noise. Clearly, the designers had thought of everything. She checked her personal terminal instinctively—a stream of messages appeared from her friends, but nothing from her parents—and sat down at the wooden desk. The terminal opened at her touch, revealing an access screen. She pressed the telltale against the reader and watched as the system unlocked.

The telltale must be configured to me, she thought crossly. She hadn't seen anything that separated hers from Nancy's, but that proved nothing. The telltale was larger than it needed to be. *They'll know if I leave the deck.*

The steward had been right, she discovered. She couldn't set access rights for the entire suite. Her father had *that* power, but she could set them for her bedroom. Smirking, she spent ten minutes trying to exclude Marie . . . and then, cursing her own mistake, set the system to exclude everyone apart from Nancy and herself. As annoying as her younger sister could be, Angela wouldn't begrudge Nancy the chance to hide from their mother. Nancy would probably be put on display once their mother had started her endless round of tea parties with rich or titled women.

She bit her lip, then brought up the starship's details. She'd hoped for a detailed diagram, but what she got was a cheery brochure praising *Supreme* to the skies. Whoever had written the blurb probably deserved a reward for use of superlatives, having skipped the course in basic writing and comprehension. She had to parse her way through the text to determine that *Supreme* had the largest swimming pools, the largest adventure playgrounds, the largest . . . there was a whole list, little of which was actually useful. The deck diagram seemed to leave off all the interesting places.

Just like the diagram back home, she thought. The mansion had a whole network of secret passageways and compartments, some known only to the family. They didn't appear on any building diagram, but anyone who knew they existed might be able to work out where they were. *The crew won't want us to see them.*

There was a knock at the door. She checked the scanner and saw a trio of maids carrying her bags. Angela opened the door quickly and invited them to put the bags on the deck, then leave as quickly as possible. She'd have to argue when Marie discovered she wasn't allowed into Angela's room. The longer she could put that off, the better. She watched the maids go, feeling an odd flicker of envy. They were far poorer than she was—she'd calculated once that blowing through her entire trust fund would be difficult—but they were also freer. No one expected them to uphold the honor of the family.

Angela looked down at her bags, silently noting where they'd been opened. Her father had warned her, bluntly, that their luggage would be searched. She smiled at the memory of her mother's reaction; the older woman had thrown a fit at the thought of strange hands pawing through her underwear. Then Angela sobered. The incident was yet another reminder that she hardly had any control over her life. The giant starship might as well be a prison.

A gilded cage, she thought as she peered into the bathroom. It was small compared to the bathroom at home, but still large enough to house a dozen people comfortably. A giant bath, a shower, a mirror . . . she wished, suddenly, that she had someone to share it with. But there was no one. *I'm trapped in a gilded cage.*

She paced the bedroom, then started to unpack her bags. Marie would offer to do it for her, of course . . . as if Angela would let her. The governess would take the inch and turn it into a mile, using her control over Angela's clothes to control Angela herself. She promised herself, again, that she would fire the governess as soon as she came of age at twenty-one. She wasn't a child any longer.

Her terminal bleeped. PARENTS ON WAY, Nancy had typed. COME OUT?

Angela was tempted to hide, but she knew to do so was futile. Instead, she checked her appearance in the mirror, scanning her rumpled dress, and strode out into the antechamber. Nancy was sitting on a comfortable sofa, holding an elaborate drink in one hand. Angela eyed it warily and told herself not to worry. The ship's crew wouldn't give her younger sister anything dangerous. Besides, even if they did, the nanites in Nancy's body would scrub any toxins out before it was too late.

"A lemon, lime, and orange mocktail," Nancy said, holding out the glass. She shot her older sister a challenging look. "You want?"

"No," Angela said, biting down the urge to insult the little brat. She'd never liked mocktails, and Nancy knew it. They were either unbearably pretentious or completely worthless. "Did you call room service?"

"Yep," Nancy said. She jabbed a hand towards the rear doors. "Their luggage arrived too."

Angela hurried over to the master bedroom and peered inside. She couldn't help a stab of envy as she saw the giant window, allowing her parents to sleep under the stars. If someone had offered her a room like that . . . she glanced around, noting no other way out of the compartment. Maybe she should be glad with what she had, she told herself. She could slip out at any moment.

Unless Father decides to put a guard on the hatch, she thought. He had grown increasingly protective over the last few years, pointing out that his daughter was a prime kidnapping target. Angela wasn't so sure. The family would move heaven and earth to recover her and capture the kidnappers, dead or alive. *He's trying to keep me from growing into my own person.*

She slipped into the room, peering through each of the doors. A bathroom, larger than hers; an office, tastefully decorated in a manner that matched her father's private suite back home; a gargantuan walk-in closet, probably too small to cope with *all* her mother's luggage . . . Angela shook her head in amused disbelief. They were going to be traveling nearly fifty light-years from their homeworld, yet they would have all the comforts of home . . .

Better than the early starships, she thought, although she wasn't sure if that was true. The starship crews had been trapped in tiny ships, but they'd had a freedom she knew she'd never enjoy. *And at least we'll be visiting a handful of strange new worlds.*

"I don't have a window," Nancy said, peering into interplanetary space. "Aren't they lucky?"

Angela shrugged. There *was* something awesome about being able to stare out into space and watch the stars peering back. But the view was also boring. A good projector could turn her room into her private theater, if she wanted it. She could plunge into a gas giant and even fly through a star, all in perfect safety. Reality seemed a trifle . . . *unrealistic*. She heard the outer door opening and hurried back into the antechamber, closely followed by her sister. Their father would not be pleased if he caught them in the master bedroom. He guarded his office as carefully as their mother guarded her reputation.

Angela sat on the sofa and watched as Robert Cavendish entered the compartment, followed by the captain and a younger man. Angela's eyes narrowed as she recognized him: Finley Mackintosh, one of her father's cronies. She hadn't known he'd been on the yacht, although she did have to admit that she hadn't paid much attention. Finley was a minor nobleman, from a family of minor nobility. He certainly wasn't on her level.

Probably trying to suck up to Father, Angela thought.

She eyed Finley, feeling an odd flicker of disquiet. He was handsome thanks to genetic engineering or the bodyshops, but something about him bothered her. She couldn't put the feeling into words. He didn't seem quite used to his face, perhaps . . . he'd had his countenance altered, time and time again, until it was no longer his. The brown hair, flawless skin, and strong jaw looked like a mask covering his true self. His looks held no sense of danger, merely something . . . *bland*. There was no fire in Finley Mackintosh, she decided finally. He wasn't one to challenge her father, let alone reach for the brass ring.

Finley looked back at her. Angela felt herself flush, just for a second, before he looked away again. His reaction was . . . odd. No frank admiration, no half-hidden lust . . . not even embarrassment at being caught looking. He could be good at controlling and hiding his reactions, but . . . she rather thought he'd felt nothing. She'd met enough entitled rich kids during her life to know they weren't good at hiding their feelings.

I'll have to look him up, she thought. Her father had made her memorize the important families, along with quite a few other pieces of useless knowledge, but the Mackintoshes had never been considered important enough to study. *I should be able to get the basic file from the database, if nothing else.*

She made a face as Marie and a dozen other servants bustled through the door. It didn't look as though the security officers had discomforted them, unfortunately. Angela watched Halle Cavendish issue a string of orders, directing the servants into the master bedroom and putting them to work. Thankfully she swept Marie into her bedroom as well. Angela made a mental note to thank her mother, afterwards. Hopefully unpacking a dozen heavy suitcases would take some time.

"Very good," her father said, loudly enough to catch her attention. "I'll see you at dinner."

Finley bowed, then retreated. Angela watched him go, trying to read his body language. But it was impossible. Finley didn't seem to resent being her father's crony, any more than he seemed to be using her father for his own purposes. Angela snorted rudely as her father cleared his throat, dismissing the thought. Perhaps Finley was just a glorified servant, whatever his title happened to be. Quite a few families had suffered financial difficulties because of the war.

"A nice young man," her father commented. If he hadn't been looking at her, Angela would have wondered if he was talking to himself. "What do you make of the ship?"

Angela blinked. Her father rarely asked her opinion. She could see why he thought highly of Finley, if she was right about the young man's character. He didn't ask questions, he didn't argue . . . he just did as he was told, precisely what her father wanted in his children. He'd rebuked Angela for asking questions more than once.

"It's a ship," she said. "It's nothing . . . nothing *special.*"

Her father's lips twitched. "It will be playing host to hundreds of very important people," he said. "It will be very special indeed."

Angela realized it wasn't a family holiday then. She'd never really had a family holiday with her parents, not when her father brought his business with him. Finley and the servants were just the tip of the iceberg. No doubt he had an entire staff on the lower decks, just waiting to be put to work. By the time they reached their first destination, she had no doubt her father and his cronies would have ironed out a plan to take advantage of the postwar situation and secure the Cavendish future. He wouldn't have any time for *her.*

She couldn't help feeling a pang of envy for her friends who had decent relations with their parents. She didn't want to be supervised constantly, but she did want to spend quality time with her father. It didn't have to be much, she thought . . . she'd settle for a walk around the grounds, just her and her father, without the family business constantly butting in. Her best friend's father had taken his daughter on camping trips and sailing voyages and . . .

Her father was still talking. Angela groaned. Whatever he'd said, she'd missed it.

"I'm sorry," she said. He wouldn't be pleased she'd zoned out, but it couldn't be helped. "Please, could you say that again?"

"I was saying that this voyage is incredibly important," he said. His tone was patient, but she caught a hint of annoyance in his words. "I expect you to behave yourself."

"I always do," Angela said.

"That's true," Nancy put in. "Angela is *boring.*"

She shot her younger sister a death glare. Being the older sister wasn't easy. Nancy was still young enough to play dumb. Angela was too old to get away with such behavior, yet too young to simply take her trust fund and go. On the other hand, escaping her mother had grown easier as she'd gotten older. Nancy couldn't do that just yet.

Lucky we don't have any younger siblings, Angela thought. Their mother seemed to believe, at times, that her daughters were little older than five. *That would be bad.*

Her father caught her attention. "I'll be speaking to you later about other matters," he added flatly. "Until then, try not to do anything I might hear about in the papers."

Angela nodded, not trusting herself to speak. Her father was behaving oddly, but . . . at least he was paying attention to her. She knew it wouldn't last. He wouldn't care what she did as long as she didn't bring scandal down on the family. *That* wouldn't be easy on a cruise ship, she knew. What happened on a cruise liner largely stayed on a cruise liner.

"Yes, Father," she said. "Is there anything else?"

"There'll be a formal dinner once the ship leaves orbit," he told her. "Finley will be escorting you."

Angela blinked, genuinely shocked. "He will?"

"He will. You will be a good conversationalist."

"Oh," Angela said. Finley could have asked her out if he'd wanted, she supposed, but she wouldn't have agreed. She'd dated boys she'd come to regret giving the time of day, yet . . . at least they'd had the nerve to ask her out. Finley . . . if nothing else, she doubted *he* would be a good conversationalist. "Do I have a choice?"

"No," her father said.

Angela looked at him for a long moment, then nodded shortly. Arguing was pointless. It wouldn't be the first time her parents had selected her dinner companion for the evening. Politics trumped personal preference, her father had told her. She might dislike her dinner companion, she might detest him with all the passion of a million white-hot, burning suns . . . no matter. As long as she remained unmarried, she was expected to play her role in family dinners.

At least he probably won't try anything, she thought. *He probably doesn't have the imagination to try.*

"Yes, Father," she said. "Will that be all?"

"For the moment," her father said. He gave her a dismissive look. "I'll talk to you later."

Or never, Angela thought as she walked back to her bedroom. *You'll forget about it within the hour.*

She closed the door behind her, then sat down on the bed. The remainder of the passengers would already be arriving, she was sure. Soon the facilities would start to open . . . she could go to the giant swimming pool, if she wished, or lose herself in a VR adventure. Or find something, anything, to take her mind off her life. *Someone* on the ship had to be worth talking to.

She heard a knock. She glanced at the scanner. Marie was standing outside, looking irked. A moment later, she knocked again. Angela ignored the rapping. No doubt Marie had tried the door first, only to discover it wouldn't open. The wretched woman had blanket access to Angela's rooms back home . . .

At least she can't get in here, Angela thought. Perhaps she could have a little nap before dinner. The farewell party had kept her up half the night. *I can finally get some peace.*

CHAPTER SIX

"This would go a great deal quicker if we were docked at the orbital tower," Raymond Slater said. The security chief looked tired. "Corporate didn't change their minds?"

Paul shook his head. Slater was right. Insisting that guests take shuttles to *Supreme*, rather than riding the car up the orbital tower and walking across, was creating all sorts of bottlenecks. Loading had slowed, and he was doubtful they'd make their planned departure date. But, on the other hand, he saw Corporate's point. The bottlenecks would make smuggling something onto the ship more difficult.

Unless they have someone on the inside, he thought wryly. *But we don't let our staff board without being searched too.*

"They insisted on it," he said. He cocked his eyebrows. "Did you turn up anything interesting?"

"No, sir," Slater said. He didn't bother to point out that Paul would have been informed at once if something posing a genuine threat had been discovered. "A couple of the bodyguards had unregistered weapons, which we confiscated until we could get them cleared, but very little else."

Paul allowed himself a moment of relief. The story about the nine-year-old who'd managed to smuggle a nuke through security had never struck him as plausible, but he had seen trained experts sneak all kinds of things through the screening. Better to be careful, even if it meant inconveniencing passengers, than having to clean up the mess afterwards. Like it or not, he had hundreds of important guests on his ship, and their safety was his first concern.

He resisted the urge to roll his eyes. The techs had quietly alerted him that nearly a hundred complaints had already been forwarded to Corporate. Paul knew he was covered as Corporate had issued the orders, but the whining might prove a nuisance. People bitched and moaned about security screenings until something happened, whereupon they bitched and moaned that the screenings weren't tough enough. The balancing act was made all the worse by the long-term effects of the war. A handful of hijackings and terrorist attacks had forced the Commonwealth to tighten security and try to cover all the bases. The costs of that had been worse than the attacks themselves.

It can't be helped, he told himself firmly.

"That's good to know," he said. "Any new matters of concern?"

"I've had to lay down the law to a couple of bodyguards," Slater said. "They figured they'd have access, even read-only access, to our internal network. Corporate vetoed it, so . . ." He grimaced, then relaxed. "Apart from that, there aren't any serious problems. No criminal records, no open police cases . . . no reason to think that any of our guests are anyone but who they claim to be. And no sore losers in the casino either."

Paul smiled. "*That* will change."

"Yes, it will," Slater agreed. "And it will be followed by charges that the house has rigged the games again."

"We'll deal with it when it happens," Paul said. The casino didn't rig the games, he'd been assured, but a sore loser might not believe it. And a smart dealer could probably rig the games without leaving any evidence behind. "Alert me if anything changes."

"Yes, sir," Slater said. He rose. "So far, everything seems to be fine."

"Just moving slowly," Paul said. Another advantage to no longer being in the military was that Corporate would be far more understanding than the Admiralty if *Supreme* didn't leave on time. The interstellar shipping schedules had always had a great deal of slippage built into them. "Did you run any additional drills?"

"I slipped a handful of ringers into the screening lines," Slater said. "All were caught."

He saluted, then walked out of the hatch. Paul smiled, then turned his attention to the holographic display. It was starting to fill up, informing him that two-thirds of the guests had already boarded. There would be four thousand passengers in all once loading was complete . . . unless some people canceled. Corporate's last update had warned that seventy passengers had canceled their cruise at short notice, choosing to pay the penalties instead of taking their cabins on *Supreme*. Paul knew Corporate wouldn't be pleased about *that*, although they were already offering the empty cabins and staterooms at a reduced rate. They'd been harping on about the importance of filling all the space for the last couple of months.

We only need to sell half the cabins to meet our operating expenses, he thought as he picked up his terminal. *But having empty compartments is annoying.*

He abandoned the thought. The latest set of updates confirmed that *Supreme* was fully supplied with everything she needed, ranging from reactor mass to food, alcohol, and medical equipment. He had no doubt that *some* bean counters were bitching about the cost, but Corporate didn't seem inclined to listen to them—a refreshing change from the navy. There, the treacherous bastards in logistics had done their level best to keep vital supplies out of his hands.

His terminal pinged, blinking up a message. He glanced at it—another update, noting that all the second-class passengers had boarded the ship—and then sent back an acknowledgment. Perhaps *Supreme* would make it out on time after all, he told himself. The passengers probably wouldn't notice. Now that the casino was open and the bars were distributing drinks, they had every reason to just relax. Who knew? Maybe the flight would go smoothly.

Let us hope so, he thought. He'd joined the navy for excitement, but as an older man, he was less keen on the idea. An exciting cruise on *Supreme* would mean that he hadn't done his job properly. *The less that goes wrong, the better.*

———

Matt's earpiece buzzed. "Evans, an alert just went off in cabin S-134," the dispatcher said. "Go check on it, would you?"

"Yes, sir," Matt said. He was tired, his body aching, but there was no point in arguing. The dispatcher wouldn't have called him if he wasn't the closest steward to the cabin. "I'm on my way."

He picked his way down the corridor, trying to move as fast as he could without looking as though he was hurrying. It wasn't easy. Silver Deck was crammed with guests and their servants, the former exploring with interest while the latter used tiny antigrav units to float luggage down the passageway. A gaggle of kids ran past him, laughing carelessly as they hurried into the distance. Matt felt a stab of envy mixed with annoyance. The brats would probably cause all sorts of problems for the ship's staff.

Cabin S-134 was second class, he reminded himself as he reached the hatch, which was closed and thus suggested that the problem wasn't serious. He told himself, sharply, that whoever was in the cabin considered it to be serious, then pushed the buzzer. It didn't look as though he had any reason to walk straight into the cabin without waiting for permission. *That* would be a good way to get dismissed from the company without a reference.

The hatch hissed open, revealing a large stateroom. It was small, compared to the private apartments on Gold Deck, but large enough to pass for a cheap apartment on the surface. A middle-aged woman stood by the washroom door, glaring at him. Beyond her, Matt could see into the bedroom. A young girl was sitting on the bed, looking dreadfully embarrassed. Matt rather suspected he knew the feeling.

"Young man," the woman said, "I paid for a cabin with two beds. Instead . . ."

She waved a hand into the bedroom. A large double bed was clearly visible. "This is not acceptable," she said, holding out a terminal as though it were a weapon. The confirmation message was clearly visible. "I booked two beds, not one. Are we meant to share?"

"No, My Lady," Matt said. He kept his voice calm. He'd been taught to remain calm, whatever the situation. Customers who felt they'd been cheated reacted badly to anything else. "Please give me a moment to check the manifest."

He took the terminal and scanned the message, then used his own terminal to check the passenger manifest. Carla had warned him that guests sometimes tried to scam their way into an upgrade, but it didn't look as though the woman—her name was Maris Simpson—was trying anything of the sort. The manifest clearly indicated that she *had* booked two beds. He looked at the bed, just in case two beds had been pushed together, but clearly that wasn't the case.

"There seems to have been a mistake," Matt said. "I—"

"I'd say there's been a mistake," Maris snapped. "Susan and I booked this cruise to coincide with her holidays *and* visit the deadbeat she calls her dad! I will *not* stand by and let her cruise be ruined. I'll call my lawyers if this is not rectified!"

Matt was tempted to point out that the stewards practically lived in one another's clothes, but he knew such a statement wouldn't help the situation. There *had* been a mistake. Maris had every right to be annoyed. Instead, he keyed his terminal, trying to determine if any of the reserved cabins had been allocated yet. He'd need authority from Falcon to reassign Maris to one of the cabins, but he didn't think the man would object. Maris's threat to sue would guarantee some bad publicity, whatever else happened. Corporate would probably prefer to upgrade her rather than risk a lawsuit.

"I've found a potential cabin," he said. His fingers danced over the display. "If you'll give me a moment, I'll try and get it assigned to you."

"Susan has been looking forward to this trip for months," Maris said. "The chance to visit Homestead and her father . . ."

Matt forced himself to listen as Maris ranted, telling him things he didn't want to know about her love life, her former partner, and how unfair it was that Susan had to grow up without a proper father. Carla had warned him that he'd hear more than he needed to know, but he hadn't really believed her. Maris didn't *have* to rant at him, did she? He was just a junior steward, the lowest of the low. But then, she did have a point. The cruise had probably cost more than she could reasonably afford.

His terminal bleeped. "You've been allocated a new cabin," he said. Falcon had approved the upgrade as well as the transfer. "I'll help you move your luggage there."

Susan jumped off the bed and held up her wrist. A silver band was clearly visible against her brown skin. "Will this still work?"

"It will," Matt assured her. He wasn't at liberty to talk about the security features built into the telltales—the less people knew, the harder it would be to reprogram and subvert the little devices—but Susan's telltale wouldn't work for anyone else. Her onboard records would already be updated. "Can I take your bags?"

"Thank you," Maris said grudgingly.

He picked up the suitcase. Maris had only one, somewhat to his surprise, and Matt carried it through the door. Susan followed him, looking around eagerly. Her eyes went everywhere as they walked down the corridor, leaving the cabin to seal itself until a housekeeping crew arrived.

"You have a cool job," Susan said. She looked up at Matt, her eyes wide. "Have you seen many planets?"

Matt hesitated, then told the truth. "This is my first cruise," he said. "I haven't gone further than the edge of the system."

Susan looked disappointed. "I'm going to join the survey corps when I grow up," she informed him. "I'll be boldly going where no woman has gone before."

"That would be fun," Matt said. The UN Survey Service had died with Earth, as far as he knew. The Commonwealth hadn't been particularly interested in picking up the slack. But now that humanity had recovered from the Breakdown and the Theocratic War was over, he could easily imagine the Commonwealth starting to probe beyond the Rim. "Did you watch every episode of *Space Trek*?"

Susan smiled. "Do you know that show was based on an even *older* show called *Star Trek*? It was about aliens and . . . um . . . stuff like that. They even stole the motto for the newer show."

Matt had to smile. *Space Trek* had been about the UNSS. He'd watched a couple of episodes, but he hadn't thought much of the program. Humanity hadn't encountered a single alien race in nearly four hundred years of exploration, not even the remains of a long-dead civilization. He'd heard the rumors, of course, but none of them had been anything more than the kind of tall stories spacers told one another in bars.

"I haven't watched the show," he said. "Is it good?"

"Her father loved it," Maris said. Her tone was forbidding. "He passed that love to his daughter."

Matt kept his expression blank as they reached the new cabin. Susan ran inside as soon as he opened the door, looking around with interest. Matt heard her whoop with joy as she realized there were two bedrooms, not one. He didn't blame her. Susan was probably around nine, old enough to dislike the idea of sharing a bedroom with her mother. Matt had felt the same way when he'd been a child.

"This is great," Susan called. "Mum! I want *this* bedroom!"

Maris caught Matt's arm. "This upgrade is free, right?"

"Yes, My Lady," Matt assured her. He smiled as he saw her face relax. Both cabins were on Silver Deck, but the larger one cost more. "The upgrade is free. All the snacks and suchlike are complimentary. Your overall access rights won't change."

"Very good," Maris said.

Susan poked her head back through the door. "Can we go to the adventure playground now?"

"Let me unpack," Maris said. She looked at Matt. "Is she safe outside the cabin?"

"She can't get off Silver Deck," Matt said. Susan was too young to be allowed to wander freely. "She should be safe enough, as long as she stays out of the way."

"I see," Maris said. She reached into her pocket and produced a credit chip. "Your terminal, please?"

Matt smiled, holding out his wristcom. Corporate insisted on taxing tips, particularly ones handled through the onboard banking system, and distributing the revenue to crewmen who didn't interact with the guests. Matt still wasn't sure how he felt about that. He was the one who'd earned those tips, but he could see the sense of the procedure.

"Thank you," he said. Carla had told him that he'd end up with a big bank balance as long as he was careful. "Please don't hesitate to call if you need anything else."

He bowed politely to Maris, then walked out of the cabin and strode down the corridor. The dispatcher took his report and directed him to another problem. An older passenger was concerned about his luggage not arriving. Matt checked the records, discovered that the luggage hadn't been screened yet, and informed the passenger that it would arrive as soon as possible. Unimpressed, the passenger dismissed him with a grunt. No tip.

"Some people are like that," Carla said when their duty shift finally ended and they were on their way to eat. "Trust me, Matt. You'll encounter worse people on the voyage."

They walked past the adult swimming pool. A number of young women were splashing in the water, followed by a crowd of young men. He couldn't avoid noticing that half of the women were topless, their breasts glistening under the light. It was hard not to stare. Women on his homeworld did not go nude, any more than their male counterparts. And yet . . . he drank in the sight, watching the girls as they swam through the water. There was something strikingly . . . *admirable* . . . in their un-self-conscious nudity, as if they had no reason to be concerned. He looked for Angela, half expecting to see her with the women, but there was no sign of her. He felt disappointed.

"I'll take your word for it," he said.

"You should," Carla said. Her voice was cold. "Be glad if that's the worst problem you encounter on this voyage." She smiled. "Back on my first cruise, there was an emergency call from a cabin, so I hurried down and opened the hatch, only to see the passenger and his wife . . . stark naked . . . and tied up in a bondage net."

Matt stared. "You're fucking with me."

"I swear," Carla said. She giggled. "They'd messed up the settings, somehow. They were trapped, barely able to move their hands and feet . . . it was lucky they could reach the emergency button. There I was, expecting a medical emergency, a medical team already on the way, and . . . well, there they were."

"Fuck," Matt said. "What happened?"

"I released them, of course," she said. "They gave me a *massive* tip. I think they were too embarrassed to do anything afterwards . . . I never saw them again, even during disembarking. God alone knows what they thought I'd said to my superiors."

Matt eyed her. "What *did* you say?"

"The truth," Carla said. She snorted. "There are times when you just have to be a little blind, Matt. And times when you have to swallow your embarrassment and help someone."

"I know," Matt said. He smiled as he pictured the scene. He'd never played with a bondage net, but he'd heard rumors. "Did it ever happen again?"

"Not to my knowledge," Carla said. They reached the dining hall and walked inside. "But you never know."

"No," Matt agreed. "You don't."

CHAPTER SEVEN

If he were forced to be honest, Paul had always considered *Supreme's* bridge to be faintly ridiculous. Whoever had designed it had clearly been more inspired by fantastical entertainment shows than by anything else. The bridge was bright, elegant, and far too inefficient for his peace of mind. He'd actually suggested moving operations to the secondary bridge, which was more efficient, as the guests wouldn't be expected to visit, but Corporate had overruled him. All they'd allowed him to do was establish his XO on the secondary bridge, just in case.

And if we really do run into problems, he thought as he looked towards the porthole overhead, *we'll have no time to move operations before it's too late.*

He sat in his sinfully comfortable armchair and glanced from station to station. The bridge resembled a luxurious office with a handful of workstations scattered around the compartment. Only the hatch and giant hologram detracted from the illusion. If nothing else, his crew could easily *look* busy, which would keep guests from filing complaints with Corporate about staff doing nothing while manning their stations.

Shaking his head, he glanced towards the operations officer. "Commander?"

"All planet-bound shuttles have departed," Commander Tidal Macpherson reported. She was young for her role but did have genuine military experience and rarely had to interact with the guests. "External hatches are closed and locked. Cross-checks have been completed."

"Internal security systems online," Slater added from his station. "All guests are within the guest sections."

Paul nodded, relieved. He'd hoped they wouldn't have any incidents before they departed, but he'd been unlucky. Three guests had been caught trying to sneak into the engine rooms, although security had collared them before they managed to get inside. They were teenagers rather than potential saboteurs, but he couldn't help feeling that their attempt was a bad omen.

"Better check that no one removed their telltales," Jeanette said. Her face hung in the center of the holographic display. "Someone's *bound* to think of that, sooner or later."

"So far, no one has flagged the alarm," Slater assured her. "And they couldn't get out of their section without a telltale."

"I hope so," Jeanette said.

Paul tapped his armrest, meaningfully. Jeanette had a point—every security system could be spoofed, with enough planning and effort— but they'd covered as many bases as they could. There was no reason to think that passengers were trying to evade their telltales, let alone leave the guest compartments. He'd made it clear, via shipboard announcement, that no one was to leave during departure.

"Communications, check with System Command," he ordered. "Are we cleared to depart?"

There was a pause. "Yes, sir," Lieutenant Stuart Hazelwood said. "They've cleared us to open a vortex as planned. *Hawk* and *Fisher* are standing by to escort us."

Paul nodded, relieved. Corporate had *finally* managed to convince the Royal Navy to assign *Supreme* escorts, at least as far as Williamson's World. It wasn't much, but as long as the two destroyers stayed with the starship, she'd be relatively safe. Very few pirates would willingly tangle with a warship, even one seemingly weaker than their ship. He'd never heard of a pirate crew prepared to put their lives on the line, whatever the payout.

"Inform them that we will be departing in ten minutes," he said. He keyed his console. "Engineering?"

"Drive systems online, Captain," Chief Engineer Conrad Roeder said. He had a strong Rosina accent, but Paul had no trouble understanding him. "All systems are at full efficiency, sir—ready and raring to go. All drive nodes are powered, all power curves normal."

"Good," Paul said.

He concealed his relief. He wasn't sure Corporate would understand any further delays. And yet if there had been a problem, he wouldn't have had any choice. The military might risk flying a starship that had lost one or two of its drive nodes, but the civilian world didn't have that luxury. *Supreme* would have had to hold position and wait for a replacement to arrive and be installed, which would not have gone down well with stockholders.

And there may be problems, he thought. Robert Cavendish hadn't been very clear, but, reading between the lines, Paul was fairly sure something was wrong. Corporate had certainly been very insistent that *Supreme* departed on schedule. *We cannot afford to delay any further.*

He took one last look at the status display. Green, right across the board. He couldn't help finding it impressive. *Supreme* had so many redundancies built into her hull and internal systems that she could still fly with half her systems out, although Corporate would never allow it. They'd over-engineered the starship, he thought. So many of the safety measures built into her hull were designed for possibilities that even the red teams—those charged with coming up with worst-case scenarios—had trouble putting them into words. He had difficulty imagining a scenario where *Supreme* had to land on a planetary surface yet was still intact enough to survive the descent.

"Alert all stations," he ordered. "We will depart on schedule."

"Aye, Captain," Tidal said.

Paul leaned back in his command chair. The near-space display was clear save for the two destroyers holding station near *Supreme*. He felt a flicker of envy for their commanding officers, mingled with grim awareness that he would probably feel differently if he were in their shoes. The military life was simpler in many ways, and yet didn't bring challenges like a cruise liner . . .

Problems that can't be resolved by shooting at them, he thought. *Or even just waving our weapons in their general direction.*

"Helm, begin nodal ignition series," he ordered. "Stand by to open a gateway."

"Aye, Captain," Lieutenant Rani Jackson said. Her fingers danced over her console as a low thrumming echoed through the ship. "Gateway sequence keyed, ready to go."

Paul felt . . . nervous. He knew it was absurd, yet he *still* felt nervous. It wasn't the first time he'd taken *Supreme* into hyperspace; their shakedown cruise had been almost painfully exhaustive, with the drives and internal systems pushed right to their limits. But it was the first time his ship had been crammed with passengers. Four thousand guests . . . they'd be watching through the portholes or the internal displays as the ship slipped into hyperspace . . .

We'd better not screw up, then, he thought.

"Open the gateway," he ordered. "Take us out."

He leaned back in his chair as the gateway, a spiraling vortex of golden light, blossomed to life in front of his ship. Cold logic and experience told him he shouldn't feel anything, but cold logic meant nothing. Paul had a sense, a very vague sense, of *falling* as *Supreme* moved forward into the gateway. And then a low quiver ran through the ship as she entered hyperspace.

"Transit complete, Captain," Rani informed him.

"The two destroyers have followed us in," Tidal added. "Local space is clear in all directions."

Insofar as that proves anything, Paul thought. *Supreme* had the best sensors money could buy, but they were still a stage or two below mil-grade. Even Corporate hadn't been able to convince the Royal Navy to share its latest designs. *Someone might just have a lock on us from a distance.*

"Helm, set a course to Williamson's World," Paul ordered. "And take us out."

"Aye, Captain," Rani said. The course flashed up on the main display almost as soon as Paul had finished speaking. Rani would have worked their route out while the ship was making the final preparations to depart, then uploaded it to the navigation computers. *Supreme* thrummed, again, as the drive systems engaged. "We are under way."

Paul let out a breath he hadn't realized he'd been holding. He hadn't expected anything to go wrong, but he had enough experience to know just how quickly things could move from stable to disastrous. The two destroyers were clearly visible on the display, and a handful of other icons had popped up, now that *Supreme* had begun to move, but no one seemed to be taking any particular interest in her.

"Continue to update the course if necessary," he ordered. "And hold us steady."

"Aye, Captain," Rani said.

———

"And we made it into hyperspace," the DJ boomed. "Anyone who bet we *wouldn't* make it into hyperspace is screwed!"

Laughter ran around the casino. Matt felt his head start to throb. Casino duty was supposed to be lucrative, as he'd had quite a few credit chips and coins shoved into his hands, but he was tempted to see if he could get off the casino roster entirely. Crowds of half-drunk people looming over gaming tables, betting on everything from a successful transfer into hyperspace to the date *Supreme* returned to Tyre . . . the scene was loud, brash, and thoroughly annoying. The noise alone was getting to him.

"That's five people, ladies and gentlemen," the DJ added. "Five people bet we wouldn't get into hyperspace. I don't know how they planned to collect!"

Matt used his implants to keep his face expressionless as he moved around the rear of the giant compartment, doing his best to avoid the crowd. He had no idea how the gamblers had planned to collect either unless they'd assumed that an unsuccessful transit would dump *Supreme* back into realspace. They might have been right, he conceded, but the odds were against them. The entire starship would have far more likely been ripped to shreds.

A cheer went up from the nearest table. A young man was raking in the chips, grinning from ear to ear. The dealer, a woman wearing a colorful uniform that made her look like a walking parfait, whispered sweet nothings in his ear. Matt watched, torn between envy and pity. The lucky winner would be seduced back to the gaming table soon, Matt was sure, and all his earnings would vanish into thin air. Carla had told him that the games weren't precisely rigged, but they *were* tilted in the house's favor. In the long run, all the money would flow to the house . . .

His terminal bleeped an alert. Matt glanced down at it and swore, then hurried around the edge of the room. An emergency, a *medical* emergency. He was allowed to run for that, thankfully. The crowd was already falling back from an elderly man who'd collapsed, another man kneeling beside him. Matt pushed his way through the throng and keyed his wristcom.

"Medical emergency," he said. He pressed the wristcom against the victim's telltale. The medics would be automatically updated on any preexisting conditions. "One emergency . . ."

"He just fainted," the other man said. "He looked pale and fainted."

The medics arrived, three of them. One checked the victim while the other two assembled the portable medical kit and stretcher. "Looks like a case of delayed hyperspace shock," the first said. He pressed a tab against the victim's neck and triggered it. "We'd better get him to Sickbay."

"I'll come too," his companion said. "Steve *needs* me."

"I'll take you," Matt said. The medics would get Steve to Sickbay via the intership cars. "Come with me?"

"Steve's always been so strong," the man said. He sounded pained. "I'd say to him, you'll go on forever. And he'd say . . . don't be silly, Bernie. I'll be dead before you."

"Hyperspace shock is rarely fatal," Matt said. Steve wouldn't have been allowed to board if he'd had a health condition that would have *made* it fatal. The preboarding medical checks would have seen to that. "He'll survive."

Bernie grasped his arm. "What if he *can't* survive?"

Matt gritted his teeth. Bernie was stronger than he seemed. "The medics will handle him," he said with more assurance than he felt. "If they can't help him, they'll pop him into a stasis pod and leave him there until we return home."

"Hah," Bernie said. "They won't turn the ship around?"

"Probably not," Matt said. There was no point in lying. *Supreme* wouldn't reverse course unless someone *far* more important than Steve—Robert Cavendish, perhaps—was in serious danger. The costs involved would be staggering. "But he'll be safe in the stasis pod."

They walked down the corridor and into an inter-ship car. Matt half expected Bernie to keep talking, but instead, he remained quiet as the car made its way through the ship and came to a stop outside Sickbay. Matt used his telltale to clear the way into the department, then looked around for the receptionist. She was sitting just inside the door, studying a datapad. Matt cleared his throat, trying to decide what to say. There hadn't been any time for a formal briefing.

"Where is he?" Bernie demanded. "Where's Stevie?"

"Mr. Garston is currently recovering," the receptionist said. Her eyes alighted on Bernie and stayed there. "The doctors may wish to speak to you about his condition."

Bernie's eyebrows raised sharply. "His condition?"

"The doctors will discuss it with you," the receptionist said. She looked at Matt. "You're dismissed."

"Understood," Matt said. He wasn't sure if the receptionist had any power over him, but her superiors definitely did. "Please inform Steward Falcon if you need to speak with me later."

"Thank you, young man," Bernie said. He reached into his pocket and produced a coin. Matt took it with practiced ease. "You may have saved Steve's life."

Matt nodded. He hoped that was true.

He keyed his wristcom as he hurried back to the casino. The dispatcher would have noticed him leaving and sent one of the reserve stewards to take his place. As Matt expected, there was an update in his inbox, ordering him to go to the reserve himself. He smiled, relieved. He wouldn't have to go back to the casino.

Not for a while anyway, Matt thought.

———

Paul looked down at the report in disbelief. "Mr. Garston concealed a health condition?"

"Yes, Captain," Dr. Joan Mackey said. She sounded cross. Her face, designed to suggest endless care and compassion for her patients, looked angry. "He was lucky to survive his bout with hyperspace shock. There's no way he should have been cleared for hyperspace travel, not outside a stasis pod. The doctors could *not* have missed this."

"I see," Paul said. He resisted the urge to swear. "What . . . precisely . . . was wrong with him?"

"*Is* wrong with him," Joan corrected. "In layman's terms, he has a *very* weak heart and a major genetic disorder. Standard rejuvenation and regeneration techniques appear to be useless. His body would probably reject a clone transplant. I've checked the medical records he *did* give us, but . . ." She slapped the table in frustration. "There is *no* way he didn't bribe someone to get clearance. I just hope he paid them enough to make up for losing their license."

"I doubt it," Paul said. Corporate would litigate to recover damages, such as they were. A good lawyer could probably parley the whole affair into a major suit. God alone knew how many people could reasonably claim to have been traumatized by watching Steve Garston's collapse. "I don't think there's enough money in the universe to make up for criminal charges and civil suits." He took a final look at the report. "Can you do anything for him?"

"Not immediately," Joan said. "Under normal circumstances, I'd recommend replacing his heart with an artificial one. I do have a couple in storage, but Mr. Garston would probably require one specifically tailored to his requirements. We might be able to alter one of the ones we've got in the machine shop . . . that said, I'd prefer to put him in stasis and hand him over to a specialized clinic once we get home."

"Understood," Paul said. Dr. Mackey had a solid record of dealing with medical problems on cruise ships. If she thought that trying to perform the procedure was risky, he trusted her judgment. "He can wait until we return home."

"I must also inform you that I will be filing an official report with the General Medical Council," Joan added. She sounded as though she expected Paul to argue. "Whatever his motives, Mr. Garston forged a medical certificate. I have a duty to report it to the authorities. The people who certified him were, at best, grossly negligent. There's no way this condition should have escaped detection."

"You can file a report once we reach the StarCom at Williamson's World," Paul said. He'd heard of portable StarComs, but *Supreme* didn't carry one. "Make sure you send me a copy. I'll ensure that Corporate knows you have my full support."

Joan appeared to be relieved. Paul didn't blame her. Corporate would be tempted, very tempted, to sweep the whole affair under the rug. Garston's collapse wouldn't look good, no matter how they spun it. But Joan would face sanctions of her own if it were ever discovered that she'd played a role in covering the affair up. If nothing else, the truth had to be dragged into the light before the rumors got out of control.

"Thank you, sir," she said.

"You're welcome," Paul said. "What about Garston's partner?"

"I do not believe that he was aware of Garston's condition," Joan said. She sounded oddly sympathetic. "And, in any case, he had no obligation to report it. My gut feeling is that we should leave him alone, at least until we return home. Corporate will want to speak to him."

"Yeah," Paul agreed. He felt a flicker of pity, mingled with annoyance. What *had* Garston been thinking? This would never have happened in the navy. "I'm sure that'll be enough punishment for anything."

"Yes, sir," Joan said.

"Make sure you record everything," Paul warned. "Dismissed."

"Yes, sir," Joan said. "I already have."

CHAPTER EIGHT

"There you are," Marie said. "I've been looking all over for you."

Angela felt her heart sink. She'd been doing her best to hide on the beach—technically, a massive swimming pool with *real* sand—but Marie had tracked her down. She looked down at the telltale on her wrist, thinking unprintable thoughts. The starship's crew wouldn't refuse her father if he asked them to find his daughter for Marie. Maybe she could just swap it for Nancy's . . .

"The dinner is in two hours," Marie continued, scowling down at her. "You have to come with me."

Her eyes flickered over Angela's bathing suit. "And what . . . *exactly* . . . do you think you're wearing?"

Angela rolled her eyes. She knew it made her look childish, but she didn't care.

"It isn't a very *daring* suit," she said, looking down at herself. Two triangles of cloth over her nipples, a third over her vagina . . . it left very little to the imagination, but there were girls and boys on the pretend beach who were leaving *nothing* to the imagination. *She* wasn't getting much attention. "I could be naked."

Marie sighed. "On your feet, young lady," she said. "We have to get you dressed."

"I don't have to go," Angela said. "I'm sure everyone would be much happier without me."

"Your father says otherwise," Marie said. Her lips thinned, a sure sign she was running out of patience. "Do you want to argue with him?"

Angela considered it. Marie wasn't going to physically drag her back to the stateroom, was she? She found it hard to imagine. Her family would never live it down. And yet she knew better than to argue with her father when he was in one of his moods. She hadn't seen much of him since they'd boarded, but when she had, he'd always given the impression of being preoccupied.

He could be enjoying himself instead, she thought. There was an elderly couple sitting farther down the beach, sipping martinis. *He could relax.*

Her lips quirked. She couldn't imagine her staid father sitting on the beach drinking wine, let alone eyeing girls young enough to be his granddaughters. Logic told her that her parents must have been young once, but she found the concept difficult to grasp. Her father had probably been wearing one of his trademark suits when he was born. The idea of him running around like one of the younger scions of the aristocracy, chasing girls and spending money as though it would never run out . . .

"Come with me," Marie snapped. "Now."

Angela sighed and stood, brushing sand off her body as she took one last wistful look towards the water. The beach was impressive, she had to admit, giving the impression of running for miles in all directions, even though she knew that the entire chamber couldn't be much larger than a couple of football fields. The combination of holographic projections and privacy fields gave the illusion that there was no one near the revelers.

"I need to shower," she said, heading towards the towel rack. "And change into something a little more fitting."

"And there I was thinking you'd want to walk through the ship wearing that," Marie said from behind. "Put on a robe and move it."

Angela rolled her eyes again. She was fairly sure no society reporters were lurking on Gold Deck, but she knew better than to take that for granted. Someone might just record footage of her walking through the corridors in her skimpy costume, then sell it to the tabloids or merely upload it to the datanet when they returned home. It was pathetic, but there were people who'd pay good money for *real* recordings of famous people.

Not that I'm that special, she thought. The tabloids had never paid much attention to her, not when her cousins were so much more scandalous. There were girls and boys who would have found the lack of attention annoying, but she thought it was a relief. *They'd be more interested in some of the other socialites.*

She pulled a robe over her swimming costume, then glanced at her reflection in the nearest mirror. Her hair was untamed, giving her a wild look. There were boys who *liked* that sort of look, she thought. Perhaps, if she showed up at the dinner with unkempt hair, she'd set a new fashion trend. She'd never cared *that* much for fashion, but her father's money and power made her a trendsetter . . .

Behind her, Marie cleared her throat. Angela sighed as she led the way to the door. Right . . . there was no way her governess, or her mother, would let her attend a fancy dinner without making sure she was as pretty and perfect as a doll. By the time the staff were done, she'd look utterly unrealistic, as fake as some of the pretty-boy stewards walking around.

And some of the older women, she thought nastily. *They look young, but it's clear they're old.*

She walked down the corridor, silently trying to pretend that Marie wasn't with her. Gold Deck had livened up over the past few days, with guests gambling in the casinos or splashing their way through the swimming pools. She had no doubt that a number of shipboard romances had already started. What happened on *Supreme* stayed on *Supreme*. She had no idea what the ship's actual motto was, if there even *was* an official motto, but she was fairly sure she knew what the unofficial motto was. A trio of guests—one man, two women—walked past her, the women wearing outfits sparkling with electric light. They'd better *hope* that whatever happened on *Supreme* stayed on *Supreme*.

Behind her, Marie sniffed. Angela allowed herself a slight smile, knowing that the older woman couldn't see her. Marie must have been irked if she was allowing her emotions to show so freely; normally she was very unemotional in public. Angela thought she should be relieved instead. The governess's charge was a trial at times, Marie had told Angela often enough, but at least she didn't follow the stupidest fashions . . .

But I might have done so if I'd had more freedom, she thought.

A disconcerting thought, too disconcerting for her to want to consider it. She'd seen too many trust fund brats go into rehab only to destroy their lives again and again. They drowned themselves in pleasures, going further and further for the ultimate high. She'd resented her parents for being controlling, but . . . they might have saved her life. Some of her peers had known the worst too soon.

She walked into the cabin. The space had changed over the last couple of days; her mother's staff had moved boxes of clothing into the antechamber and piled them up against the far bulkhead. The setup was chaotic, Angela thought, although *that* wasn't a bad thing. Her mother wouldn't be inviting many guests over while everything was in disarray. She had an uncle who lived in a messy mansion and never had to worry about unwelcome visitors. Angela rather admired him.

"Open the cabin," Marie said. Her lips thinned again. "Please."

Angela concealed her amusement. It was petty, but it was power. She nodded and pressed her fingers against the reader, opening the door and striding inside. Marie cleared her throat in annoyance as she saw the mess—Angela had left clothes everywhere when she'd been unpacking her bags—but said nothing.

"Get undressed," Marie ordered as she opened a clothes bag. "We don't have much time."

"We have one hour, forty-seven minutes, and twenty-five seconds," Angela said. She shrugged off her robe, followed by the wisps of costume. "I'm sure we have plenty of time."

Marie ignored her. "This is a formal dinner, My Lady," she said. "Do you understand the protocol?"

"Yeah," Angela said. "I know *precisely* what to do." She sighed. "Why couldn't it be a dance? Or a masked ball?"

"Because the captain wishes to welcome his most important guests properly," Marie said curtly. She walked into the bathroom and turned on the shower. Her voice echoed back through the door. "There'll be masked balls later."

"They're on the schedule," Angela muttered. She *liked* dancing. She would happily sit through a couple of hours of boring speechifying if she knew there would be dancing afterwards. "But why can't we dance *now?*"

"Because it wouldn't be proper," Marie reminded her. She stuck her head out of the bathroom. "Come."

Angela groaned. It was going to be a long evening.

———

"Stand up straighter," Senior Steward Falcon said. He paced the compartment, inspecting each of the stewards in turn. "You're serving the *captain* and his handpicked guests tonight. I'll pitch you out the nearest airlock if you make a mistake."

Matt kept his face expressionless. Falcon sounded pissed. He was stamping around the deck like a bear with a toothache, snapping and snarling at anyone who wasn't practically perfect in every way. He'd dragged the evening staff off their regular shifts to drill them remorselessly, then barely gave them a chance to eat before forcing them to get dressed in their serving uniforms. Beside him, Carla was silently fuming. Falcon had told her to tighten her shirt.

"Do not speak unless spoken to," Falcon reminded them. Matt couldn't help thinking that he sounded like a bad impression of a drill sergeant. "Keep your eyes to yourselves . . ."

"He means you," Carla muttered quietly.

Not quietly enough. Falcon swung around to glare at her. "France! What is the correct response to a complaint about the food?"

Carla straightened. "Abject apologies, followed by an offer to replace the meal with something more suitable," she said. "And a great deal of groveling."

"Right," Falcon said. His gaze moved to another steward. "Lucas! What is the correct response to a request to have one's seating assignment changed?"

"Check with the datanet for free seats; then reassign them," Lucas said. "And make sure that the files have been updated to reflect the new seating pattern."

Matt nodded. The vast majority of the guests were wealthy enough to afford biological enhancement and nanotechnology supports—they probably wouldn't be allergic to anything on the menu—but there was no accounting for taste. The staff had already worked out the menu, ensuring that everyone received a meal they could and would eat. There would be no surprises, Matt thought, and very little wastage either. *That* wouldn't matter—biological waste could be recycled—but it was important. The captain didn't want people saying that he didn't offer a good table.

And the first set of guests are all rich and powerful, he thought. *They'll complain loudly if they can't eat the food.*

Falcon barked orders. Matt strode forward, stopping in front of the reflective field. An image of himself appeared, wearing a white uniform that made him look a year or two younger. Everything was right, from the jaunty cap to the shoes . . . he even wore white gloves! A stain could seemingly ruin everything, but he knew from experience that the uniforms were designed to resist staining. He could wipe a spill off with a cloth and go straight back to work.

"It makes your butt look big," Carla whispered.

Matt fought the urge to giggle. He thought Falcon was joking about tossing people out the airlock, but the senior steward had plenty of other ways to punish anyone unlucky enough to screw up. And he'd have a point. Falcon would get a share of the blame if someone accidentally splashed soup on a guest, even if he was on the other side of the dining room at the time. Perhaps he'd be tossed out the airlock too.

"It makes your chest look bigger," he retorted. "Can you even breathe in that?"

"Barely," Carla said. "If I pass out midway through the dinner, remember to drag me out of the room before opening my shirt and performing CPR."

"I'll do my best," Matt promised. "I'm sure you'll get lots of tips."

"Hah," Carla said. She tilted her head, inspecting her reflection. "They come with a high price, don't you know?"

Falcon cleared his throat loudly. "The dinner will start in thirty minutes," he said. "We will now proceed to the dining antechamber."

"Hurry up and wait," Carla muttered. "Are you surprised?"

Matt shook his head. Captain VanGundy had told everyone that dinner would be served at 1700 precisely. He wouldn't be pleased with delays. There were quite enough logistic problems with feeding forty people at the same time without the staff being late. And the captain's displeasure would make itself known quickly. Falcon had taken a perverse pleasure in reminding his staff that the captain could order someone dismissed and thrown in the brig until the starship reached the next civilized world, then deposited there. Being a castaway sounded romantic until the reality sank in.

"No," he said. "It's just what I expected."

———

"You look adorable, sir," Jeanette said.

Paul gave her a dark look. He'd never liked hosting formal dinners, even when he'd been the captain of a superdreadnought. His fellow commanding officers had made good company, but admirals and reporters hadn't been quite as tolerable. And yet, they'd been navy or dependent on the navy. They'd had an incentive to behave that *Supreme*'s guests lacked.

He glowered at his reflection. His black dress uniform, liberally sprinkled with gilded braid, made him look like an admiral from a tinpot navy on the other side of the galaxy. The cynic in him wondered if there was enough gold on his jacket to purchase a starship, although he knew that was rather unlikely. He couldn't help wishing that he'd been allowed to keep his military uniform, which might have impressed some of the guests.

"You're meant to be on the bridge," he said crossly. Jeanette couldn't host any of the dinner parties, unfortunately. "Unless you want to swap jobs right now . . ."

Jeanette gave him an angelic smile. "Only if I get to keep the rank afterwards," she said. "I don't want to be captain for a day."

"I don't blame you," Paul said.

"We're still getting applications to actually *be* captain for a day," Jeanette said. "Quite a few duplicates too. Some girl called Marissa put in a dozen separate applications."

Paul resisted the urge to groan. An old tradition of putting an ensign in command of the ship for a day had existed, but the practice hadn't survived the war. The Royal Navy had too many other things to worry about than maintaining a tradition that most senior officers regarded with a complete lack of enthusiasm. He would have preferred not to even raise the possibility of having a civilian preteen pretend to be a commanding officer . . .

And there'll be complaints if we don't pick a winner, he thought. *It's too late to avoid having the contest altogether.*

He looked at his XO. "Is it just me, or are we expected to be party clowns as well as starship officers?"

Jeanette shrugged. "Doesn't the military have its silly moments?"

"No," Paul lied. "Well . . . nothing I want to talk about anyway."

His XO grinned. "We're meant to keep the customers happy," she said. "If that means putting a child in the captain's chair for a day and pretending to take her seriously . . . well, it's what we have to do. If there's a real emergency, we'll drop the facade and do everything in our power to handle the problem . . . as you know, sir."

"Yes," Paul said. He had faith in his crew. They'd handled a small number of emergencies already, although none of them had been particularly serious. And they'd done well during the simulated emergencies. He hoped they'd never have to face a *real* emergency. "It just feels odd."

"So does half the spit-and-polish we see from you military types, sir," Jeanette said. "But it makes sense in context."

Paul nodded, then took one last look in the mirror. "Time to face the music," he said. He felt almost as if he were going to his execution. God alone knew what Robert Cavendish and his ilk would want to discuss. "Good luck on the bridge."

"So far, we've had an uneventful cruise," she said. "None of the starships we've detected have shown any signs of interest in us."

"And let's hope it stays that way," Paul said. He donned his cap. "Wish me luck."

Jeanette smiled. "I can sound an alert at 1730 to get you out of there?"

Paul considered the option longer than he should have. "No," he said finally. The offer was tempting but would undermine passenger confidence in his ship and crew. "Just inform me if anything happens that requires my attention."

"Yes, sir," Jeanette said. "Good luck!"

"Hah," Paul said.

CHAPTER NINE

Five minutes into her semi-date with Finley Mackintosh, Angela was already certain that it was going to be a disaster. Not in the sense that he would turn out to be all hands, or that he would monopolize her attention and prevent her from talking to anyone else, but in the sense he was *boring*. He hadn't shown a hint of interest in her. His eyes hadn't even flickered to her chest when he'd first laid eyes on her. Instead, he'd merely bowed and offered her his arm.

She pasted a faint smile on her face as they walked down the corridor and into the dining room. The corridor itself was open, a transparent canopy allowing passengers to stare out into the flickering lights of hyperspace. Brilliant flashes and flares of energy danced around the starship, a private fireworks display that took her breath away. Angela wanted to stop and watch the lights, to admire the colors no one ever saw outside hyperspace, but Finley gently pulled her onwards. Naturally, the dining room itself was covered. No one could see outside.

Of course not, she thought as a white-garbed steward led her to their table. *We wouldn't want to distract people from the blather.*

Her eyes swept the compartment as more and more people were seated. Their table was slightly raised, allowing her to look down on the rest of the compartment. She couldn't help wondering, as she watched the room fill, just how many noses would be put out of joint. She'd seen feuds start because the wrong people were seated together.

Or because two society bitches were wearing the same dress from very exclusive designers, she thought. That had been amusing, although her mother had not agreed. *They were tearing each other apart in public.*

She tried hard not to be bored, but it wasn't easy. Finley wasn't talking to her . . . or anything. He was just sitting there, quietly. No wry remarks, no flirting or teasing . . . she was tempted to believe that he didn't even know she was there. She wondered, absently, what he'd do if she pulled down her dress, then squelched the thought. Finley's opinion didn't matter. It was her father who would go ballistic if she embarrassed the family so badly.

I should be sitting next to Nancy, she thought. *At least I'd have someone to talk to.*

She groaned to herself. Her younger sister was at the lowest table, chatting to a boy who looked a year or two older. He looked bored already. Angela felt a stab of pity, mingled with a certain understanding. She'd hated going to dinners when she'd been twelve. Sitting still for three hours while the grown-ups babbled about nonsense was awful, particularly when she wanted to run and play. It was no place for a child.

And she's the youngest person here, Angela thought. She rather suspected that she and Finley were the next youngest. Would Nancy have even been invited to the dinner if she hadn't been famous? *That poor boy might have been ordered to escort her too.*

A steward poured her a glass of wine. Angela eyed the drink lovingly, but she knew better than to touch it until everyone was served. Her parents entered the room, her mother giving Angela a bright smile as they took their seats on either side of the captain's chair. The captain himself entered a moment later, wearing a black jacket covered in braid. Angela couldn't help thinking that he looked uncomfortable. She didn't blame him. Formal dinner parties were always the worst.

We could have pushed the tables against the walls and turned the compartment into a dance floor, she thought. *And then had a buffet rather than table service.*

The captain tapped his knife against his glass. Angela turned, silently cursing under her breath. Being at the high table was supposed to be prestigious, but the placement also made it impossible to avoid paying attention. Everyone would notice if she shunned the captain, no matter how boring his speech was. Her father would be annoyed. He'd be annoyed even if he agreed that the speech was boring.

"There was a time," the captain said, "when interstellar travel was dangerous . . ."

Angela managed to keep a look of polite attention on her face, somehow. Whoever had written the captain's speech wasn't very good. A combination of mindless platitudes and unsubtle references to the immense cost of building such a cruise liner . . . she'd heard better speeches from her friends who intended to go into politics. But then, the captain did have a captive audience. He could drone for hours if he wished.

It *felt* like hours before the speech finally came to an end. "We have many special guests on this ship," the captain concluded. "But I ask you all to raise your glasses to one in particular: Nancy Cavendish, the first child to be born in hyperspace."

Angela raised her glass, torn between sympathy for her sister, who looked as though she wanted to drop dead on the spot, and the old irritation. Nancy was the first child to be born in hyperspace . . . big deal! Hell, Angela wasn't even sure that Nancy *was* the first . . . it wasn't as if she'd been born when humanity had learned how to open gateways and begin to explore hyperspace. Quite possibly there had been other births . . .

Nancy was definitely the first to be born on one of our ships, she thought. Normally, pregnant women would spend the trip in stasis. *Mother insisted on staying out of the pods.*

She glanced at Finley. "Do your siblings have any undeserved claims to fame?"

Finley looked back at her. "No."

Angela sighed. She'd been right. It was going to be a *very* long evening.

———

Matt took the plate, then carried it into the dining room. He could feel hundreds of eyes on him as he walked to the high table and carefully placed the plate in front of the captain, then walked back to the entrance. Carla and the others were carrying plates themselves, executing a choreographed dance designed to get as many plates out as quickly as possible. The guests wouldn't want to wait for their food.

They should have set up a buffet, he thought, as he picked up another plate, checked the tag, and carried it into the compartment. *That would be quicker.*

He placed the plate in front of Nancy Cavendish, who winked at him. Matt resisted the urge to wink back, knowing that someone would spot him. The entire dinner was being recorded for posterity, although he had no idea who would be interested. Corporate wouldn't allow the footage to leak out without permission from everyone at the dinner . . .

Carla passed him, her face expressionless. Matt noticed a number of hungry eyes, male and female, following her as she walked back to the door. It was odd. The women at the tables looked like butterflies, wearing fine clothes that revealed too much flesh for anyone's peace of mind, but the guests were staring at Carla or him instead of their peers? He could feel eyes watching him as he returned to the antechamber. The next set of plates was already waiting for them.

———

"The cheese is very good," Robert Cavendish said. "Highlands cheese, I believe. From Hebrides?"

"Yes, My Lord," Paul said. Thankfully, Jeanette had insisted that he read up on the food. "It was purchased five years ago and kept in storage."

"A good thing too," James Tasman said. He wasn't nearly as wealthy as Robert Cavendish, but was rich enough to buy himself a stateroom on Gold Deck. "There won't be any more like it."

"No, My Lord," Paul said. He gritted his teeth. Hebrides had been nuked, the surviving population largely evacuated, the world itself utterly beyond repair . . . and Tasman was moaning about a lack of *cheese*? "This may be the last surviving batch."

"One would imagine that they could set up cheese farms on their new homeworlds," Cavendish said. "It would bring in additional funds, I suppose."

Paul resisted the urge to shrug. It wasn't his place to point out that selling cheese, even the most expensive cheese in the galaxy, wasn't going to bring in enough money to terraform Hebrides. The planet was a radioactive wasteland. He doubted the refugees were going to find settling another world easy, no matter where they went. They'd either quickly lose their culture or find themselves resented by the locals. Either way, something would be lost.

Cavendish cleared his throat. "The king is talking about doubling the military budget," he said slowly. "Is that reasonable?"

"Perhaps," Paul said. "It would depend on what they spent the money on."

"It's not," Tasman said. He took another bite of his cheese. "The war is over. Building up the military is just another excuse to keep war-level taxation in place."

"Perhaps," Cavendish repeated. He ignored Tasman with a thoroughness Paul could only admire. "Can you elaborate?"

Paul tried to keep his face impassive. Both military and corporate worlds had superior officers who liked hearing things that confirmed what they already believed, or, for that matter, hearing what they wanted to hear. He *did* have an opinion, he *could* offer it . . . but he had no idea what Cavendish wanted to hear. Would he be penalized for telling the truth? Or . . . or what?

"The Theocracy isn't a threat any longer," Paul said. There were a handful of rogue starships, according to the latest set of updates, but they would be hunted down and destroyed eventually. "Right now, we don't face any other serious threats. The other galactic powers aren't interested in confronting us."

"That's because we kicked the Theocracy's ass," Tasman said.

"Yes, sir," Paul said. He held up a hand to make his point. "Right now, we have two problems. On one hand, we have to patrol the spacelanes throughout Commonwealth *and* Theocratic space. That requires a considerable number of smaller units, with larger capital ships held in reserve. On the other hand, we have to maintain a powerful deterrent to ensure that none of the other galactic powers start considering a smash-and-grab of their own."

"You just said that the other galactic powers aren't interested in confronting us," Tasman said.

"No, because we can defend ourselves," Paul pointed out. "If that changes, if one of them thinks they have a decisive military advantage, they might be tempted to try something. They may well feel that the *inner* powers are trapped, hemmed in by the outer powers. It would tempt them to go for us."

Cavendish looked like he'd bitten into a lemon. "You think that they would?"

"Weakness invites attack," Paul said. "Human history teaches us that much, at least."

"It's also expensive," Tasman said. "The money lavished on the military could go elsewhere."

"Except then you look both wealthy and weak, an irresistible combination," Paul countered dryly. "Having a strong military is like buying insurance. If you never need it, you've wasted all that money; if you do need it, you'll really need it."

"Good point," Cavendish said. "I thank you, Captain."

"But what are the odds of being attacked?" Tasman asked. "You have a cold view of the universe, Captain."

"I do," Paul agreed. "The universe does not bend to wishful thinking."

Cavendish chuckled. "And sometimes you have to make the hard decisions," he said. He smiled. "Do you think the king's reconstruction program is a good idea?"

"I don't know enough to offer a comment," Paul said. "But it might be cheaper than clearing up the mess afterwards, if the postwar universe collapses into chaos."

"If," Tasman said.

"If," Paul agreed.

————

The cheese, Angela decided, was expensive rather than tasty. Muttered comments about it being the last of its kind didn't help. The next two plates of food, lamb pieces and something she couldn't identify, weren't much better. She understood how important it was to show off one's wealth, but merely booking a Gold Deck stateroom would do that. Why not have some decent food?

Finley nudged her gently. "What do you do all day?"

Angela blinked in surprise. That was his first question? He hadn't said anything to her since the food had arrived . . . did that mean he was trying to make conversation? Or was he just awkwardly plodding his way through the dinner? Perhaps he was bored too.

"Not much," she said. It struck her, suddenly, that her reply was literally true. She *didn't* do much all day. "I was at the beach this morning . . ."

Finley's eyes raised. "A beach?"

"Yeah," Angela said. A sudden sense of wickedness made her lean forward and whisper in his ear, "And guess how much I was wearing?"

She wasn't sure what sort of reaction she'd expected, but she saw nothing. She'd known boys who would have blushed; boys who would have told her what *they* thought she should have been wearing; and boys who would have told her, in great detail, *precisely* what they'd like to do with her when they were alone. But Finley showed no reaction at all. Perhaps he just wasn't interested in her—or women in general. Or perhaps he simply didn't like her.

Father arranged this date, she thought, feeling a flicker of sympathy. Finley might not have wanted the date. *He didn't ask me out on his own.*

"A beach," Finley repeated. "What *else* do you do all day?"

"Back home, I have a social life," Angela said. It was true, although her social circle had been starting to come apart. All of her friends were marrying or taking up positions in the corporate hierarchy. "I go to parties, I shop, I . . ."

She sighed. She knew she was lucky, insanely lucky. Her trust fund would keep her solvent for her entire life, unless she tried to purchase her own starship or mansion. She would never have to work, never have to do anything. And yet, her life was empty. Angela had no challenges, nothing to overcome . . . just an endless cycle of pleasure. What was she worth, really? Would she grow into someone as vapid as her mother? Or eventually go off the rails and self-destruct in a manner that couldn't be covered up?

"I don't know," she said. She looked at him. "What do *you* do all day?"

"Father trained me to manage his business accounts," Finley said. "I will take over when he retires. Your father has offered additional training."

"How nice," Angela said. She doubted the gesture was *free*. Her father rarely did anything out of the goodness of his heart. "I hope you have a nice time."

Finley, for the first time, smiled. "I hope so too."

Angela looked up as another steward approached, carrying yet another plate. A piece of pie. She wondered, suddenly, what it would be like to work as a steward. Or anything, really. Did they feel accomplished? Or were they too desperate to save money to care about what they actually did?

And now we're starting dessert, she thought sourly. *Another three hours to go.*

———

"Your girlfriend is at the high table," Carla said as they waited to go back into the dining room. "That guy she's next to looks constipated."

"It must be the food," Matt said. Angela glowed like an angel—the white dress made her look like a bride on her wedding day—but Finley Mackintosh seemed to be a weakling, the kind of young man who would be mercilessly bullied at school and grow up into a colorless accountant. "There isn't enough fiber in their diet."

Carla shot him a warning glance. "Be careful you don't say that too loudly," she said. "You never know who might be listening."

Matt nodded reluctantly. Angela wasn't the only beautiful woman in the dining room, but there was still something about her that drew his eye. He'd thought too much about her over the last few days. It was silly, it was stupid, it was dangerous . . . and yet he was doing it anyway. It was enough to make him wonder why he didn't use one of the VR chambers or the brothel. The stewards *were* allowed to use them if they weren't already reserved.

"Yeah." Matt glanced back. Falcon was issuing orders, pointing to the final set of plates. He suspected that Angela would be relieved when the evening finally came to an end. "Do you think they'll tip us?"

Carla gave him an exaggerated shrug. "The rich tend to give better tips, when they think to do it, but the poorer guests tend to be more consistent about *giving*."

"Oh," Matt said. "Is *that* why Jonny and Kate were so pleased to be assigned to Silver Deck?"

"A gamble," Carla said. "Will they take more tips, but less money? Or not?" She smiled. "There are men out there who could buy a whole starship with pocket change."

Matt believed her. He'd looked up the figures. Robert Cavendish wasn't the only person on the ship so wealthy that anyone who wanted to talk about it needed to resort to imaginary numbers. If Carla was aiming for a rich husband, she could hardly do better for a hunting ground. But would she find happiness or a ball and chain? She was no more the social equal of any of the guests than Matt himself.

Or maybe I'm overthinking it, he thought as he hurried to pick up the next plate. Carla had always struck him as sensible. *She might just want to finish this cruise with as little trouble as possible.*

CHAPTER TEN

The "date" hadn't been *entirely* a disaster, Angela decided as she walked into the antechamber, but it could have been a great deal better.

She snorted at the thought. Finley had gallantly offered to walk her around the promenade after dinner, and she'd agreed, reluctant to risk her father's displeasure by ending the date so soon. And yet, it had been boring, tedious beyond words. Finley talked more when they were alone, but his conversation was as boring as everything else. There were only so many times that he could talk approvingly about pieces of expensive—and overpriced—artwork before she wanted to scream.

She didn't have any feelings for him, positive or negative. Even the dull resentment that she'd been forced to waste an evening was more aimed at her father than her fake date. *He probably found me as boring as I found him.*

She looked up as she heard someone clearing his throat. "Angela," her father said. He was sitting on the sofa, reading a datapad. "If you'll come with me . . . ?"

Angela felt a chill running down her spine as her father rose and led the way into his private office. As she'd expected, it had been remodeled into something very similar to the office he had in the mansion, right down to the secure cabinets and a large wooden desk. The only things missing were the bookshelves and their contents. She'd always believed her father never actually read the books.

"Please, take a seat," he said. "Your mother will be joining us in a minute."

Angela's mouth felt dry as she sat on the comfortable chair. She was rarely allowed in her father's office, and the only times she'd been summoned had been when she had perpetrated a crime so awful that her last governess had marched her to Robert Cavendish rather than tell her off personally. Angela had never really had the sense that her father actually cared what she did—he'd always seemed simply annoyed that he'd been interrupted—but she'd never enjoyed his lectures. They'd always ended with her in tears, promising to be better.

Her mind raced. What had she done wrong?

She'd managed to keep her room private, but her parents had *days* to lecture her for that. She'd gone on the damned date with Finley, hadn't she? Maybe she hadn't hidden her true feelings as well as she'd thought, and her father was about to yell at her for looking bored in public. It was all his fault, damn it. She had no idea *what* he'd been discussing with the captain, but . . . she was sure it had been more interesting than Finley's toneless babblings.

She looked up as her mother stepped into the room and closed the door behind her. Was she being blamed for some act Nancy had committed? She doubted it. Her sister's governess was usually good at figuring out when Nancy had done something wrong, but they'd left Suzie on Tyre. Marie might not have realized that *Nancy* was to blame for some heinous crime. Or maybe her parents were about to give another lecture on proper decorum in public, with her mother there to drive the lesson home.

"Angela," her father said, "we have something important to discuss with you."

She could feel her heart racing in her chest, pounding. She was surprised the other two couldn't hear it. Her thoughts ran in all directions, mocking her. She didn't think she was in trouble, yet . . . yet part of her wondered if that was actually a good thing. This was starting to feel worse than the day she'd accidentally damaged her mother's prize rosebushes during a particularly noisy game.

"Yes, Father," she managed. "I am here."

Robert Cavendish cracked a faint smile that didn't quite reach his eyes.

"You are nineteen," he said. "You are old enough to sit at the high table and make conversation with the adults."

Angela cringed. It *was* about Finley, then. She'd been right at the end of the table, and there'd been no one else to talk to unless she spoke over Finley. Her father had noticed that they'd barely conversed . . . she gritted her teeth, wondering what form the rebuke would take. They couldn't bar her from visiting her friends when they were uncounted millions of light-years away.

Not millions of light-years, her thoughts pointed out. *Just one or two, perhaps.*

She fought to keep her face expressionless. On Tyre, she could take an aircar and fly halfway around the world for an afternoon with her friends. God knew she'd done it a few times, although the war had cut down on such little pleasures. On *Supreme*, she could no more visit her friends than she could fly under her own power. They were all back on Tyre. The only person she knew who was close to her own age was Finley, and he was twenty-four.

Her father made an irritated sound. Angela flushed. He'd been talking, and she hadn't been listening.

"I'm sorry," she said. "I was light-years away."

"I noticed," her father said. He didn't sound angry. That worried her. He was *definitely* distracted by some greater thought. "It is time for you to embrace some of your adult responsibilities."

Angela blinked. "Father?"

"You and Finley will marry," her father said. "The wedding will be concluded the day before we return to Tyre."

For a long moment, Angela honestly couldn't comprehend what her father had just told her. Marriage? To Finley? To . . .

"He's a very decent young man," her mother said. "He's intelligent and caring and—"

Angela found her voice, somehow. "We *are* talking about Finley Mackintosh, right?"

"Yes," her father said. He sounded irked, his eyes darkening in displeasure. "You went to dinner with him, remember?"

Angela felt a flicker of annoyance—she hated it when people talked down to her—but it was buried under her shock. She was nineteen . . . her parents couldn't just marry her off, could they? She . . . she swallowed, hard. She'd known other girls who *were* married off, just to ensure that the aristocracy remained in power, but she'd never thought such an arrangement would happen to her. She'd always assumed that she'd simply inherit her father's position one day. She would never be the duchess, but she'd have power . . .

At least you actually know Finley. Her thoughts mocked her. Perhaps she would've been more enthusiastic if she *didn't* know Finley. *There are some boys and girls who meet their partners on the day of the wedding.*

"He's boring," she managed. "He's the most boring man in the world."

"He's intelligent and capable," her father said crossly. "And he can discourse on a wide range of subjects."

Angela made a rude sound. *That* was a lie. Or . . . perhaps Finley *could* talk about things that interested her father. She had no idea. Perhaps they chatted happily together about the Norwegian leather industry. Or, more likely, the postwar reconstruction of worlds no one had ever heard of until they'd suddenly become part of the Commonwealth. She had no doubt the old fogies could babble for hours about . . . about anything.

Finley isn't that old, a treacherous part of her mind pointed out. *He's only six years older than you.*

"He's a tedious little man," Angela insisted. "Father, I don't want to marry him."

"You must," her mother said.

Angela rounded on her. "Why?"

"You must," her mother snapped. "Angela—"

"I am *not* desperate to rise in the world," Angela snapped back. "I don't gain *anything* from marrying Finley!"

Her mother recoiled as if she'd been slapped. Angela felt a moment of guilt, but she was too angry to care. She wasn't going to be married off, damn it. If they wanted to kick her out of the family, she'd take her trust fund and go! She wanted . . . she wasn't sure *what* she wanted. In hindsight, maybe it had been a mistake to do nothing with her life. She could have joined her cousins in preparing to take over the family business or followed Kat Falcone into the navy . . .

I did nothing, she thought grimly. *My only value lies in breeding stock.*

"That will do," her father said. He sounded angry. Normally his tone would have been enough to make her submit at once. "You do not talk to your mother like that, young lady."

Angela was too angry to care. "And what will you do if I *refuse* to marry him? Ground me for a million years? Beat me? Kick me out of the cabin or the family or the airlock? Or . . . or what?"

Her father met her eyes evenly. "I'll tell you the truth," he said. His voice was surprisingly calm. "You owe it to the family to marry well."

Angela swallowed. She'd expected her father to shout. Instead . . .

She took a long breath. "I understand that I owe you . . . that I owe the family," she said. "But I . . . I do not *have* to marry anyone. I don't *want* to marry anyone."

"I understand exactly how you feel," her father said quietly.

"No, you don't," Angela yelled. It was hard, so hard, to try to be calm. "You're not the one who has to open her legs and let a boring trust-fund brat fuck her in a loveless match!"

The blatant crudity should have shocked her father. She'd certainly expected the words to make an impact. Instead, he seemed prepared to ignore them.

"Like I said, I'll tell you the truth," her father said. He was *still* calm. "Do you want to listen?"

Angela nodded, once.

"I believed it would be better if you chose for yourself if you wanted to join the family business," her father said. "My father . . . my father forced me to learn everything, back when he thought I would be the next duke. I didn't like that life, Angela. I thought that if you were interested, you'd come to me and ask for training. Instead . . ."

"I did nothing," Angela said.

"Yes," her father agreed. "Perhaps I should have forced you to learn. It would have given you more background information."

He paused. "You are dangerously ignorant of many things," he added. He looked down at the desk for a long, chilling moment. "And one of the things you don't know is that Cavendish Corporation is in serious trouble."

Angela stared at him. "We are?"

"Yes," her father said.

He rose and started to pace. "We contributed a significant sum of money to fund the Commonwealth, back when King Travis was on the throne. I'm not talking about mere *billions* here. My father felt the investment was worthwhile, as long-term projections indicated that the Commonwealth would be successful. Indeed, we saw a number of those investments start to repay themselves over the last decade.

"And then there was the war. All of a sudden, those investments were either frozen or lost completely. The Theocracy destroyed a number of our investments when they occupied worlds along the front lines. Worse, there was a sudden rise in taxation on Tyre, matched with economic disruption caused by the war and terrorist attacks and . . ."

He laughed, humorlessly. "Building this class of ship might not have been a bright idea," he said, waving a hand at the bulkhead. "Sure, it's pocket change . . . but pocket change adds up."

Angela couldn't believe her ears. "Father . . . are we *broke?*"

"Not yet," her father said. "Our best-case projections, assuming that there are no further economic shockwaves, suggest that we might be able to secure ourselves over the next five to ten years. Our worst-case projections suggest we might be looking at complete collapse within the next five years. A lot depends on factors completely beyond our control, Angela. The king's elaborate reconstruction plan will create new work for us, but it will also put more stress on our finances at the worst possible time."

"Oh," Angela said. She still couldn't believe her ears, but there was a certainty in her father's voice that made it impossible to disbelieve him. "The government can't help?"

Her father snorted. "Sweetheart, the government is a major part of the problem," he said sardonically. "And even if politicians wanted to help, they couldn't. Even *trying* would bring on the disaster."

Angela's eyes sharpened. "Are you sure?"

"Yes," her father said. "Right now, we've covered our weakened position as completely as we can. Very few rumors, nothing credible, have managed to leak out. But . . . if we run into another financial problem, we're going to be in trouble. Any attempt to rationalize our expenses will probably set off the crisis. Our stockholders will pull out. Entire sub-businesses will collapse or be snapped up by other corporations."

He turned to face her. "We're in a very delicate position, Angela," he said. "And the slightest wrong move, or even a right one, might be enough to cause a disaster."

"I see," Angela said. She saw no point in trying to debate finance or economics with her father. He'd been playing with both for longer than she'd been alive. "How will Finley marrying me help?"

"Finley's family wishes to move up in the world," her father said. "A match between you and Finley will give them more prestige, something they want desperately. It also gives us access to their coffers, something *we* want desperately. Merging some of their sub-businesses into ours will give us an infusion of ready cash without raising eyebrows."

"Too *many* eyebrows," Angela's mother said.

Her father nodded. "And, in the long term, Finley will also bring a number of stocks, shares, and other business interests to the combine. The move will help secure our position long enough to adapt to the postwar universe."

Angela looked from one parent to the other. "And if I refuse to marry him?"

"Good question," her father said. "We won't kick you out of the family, if that's what you're asking. But I don't know what will happen to the family. None of the Big Twelve have ever gone bankrupt before. If we can't meet our debts, we'll be sunk."

". . . Shit," Angela said.

She wasn't sure she believed him when he said he wouldn't kick her out of the family. Her father had a pronounced streak of ruthlessness, one that had occasionally shocked her in the past. *And* Finley's family would have conducted the negotiations with a view to getting all they could from the Cavendishes. They'd demand satisfaction if the marriage never went through. Even if they didn't know precisely why Angela's family needed the money, they'd know that something was wrong. The merest hint of a credible rumor might destroy the corporation.

"Millions of people will be affected," her father said, quietly. "Some will find work for other corporations; others will find themselves unemployed for far longer. Most of our assets will probably be seized to pay off our debts: the mansions, the penthouses, the estate in the hills . . . your mother's extensive collection of dresses. If the collapse is limited to just us, it will be bad enough. If it weakens or destroys other corporations, it will be a great deal worse. The entire Commonwealth might be threatened."

Angela looked down at the deck. She might not have her father's experience, but she knew a guilt trip when she heard one. The family itself was at risk. She thought, suddenly, of her cousins, trying to learn the ropes. Did they know about the crisis? Or had it been kept from them? She doubted more than a handful of people knew the full extent of the problem . . .

"I know this won't be easy," her mother said. "It wasn't easy for me either."

"Of course not," Angela snarled.

Her mother placed a hand on her shoulder. "You marry him and have two children," she said softly. "Five years from now, or ten, you decide you want to leave. You have over a century ahead of you. No one will expect you to spend your entire life with the same man."

Angela glared. Had her mother faced the same dilemma? What deals had been made, in the dark, before she married Angela's father? Or was she just the social climber Angela had always taken her to be.

She didn't look up. The collapse of an entire corporation would be disastrous. She thought of the gardeners who'd built her a treehouse, of the young servants who kept the mansion running . . . they'd all lose their jobs. She couldn't even *begin* to understand what might happen if she refused the match . . .

Her fists clenched. She had no choice. Her father knew she had no choice. Hot tears prickled at the corners of her eyes. She didn't know—she had no way to know—if Finley had wanted the match or if he'd been strong-armed into it too. But the union would be easier for him, wouldn't it? He could just sleep with her a couple of times, then leave her alone. He didn't have to be a complete asshole to turn their marriage into a farce. The mere act of marrying under such conditions would do that for him.

And if I don't marry him, she thought numbly, *untold numbers of people will suffer.*

"Fine," she shouted. She rose. She'd go to her bedroom, then . . . then what? "But don't expect me to be happy!"

CHAPTER ELEVEN

"That was an . . . interesting evening," Matt said as they stepped into their sleeping quarters. "I don't know how they put up with the speeches."

"It's astonishing how interesting someone becomes if they have enough money to buy and sell a million people like us," Carla said. She closed the hatch behind them. "What happened to the others?"

"They were talking about hitting the mess," Matt said. He didn't feel particularly hungry himself. Going to the crew bar would be fun, but right now he needed sleep. "Was Falcon joking when he said there'd be an after-action review?"

Carla laughed, humorlessly. "No," she said. "He'll be telling us what we did wrong all week."

"Oh dear," Matt said. "Nothing actually went wrong, did it?"

"No," Carla said. "They would have heard the shouting at the other end of the ship if something had gone awry."

Matt sat down on the bunk. "I made seven hundred in tips," he said, checking his credit balance. Some of that would go to the general fund, he knew, but the remainder was his to keep, untaxed. "How about you?"

"Two thousand," Carla said. Her face turned sour. "Trust me, I earned it." Her voice was grim.

Matt looked up. "What happened?"

"Oh, all the usual things that happen when rich elderly men and women see a pretty young girl serving their table," Carla said. "Don't *you* get your ass squeezed from time to time?"

Matt flushed. "Not on duty."

"Just you wait," Carla said. She smirked, her lips curving into a cruel smile. "Some of those *really* old women will try to drag you into their cabins, if you're not careful. Maybe some of the middle-aged men and women too."

"You make it sound like a bad thing," Matt protested.

Carla laughed, harshly. "I dare you to tell Falcon that you were late for morning briefing because some elderly cougar lured you into her bed and kept you up all night," she said. "I assure you he won't like it."

"Probably not," Matt agreed. The idea sounded amusing, but he knew it had its darker side. "Are you all right?"

"I've been better," Carla said. She shot him a sidelong glance. "You spent half the evening staring at Angela, by the way. Don't think I didn't notice."

Matt blushed furiously. "Did anyone else notice?"

"I don't know," Carla said. "But I suggest you keep your eyes to yourself."

"She didn't look as if she was enjoying herself," Matt said. A thought struck him. "Is her sister *really* the first child to be born in hyperspace?"

Carla shot him a mischievous look. "If you say otherwise, I dare say Mr. Cavendish's lawyers will want a word with you," she said. "They made quite a big deal out of it at the time."

"I didn't notice," Matt said. How old would *he* have been, back then? Seven? Eight? He made a mental note to look the story up, when he had the time. "Angela didn't seem impressed."

"I imagine she wouldn't be," Carla said. "How many bad movies have started with an older child being jealous of a younger sibling's fame?" She elbowed him. "Go get a shower; then get into your bunk," she said firmly. "Mornings always come too soon."

"Yes, My Lady," Matt said.

Carla gave him the finger as he stripped off his uniform, carefully hanging it in the locker to be cleaned. The staff would pick the clothing up to wash the following morning. He couldn't help feeling a stab of relief as he stood naked in front of the mirror. The uniform was tight in all the wrong places. Perhaps he should have been surprised that no one had tried to grab his ass. He knew that some of the male guests swung both ways.

He stumbled into the shower and bathed, hastily. Carla was right. Falcon had told the evening staff that they could stay in their bunks until 1000, but that would give him only seven hours of sleep at best. The others would be coming back soon too. He was used to sleeping in the wardroom now, despite the complete lack of privacy, but it was still easy to jerk awake at the slightest noise. His instructors had told him that was a good thing.

Bastards, he thought as he finished showering. *They just wanted to make sure that none of us had a good night's sleep.*

Carla was undressing when he walked back into the cabin, removing her uniform piece by piece. Matt forced himself to look away. His cock twitched, and he dived into his bunk. He was too tired to hide anything from his bunkmate, and yet . . .

He turned his gaze to follow her as she walked to the shower. Her rear was as perfect as the rest of her, drawing his eyes to her bare legs, yet . . . there was a nasty bruise on her right buttock. Had someone pinched her hard enough to leave a mark? Matt shivered, torn between anger and a sour realization that there was no point in complaining. Corporate might believe Carla if she filed a complaint, but they wouldn't do anything about it. The customer was always right. They might even retaliate against Carla if she made too much of a fuss.

Matt leaned back in his bunk, trying to think. There'd been forty guests in the dining compartment, half of whom were men. But it didn't *have* to be a man, did it? Carla had pointed out that women could be predators too. Who had it been? He wanted to know, even though cold logic told him that it would be pointless. He couldn't do anything about it.

Poison the bastard, the vindictive part of his mind suggested. *Or shove him out the nearest airlock.*

He shook his head in frustration. The entire ship was monitored. Security would track down a murderer in record time, unless . . . he'd seen movies where the security net was compromised, but he didn't have the faintest idea how to begin. Come to think of it, he wasn't sure he could get his hands on poison or open an airlock from the inside. He'd need security codes he didn't have. No, murder wasn't an option. The whole thing was a pointless revenge fantasy.

Carla stepped back into the cabin. Matt looked away, hastily.

"Good night," he said.

"I'll kick you out of bed at 1000," Carla said. She sounded like her old self again, no hint of disquiet. "You're back on casino duty tomorrow afternoon."

"Joy," Matt said.

———

"All systems remain nominal," Jeanette said as Paul stepped onto the bridge. "I've ordered a slight course change to avoid a prospective energy storm, but we should still make our destination within the time window."

Paul studied the display. The energy flickers might turn into a storm, or they might just fade back into the background, but there was no point in taking chances. A superdreadnought wouldn't have a hope if it got caught up in an energy storm. *Supreme*'s defenses were good, but still flimsy by comparison. Better to be late, even pushing the edge of their destination window, than try to skirt the edge of a storm.

"Very good," he said.

He smiled to himself, thinly. It was one of the things natural-born groundpounders would never understand. Space travel held a hint of unpredictability, even hundreds of years after the first starships had traveled into hyperspace. He'd love to be able to promise that *Supreme* would reach her destination on a specific date and time, but he knew better. The universe was rarely so obliging.

"Thank you, sir," Jeanette said. She glanced at her terminal. "There was a minor incident on D Deck, a rowdy party that got a little out of hand. Security cleared up the mess."

"Glad to hear it," Paul said. "Is it likely to cause long-term problems?"

"I don't believe so," Jeanette said. "It sounds like a leaving party that turned into a drunken riot. No significant injuries or damage, just a handful of frightened people. I don't see any need to drop a hammer on them."

Paul pursed his lips. He was far too used to military discipline. Crewmen caught fighting could expect to spend the next few weeks on punishment duties, even if they weren't formally disciplined. Hell, most of them would probably prefer an informal punishment rather than anything else. Spending the week cleaning the shuttlebay was better than a black mark on one's record. But he doubted a civilian would see it that way.

"I'll read the full report in the morning," he said. Someone would second-guess him, of course. Someone always did. "But as long as no one was seriously hurt, I dare say there's no need to take sterner measures."

"Yes, sir," Jeanette said. She smiled. "They were just letting off steam."

"I can't put *that* in my report," Paul said. He'd thought military bureaucrats were bad when it came to demanding that everything be reported, then filed in triplicate. Corporate was even worse. "But guests will be guests."

He looked at the display. *Supreme* hung in the center, escorted by the two destroyers. He considered, briefly, asking their captains to dinner. The request was within his purview, and it would be good for civil-military relationships. But he didn't want to take the captains off their command decks with the possibility they'd be attacked. Pirates might be shadowing *Supreme* even now.

And that's another problem with commanding a cruise liner, he thought. *I can't afford to ignore any sensor contact.*

"Hand the bridge over to your relief when the time comes," he said. "And make sure you get some sleep."

"Yes, sir," Jeanette said.

Paul nodded curtly. Leaving didn't please him. He wanted to spend more time on the bridge, but he had no choice. He was expected to spend time with the wealthy passengers when he wasn't actually sleeping . . . He'd heard that some corporate installations had building managers and business managers. Corporate might see the sense in appointing a guest captain as well as a starship captain. But if he wasn't careful, he might wind up with the wrong job.

"I'll be in my quarters," he said.

He turned and strode off the bridge. The corridor lights were dimmed, a droll, unnatural reminder that it was shipboard night. The dull lighting sent warning shivers down his spine. Military warships didn't pay more than lip service to shipboard night, whatever the hour. The gamma and delta crews couldn't afford to start thinking that they should be asleep when they were on duty. They never dimmed the lights outside crew quarters.

It felt weirdly *off* as he walked down to his cabin hatch. *Supreme* was sleeping, with most of her passengers in their beds. Some guests would be up all night drinking, he was sure, but the remainder would be asleep. The hospitality crews would be asleep too. There was something eerie about the missing background noise . . . even the dull thrumming of the drive was gone. He couldn't help feeling a flicker of disapproval. He'd been taught that hearing the drives was a good thing.

The passengers disagree, he thought. Corporate had drilled that lesson into his head, along with a number of others. *And the passengers are always right.*

He opened his hatch and stepped inside. The steward had already cleaned the compartment, made the bed, and refreshed the coffeepot. He wasn't sure he liked that either, although he had retained a steward when he'd been in the navy. The only thing missing was the prelaid breakfast . . . but then, he was supposed to take his breakfast in the dining room. No doubt the passengers would complain loudly if he didn't eat with them.

Eating with the captain is part of the attraction.

Paul undressed quickly, then checked his terminal. Security's preliminary report on the fight was already waiting for him but contained few details. Paul suspected that any future investigations would be perfunctory. No one had been seriously hurt, the ship hadn't been damaged . . . and besides, the passengers were always right. As long as they didn't do anything Paul had to take official notice of, he was supposed to turn a blind eye.

I miss the navy, he thought as he walked into his bedroom and climbed into bed. *Things were so much more understandable there.*

He closed his eyes. Sleep came quickly.

———

Angela couldn't sleep. Her thoughts were churning.

She'd never *thought* she'd get married, not really. She was *nineteen* . . . even her mother had been in her early thirties when she'd married. There was certainly no hurry to wed and start having children. Her fertility cycle had been frozen, thanks to the wonders of modern medical technology. She didn't have to get married quickly to have babies, let alone do anything else.

But now she *had* to get married . . .

Her mind spun as she tried to process everything she'd been told. It was impossible to believe, truly believe, that the family corporation was in dire straits. And yet . . . she was sure, somehow, that her father wasn't lying. He wouldn't seek to marry her off to someone below her, certainly someone who didn't have a hell of a lot of talent, unless he was desperate.

The thought made her cringe. She just didn't like Finley. She certainly didn't want to bear his children! And tradition dictated she *had* to bear his children. They couldn't use an exowomb or a surrogate mother . . . their children had to be hers. She damned the tradition as savagely as she could, using words she knew Marie would have told her off for saying.

She leaned back in her bed, trying to think. She couldn't just leave. She didn't know if her father could or would cut her off from her trust fund, but the fund itself might not survive if the corporation crashed. If she'd thought to learn . . . she cursed herself too, just as savagely. She didn't know enough to check her father's words . . . she had no way to ascertain for herself if he was right. In hindsight, she should have forced herself to study as if her life depended on it.

My life did depend on it, she thought.

She fought down an insane urge to giggle. She'd watched period romances with her girlfriends—when men were men, women were women, and children were either bratty as hell or impossibly pure—and she'd never understood them. Everyone seemed to be bound into their roles, even the children. The men and women had acted foolishly because they never seemed to think! And yet . . . she understood them now. They'd been bound by invisible chains of duty and honor and obligation, just like her. The only real difference was that she'd never realized she was chained as well until it was too late.

Her fists clenched. *She* hadn't been born to a world that limited her because of her sex. There had been all *kinds* of opportunities, if she'd chosen to take them. She could have studied and joined the corporation; her name would have ensured her rise if she'd had a smidgeon of talent. Or she could have joined the navy or a trading ship or . . . instead, she'd just stayed where she was. And now she was trapped.

She closed her eyes, trying to summon the merest hint of feelings for Finley. She'd started experimenting with boys, and girls, almost as soon as she'd come of age. She had experimented in a way she was sure would shock her parents, if they knew . . . and yet, she couldn't imagine sleeping with Finley.

Fuck it, she thought. Her eyes snapped open. *What the hell do I do?*

Angela cursed again. There was no one she could ask for advice. No one who might help her. No one who might . . . do what? Fight her father? Give him a way out that didn't include bartering away his daughter's life?

And now I'm trapped. There was no way off the cruise ship, at least until it stopped at Williamson's World. And then . . . she wasn't even sure if she'd have access to her trust fund there. *What do I do now?*

Slowly, bitterly, she drifted off to sleep.

CHAPTER TWELVE

"You look like hell," Nancy said when Angela staggered out of her cabin. "What were you and Finley *doing* all night?"

Angela glared at her, trying to push all her fury and fear into her expression. Her sister stumbled backward, her eyes going wide with shock. Angela knew she should feel ashamed for frightening the younger girl, but right now all she felt was envy. Nancy wouldn't be old enough to marry for at least another six years. She'd have ample time to carve out a career for herself, or something, if she wished.

"I just asked," Nancy managed. She tried to peep into the cabin. "Is he still there?"

"Shut up," Angela growled. If their mother heard Nancy talking like that, they'd both be in big trouble. "You—"

"Ah, Angela," Marie's voice said. Angela turned just in time to see her governess emerge from the rear chamber. "Your mother requests the pleasure of your company in her private dining room."

"Oh," Angela said. "And what if there *isn't* any pleasure to be had in my company?"

Marie eyed her disapprovingly. Angela had to smile. She'd changed into a nightgown that was practically translucent, but she hadn't bothered to wash her face or fix her hair. Her makeup was smeared. Her cosmetic scales were damaged, and she looked like a witch. She wondered, absently, just what the first boy she'd dated would make of her. Would her nightgown make up for her ghastly face?

Maybe Finley will take one look and run away, screaming, she thought. A giggle slipped from her lips. *That might get me out of this nightmare.*

"Go wash your face and put on a robe," Marie ordered. "And then inject yourself with a detoxicant. You probably had just a little too much to drink last night."

"More than just a little," Nancy put in. "You were quaffing wine like it was—"

"Be quiet, you little brat," Angela snarled. *"Please."*

She turned and stalked into her bedroom, silently daring Marie to follow her. Maybe Nancy would distract the governess long enough to let Angela clean herself up in peace. The last thing she wanted, right now, was a lecture on The Proper Behavior of a Young Lady in Polite Society or something even more tedious. She'd had a nasty shock last night, and she doubted it would get any better in a hurry. What if . . . she sighed, gritting her teeth as she glared at herself in the mirror. It was a minor miracle that the glass didn't shatter instantly.

Perhaps I should just take one of those prank sweets before bed, she thought. *Finley won't want to kiss me if my lips taste like shit.*

She dismissed the thought, angrily, as she wiped her face clean. There was nothing to be gained from laying on the makeup with a trowel, not now. Maybe she'd fix her face later, before she went out . . . or maybe she wouldn't bother.

She glared down at the telltale on her wrist, then donned a robe and hurried outside. Nancy was gone, unsurprisingly. Marie was waiting, impatient. Angela glowered at her—the governess stared back evenly—and then turned to the door. Marie walked behind her all the way to Halle Cavendish's private dining room as if she expected Angela to run.

The thought would have made Angela laugh if it hadn't been so serious. Where the hell was she expected to *go*?

"Angela," her mother said as Angela paused at the door. "Come on in."

She braced herself and walked inside. Her mother was sitting, a tiered cake table in front of her loaded with brightly colored cakes and macaroons. The breakfast threatened to make Angela's stomach churn. She would have loved it when she'd been a child, she thought, but now . . .

She took the seat facing her mother and forced herself to relax. One of the servants filled her cup with coffee, then withdrew. They were alone in the room.

"You should try a piece of Battenberg," her mother said, holding out a piece of tennis cake. "It's really very good."

Angela rolled her eyes, then took a cupcake. Knowing her mother, each individual cake had probably cost enough to feed an entire family for a week. She wouldn't have thought about such details normally, but now . . . if the family was hurting for cash, why were they wasting money on fancy cakes? She was sure the money could have fed them all for months.

Because we have to maintain standards, her thoughts reminded her. She'd once known a boy who'd brought tons of cheap chocolate to a party. Everyone had laughed at him, then gorged themselves silly. *If we don't look rich, people might start to wonder.*

"I don't feel like eating," Angela said instead. She took a sip of her coffee, grimacing at the taste. "Mother . . ."

"Sugar is good for you," her mother said. She held up her cup and smiled. "It cheers you up."

"I don't think sugar will make me feel any better," Angela snapped. "Mother . . . I'm going to marry a total fool because the family demands it of me. What more do you want?"

Her mother put down her cup. "To help," she said. "We are both in this together."

Angela felt her temper fray. "The only thing you could do to help is murder Finley!"

"This isn't his fault," her mother said. "And his death would not save us one little bit."

"Of course not," Angela snarled.

Her mother's lips thinned until they were almost invisible. Angela sighed, then braced herself for the lecture. She had a duty to the family . . . blah, blah, blah . . . and she was expected to uphold that duty because it was the price she paid for being part of the family. She'd heard the lecture before, several times.

"We are both women," her mother said instead. "And I do want to help you."

Angela blinked in surprise. "Did you . . . did you get pushed into marrying Father?"

"Yes," her mother said. "Your grandfather and *my* father arranged it. Agreements were made behind the scenes. I wasn't told I would be marrying your father until it had been arranged."

"Oh," Angela said. "And you just went along with it?"

Her mother held up a hand. "Just listen," she said. "Your father knew that he would be getting married, but he didn't make the choice. I'm not sure just how much influence he would have had, if push came to shove. Your grandfather was very set in his ways."

Angela rolled her eyes. The aristocratic world was divided into those who had influence and power and those who didn't. She found it impossible to imagine Robert Cavendish as a powerless young man . . . he'd never been young to her. How could he have been at the mercy of his own father?

"I understand it won't be easy," her mother said. "It wasn't easy for me either."

"You married Father," Angela said stiffly.

"He was practically a stranger to me," her mother pointed out. "We didn't know each other."

"And now you're still married," Angela said.

"Yes," her mother agreed. She took a long breath. "You and Finley need to have a mature conversation about your marriage. Your children will have to be his, of course, but there is a great deal of leeway outside childbirth. You don't have to live together, as long as there are children and you're formally wed. Angela . . . this is not the end of the world."

"It is for me," Angela said.

Her mother sighed loudly. "You're your father's daughter, all right. You have his sense of drama."

She went on before Angela could think of a comeback. "This is a three-month cruise," she said. "You and Finley will have plenty of time to get to know one another"—she winked in a manner that made Angela cringe—"and hold a mature discussion about how you're going to organize your marriage. I dare say he will be tolerant if you are tolerant too. You *do* have power in this relationship."

Not much, Angela thought. How long would she need to stay married to give her father a chance to rebuild the family finances? *And once we have children, Finley and I will always be connected.*

She looked down at the table. She did have some advantages, but not that many. She could easily imagine the marriage contract including a list of clear terms for everything, from having children to permanent separation. She and Finley would be expected to have the first child as quickly as possible, then the second . . .

"Fuck," she said.

"Language," her mother said sternly. "We *are* in this together, Angela. I want to help you."

"I already know how babies are made," Angela said, just to see if she could provoke a reaction. "I learned that in school."

"There's more that goes into making a marriage work than just having sex all the time," her mother said. Her lips twitched. "Although most men would probably be happy if they got sex every day or so."

Angela flushed. She didn't want to *think* about her parents . . . *doing it.*

"I'm marrying him for the family," she said. "Not for Finley . . ."

"Then you need to make sure he knows it," her mother said. She pointed at the cakes. "Eat one or two, Angela. You'll need to build up your energy."

Angela eyed her suspiciously. "Why?"

"Because Finley is going to propose marriage to you in a couple of hours," her mother said placidly. "You'll need energy to accept his proposal. You can't look as if you're on the verge of fainting on the promenade."

"Oh," Angela said. The fix was in, wasn't it? No doubt the marriage contract had already been signed, sealed, and delivered. Did she have to sign the contract herself? Did Finley have to sign it? Their respective parents would have done the dickering well before either of them knew they were going to get married. "And what if I refuse?"

Her mother pointed her fork at Angela. "If you never listen to any advice I give you ever again, listen to this now," she said. "Do not . . . *ever* . . . humiliate your husband in public."

Angela bit down several sharp retorts, starting with an observation that Finley wasn't her husband *yet.* "Why?"

"Because it makes it harder for the poor dears to think straight," her mother said. She smiled rather coldly. "Men are quite limited creatures in so many ways. They cannot handle two different aspects of life colliding. They present one face to you, one face to their best friends, one face to their superiors, and yet another to their inferiors."

"No multitasking," Angela said.

"Exactly," her mother said. She picked up a cupcake and bit into it with full evidence of enjoyment. "A man might know how to talk to his wife, or to his friends, but he can't do both at once. The feat gives him headaches." Her smile widened slightly. "Which is why you see men who kiss up to the boss while stamping on everyone below them."

"I've known women who act like that," Angela said.

"Quite," her mother agreed. She looked down at the table for a long moment. "Men are smart when their emotions aren't getting in the way," she said. "They say the same about us, of course."

"Of course," Angela said. She reluctantly took a bite of a cupcake. The treat tasted like ashes in her mouth. "How do you know all this?"

"When I was your age, darling, my mother knew nothing," her mother said. "Ten years later . . . by golly, how smart that woman had become!"

Angela felt a moment of sympathy for her mother. Her maternal grandmother had been a proud and overbearing woman, endlessly pushing her children to excel. It was hard to imagine Halle Cavendish resisting *her* mother's advice.

Her mother reached out and patted Angela's shoulder. "I am here for you," she said. "And if you need advice, I will give it."

"And you'll tell Father," Angela said.

"No," her mother said. She paused. "Not without asking you first."

She clapped her hands. The door opened, revealing Marie. "Take Angela to her bedroom and get her ready," she ordered. "She must look her best."

"Yes, My Lady," Marie said.

Angela barely had any time to think over the next hour or so. Marie was ruthless, scrubbing every inch of her body and then combing through her hair until it shone. Angela would have resisted if she hadn't been lost in her own thoughts. The fix was definitely in. Finley was going to propose to her in front of hundreds of people, all of whom were wealthy and powerful . . . apart from the ship's crew, she supposed. But they didn't really count.

"I hope you're planning to give me underwear," she jibed as Marie laid out the dress, a soft blue design, elegant and understated. "I'm not walking through the ship without panties."

She half hoped to provoke an argument—a shouting match might have made her feel better—but Marie didn't rise to the bait. Instead, she opened a small box and passed it to Angela. A small pair of panties waited for her, clearly designed not to be visible under the dress. And probably expensive as hell . . . she looked at the jewels on the table and shook her head in disbelief. She hadn't seen them before, which meant they were probably new. God alone knew how much money her father had spent on her proposal dress . . .

Mother must have crammed them into her bags, she thought. She wondered, suddenly, just how much money her father had spent on her wedding. He'd have to make it look good, even if it *was* on a cruise liner. *Perhaps we could save enough money to avoid bankruptcy if we canceled the wedding.*

Of course not, her own thoughts replied. *Do you really think your wedding will cost trillions of crowns?*

"You look lovely," Marie said. "Don't you just?"

Angela eyed herself in the mirror. The blue dress suited her, she admitted crossly. It flattered her figure without revealing much and brushed against the deck . . . she was tempted to wonder if she could go barefoot. Gold Deck was carpeted everywhere, and no one would notice, but she knew it wasn't possible.

"I look like I'm going to my own funeral," Angela said.

"Then put a smile on your face," Marie said. "You'll feel better."

Angela didn't feel better, not when she met Nancy outside or when her mother escorted her out of the compartment. A handful of others met them as they walked, her father's cronies or her mother's hangers-on. Angela felt bitter, grimly aware that she would have no opportunity to protest or escape.

And Finley's proposal is about as spontaneous as . . . as this trip, she thought sourly, as they turned onto the promenade. The lights of hyperspace winked at her. Angela suddenly understood why so many people believed that *life* existed in hyperspace, even though nothing had ever been proved. *This is a farce.*

Finley was waiting midway down the corridor, escorted by three young men. His family or cronies, Angela assumed. Or maybe his governor . . . did Finley *have* a governor or governess of his own? He was certainly old enough to refuse if one was offered. But a bodyguard would make perfect sense. Angela hadn't been allowed to leave the estate, even to go to shop, without an escort. Thanks to the war, there had been times when she hadn't been allowed to go at all.

Her mother touched her arm lightly, warning her to stop. Angela forced herself to paste a smile on her face as Finley knelt in front of her, moving with a surprising awkwardness for a man of his size. She wondered, sourly, if he'd made full use of the bodyshops . . . or if he was as nervous as she was. Perhaps he hadn't been consulted before the deal had been done either. His family would be pissed if he screwed the union up before everything was sorted out.

"Angela," Finley said. His voice was quiet, too quiet. He had to clear his throat and start again. "Angela, I ask that you do me the honor of accepting my hand in marriage."

Angela couldn't move. The world seemed to be graying out around her. He opened a box, revealing a ring . . . it would be perfect, of course. A simple gold band, topped with a diamond . . . exactly what she'd wanted back when she'd been a little girl. She hadn't understood what marriage meant until she'd grown older . . .

She was trapped. She couldn't refuse. She was trapped.

Carefully, very carefully, she took the ring from the box. A mad impulse struck her, a desire to throw the ring down the promenade, but she knew she couldn't. Her family and millions of others were depending on her. Their human sacrifice.

"I accept," she said. She slid the ring onto her finger, even though she knew the gesture was meant to be his job. A flicker crossed his face, so quickly that she barely registered the expression before it was gone. "Thank you."

Gritting her teeth, she took his arm, helped him to his feet, and leaned in for a kiss. His lips were warm, but she felt nothing.

Nothing at all.

CHAPTER THIRTEEN

"You do realize you're being silly," Carla said. "There is no way she was *yours*."

Matt scowled at her as they walked down the crew corridor. Four days had passed since the captain had announced the engagement of Finley Mackintosh and Angela Cavendish, and the datanet was buzzing with gossip. The hearts she'd broken . . . everyone was twittering about how beautiful she was and his handsomeness. Matt felt sick, even though he knew Carla was right. Angela had never been his.

He looked around the corridor, unwilling to meet his colleague's amused gaze. The crew corridors were bare, so bare that the absence of paintings and carpeted floors was all too clear. He could see patches of dust in places no passengers would ever see, while the passageways on the far side of the bulkheads were swept every day—one hell of a dance for the cleaning crews, who weren't supposed to be seen, and one hell of a sign that Angela and he came from very different worlds. He was, most definitely, being silly.

"Bah," he said finally.

Carla poked him, none too gently. "If you walk around some of the lower decks with a boyish smile, I'm sure *someone* will lure you into their cabin," she said. "And if you're careful, you probably won't even miss your shift!"

"Thanks for nothing," Matt said. He gave her a sharp look. "And how many guests have *you* slept with?"

"Enough," Carla said tightly.

Matt looked away, embarrassed. The old sweats hadn't made any bones about it. Being ogled—or worse—was just part of the job. He didn't think he'd mind *too* much if a middle-aged woman dragged him into her cabin for a few hours of bedroom gymnastics, but Carla might feel differently. She probably *did* feel differently. Matt found it hard to imagine having a fat middle-aged man riding him . . .

He swallowed, hard. Carla was young and stunningly pretty. She'd attract attention, and some of her admirers wouldn't be gentle. Nor would they be shy about pressuring her into their bed. And, he told himself again and again, there was nothing he or anyone else could do about it without losing their job. As long as there was a fig leaf of consent, Corporate would look the other way.

"I'm sorry," he said. "I didn't mean to be rude."

Carla sighed. "It's part of the job," she said. "But I'll be handing in my notice when we return home."

Matt winced. "I'll miss you."

"You'll miss the chance to ogle me at night," Carla teased. "Or did you think you were being subtle?"

". . . No," Matt said. His face was as red as her hair. "I'm sorry."

"Keep it in your pants," Carla advised. She held up a hand as they reached the service hatch and keyed the access panel. "You'll get into less trouble that way."

The hatch opened, revealing a half-hidden entrance to the passenger deck. Matt followed her through quickly—Corporate demanded that the entrances were to be kept as secret as possible—and closed the hatch behind them. A handful of young men were marching down the corridor, arms interlocked as they bawled out a bawdy song about a girl who had a different boyfriend for every day of the week.

His earpiece bleeped. "France, you are summoned to Cabin Gold-17," the dispatcher said. "Evans, you are ordered to check the observation blister."

Matt and Carla exchanged glances. "The observation blister, sir?"

"The intruder alarm sounded," the dispatcher said. "Security is standing by, if you need them."

"Joy," Matt muttered. Carla was going in entirely the wrong direction. The observation blister was supposed to be sealed. Whoever had managed to get inside might not like being caught. "I'm on my way."

"It's probably someone making love under the stars," Carla said reassuringly. "You'll be fine."

Matt jabbed a finger towards the bulkhead. "There are no stars out there."

"You know what I mean," Carla said. "Good luck."

Matt watched her go, then walked slowly towards the access hatch. Technically, the observation blister was part of Gold Deck, but . . . the guests weren't meant to get inside without permission. There was no *need* for them to get inside. If they wanted to see the stars, or hyperspace, they could just walk into the promenade. Dozens of rich guests were doing just that, taking their exercise under hyperspace. He didn't care to understand what they thought they were doing.

Probably just making it clear that they're actually here, he thought as he passed a handful of older men going in the other direction. *Just being able to take a cruise with us is a sign of vast wealth.*

He tensed as he reached the access hatch and checked the panel. A light was silently burning, warning him that someone was inside. A happy couple, making love? Or someone who merely wanted privacy? Or . . . he wished, suddenly, that he had a weapon. If he was about to interrupt someone planning to sabotage *Supreme*, he was probably about to die. All the horror stories of guests who smuggled WMDs onboard suddenly seemed very plausible.

The hatch hissed open, revealing a tiny bubble peering out into hyperspace. It was completely bare, save for a single bench in the exact center of the tiny room. A girl was sitting on the bench, her back to him. Matt allowed himself a moment of relief—at least he hadn't interrupted people making out—and then cleared his throat. The girl started, then turned around.

"Nancy Cavendish," Matt said. He frowned as he took in her appearance. Her eyes were so pale that they were almost gray. She was chewing on a strand of hair, meditatively. He wondered, just for a moment, if he should take her to Sickbay. She didn't look well. "What . . . how did you get in here?"

Nancy smiled. "The security panel is easy to twist, if you try," she said. "It needs to be unlocked from the main system first."

Which is probably what set off the alarm, Matt thought. Nancy was very lucky a security team hadn't come crashing in to find out what had happened. *She disabled the lock, but not the monitoring circuit.*

"This place is off-limits," he said as gently as possible. "Why are you here?"

Nancy jabbed a finger towards the transparent blister. Outside, hyperspace flashed and flared around the giant starship. "I *like* hyperspace," she said. "Feels like coming home."

Matt lifted his eyebrows. "Because you were *born* here?"

"Perhaps," Nancy said. "Sometimes I hear voices out there."

"Voices?" Matt repeated. "What do they say?"

"I don't know," Nancy said. "I can hear them, but . . . but it's like they're talking so quietly that I can't make out the words."

Matt had no idea what to make of it. He'd heard the stories . . . alien sightings, unknown starships, incidents that defied rational explanations . . . but none had ever come with hard proof. They were just stories, the kind spacers told groundpounders when they wanted to mess with their heads. He didn't believe that anything could actually *live* in hyperspace.

"The universe is a big place," he said instead. "There could be anything out there."

Nancy glanced at him. "You don't believe me, do you?"

Matt hesitated. The honest answer was no, but that might upset her. And if she complained to her father . . .

"No one does," Nancy said. "They say it's just my imagination." She smiled. "Unless they're saying that I belong in hyperspace."

"Perhaps you do," Matt said.

He shrugged to hide his confusion. He'd looked up the regulations governing pregnant women in hyperspace and discovered a puzzling mystery. There didn't seem to be any legitimate reason for insisting that pregnant women travel in stasis, although most women wouldn't be offered a choice. Trying to sneak a pregnant woman onto a ship when most passengers received a medical check before they boarded was grounds for having one's travel permit revoked. Nancy was nearly unique—*completely* unique, if one believed her family's publicity department—for good reason.

And hyperspace shock is real, he thought. He didn't need to swallow poison to know it was a bad idea. *Who knows what it might do to a pregnant woman?*

He pushed the thought aside. "I think I should escort you back to your cabin," he said. He indicated the door. "Please come with me."

Nancy looked reluctant. "It's boring in the cabin," she said. "And I don't want to hang out with the other kids."

"You can't stay here," Matt said. "But if you let me escort you back now, I won't tell your father where you've been."

"Fine," Nancy said. She stood and marched towards the hatch. "You'd *better* keep your mouth shut."

Matt keyed the hatch closed as soon as they were both inside, then sent an alert to maintenance. Nancy's handiwork—he wondered, absently, where she'd learned to manipulate access hatches like that—would have to be undone as soon as possible. And then the other hatches would have to be checked too.

He had a thought. "What happened to your telltale?"

Nancy smirked. "I *accidentally* left it on the table by the door," she said. "Oops."

Matt silently congratulated her. She'd used the telltale to get out of the cabin, then left it behind. As long as she didn't try to get off Gold Deck, she could go anywhere public . . . it wasn't something he would have considered, at her age. But then, Nancy had a strikingly safe life. No one would dare to hurt her, not when they knew her family would take a terrible revenge.

And this ship is very safe, he thought. *She'll be fine as long as she stays on Gold Deck.*

"I've always wanted to join the Survey Service," Nancy said. "Do you think they'd take me?"

Matt smiled. Susan Simpson had had the same thought, hadn't she? Susan was three or four years younger than Nancy . . . perhaps he should introduce them. Or perhaps the age difference would be too great. At that age, even a year seemed an unbridgeable gulf. He made a mental note to see what events both girls might attend in the future. They might hit it off at once.

"Perhaps they would," he said. If, of course, there *was* a Survey Service by the time Nancy reached adulthood. "You'd go into the unknown."

"That's the point," Nancy said. She waved a hand at the bulkhead. "What am I going to see, on this cruise, that other eyes haven't already seen?"

"Nothing," Matt said. They reached the stateroom hatch. "But *you* won't have seen it . . . before, I mean. I think that's the point."

"It's not the same," Nancy said as the hatch hissed open. "I . . . oh, *hello*, Angela."

Matt flushed helplessly. Angela stood there, wearing a black sweater and skirt that hung down to her knees. A surprisingly simple outfit, one that drew his eyes to her face. And yet it was all he could do to keep from stammering like a schoolboy. He felt very, very unsure of himself.

"Nancy," Angela said, "what have you been doing?"

"Nothing you need to know about," Nancy said. "Why don't you two have a nice chat? I have to run."

She darted past her sister and hurried farther into the stateroom. Matt stared after her, wondering just what Nancy was playing at. Maybe she'd just wanted to embarrass her older sister. Matt had always found his sisters to be unbearable when he'd been twelve. But he'd never put them on the spot like that.

"I found her in a restricted area, My Lady," he said. "I had to bring her back here."

"Thank you," Angela said. She looked back at him for a long moment. Matt could barely maintain eye contact. "I . . . what are you doing now?"

Matt fought to keep his face expressionless. "I'm on roaming duty," he said. "Ah . . . that means I handle any problems that come up."

"Sounds like a fascinating job," Angela said, a bitter curve to her smile. "I . . . would you like to come in and chat?"

Matt felt his heart skip a beat. A chat . . . or something more? He'd heard a couple of the older stewards bragging about scoring with rich girls, although he wasn't sure he believed them. He'd heard similar stories when he'd been in high school and . . . well, no one would have got any work done if half of those stories had been true. He honestly wasn't sure what to do. Technically, he was on duty . . . but he could hardly deny a request from a wealthy guest . . . could he?

"Only for a short while, My Lady," he managed. "I have to keep patrolling the decks."

Angela's lips twisted. "It must be a job with a lot of responsibility," she said. She turned and led the way into her bedroom. The rest of the giant stateroom seemed empty. "Do you enjoy it?"

Matt thought for a moment. "It has its moments," he said. He took the seat she indicated and smiled, choosing his words carefully. "I meet a great many interesting people."

"I'm sure you do," Angela said. She sat down, crossing her arms. "Is that what you truly believe, or . . . or is it what you're told to say?"

"I do meet interesting people," Matt said. He remembered, too late, that "meet interesting people" was one of Corporate's slogans. "Sometimes they're *very* interesting people."

"I bet," Angela said. "Who's the most interesting person you've met?"

You, Matt thought.

He didn't dare say *that* out loud. God alone knew how she'd take it. But who else *was* there? The military vet on Silver Deck? The trio of performers playing in the lower decks while traveling to their next gig? Or the pop star sensation five doors down, who had somehow managed to use her sex appeal to cover up a voice that sounded like someone scraping nails over a blackboard?

"There are three performers down on the lower decks," he said. "They trade singing for travel tickets. They perform for us during transit, then . . . they'll perform on Williamson's World."

Angela smiled, as if he'd unintentionally said something funny. "Do their performances pay for their tickets?"

"Corporate thinks so," Matt said. He doubted Corporate cared very much. The performers entertained the lower decks at a low cost. No doubt something in their contracts ensured they didn't earn too much. "Have you been to see them?"

"No, but I will," Angela said.

She still appeared to be smiling at a joke. Matt wanted to know what she was smiling at, but he didn't dare ask. For all he knew, she was smiling—laughing!—at *him*. He wouldn't blame her either. God knew he must sound like a yokel.

"They're good," he assured her. Carla had forced him to see the performers two days ago. "They really should be invited up here."

"You should suggest it to the captain," Angela said.

Matt blinked in shock. "The captain wouldn't listen to me," he said. He could mention the idea to the entertainment director, but there was a good chance the older man would laugh in his face. The wealthy and powerful didn't want to listen to a bunch of cheap musicians, did they? They wanted cultured entertainment. "I'm low on the totem pole."

"Oh," Angela said. She looked embarrassed. "I should have thought."

"Don't worry about it," Matt said.

They talked for nearly an hour before Matt slipped out of her cabin. He hoped no one would ask questions—technically, Angela had every right to ask for his services—as he made his way back to the swimming pool. He saw no sign of Carla when he arrived . . . he frowned, unsure what to do. Where was she? Their shift would be over in twenty minutes, and they'd have to report in before they went off duty. And yet . . .

He found himself smiling, helplessly. He'd just spent an hour with a beautiful girl.

One who's getting married, he told himself sternly. All the stories the old sweats had told him paled next to that simple truth. *She was just interested in talking to you.*

Still, he couldn't keep himself from smiling.

CHAPTER FOURTEEN

Being engaged, Angela had decided shortly after the formal announcement, was even worse than she'd feared. She could never be alone. *Everyone* wanted to compliment her on her forthcoming nuptials, from the starship's crew to every last guest on Gold Deck. She wanted to run and hide, but Marie was always right behind her. Her mother's daily chats didn't make life easier either. When she wasn't talking about married life in embarrassing detail, she was talking about the importance of making the union work. Angela wasn't even married yet, and she was already sick of it!

It was almost a relief, therefore, when the captain held a masked ball the night before planetfall. Angela dressed up as a pirate girl and strode around the dance floor, muttering catchphrases she was fairly sure that no real pirate had ever said. She danced with a dozen different men while Finley chatted to her father in the far corner. Angela was torn between annoyance and relief. On one hand, he was clearly ignoring his bride-to-be in front of everyone; on the other, she was glad to be ignored. Their daily walks down the promenade were *boring*.

She swept around the floor, moving from partner to partner with practiced ease. The different costumes didn't impress her, although she knew they'd probably been stitched together on the ship. A man dressed as a king from a bygone era, a wizard in long white robes, a soldier who couldn't possibly have worn such an ornate uniform in a real battle . . . she found it hard to care. It was more important to her that they were good dancers. She would have forgiven Finley a great deal if he'd danced with her.

The night went on, slowly starting to drag. She picked up a plate of food at the buffet and watched with a certain sisterly amusement mingled with envy as Nancy was sent back to the stateroom. No doubt Nancy would take the opportunity to make sure she went the long way home, but at least she would be alone. Or as alone as anyone got on *Supreme*. Angela had done some research and discovered there was no legitimate way to escape surveillance completely. Removing the telltale wouldn't be enough to spoof the system.

She turned as the captain called for silence. He stood on a small podium, wearing his seemingly uncomfortable dress uniform. Angela had worn enough formal clothes to see the signs. And yet there was a confidence about him that she admired. Captain VanGundy was a man who'd done something with his life.

And I won't, she thought numbly. *I won't ever get the chance.*

"It has been a lovely evening," the captain said. "I hope you all enjoyed the dance."

A low rumble of assent emerged, mainly from the younger guests. The older ones had spent the evening chatting, either discussing their long-term plans or, more likely, engaging in tedious male bonding. Or whatever the interactions were called when women were involved as well as men.

"Tomorrow, we will arrive at Williamson's World," the captain said. "We will remain in orbit for a week, then depart for our next destination. You will all have ample opportunity to see the sights, if you wish. If not . . . we will be bringing local performers onto the ship. You can watch them from the comfort of your staterooms."

Pathetic, Angela thought. She knew very little about Williamson's World, but she was looking forward to going down to the surface at least to get some fresh air. *Why would anyone want to stay on the ship?*

"Remember to read the briefing notes first," the captain concluded. "Anyone who doesn't have the right documents will not be permitted to disembark."

He stepped down. The music started again, but the captain ignored it. Instead, he walked to the nearest hatch and stepped through. Angela nodded to herself in understanding. The party was now officially over, although some of the younger guests would probably keep dancing and singing into the wee hours. She could leave—everyone could leave— without giving offense.

Although the captain probably doesn't want to be here either, she thought. *And who could blame him?*

A hand fell on her arm. She jumped.

"Angela," Finley said.

She turned to see him standing behind her, his face looking as bland as ever.

"Finley," she said. She struggled to keep her voice calm. She was tired, too tired. Her body was starting to ache. She needed a long bath and sleep, perhaps not in that order. "What do you want?"

Another flicker crossed Finley's face. "I would *like* you to accompany me back to the stateroom," he said. He held out a hand. "Please?"

It wasn't a request, Angela knew. Sure, she *could* say no and dart back onto the dance floor, but her parents would never let her hear the end of it.

She held out a hand, reluctantly. Finley took it and slowly guided her towards the main entrance, leading out onto the promenade. Behind her, the MC called the next dance. Angela felt a pang; the song was one of her favorites. Just for a moment, she considered inviting Finley onto the dance floor, but she knew he would never agree. The music cut off behind them as they walked through a sound-dampening field, then down the promenade. It was largely empty save for a handful of people peering out into hyperspace.

"Hyperspace is creepy," Finley said. "It makes me feel uneasy."

Angela gave him a sharp look. It was the first hint of actual human feeling she'd seen from him, although it was weedy. Finley was going to be related to Nancy, after all. How would he cope with being linked to the first child to be born in hyperspace? She told herself, firmly, that she was being silly. Being born in hyperspace hadn't given Nancy superpowers or anything else worth having, save for a fame she'd done nothing to deserve. Finley was hardly the only person to feel that hyperspace wasn't safe for humanity. Just looking out into the eerie lights surrounding the ship made her feel small, insignificant.

"You'll get used to it," she said, a little sharper than she'd intended. How much had she drunk at the ball? She couldn't recall. There had been at least five glasses of various wines, hadn't there? "Are you planning to stay on Tyre once we get home?"

"I think we'll have to stay on Tyre," Finley said. "There's work to be done."

Angela looked up. She hadn't missed the *we*.

"Father has taken three months off," she said as they left the promenade and walked down to the stateroom. A handful of youngsters were splashing in the pool, although it was well past midnight. They'd be awfully cranky in the morning when they went down to the planet. She wondered, absently, just what their parents were doing. "You could do the same."

"I doubt it," Finley said. "There's work to be done."

They reached the stateroom. Angela touched her telltale to the scanner, opening the door. It was dark inside, the lights coming on as she walked into the compartment. She hoped Finley would take the hint and leave—she didn't want to give him the traditional good-night kiss—but he followed her. Angela was honestly shocked. She didn't think that Finley had the imagination to be so forward.

"We need to talk," Finley said. "Privately."

Angela hesitated. She didn't want to let Finley into her bedroom. She was fairly sure he'd behave himself, but . . . it was her private place. Still, she had no doubt that the servants had already been awakened if they'd been sleeping. Soon, one of the maids or Marie would come to see what they could do for their mistress. She certainly didn't want to have any discussions in front of her governess.

"Fine," she said.

She opened the door to her bedroom and stepped inside. Boxes lay everywhere, some opened to reveal their contents; dresses and underwear lay spread on the bed. Marie hadn't been able to get inside to clean up, of course. Angela felt a flicker of embarrassment, which she ruthlessly squashed. She was a slob at times, naturally. Finley had better learn to put up with it if he wanted to marry her.

"Please, take a seat," she said, clearing a pile of underwear from one of the chairs. She'd hoped to provoke some kind of reaction, but she saw nothing. Not normal, she decided as he sat down. "What do you want to talk about?"

"We're going to be married," Finley said.

"So it seems," Angela agreed. She remembered what her mother said. Finley seemed to present one face to her father and another to her. She suddenly realized that she might not know Finley as well as she thought. She might not know him at all. "It might have been pointed out, once or twice."

Finley didn't smile. "A great deal rests on this match," he said. "I believe your father might have mentioned it to you."

Angela couldn't quite keep the dismay off her face. She'd been lectured by her father, her mother, and several distant relatives who just *happened* to be on *Supreme*. She could practically parrot the lectures back to them. Was Finley going to lecture her too? She was damned if she was taking it from her husband. It was bad enough hearing lectures from old biddies who had nothing better to do but ask when she was going to have children.

"He did," she said.

Her mind raced. How much did Finley actually *know*? Did he realize just how much was actually resting on the match? Or did he think that Angela's family had other options? She had no way to ask without giving away the secret . . . if, of course, it actually *was* a secret. Her father might be able to handle the complex mixture of intrigue and lies that pervaded the corporate world, but she couldn't. Angela silently promised herself that she would do everything in her power to start learning once she got home. Ignorance was no defense against reality.

"Your family needs this match," Finley said. His voice made her blood run cold. "And so does mine."

"Yeah," Angela said. She felt out of her depth. "I know."

She forced herself to think. Who was dependent on whom? Finley's family would take a hit if the Cavendish Corporation collapsed. She was sure of that, but would the failure destroy them? She didn't know. If it would, then the two families were locked together; if it wouldn't, Finley had more leverage than he perhaps realized. She cursed her own ignorance again. She just didn't know enough to make a reasonable guess, let alone gamble for the very highest stakes.

"We must make this marriage work," Finley said. "We cannot afford to be distracted."

Angela felt a hot flash of anger. She was going to marry him. She was going to marry him . . . and he was talking to her like she was a particularly stupid child?

"No, we can't," she snapped, allowing her anger to show. She wanted to get undressed and into bed. She'd have a bath tomorrow, before disembarking. "Get to the point!"

Finley looked bemused. "The point?"

"You insisted on talking to me," Angela said. She didn't bother to calm her voice. "What. Do. You. Want?"

"You will comport yourself with the very highest decorum," Finley said. He sounded as though he was laying down the law. "I want you to remember that you *are* going to marry me."

Angela controlled her anger with an effort. The only person who'd *ever* talked to her like that was her father, and only when he was in a particularly foul mood. She'd never liked his tone on those occasions, although honesty compelled her to admit there were times when she'd deserved it.

"I know that," she snapped. "What's your point?"

She saw a hint of anger on his face. "You will remain with me when we go to dances," he said. "You will *not* do anything to call our marriage into question."

Angela leaned forward. "I won't, will I?"

"No, you won't," Finley said. "You will stay with me. You will *not* dance with strangers or—"

"I am not your slave," Angela hissed. "I am not some . . . some woman from a historical fantasy! You do not *own* me!"

"We have to get married for the good of the family, both families," Finley snapped back. He sounded angry himself. Part of her mind noted that it was the first time he'd showed any sign of strong emotion. "I will *not* let you threaten it!"

"Me dancing with one man or ten men or a hundred men will not threaten *my* family," Angela said. "And it won't threaten yours either."

"Regardless, you will behave yourself," Finley said. "I expect you to remain with me at all times."

"Oh," Angela said. "Would you like me to call you Lord and Master too?"

Finley flushed. "No."

"Oh, *goody*," Angela mocked.

"You will remain with me," Finley said. "I expect you to—"

"Then dance with me," Angela said, cutting him off. "Come onto the dance floor and *dance!*"

"I can't do that," Finley said.

Angela rolled her eyes in a manner that often annoyed Marie. She knew there were some boys and girls who were nervous when they stepped onto the dance floor, but they usually got over it. Wallflowers didn't last long in high society. Finley was certainly young enough to still be a wallflower, particularly if he'd spent his adolescence preparing to take over the family business, but . . .

She sighed, inwardly. He was just being silly.

"Then I can't stay with you," Angela said. She schooled her voice into something resembling a reasonable tone. "Finley, our marriage will not be threatened by me dancing with other men."

"We're going to be together for a long time," Finley said. "It will."

"Then dance with me," Angela said. "It isn't *that* hard to pick up the basics."

Finley gave her a sharp look. "Do you have any idea at all just how *much* is riding on this match?"

"Yes," Angela snapped.

"Then I'm sure you can understand why it is *important* that this match doesn't fail," Finley said, coldly. "You *will* comport yourself as I say."

Angela's temper flared. No one had *ever* tried to dictate to her like that before, not even her father. How dare he? Married or not, she wasn't his property. They'd have two children, as per the contract, then forge separate lives. She didn't give a damn if he wanted to bring home a score of lovers or waste his days in the office. And she didn't care if he felt otherwise.

"No," she said flatly.

"Yes," Finley said.

"Get out," Angela said. She jabbed a finger at the outer door. "Now!"

Finley rose. "I meant it," he said. "Too much is at stake for you to act badly."

Angela fought down an insane urge to giggle despite her growing rage. He wasn't concerned about *her*; he wasn't jealous . . . he was concerned about the family corporations. He . . .

"Out," she said.

Finley looked down at her for a long moment, and then he turned and walked through the hatch, into the corridor. Angela jumped up and bolted the hatch closed as soon as he was gone, even though she knew the portal was codelocked. Sweat trickled down her back as she returned to the bed, feeling oddly vulnerable. Finley . . .

She lay down, feeling bitter. What sort of life could she expect once they were married? If Finley was so concerned about keeping up appearances, what would he want from her?

I'll be going down to the planet tomorrow, she thought.

The idea gnawed at her mind. Could she transfer her trust fund to Williamson's World? Plot an escape? But if she did, the entire corporation would suffer. She was trapped, and Finley, the bastard, knew it. She had no way out.

Uncomfortably, she slowly drifted off to sleep.

CHAPTER FIFTEEN

"We have entered orbit, sir," Lieutenant Rani Jackson reported. "Orbital position is nominal."

"System Command confirms," Lieutenant Hazelwood added. "They're clearing our shuttles for fast-track now."

"Good," Paul said, relieved. He hadn't expected trouble. Williamson's World had been a success story even before it had joined the Commonwealth. But *Supreme* was just too big a target for his peace of mind. "Inform the hospitality staff that they can begin disembarking the passengers."

"And remind them to ensure that they have their papers," Jeanette added. "Williamson's World is a little odd."

Paul nodded. "They'll be checked on departure," he reminded her. "And upon returning to the ship."

He smiled thinly. Dozens of horror stories circulated freely about passengers who forgot their papers and therefore couldn't return to their ships, although very few of the tales were rooted in reality. If Robert Cavendish or one of his ilk forgot their papers, all that really needed to be done was a quick check against the ship's records. It was vaguely possible, Paul knew, that an infiltrator could rewrite their DNA enough to fool a basic sensor, but the process would leave traces if someone knew where to look. He'd make sure to be careful if someone claimed to have lost their papers.

Hazelwood's console chimed. "Captain, you have a priority call from the surface," he said slowly. "They're requesting an immediate chat."

Paul rose. "I'll take it in my office," he said. "Commander Haverford, you have the bridge."

"Aye, sir," Jeanette said.

Paul stepped through the hatch and walked over to the desk, his mind churning. Cruise liner captains did receive priority calls, but they normally came after passengers had disembarked. A guest might have had an accident . . . or run into trouble with the local law . . . but he hadn't even disembarked anyone yet! He sat down and pressed his fingertips against the terminal reader. No doubt it would resolve itself soon enough.

A stoic face appeared in the display. "Captain VanGundy?"

"Yes," Paul said. There was no point in trying to deny it. "What can I do for you?"

"Captain Harness, Commonwealth Investigative Service," the man said. "I'll get right to the point. You're taking passengers onboard, aren't you?"

"Yes," Paul said. *Supreme* had a number of new guests lined up if they hadn't canceled between departure and arrival. It wasn't uncommon. The ones who hadn't canceled would be making their slow way to the spaceport now. "Do you believe I need to deny boarding?"

"Rather the opposite," Harness said. His face twisted, oddly. "I need you to take on a particular guest."

Paul's eyes narrowed. If the Commonwealth Investigative Service was involved . . .

It clicked. "A criminal?"

"Yes, Captain," Harness said. "A man called Roman Bryon. I'm sending you the file now."

Paul frowned as the file popped up in front of him. "A serial killer?"

"Yes, Captain."

"Are you *mad?*" Paul forced himself to remain calm. "You want to put a serial killer on a cruise liner?"

Harness looked embarrassed. "The CIS arrested him, with the cooperation of the local authorities, after a request was received from Britannia. Bryon managed to escape the long arm of planetary law by somehow boarding a freighter and fleeing to Williamson's World, but they tracked him down."

"How reassuring," Paul said. The file's list of murders did not make pleasant reading. "Put him on another ship."

"That's not an option," Harness said. "The treaties we signed insist that he be put on the first available vessel."

"Then hire another ship," Paul said. He waved a hand at the bulkhead, indicating the planet below. "This is not some stage-one colony world where there's only one ship every five months, if they're lucky. There are hundreds of starships coming and going."

"Yes, but you're the only one going straight to Britannia," Harness pointed out. "The budget will not allow us to hire a ship."

Paul groaned. Corporate would not be pleased. It wouldn't be the first time their ships had been used to transport prisoners, and he'd never heard of an escape, but no one would feel comfortable with a man like Roman Bryon on their ship. Paul had reviewed the treaties back when he'd been retraining. If *Supreme* really was the first available vessel going in the right direction, and if it was technically feasible, Paul had to take the criminal.

It isn't as if we're short of brig space, he thought tartly. *Or we could just put him in a stasis pod.*

"I'll have to clear it with my superiors," he temporized. Corporate might authorize him to hire a second starship rather than risk taking a serial killer on *Supreme.* "They'll have to sign off on the risk."

"They don't have a choice," Harness said. "The treaty—"

"I don't know how well that interpretation will stand up in court," Paul said. "Tell me . . . is there any good news?"

"Bryon will be escorted by one of my people," Harness said. "He has both the training and enhancements necessary to keep someone in line."

"Bryon will be going straight into the brig," Paul told him. "There's no way in hell I'm giving him a goddamned cabin."

"Understood," Harness said.

Paul glowered down at the file. Had someone planned the timing to ensure that Bryon had to travel on *Supreme*? Was the escort hoping for a free holiday? Or was Paul just being paranoid? Every spacer knew that sometimes the timing just didn't work out.

And we might well be the only ship bound for Britannia, he mused. *Crap.*

"I'll check with Corporate, then get back to you," he said. He cursed under his breath. Technically, he *did* have the authority to deny boarding, but such hubris would probably cost him his career. Harness would have plenty of time to appeal to Corporate and convince Paul's superiors to override him. "You'll have an answer before we depart."

"Very good, Captain," Harness said. "And thank you."

His face vanished. Paul swore out loud, then keyed his wristcom. He needed to write an urgent message, then make the arrangements. If Harness was right . . .

Fuck, he thought. *The guests will throw a fit.*

———

Matt was looking forward to going down to Williamson's World himself, although the stewards would have only a few hours on the surface— hardly enough to do more than visit Spaceport Row and maybe a few landmarks. Two-thirds of the passengers were taking full advantage of the opportunity to disembark, booking rooms in planetary hotels and lining up strings of touristy activities. *They* got to spend a full week on the planet.

The airlock was a bottleneck, he reminded himself, as the guests slowly filed past the stewards. Matt and Carla checked their telltales to make sure they were authorized to leave the ship, then waved them through and into the shuttles. The process struck him as disorganized, but it didn't really matter. Getting the guests back onto the ship would be a great deal harder.

He smiled as he saw Maris and Susan Simpson, the latter grinning from ear to ear. Matt waved to the little girl, wondering if he'd ever been that young. Susan was clearly excited to see another world . . . he felt a flicker of envy, mixed with concern. He hadn't had the impression that Maris was rich enough to afford a hotel in a good neighborhood, but there was nothing he could do.

"We're going down to the surface," Susan said when she reached the checkpoint. "It's going to be fun!"

"I hope so," Matt said. He scanned her telltale. It bleeped up a warning: Susan was not allowed to leave the ship without her mother or a duly authorized guardian. "Just let me check your mother."

"We'll be coming back in the evening," Maris said. Matt checked her telltale, making sure to link it to Susan's. The last thing he needed was an alert going off when Susan tried to board the shuttle. "What time is the last shuttle?"

Matt checked his terminal. "Twenty-three hundred, unless you hire a private craft," he said. "You can split the cost with other passengers, if you wish."

Maris looked irked. "Thank you," she said. "Susan, come."

Susan waved goodbye, then hurried through the hatch. Matt smiled and turned back to the line. A whole string of people walked past without any alarms, just enough to make him relax before he heard a warning bleep. The guest was disembarking permanently and needed to take another shuttle.

"It's vitally important that I disembark at once," the guest said. He was a tall man with a long dark goatee and a grim expression. "I have meetings . . ."

"You need to pass through immigration," Matt said, keeping his voice calm. "That's the shuttle departing from the lower hatch . . ."

The guest bit off a curse, then stamped off. Matt watched him go, hoping he wouldn't lodge a formal complaint. The captain would understand—regulations were tighter when someone was disembarking permanently—but Corporate might take a dimmer view. And yet, they *wrote* the damn regulations. If someone went down to the surface without following proper procedure, they might well be arrested and deported. At the very least, Matt would be unceremoniously fired for landing Corporate in the shit.

"Matt," a familiar voice said. He looked up to see Angela Cavendish. His breath caught in his throat. "How are you?"

"Fine," Matt managed. He was aware, all too aware, of Carla looking at him. He had to keep it professional. "Can I see your telltale?"

Angela held out her hand. Matt scanned the telltale, then blinked in shock. The response was clear: Disembarking Denied.

"I have to leave the ship," Angela said. She leaned forward, her perfume drifting through the air. "Please . . ."

Matt swallowed, hard. Angela had been *denied* disembarking? It would make sense for Nancy, he supposed, but Nancy was a child! Angela was nineteen, easily old enough to travel down to the surface on her own. Unless . . . he looked at the tag, then called up her file. No conditions, merely a blanket ban. Angela was simply not allowed to leave the ship.

"I can't clear you to leave," he said. He tried to find out who had barred her from travel, but there was no ID mark on the file. "You'd need to appeal to the captain."

Angela stared at him. "But I need to leave!"

Matt looked back, trying to remain calm. There was something plaintive in her voice. She was begging him to help. And yet . . .

"I can't let you board the shuttle, My Lady," he said carefully. "You wouldn't be allowed to disembark at the far end."

"You have to," Angela said. Her voice started to rise, hysterically. "You have to let me through!"

Carla came forward. "You need to speak to the captain," she said briskly. Matt was torn between relief that she'd intervened and irritation. "Miss Cavendish, we cannot clear you through the hatch. You have been denied permission to leave the ship."

Angela's face crumpled, then twisted with rage. "He did it," she screamed. Matt recoiled in shock. The other guests were already backing away. "He did it!"

Matt stared as Angela broke down completely, alternatively railing at the two stewards and screaming insults in all directions. Who had done it? Robert Cavendish? Or someone else? Or . . . he glanced at Carla, unsure what to do. A hysterical guest needed to be removed as quickly and quietly as possible, but that was clearly impossible. Angela might be faking it—he'd seen a few people fake hysterics to get what they wanted—yet the tirade looked real. She sounded as though she had reached the limits of her endurance . . .

"Come with me," Carla said.

Carla took Angela's arm and marched her down the corridor. Matt stared after them, unsure what to do. The rest of the guests seemed equally shocked. He keyed a report into his terminal, then started to check the next telltale. Carla didn't come back; another steward arrived to replace her. The rest of the shift passed without incident. Matt couldn't help being relieved.

He headed back to the wardroom as soon as his replacement arrived and found Carla sitting in front of the terminal. "I can't tell *who* put the block on her," she said. "But she was definitely forbidden to leave the ship."

Matt nodded. He'd looked it up for himself. "What happened?"

"I managed to get her to calm down once she was away from the hatch," Carla said. She looked up at him and smiled. "Still like that girl, honey?"

"Did she say what was wrong?" Matt asked, ignoring her question. "Or anything useful?"

Carla shrugged. "If that's her reaction to a minor setback," she said, "I dread to imagine what she'd do if she suffered a real blow. Or took a pratfall. Or . . ." She snorted. "Maybe she just needed a bodyguard," she added. "Williamson's World isn't Ahura Mazda, but it isn't exactly safe either."

"Not around the spaceport," Matt agreed. If some of the old sweats were telling the truth, there were ports no one would want to visit without full combat armor and a company of heavily armed marines. "I'm sure Angela would have been fine."

"So it's *Angela* now, is it?" Carla teased. "Watch yourself, really."

"I will," Matt promised. He peered over her shoulder. "Do you think she needed a bodyguard?"

"I don't know," Carla admitted. "Didn't you check? There's nothing on her record to suggest that she had to go with someone. There's just a blanket ban on leaving the ship."

Matt frowned. "Is that common?"

"Not for anyone over eighteen," Carla said. She bit her lip. "I suppose someone could program in an exception, but . . . Matt, the captain would have to sign off on it. Perhaps it would be better not to ask too many questions."

"I see," Matt said. "Ouch."

"Ouch indeed," Carla agreed. She rose. "Let's get something to eat, shall we?"

———

Angela stumbled into her stateroom, feeling wretched.

She hadn't meant to break down, not like that. She . . . she'd hoped to leave, to see what she could do on the surface. She'd even booked a hotel room for herself. But when she'd tried to leave . . . it hadn't been Matt's fault, she knew, but she'd screamed at him anyway. The entire ship would be buzzing by the end of the day. *Everyone* would know she'd thrown a tantrum that would have disgraced a five-year-old child.

It might be a good excuse not to attend parties, she thought. *Or perhaps I should go anyway, just to make it clear that I don't listen to my wretched fiancé.*

She strode across the carpeted floor and pressed her finger against her father's bell. There was a long pause, long enough to make her wonder if he was somewhere else, and then the door opened, allowing her to step into his office. Robert Cavendish was seated at his desk, his eyes disapproving. Someone had called him already, she realized dully. She hoped it hadn't been Matt.

"Tell me something," her father said. He sounded tired, but angry. "What were you thinking?"

Angela glared at him, then threw herself into an armchair. "I was thinking that I wanted to leave the fucking ship."

Her father looked stern. "Without clearing your departure with your parents first?"

"I'm *nineteen*," Angela protested.

"And you have the mentality of a toddler," her father said. He went on before Angela could think of a retort that wouldn't sound childish. "You *were* going to go down to the surface as part of a group. Now you will remain on the ship."

Angela stared. "You're *grounding* me?"

"Your behavior towards Finley has been unacceptable," her father said. Angela grasped that he wasn't talking about her breakdown. "I need you to be mature and responsible, not . . ."

"Not *what?*" Angela demanded. She'd never dared talk to her father so rudely before, but she found it hard to care. "He doesn't *own* me." She paused. "Or do I have to keep him sweet?"

"Yes," her father said. "Right now, we need him more than he needs us."

"He won't get the title without us," Angela pointed out.

"Money would be better than a title," her father said. "Would it not?"

Angela bit down on a snide remark about society bitches who would probably disagree.

She sank back in the chair, feeling bitter and depressed. There was no way out. There was no way . . .

I can't even get off the ship, she thought. *They won't let me go.*

"It's not fair," she said.

Her father raised his eyebrows. "If you genuinely believe the universe should be fair," he said, "I have committed a severe blunder in your education. Or do you believe that there is *no one* who would gladly marry Finley, if it was the price to swap places with you?"

". . . No," Angela said.

"True," her father agreed. "One does not have to look very far to find people who lack the advantages you were born with."

"I know that," Angela said.

"Then stop moaning," her father told her. "There's a price for everything."

"Like marrying Finley," Angela said. The depression grew stronger, mocking her. "And if I don't marry him, I lose everything."

"Yes," her father said. "And so does everyone else."

CHAPTER SIXTEEN

"It's not as bad as it seems," Raymond Slater said. He sipped his coffee thoughtfully as he sat in front of Paul's desk. "We can put the bastard in a stasis pod and put the pod in the brig. That should satisfy Corporate."

Paul snorted as he paced his office. Corporate had flatly refused his suggestion of hiring another ship. He'd attempted to convince Robert Cavendish to StarCom home and pull strings, but Mr. Cavendish had been oddly reluctant to comment. It made no sense. Paul had even considered trying to deny Bryon permission to board at the last possible minute, but the decision would have been a career-wrecker.

"I hope so," he said crossly. He scowled, cursing diplomats and bureaucrats under his breath. Surely someone would have reasoned out the problem with the damned treaty before a starship and her crew got stung. But then Bryon was being extradited somewhere a little farther away than Tyre. Britannia wasn't part of the Commonwealth. "And his escort?"

"Constable Hamish Singh, retired marine," Slater said. He sounded pleased. "We had a brief chat, sir. He's quite willing to accommodate us. He thinks the stasis pod and cell combination is workable."

"I bet he does," Paul said. The constable would have an easy trip if his charge remained in stasis. There would be plenty of opportunity to sample *Supreme*'s delights. "I trust that Mr. Bryon doesn't have anything that might interfere with the stasis field?"

"Not according to his file," Slater assured him. "We'll do our own checks, just in case, but I'm fairly sure he doesn't have anything military-grade."

"We shall see," Paul said. He cleared his throat, changing the subject. "Anyone *else* we should be worried about, Chief?"

Slater didn't bother to look at his datapad. "There's a missionary group heading to Britannia, sir," he said. "They've booked a couple of cabins in third class. I don't think they're going to cause trouble, but we should probably be aware of the dangers. Other than that . . . nothing that really makes me sit up in alarm."

"Good," Paul said. "One serial killer is quite enough."

"*No* serial killers would be better," Slater said. He shook his head in wonder. "What was Corporate drinking when they signed off on the treaty?"

"I don't know," Paul said.

He cursed under his breath. In theory, there wouldn't be any problems with transporting the bastard to Britannia. No one could escape a stasis field without outside help. In practice, the guests would not be pleased when they heard about transporting Bryon. Paul had seriously considered accidentally leaking the information, secure in the knowledge that most of the guests would start screaming at Corporate. But his lords and masters would turn Paul into the scapegoat and fire him.

"Make sure the brig is secure at all times," he ordered. "There's no point in taking chances."

"No, sir," Slater said. "I'd like to give Mr. Bryon a modified telltale too. Might make his chances of escape even slimmer."

"Do whatever you need to do," Paul ordered.

He returned to his desk and sat down. Bryon's file was horrifying reading. He'd made his first kill at thirteen, apparently, then gone on to kill at least seven others before the local authorities finally started to close in on him. Somehow—the file didn't say—Bryon had realized he was under investigation and fled. And he'd made it all the way to Williamson's World. He'd been damn lucky the local authorities hadn't killed him on the spot.

"We'll be leaving orbit this evening," Paul said slowly. "At least we'll still have our escorts."

"Until we leave the system," Slater reminded him.

Paul resisted the urge to bang his head onto the table several times. No escort . . . if even one of the destroyers had stayed with *Supreme*, he could have transferred Bryon to a military brig, to be watched by a military crew. That would have satisfied the treaty without putting his passengers in even the slightest hint of danger.

Something must be wrong back home, he thought. Corporate might not give much of a damn about his opinions, but they'd care about the guests'. The customer was always right . . . why put passengers at risk, even if the risk was minimal? He didn't like the implications. *I should have stayed in the navy.*

"We could put Bryon out the airlock," he said, knowing even as he spoke it was wishful thinking. Serial killer or not, he couldn't be simply executed out of hand. Paul lacked the sweeping authority of a warship captain. "Blast it."

"I'll keep him under control," Slater promised. "And when we reach Britannia, we'll make sure he gets bundled down to the surface before anyone sees him."

"Very good," Paul said.

He sighed. *I really should have stayed in the navy.*

"Remember you had some shore leave," Falcon boomed as the stewards gathered outside the airlock. "Put smiles on your faces!"

Matt pasted a grin on his face. Shore leave had been fun, but far too short. He'd wandered around Spaceport Row with a few of his friends, sampling the local bars. Most of them had been effectively identical, right down to the stench of shipboard rotgut, whores lining the streets, and spacers trying to drink themselves into a stupor. He rather suspected that someone, somewhere, owned a franchise. Every Spaceport Row looked the same.

He glanced at Carla and frowned. She looked pale and hungover, something that bothered him more than he cared to admit. They were flatly forbidden alcohol onboard the ship . . . there wasn't even an illicit still, as far as he knew. Had she been drinking with a guest? Possibly, Matt supposed. She hadn't come down with them for shore leave.

"Check ID cards, hand out telltales, then pass them onwards," Falcon added, striding up and down like a demented drill sergeant. "Don't worry about escorting guests to their cabins."

Because these are mere third-class passengers, Matt thought. *They don't get even a lick of special treatment.*

He leaned forward as the first group of guests walked through the airlock. Three families, one with over a dozen children. A check of the manifest told him that it was a line marriage with seven adults . . . half of the adults seemed to have been held back. He wondered how the arrangement worked—he wasn't sure he could have shared his wife with anyone, if he'd had a wife—and then started to check ID cards. The children were remarkably well behaved.

He ran the children through the scanner . . . no alerts popped up . . . and handed out telltales. The kids all had telltales covered with popular cartoon characters, although the older children didn't seem too impressed. Matt didn't blame them. The telltales looked cheap and nasty and not particularly secure.

"Thank you," a harassed-looking mother said. "Which way to our cabin?"

Matt pointed towards the inner hatch. "Through there; then follow the numbers down to your compartment."

He turned back as the next set of guests arrived . . . and blinked in surprise. Nine men walked through the hatch wearing monkish cowls that hung over their eyes. He had no idea how they actually *saw*. Their robes were as dark as space itself, covered in strange designs that made his head hurt. Matt rather thought that some of the designs looked like a cross between an octopus, a spider, and a giant eyeball.

"Greetings," the leader said. His voice was almost unaccented. Matt would have bet good money that he hadn't been born on Williamson's World. "I am Brother John, Speaker of the Brethren of the Holy Voice."

"Welcome onboard," Matt said automatically. Falcon had said something about the Brethren, hadn't he? He kicked himself for not paying more attention to the morning briefing. "Please, can I see your papers?"

"You may," John said.

Matt waited, then said, "Please, *may* I see your papers?"

John smirked as if he'd won something worthwhile instead of a petty little power game and passed over an ID card. Matt inspected it thoughtfully, then inserted the card into the reader and ran the scan. Biographical details flashed up in front of him. He'd been right. John had been born on Rockall. His parents had probably come from Tyre.

"I trust there are no problems," John boomed. "The Holy Voice moves us."

Matt bit down a sarcastic reply. He couldn't remember much about the Brethren, but what little he could recall hadn't impressed him. He'd sooner have started worshiping the old gods than super-advanced aliens who lived in hyperspace and watched humanity from their lofty perch. There were *no* aliens. But there was no point in questioning the Brethren. No doubt they'd see it as an attack on freedom of religion.

"You're cleared to board," Matt said. He checked twice, just to be sure. No warning flags appeared in John's file, save for a note that he'd been deported from Satilla. Probably religiously motivated, Matt decided. Nothing suggested that he'd been convicted of a crime and kicked off the planet. "You'll find your cabins on the lower decks."

"The Holy Voice thanks you," John informed him. He took the telltale and snapped it on his wrist. "We wish to speak our message to the other passengers."

"You'll need to clear that with the captain," Matt said. He hoped the captain would tell the Brethren to keep their faith to themselves. Trying to convert the rich and famous, or even the second- or third-class passengers, wouldn't win the group any friends. Religious freedom was part of the Commonwealth Charter, but so was freedom *from* religion. "You can send him a message from your cabin."

"We wish to speak to him in person," John said. "When can that be arranged?"

Never, Matt thought.

"You would need to request a meeting," he said. The captain would be very busy over the next few days. Matt had been listening to rumors, even though he didn't know how much credence to give them. A resumption of the war wasn't too likely, was it? And yet *something* had clearly put a bee in the old man's bonnet. A group of religious travelers probably wouldn't be a very high priority. "I can put in a request for you, but it might be a while before he sees you."

"The Holy Voice thanks you," John said.

He turned and walked off, moving slowly under his heavy cowl. Matt resisted the childish urge to stick his tongue out. Falcon was in a snit—the captain's displeasure had filtered down to the lower ranks—and Matt had no doubt he'd be chewed out royally if Falcon caught him doing anything objectionable. The other Brethren followed, moving in eerie unison.

"Well," Carla said, "*that* was interesting."

Falcon made a noise for attention. "Do I need to remind you all of the rules?" He went on before anyone could object. "They're allowed to hold services in the chapel, if they book it, and they're allowed to invite others if they wish," he said. "They are *not* allowed to harass other guests, whatever the situation. Nor are other guests allowed to harass them. If you spot either, call security and intervene."

"I hear they do nude worship," Jack said. "It sounds like fun."

"They'd be a bigger sect if they did," Carla said cynically. "I think they probably wear those robes the whole time."

"Quiet," Falcon said. He scowled. "Or do I have to force you all to reread the religious regulations?"

"Cruel and unusual punishment, sir," Matt muttered.

Falcon had sharp ears. "Cruel, but not unusual," he said. "Making you write them out a dozen times would *definitely* be cruel and unusual."

"Beats cleaning the head, sir," Carla said.

"I'll remember that," Falcon said dryly. He glanced at his wristcom. "Departure is in two hours. Get a snack; then go to your stations. And try not to *look* as though you don't believe a word they say."

"Yes, sir," Matt said. He glanced at Carla. "Shall we go?"

Carla nodded. She still looked pale. "Why not?"

———

Paul didn't need to be there when Roman Bryon was brought onto his ship. He had every confidence in Slater and his staff, who were trained to handle everything from fistfights to pirate boarding parties. But still . . . he'd made the decision to watch. It was *his* ship, insofar as Corporate let it be his ship, and he was damned if he was leaving his crew to handle the serial killer alone.

The shuttle hatch opened. Two men appeared carrying a large stretcher between them. An ordinary-looking man lay on it, wrapped in a straitjacket. There was nothing remarkable about his face, nothing that screamed *monster*. Paul would have felt slight sympathy if he hadn't known precisely what Bryon had done. He didn't even know if the file contained all of Bryon's crimes. The writer had speculated that the murderer might be responsible for several unexplained deaths before his flight from Britannia.

"Check his ID; then scan the body," Slater ordered. "And then repeat the scans."

"Aye, sir," his officer said. There was a pause. "One set of standard-issue implants, deactivated. Nothing else, as far as I can tell."

"There was nothing," a new voice said. Paul looked up to see another man stepping through the hatch. "He had a limited amount of genetic enhancement, but nothing particularly unusual."

"Constable Singh," Slater said. "Captain, please, can I present Hamish Singh, retired marine."

"Pleased to meet you," Paul said. Singh was statuesque and strongly muscled, clad in a constable's uniform. He had a marine-issue carryall slung over his back. "Is our guest secure?"

"He has made no attempt to escape," Singh informed him. His accent was odd. Paul couldn't place it. "However, he panicked when he was informed that he would be returned to Britannia to face trial."

"The second scan is clear," Slater's officer said. "His implants have definitely been deactivated."

"And codelocked," Singh put in. "We don't believe they can be reactivated."

"Good," Paul said.

Slater's men took over the stretcher and carried it through the maze of hidden corridors, down to the brig. Paul followed, feeling cold. There was no sense of *danger* around Bryon, no sense that he was an unspeakable monster. But he remembered the images attached to the file and shuddered. Bryon's normality was his danger. Hardly anyone saw him as a serious threat.

"We set up a stasis pod in the cell," Slater explained as they reached the brig. "He'll be held inside on an independent power circuit. The entire system has been isolated from the rest of the ship."

"Very good," Singh said. "I'll require access to the brig, of course."

Slater didn't look pleased. "You'll have access to the general compartment and that particular cell," he said, "but not to the rest of the cells."

Paul kept his face expressionless as the stretcher was carried into the brig, a part of the ship few realized existed, seemingly part of an entirely different vessel. The brig was clean, certainly better than some planetside jail cells, but was indisputably a prison. Each of the cells had minimal privacy, allowing guards to peer in whenever they liked.

"You don't use force fields to keep the prisoners inside," Singh observed.

"No," Slater agreed. He opened one of the doors, revealing an independent stasis unit. "We prefer to use something more reliable."

Paul nodded in approval. Force fields were good, but if the ship lost power, they'd lose the force fields too. Better to rely on something that couldn't be taken down so easily. Anyone bent on breaking Bryon out of his cell would have to decrypt a codelocked hatch rather than simply cut the power. Nearly seventy years had passed since a handful of criminals had been broken out of jail when their associates cut the power, but the Tyre Penal Service had never forgotten. Two of the crooks had never been recaptured.

He watched as Bryon was removed from the stretcher, dumped into the stasis pod, and frozen in time. Some damned bean counter would probably insist that there were better options, but those assholes weren't on the ship. Better to use a stasis pod than risk a breakout that might leave a dozen guests dead. Paul had no idea precisely what Britannia would do once Bryon was handed over, but he doubted they'd be kind. Bryon's known crimes were more than enough to get him hung.

"Thank you, Captain," Singh said. "I know this is a hassle."

"It's a security nightmare," Paul said. Robert Cavendish had asked him to a private dinner. Perhaps he'd raise the issue there. "As long as he stays in the pod, there shouldn't be a problem. But if he gets out . . ."

"I'll stop him," Singh said calmly. He sounded confident. His record suggested he had reason to be. "I have permission to use deadly force, if necessary."

"You might have to," Paul said. He looked at Slater. "I'll be on the bridge, preparing to depart. Alert me if there are any problems."

"Yes, sir," Slater said.

Two hours later, they slipped into hyperspace and set course for Britannia.

CHAPTER SEVENTEEN

"Our escort has just peeled away," Commander Tidal Macpherson said. "We're on our own."

"All alone," Lieutenant Rani Jackson said.

"Stow that chatter," Paul snapped. He wasn't in a good mood. They'd done everything in their power to ensure that no one could track *Supreme* unless vessels had sensors so advanced they might as well have come from the future, but he still felt naked. "Helm, are we on course for Britannia?"

"Yes, sir," Rani said. "Assuming we don't have to change course, we will cross the border in twelve days and reach our destination in nineteen."

Paul nodded, stiffly. They *would* have to change course. He was fairly sure of it. The weather reports warned that energy storms had been sighted along the border, blocking a straight-line course to Britannia. They might have to change course several times just to avoid disaster. Irritating, but couldn't be helped.

"Very good," he said. He looked around the bridge. "I want long-range sensors to be constantly monitored at all times. We'll change course to avoid any potential contacts."

"Aye, sir," Tidal said.

Paul sat back in his chair, cursing under his breath. No reports of pirate activity had crossed his desk. It wasn't as though he was taking the liner through the Gap and into Theocratic space, but changing course still didn't sit well with him. Ideally, *Supreme* would be escorted at all times. And yet he knew it just couldn't be helped. The Royal Navy had too many other demands on its time.

He keyed his console, requesting a status update. Everything appeared to be fine: the crew were doing their jobs, the guests were enjoying themselves . . . many of the children were even enjoying a game of hide and seek, according to the stewards. And yet he still felt uneasy as his ship moved farther from Williamson's World.

You're being silly, he told himself firmly. *What are you planning to do? Turn back to Williamson's World? Or fly all the way back to Tyre?*

His lips quirked. In theory, he could abort the entire cruise at will; in practice, Corporate would fire him as soon as they heard about the maneuver. The guests would be outraged at having their trip cut short for nothing more than their captain's unease. They'd sue . . . and they'd have a point. Paul's unease was rooted in nothing more than his own concerns about being alone in hyperspace.

"Commander, you have the bridge," he said, rising. He had paperwork to manage and a string of formal complaints to register. Corporate couldn't help him, but perhaps they could make it easier for the next commander who was asked to take on an unwanted passenger because of an outdated treaty. "I'll be in my office."

"Yes, sir," Jeanette said.

———

Nancy, Angela decided as she pressed the terminal against the sensor, was a genius.

She didn't even begin to understand the explanation her sister had given her. Indeed, she suspected Nancy didn't understand half the technobabble she'd used. But it was enough to know that the combination of her family's ID codes and the absence of a telltale was enough to open the hatch into the observation blister. Leaving the telltale behind was a risk, she admitted, but would make it harder for Marie to track her down. The governess had been so clingy over the last few days that Angela had come close to hitting her.

Probably won't be that difficult to find me, she thought sourly. *But as long as she thinks I'm in my room, everything will be fine.*

Angela walked forward and sat on the bench, peering out into hyperspace. The observation blister felt comfortable, even though the space looked like an afterthought. She didn't see why it was *needed* when there were so many windows on the starship, allowing anyone lucky enough to have one of the better cabins to look outside. The compartment was crude, the bench was hard metal . . . but it was *private*. She'd have happily borrowed a steerage cabin if it meant some privacy.

Hyperspace flickered and flared outside, waves of sparkling luminescence dancing around the giant starship. Angela watched shimmering rivers of light flaring in the distance, half wishing she could step through the bubble. It would have killed her, but . . . she closed her eyes for a long moment, trying to fight down bitter depression. Perhaps death would be better than being trapped.

It isn't going to be that bad, she told herself. *Really.*

Of course not, her thoughts mocked her. *It's going to be worse.*

Angela sighed, out loud. Finley wanted . . . what? Her to be a quiet little butterfly? To play the role of a dutiful wife? No one would care what she did, as long as she bore Finley two children . . . but it was important, apparently, that everyone believed the marriage was working. She couldn't live apart from him, she couldn't go to social events without him, she couldn't . . .

She opened her eyes and looked down at her pale hands. She was trapped. There was no way off the ship, no way out of her life. She'd marry Finley the night before they returned to Tyre, then . . . live in his mansion and do nothing. Nothing at all. She couldn't even look forward to the wedding night. It was impossible to imagine Finley doing anything but sleeping. He'd sleep with her . . .

He will *sleep with me*, she thought. She giggled, despite herself. *That's* all *he'll do.*

She cursed her own stupidity under her breath. She could have studied hard and learned how to handle the family's affairs. God knew her father needed more trusted help. Her relatives back on Tyre could keep matters ticking over for the time being, but that wouldn't last forever. The corporation needed bold and decisive leadership. Or she could have joined the navy, or gone into politics, or even used her trust fund to buy a starship or set up a business of her own. Instead, she'd just wasted her life.

It was a waste, she thought angrily. *Why didn't anyone tell me?*

Because you wouldn't listen, her own thoughts pointed out. *Would you?*

She clenched her fists. Of *course* she wouldn't have listened. As a child, she'd enjoyed herself; as a teenager, she'd sought pleasure in all its myriad forms. She'd grown into physical adulthood without ever having matured. And now she was nothing more than breeding stock. The only thing she was expected to do was lie back and think of the corporation.

The hatch hissed open behind her. Angela started, then glanced around. Matt stepped into the compartment wearing his white uniform. His eyes went wide when he saw her. Angela remembered just how she'd behaved at the shuttle hatch and blushed. She'd acted like a toddler throwing a tantrum.

"My Lady," Matt said, his voice formal. "This is a restricted area."

Angela winced. They'd had a friendly chat once, hadn't they? But that had been before she'd thrown a tantrum. She couldn't really blame him, she supposed, for keeping his tone as formal as possible. He wasn't a family retainer who'd earned the right to speak his mind, just . . . just someone so low on the totem pole that no one would care if he lost his job. A word from her would be enough to get him thrown into the brig.

"I'm sorry for how I treated you," she said. Her father hadn't reprimanded her for her behavior. Somehow, that made her feel worse. "I was out of line."

"I've had worse," Matt assured her. He kept his eyes firmly fixed on her face. "I'm just the face of someone else's decision."

"I know," Angela said. "I was a little brat."

"A *big* brat," Matt said with a hint of the old smile. Angela was glad to see it. His face was handsome enough, she supposed, but she liked the way it lit up when he smiled. *That* wasn't something you could buy in a bodyshop. "Are you feeling better now?"

"Just a little," Angela lied. "I . . . my life is a mess."

Matt quirked his eyebrows. "What do *you* have to worry about?"

"It's a long story," Angela said. There was no point in telling him. She certainly didn't really know him. What if he started a whole new series of rumors? "My life is a mess."

"I think everyone gets that feeling from time to time," Matt said. "I've had it too."

Angela found it hard to believe him. She didn't think he had anything like her problems. No one was pressuring him into an unhappy marriage with an old man trapped in a young man's body. But she supposed he had problems of his own. It was hard to imagine the scion of a wealthy family joining the crew and being berated by every last passenger. Even the steerage passengers on the lower decks spoke down to the crew.

"I was told that I should tell people to talk through their problems," Matt said. "Would that actually help?"

Angela surprised herself by giggling. "Who told you that?"

"Corporate," Matt said. "We were given lectures on conflict management and reconciliation."

"I don't think that would help," Angela said.

She shook her head in disbelief. Conflict management and reconciliation *indeed*! It sounded like something that would be applied to a planet emerging from civil war. And yet, if it didn't address the underlying problems, it wouldn't put the war off indefinitely. She'd never paid that much attention to international affairs, but it just *sounded* stupid. People were not *machines* governed by logic and reason. The Theocracy would have conceded defeat long ago if they'd allowed cold logic to trump religious fanaticism.

And no amount of talking will hide the fact we need the match to work, she thought bitterly. *I have to marry Finley, and that's the end of it.*

She groaned to herself. Perhaps it wouldn't be ten years, but longer. *Much* longer. What if she found herself trapped for *twenty* years, until the children reached adulthood? She could leave then, she was sure, but . . . she wouldn't be the same, not afterwards. She'd seen too many old women in young bodies, acting . . . acting as though they were trying to make up for lost time. It dawned on her, slowly, that parts of the aristocratic world were *sick*. How many others, men as well as women, had grown bitter and resentful over the years?

Matt cleared his throat. "I have to ask," he said, "how did you get in here?"

Angela didn't bother to dissemble. "Nancy taught me a trick," she said, holding up the terminal. "How did you know I was in here?"

"An alert went off, just as I was about to go off duty," Matt said. He inspected the terminal thoughtfully. "Your little sister is quite clever. She used an override code to unlock the hatch. I wonder how she got it."

"Probably borrowed it from Father," Angela said. Nancy had always been exploring places she wasn't supposed to go. They'd had to get her out of a chimney once . . . which hadn't been easy. "Or perhaps from one of the staff."

Matt looked displeased. "Technically, I should report it," he said. "If the codes are being misused . . ."

Angela shot him a pleading look. "She's only *twelve*."

"But someone else might have copied the code too," Matt said. "*And* be smart enough not to use it while wearing a telltale."

"Sorry," Angela muttered. She looked down at her bare wrist. In hindsight, she should have worn a long-sleeved shirt. The absence of the telltale was obvious. "I'll speak to her."

"Make sure she listens," Matt advised. He motioned for her to stand. "You can't stay here."

Angela rose slowly. The lights of hyperspace seemed to be calling to her . . . she wondered, suddenly, just how much force was necessary to break the canopy. She doubted, somehow, that her fists would be enough.

She turned. Matt looked good, great even, in his uniform. She allowed her eyes to trail over him, noting the half-hidden muscles. He was in fine shape for a man who presumably didn't go to the bodyshops each week for a touch-up. His face *was* a little babyish, she decided, but he still had a soothing smile. The form suited him.

"Everyone else is at the ball," she said. Thankfully, she hadn't been forced to attend. Her tantrum provided an excellent excuse. "Would you . . . ah . . . would you escort me back to my quarters?"

"Of course," Matt said. "My pleasure."

He opened the hatch and motioned for her to step through. Angela took one last look around the observation blister—she was sure she wouldn't be able to come back—and then stepped through the hatch and walked down to the promenade. Only a couple of guests were visible, one reading an old-fashioned book and the other snoring loudly in an armchair, his face covered by a towel. Angela smiled at the sight as she and Matt moved down towards the inner hatch, feeling a tinge of envy. The two old men had nothing to worry about, did they?

Perhaps they do, she thought. *I didn't know the corporation was in trouble until it was too late, did I?*

It was a sobering thought. She was used, too used, to being surrounded by beautiful people, by men and women who acted as though they didn't have a care in the world. Her friends back home had partied all night, slept all day, and then partied again . . . and again . . . and again. They'd never been concerned about money or power . . . they'd grumbled about their allowances from their parents, but they'd never felt *poor*. They'd certainly never lacked for anything. And yet, who knew what had been hiding behind their pretty faces?

She looked at Matt as they walked down the corridor. His handsome face wasn't real, but there was a genuineness to him that so many of her friends back home lacked. He actually had to work for a living, something she hadn't known she should value until it was too late. He exhibited no polish beyond a handful of etiquette lessons, no facade that might conceal a rotting heart. She looked at him . . .

. . . and realized, suddenly, that she'd already made a decision.

They reached her back door and stopped. "Can you open it?" she asked. "I don't want to go through the antechamber."

Matt seemed to find the request perfectly reasonable. He pressed his wristcom against the scanner, unlocking the hatch. Angela stepped into her bedroom, motioning for Matt to follow. The room was a mess—she'd thrown boxes and dresses around after her father had told her she was effectively grounded—but at least it was private. Her telltale lay on the bed where she'd left it.

She looked at Matt. "Close the hatch."

Matt did as he was told. Angela took a deep breath, then leaned forward and kissed him. His body tensed in surprise an instant before his lips melted into hers. He hadn't known what she wanted, she realized. An aristocrat would have had no trouble recognizing the invitation for what it actually was. But Matt . . . to him, she was forbidden fruit. The thought added spice as she broke the kiss, wrapping her arms around him. She could feel his heartbeat . . .

Her father would not approve, she knew. Nor would her mother . . . or Finley. Matt was a steward, one of the hired hands. He was so far below her that any relationship would be the stuff of a bad romcom.

But she found it hard to care. She wanted—*needed*—to feel as though she was desired for herself, not for her title or money. She wanted to feel like a *person*.

"Get undressed," she hissed.

She pulled at his trousers even as his hands started undoing her shirt. His fingers felt like magic on her breasts, her nipples hardening as he stroked them gently. She felt a flush of desire mingled with satisfaction as he did as he was told. *She* was in charge. He kissed her again and again as his hands roamed downward. She gasped in pleasure as they moved inside her panties and stroked her sex, his hardness suddenly pressing against her . . .

She could wait no longer. "Take me to bed. Now."

CHAPTER EIGHTEEN

Matt awoke, slowly.

His body felt . . . odd. His memories were a jumbled mess. He was tired, but it was a good sort of tiredness. His eyes opened . . .

He jerked awake. He wasn't in his bunk. He was in a Gold Deck cabin. And . . . he sat upright and turned his head, unsure what he would see. Angela Cavendish lay next to him, fast asleep. Her chest rose and fell in time with her breathing; her golden hair fanned out like a halo. Matt stared at her, his heart starting to pound as he remembered all the things they'd done. Angela had been the most determined, desperate lover he'd ever had. She'd done things he hadn't known were possible.

I fucked her, he thought dazedly. *I fucked her.*

Something bleeped. His wristcom . . . he looked around, unsure where it had gone in all the excitement. He wasn't even sure when he'd taken it off. The device bleeped again, telling him that it was buried under a pile of clothes. He stumbled out of bed, picking up the wristcom. Both Carla and Falcon had sent him messages asking where he was. He suspected that his supervisor had checked the security sensors after sending the second message. The questions had cut off rather sharply.

He knows where I was, he thought. *And that means . . . ?*

Matt wasn't entirely sure. Carla had told him that the passengers came first, so if a steward happened to be lured into one of their beds, the affair wouldn't be held against him, but Matt wasn't sure he wanted to gamble on that. Falcon had every reason to be pissed. Matt hadn't sent a message to indicate what was going on, let alone that he might be late for his next duty shift. He tapped out a message quickly, then turned back to the bed, suddenly unsure of himself. Should he stay? Or sneak out . . . he didn't know. Part of him was insistent that he should stay with Angela.

She opened her eyes. "Matt . . ."

Too late, he thought.

Angela smiled at him. Matt thought, just for a moment, that he was looking into the sun. She was utterly gorgeous, utterly stunning, so utterly beautiful that . . . he couldn't believe everything they'd done together. His eyes dropped to her breasts . . . had he really licked and fondled them? Had he . . .

"Come here," Angela said. "Now."

Afterwards, Matt headed for the shower. It wasn't entirely a surprise when Angela followed him, walking naked across the corridor as un-self-consciously as a cat. He could barely keep his eyes off her, even as he turned on the shower and water splashed down to rinse them both clean. She was *real*.

He found himself tongue-tied as he dressed, wishing he'd had a change of clothes. Or even of underwear . . . Angela didn't have anything he could borrow. And yet . . . he pushed the thought aside, unsure what to say. Was this a one-night stand? Or would she invite him again and again until *Supreme* returned to Tyre? Or would their liaison be permanent? Cold logic and stories from the old sweats told him that no shipboard romance lasted past the romance, and certainly not when the partners came from such different spheres.

Angela smiled as she pulled on a set of simple clothes. Matt wondered, as the postcoital bliss continued to wear off, if she'd thought about the future at all. Maybe she didn't think she *had* to think about it. Maybe it had all been a one-night stand for her. Someone in her shoes would have no trouble finding a different partner every night. She could work her way through the stewards, male and female alike. The thought caused him a pang, one he didn't want to look at too closely. He liked Angela more than was good for him.

"We'll go out the back door," Angela said. She shot him a smirk that suggested she was enjoying her game. "You can escort me to breakfast, then go."

Matt bowed politely. "Very well," he said. He wondered what *that* meant. "You can always send me a message through the datanet."

He opened the door. "Finally," a male voice said. "I . . . who are you?"

Matt stared. *Who . . . ?*

"Finley," Angela squeaked. "What are *you* doing here?"

"I think a better question would be, what is *he* doing here?" Finley said. He jabbed a finger at Matt. "Get out."

Matt stared back at him. Finley looked . . . *angry*. His face, normally colorless, was flushed; his delicate hands were clenched into fists. Matt was sure he could take the man in a fight, but what would happen if he did? Corporate wouldn't even bother listening to his side of the story before they dismissed him, if he was lucky. Being dumped on Britannia might be the best possible outcome.

But he didn't want to leave Angela alone with him.

Finley's gaze tightened. "You will get out," he snapped. "You will never talk to Angela again. If you do, I will destroy your career. Do you understand me?"

Matt glanced at Angela. She looked aghast. Matt honestly didn't know what to do. Finley was showing all the danger signs, all the warnings stewards had been taught to watch for so they knew when to intervene in a dispute. And yet . . . he didn't *think* Finley's threat was an idle one. He was more than powerful enough to destroy Matt's career.

Angela cleared her throat. "Jack, go," she said. It took Matt a moment to realize she'd given him a false name. She sounded angry too, but far from defeated. "Just . . . go."

Matt silently damned himself as he walked past Finley, expecting a blow at any moment, and strode down to the access hatch. Angela had told him to go, yet he felt as though he were running out on her. And he was . . . leaving her with someone who looked as though he was going to start throwing punches. He wanted to turn back, to watch from a distance in case she needed help, but he knew it wasn't possible. His career . . .

You didn't think of that when you let her take you to bed, he thought numbly. *You knew she was getting married.*

He gritted his teeth as he made his way down to the wardroom. Angela had known she was getting married, and yet she'd still taken him to bed. And yet . . . he kicked himself for a fool as he walked into the wardroom. Carla was rubbing cream on her face as he entered. She was clearly getting ready for her next shift.

"Well, look what the cat dragged in," Carla said. Her eyes narrowed as she turned to face him. "Where were *you* last night?"

"I think I fucked up," Matt said. He sat down on the bunk and checked his wristcom. Falcon had changed his duty shift, putting him in the casino in the afternoon. "I fucked, and then I fucked up."

Carla face-palmed. "Don't tell me . . ."

Matt wished that was an option. But he needed advice. "I slept with her," he said. There was no need to give names. "And then her fiancé caught us."

"Fuck me," Carla said. She banged her palm into her forehead again. "You slept with her, *then* you got caught?"

"Yeah," Matt said.

Carla eyed him for a long moment, her bare breasts bouncing in front of Matt's eyes. He felt nothing.

"You," Carla said finally, "are a fucking idiot."

"I know," Matt said.

"You have *got* to stop thinking with your dick, you . . . you *man*," she snapped. "Now you're in deep fucking trouble."

"I know," Matt said again.

Carla leaned back, one finger tracing out a line on her cheek. "You were caught by someone who could purchase a *million* horny dickheads like you," she said. It looked as if she had a faint mark on her bare shoulders. "You were—"

"He said he'd have my career if he saw me talking to her again," Matt said. "I don't know what to do."

Carla drew back her hand and slapped Matt across the face, just hard enough to sting. "This is what you are going to do," she said. "You are going to pretend she doesn't exist. If you have to interact with her, you stay professional . . . fuck . . . go ask Falcon for a transfer to Silver or even Bronze. You don't have anything to do with her. You don't *talk* to her, much less *fuck* her."

Matt swallowed. "I . . ."

"I've *met* that bastard," Carla added. It took Matt a moment to understand she meant Finley Mackintosh. "He won't hesitate to destroy you completely if he thinks you're a threat. This is not some goddamned stupid romcom where the poor suitor beats the rich suitor. You *cannot* fight him for her. Your entire fucking career is at risk because you thought with your fucking dick rather than your fucking brain!"

She paused, gasping for breath. "Come on, Matt," she said. "Is it really worth throwing away *everything* for a spoiled brat of a girl?"

"She's not spoiled," Matt protested.

"I guarantee you that she is," Carla said. Her voice rose. "Did *you* get everything you wanted as a child? Did I? Hell no! She did. Her parents could buy her anything from a stable of ponies to a private starship of her own! And they did! To her, you're just a cunt stimulator on legs!"

Matt recoiled in shock. "She isn't—"

"I know the type," Carla said. She pointed a finger at Matt's crotch. "She doesn't give a damn about you. You're just an object to her. And if you value your career, perhaps even your life, you will stay the fuck away from her."

She reached for her bra and pulled it on. "Get changed; then grab some breakfast," she said as she checked her appearance in the mirror. Matt watched her dully. "And then remember what I said. Stay away from her!"

Matt sighed. "I don't know what to do."

Carla snapped a muffled swear word as she pulled on her jumper. "Haven't you been listening? Stay away from her!"

She glowered at Matt, then walked to the hatch. Matt watched her go, feeling . . . he didn't know *how* he felt. Harsh logic suggested that Carla was right, but . . . he thought Angela and he had something more. Could that just be his hormones talking?

Of course you want to sleep with her again, his thoughts said. *But is it really worth the risk?*

He cursed. He had no answer.

———

Angela looked at Finley as Matt hurried down the corridor, feeling a stark, burning rage that threatened to overcome her. Finley's face was hot, his fists clenched . . . she wondered, suddenly, if this was the first true glimpse of emotion he'd shown her. How much of his emotionless face was a mask?

He stepped forward, entering the cabin and closing the hatch behind him. Angela realized, a moment too late, that she should have tried to close the portal. Her heart was pounding in her chest as she followed Finley's gaze around the room. She and Matt had been *very* busy. The signs were everywhere.

"Tell me something," Finley said. His voice was calm, so calm she knew it was an act. "What were you thinking?"

Angela drew herself up to her full height, crossing her arms. "You don't *own* me," she said. "We're not even married yet!"

"You shouldn't be doing anything that might call our marriage into question," Finley said. He leaned forward, looming over her. For the first time, she felt a trickle of fear. "You whoring around with a . . . a . . ."

"As opposed to whoring myself for the family?" Angela demanded. "Or marrying someone for the good of the corporation?"

Finley recoiled, almost as if she'd slapped him. "You . . . that's different!"

Angela pressed her advantage. "How?"

"You and I are getting married, despite our opinions," Finley snarled. He didn't seem to have a good answer. "I don't care if you love or hate me. God knows I don't like *you*. But our families need the match, and I will not let you ruin it."

"You don't like me," Angela said. "What *do* you like?"

Finley ignored the question. "This is the most important match in history," he added. "You will—"

Angela laughed. "What about the marriage between the king and that runaway princess?" Her circle had been faux outraged about the whole affair. They'd always assumed the king would choose a bride from the nobility. God knew there had been rumors about King Hadrian and Kat Falcone being secret lovers. "Or Baron Argyle and that woman from the wrong side of the street, or . . . ?"

"It is the most important match for our families, then," Finley barked. He loomed closer, forcing her to take a step backward. "You will *not* ruin it."

"Our match will not be ruined by us having an open relationship," Angela snapped back. She'd wanted to see *some* sign of feeling from Finley, but this . . . she gritted her teeth in fury. She was not going to put up with this. "You do not own me. I will bear your children, as stipulated in the marriage contract, but nothing else. We will live apart . . . you can handle your boring job while I—"

"Take lovers from the lower classes?" Finley asked. "Will I come home one day to find you in bed with the gardener and his wife?"

Angela felt a hot flash of anger. "I will do as I please!"

"No, you won't," Finley corrected. "You'll do as your parents want."

"So will you," Angela snapped back. "You don't want this match any more than *I* do!"

"We all have to make sacrifices," Finley said. "I will not take part in a farce of a marriage."

"It's *already* a farce," Angela sneered. "You want to marry me about as much as I want to marry you!"

Finley reddened. "Yes," he said. "That's true. I don't want to marry you. But you know what? I *have* to marry you. I *have* to make it look as though the relationship is working! If we are together, bound by blood, our families will remain bound together. If we are separate, our enemies will scent weakness and move in for the kill."

"And if that happens," Angela whispered, "at least I will be free of you."

Finley lifted a hand. For a moment, she honestly thought he was going to hit her. Part of her even thought it might be a good thing. The violence would be a major scandal; her father could use the incident as leverage to get concessions out of Finley's family. But would it be enough to save *her* family? She rather suspected that the Mackintoshes would sooner throw Finley to the wolves than give up a major advantage.

"Countless lives depend on our marriage," he hissed. He lowered his hand, slowly. "Are you prepared to threaten them because of your selfishness?"

"I'm not *selfish*," Angela snapped.

"You are a little brat who never grew up," Finley said. "You don't bother to think about the consequences of your actions. How many times have you gone through rehab?"

"Never!"

"Oh, *there's* a surprise," Finley mocked. He made a visible attempt to calm down. "You will behave yourself for the rest of the voyage . . . and married life."

"Oh," Angela mocked. "And if I don't?"

"I'll destroy your fuck-toy, for a start," Finley said. "And I'll—"

Angela slapped him. Or tried to. He caught her wrist before her palm could make contact.

She gritted her teeth, refusing to cry out. Finley was stronger than he looked.

"This is not a game," Finley said. He pushed her backward, squeezing her wrist hard enough to bring tears to her eyes. "I don't want this any more than you do, but you will behave."

"Let go of me," Angela managed. It wasn't the first time she'd felt pain, but it was the first time anyone had deliberately hurt her. Her parents had never lifted a hand to her. "Finley, please . . ."

He let go. "Remember what I said," he told her. "This match *has* to work."

He turned and stalked out of the hatch, closing it firmly behind him. Angela stared down at her wrist, rubbing it gently. The pain was already fading. She looked up at the hatch, feeling fear trickling down her back. Finley . . . she'd never liked him, but she'd never thought he could be so angry.

"Fuck," she said. Whom could she count on? No one. Her sister was too young to help, and everyone else had their own agendas. "What do I do now?"

And then the emergency alarms started to howl.

CHAPTER NINETEEN

"Having a serial killer on the ship is a little inconvenient, I agree," Robert Cavendish said as he buttered a piece of toast. "But is it really a serious problem if he's in stasis? I was given to understand that a person couldn't escape a stasis field?"

"It's the precedent that matters, My Lord," Paul said. He'd invited Cavendish to a private breakfast, partly so he could lobby the older man. "The treaties were written and signed before interstellar travel became so common. It wouldn't have been hard to charter a ship for Britannia or even hold the trial on Williamson's World if Britannia declined to pay."

"It would have cost money," Cavendish said. His lips quirked. "I dare say Williamson's World would have been less than enthusiastic about spending their own money on the prisoner transfer. Or even holding a potentially innocent prisoner."

Paul sipped his coffee, puzzled. Corporate . . . and Robert Cavendish . . . seemed to be deliberately overlooking the risk. No one would be happy if they knew there was a serial killer onboard *Supreme*, even if the monster remained in stasis for the entire trip. Indeed, he was sure that rumors were already leaking out. Corporate might find itself with a public-relations nightmare on its hands.

At least they can't blame it on me, he thought. He'd taken care to document that he'd protested the decision, up to and including sending copies of his messages to time-locked archive sites. It wasn't something he would have done in the navy, but he didn't think the navy would have been *quite* so quick to start looking for a scapegoat.

He took a breath. "Might I ask why Corporate decided not to argue the point?"

"There were politics involved," Cavendish said. "On one hand, the danger of transporting a known criminal had to be taken into account. On the other, a willingness to disregard the treaties would probably have come back to haunt us in short order. Dismantling the treaties, or even having them rewritten, will take months of high-level talks." He took a bite of his toast. "Chartering a ship would have been cheaper," he added. "But we didn't want to set a precedent."

Paul didn't understand. Chartering a vessel would be an awkward precedent, particularly if it happened time and time again. That was true enough. But Corporate regularly handled vast sums of money. Hiring a smaller ship, even a courier boat, to take a stasis pod from one world to another wouldn't cost that much in the grand scheme of things.

He took another sip of his coffee. It was . . . *unusual* . . . for Corporate to refuse to spend money. They regularly paid premium rates for expensive wine, natural meats . . . even expensive coffee. God knew it was unlikely that anyone would be able to tell the difference between natural and vat-grown meat, but Corporate insisted. Perhaps the accountants had finally managed to put a brake on the spending at the worst possible time. All those expensive bottles of wine added up very quickly.

Not that quickly, he told himself.

He cleared his throat and changed the subject. "I trust you have enjoyed the cruise so far, My Lord," he said. "Or is there anything we can do to improve your experience?"

Cavendish smiled humorlessly. "I have been working for most of the cruise," he said. "I haven't had time to enjoy myself."

Paul kept his face expressionless. *That* didn't sound good. And yet, if there was a real problem, why would Robert Cavendish go on a three-month cruise? Perhaps he was just using the time to plan out the next twenty years or so of corporate development. The war was over, and now, with the Commonwealth expanding into the Jorlem Sector and Theocratic Space, the Big Twelve had a lot of work. Cavendish would be at the forefront of reconstruction.

"I hope you'll have time to sample some of our wares," Paul said instead. "This *is* a pleasure cruise."

His wristcom bleeped before he could say another word. He keyed it sharply. "Go ahead."

"Captain, this is Commander Macpherson," Tidal said. "We may have a situation."

Paul felt his blood turn to ice. His crew knew whom he'd invited to breakfast. They wouldn't interrupt unless it was urgent. And that meant real trouble.

"I'm on my way," he said. He rose, closing the connection. "I'm sorry for the interruption."

"I quite understand," Robert Cavendish said. "Please, see to your ship."

Paul nodded, then strode through the hatch onto the bridge. The main display was right in front of him, showing two red icons steadily approaching *Supreme*. He couldn't be sure, thanks to hyperspace, but they looked to be light cruisers . . .

"Two contacts on approach vector, sir," Tidal said. She rose, offering him the command chair. "They just came into sensor range now."

"Sound quiet alert," Paul ordered. The guests wouldn't be told, not yet. Hopefully the whole affair would be settled before they had a chance to panic. "Do we have any ID?"

"No, sir," Tidal said. "There's too much distortion to get a clear image. I'd say they were prewar junk, but I can't prove it."

Not that it matters, Paul thought. He sat. *A prewar cruiser could still blow us to atoms if it wished.*

He gritted his teeth as he contemplated the vectors. Two ships . . . it was remotely possible that they were friendly, but the odds were against it. Britannia wouldn't have dispatched two warships to escort *Supreme*, not if they weren't willing to send warships to pick up Roman Bryon. No, they were either pirates or the ragtag remains of the Theocratic Navy. He couldn't afford to assume anything less.

"Prepare to alter course," he ordered. "Stand by to deploy two ECM drones."

"Aye, sir," Rani said.

Paul watched as her proposed course appeared on the display. It wasn't quite straight away from the pirates, but close enough to ensure that they'd have problems recovering *Supreme* if they lost her. The standard tactical manual insisted that starships shouldn't run in a straight line, although the cynical side of his mind pointed out that the pirates presumably had read the same manuals. But they'd still have to guess the starship's vector . . .

"Deploy drones," he ordered. "Alter course on my mark." He braced himself. *"Mark!"*

Supreme slowly, far too slowly, altered course. A cruiser or a battlecruiser, perhaps even a superdreadnought, would have been able to turn on a dime, but not his wallowing sow of a liner. The pirates were getting closer. They might not lose their lock on her hull if they got too close. Hyperspace would amplify the ECM—the pirates would suddenly find themselves chasing a multitude of targets—but they might not be fooled for long.

We have to find cover, he thought. Crashing back into realspace wasn't an option. The pirates would have no trouble locating them. *We could . . .*

"Captain," Tidal snapped. "I'm picking up a *third* unknown ship, directly ahead of us!"

Paul swore. The pirates had gotten lucky, insanely lucky. Or they'd managed to get a better lock on his hull than he'd assumed. Either way, *Supreme* was in trouble.

"Sound red alert," he ordered. "Helm, alter course, bearing . . ."

Rani coughed as the new course took shape on the display. "Sir, there's an energy distortion in that direction."

"Do it," Paul snapped. She was right, but he didn't have time to argue. *Supreme* could not afford an encounter with one pirate ship, let alone three. The energy distortion would provide some cover, he hoped. "We need cover."

"Aye, sir," Rani said.

———

"ATTENTION ALL PASSENGERS. THIS IS NOT A DRILL. RETURN TO YOUR CABINS AT ONCE. I SAY AGAIN, RETURN TO YOUR CABINS AT ONCE!"

Matt jumped, then glanced at his wristcom. An emergency alert was flashing, warning him to be ready to move if necessary. If he hadn't been in the shower, then he wouldn't have missed it. Cursing, he yanked on his jacket and ran for the hatch. He had to be at his emergency station *now*, or he'd be in deep shit when the crisis, whatever it was, came to an end. Other stewards and crew ran past him as the alarms howled louder, shaking his very bones. This wasn't a drill.

He reached his duty station and skidded to a halt. Carla was already there, taking an emergency pack from Falcon. The older man shoved one at Matt, motioning for him to check the pack. Matt unbuttoned it, making sure the stunner and other pieces of kit were clearly visible.

"Put on your stunner," Falcon yelled. He had to shout to be heard over the deafening alarm. "Hurry!"

Matt nodded, checking the power cell and then strapping the stunner to his belt. He'd been trained how to use the weapon but had never used it in real life. Sweat ran down his back as the other stewards joined them, some clearly woken up from sleep. A low vibration ran through *Supreme*, warning them that the ship was changing course. Matt's blood ran cold.

"RETURN TO YOUR CABINS!" the alerts kept repeating. Matt could feel his head starting to pound. "THIS IS AN EMERGENCY SITUATION. RETURN TO YOUR CABINS!"

"Move out," Falcon shouted. "The casino has to be cleared."

The stewards hurried through the hatch and into the guest section. Hundreds of guests ran past them, some carrying children and infants, others glancing around in panic as though they'd lost someone. A set of nude swimmers were dripping wet as they fled, their hands covering their private parts as best as they could.

The casino was a nightmare, jam-packed with guests shouting and screaming at the tops of their voices. Matt couldn't keep track of the different arguments—the constant howling made the task impossible—but he thought he had the general idea. They all thought they were going to break the bank and that their rivals had somehow triggered the alert.

"Move," Falcon shouted. His voice was barely audible over the alarms. "You have to return to your cabins!"

"I'm not leaving," a fat man shouted. He clutched a set of cards to his chest protectively. "I was winning!"

"You have to leave," Falcon said. He drew his stunner and zapped the man. Matt watched him crumple to the deck. The move was draconic but got the point across. "Now!"

Matt gritted his teeth as the crowd slowly broke up, muttering dark threats about lawyers and lawsuits. One of them even waved a terminal in Matt's face, getting a snapshot for later use. The photo wouldn't do him any good, Matt was sure. Normal procedures were suspended during an alert. The lawyers would either advise the passenger to drop the case out of court or let him go broke trying to win. Besides, *Matt* hadn't stunned the fat man.

And Falcon will be in the clear, he thought.

The alarms stopped howling as the last guest left the casino. Matt allowed himself a moment of relief, even though his ears were ringing. Emergency notes were still sounding, red lights still flashing . . . the emergency, whatever it was, wasn't over. He glanced at his wristcom, but there was no update from the bridge. He suspected that wasn't good news. If the bridge crew were too busy to update the stewards . . .

"There's a handful of others still out of their cabins," Falcon called. "Dispatch will give you the details. Go chase them back *into* their cabins."

Matt exchanged glances with Carla, then nodded. "Yes, sir."

The promenade seemed weirder, he decided, as they hurried down the passage. Hyperspace looked . . . strange. He couldn't put his finger on it. Describing hyperspace was far from easy, but something was there, nagging at the back of his mind. He wanted to stay and stare, yet he knew there wasn't time. The decks had to be cleared.

"Perhaps we'll find Finley Mackintosh out of his cabin," Carla teased. "Wouldn't you like to stun him?"

Matt ignored her as they peered into a small room. A pair of teenagers were cuddling, wearing VR suits. Matt felt a flicker of disgust mingled with a certain kind of wry amusement. There was something . . . silly . . . about making love to one person while pretending to be making love to someone else. But at least their lovemaking explained why they hadn't heard the alarms.

Carla stepped forward and tapped the off switches. "There's an emergency," she stated as the couple stared at her in shock. Being yanked out of the sim had to be slightly disorientating at best. "You have to go back to your cabins!"

"But—"

"No buts," Matt said. He did his best to sound gentle. The couple didn't need to be pressured, not while they were still trying to work out what was real and what wasn't. "Leave your gear here and go back to your cabins."

He watched them go, then glanced at the VR helmets. "He was banging a pop star and she was banging an actor," he said. "Go figure."

"I imagine it's easier that way," Carla said. She stuck out her tongue. "No drama."

Matt elbowed her. "Come on," he said. "Let's go."

Carla nodded as the dispatcher located a handful of other wandering souls. Two were sleeping on the promenade—Matt was privately impressed they'd managed to sleep through the alert—and a third was clearly sulking. He ordered all three of them back to their cabins, half wishing he could join them. Or go find Angela. She had to be out of her mind with fear.

"This isn't a drill," Carla said. She sounded worried. "What is it?"

Matt had no idea. If there had been a major drive failure, the captain would have ordered a crash-transit back into realspace. Hyperspace would murder an unpowered ship, even if the energy surge didn't trigger a storm. But something else . . . pirates? Suddenly the horror stories he'd heard about pirate crews boarding merchant ships seemed alarmingly plausible.

Carla caught his arm. "Matt, promise me something," she said. She met his eyes. "If it's pirates, don't let them take me alive."

"I . . ." Matt swallowed, hard. Angela and Nancy and the other upper-class passengers would probably be safe. They'd be held for ransom, but they wouldn't be hurt. Carla and the other stewards . . . fair game. Corporate wouldn't ransom any of the crew. The pirates would rape and kill the stewards for laughs. "If I have to."

"You will," Carla said. She sounded as if she was on the verge of panic. "I won't let them take me alive."

Matt nodded. He didn't want to be taken alive either.

———

Angela covered her ears as the alarms grew louder, then slowly made her way to the inner door and into the antechamber. She wanted to stay and hide, to think of some way to escape her fate, but she understood that she had to make sure everyone knew where she was. Marie was sitting on the sofa, her face cold and hard. Angela glared at her, not bothering to hide her dislike. One way or another, Marie wouldn't be her problem much longer.

"Sit down," Marie ordered. Somehow, she managed to be heard over the sound of alarm bells ringing. Her stern face dared Angela to argue with her. "Now."

Angela sat down, rubbing her wrist slowly. The pain was almost gone, but enough remained to remind her of everything that had happened. She forced herself to think, to distract herself from the incessant alarms . . . perhaps as a married woman she could gain control of household management and use the situation to her advantage . . . Finley wasn't going to be interested. The rich generally hired managers to run their houses for them.

Perhaps we can't afford it, Angela thought. It wasn't a particularly comforting thought, but it was something. Besides, it helped keep her mind off the emergency. *Or . . .*

She looked up as Nancy stumbled towards the sofa, eyes wide. The younger girl looked scared . . . no, *terrified*. Her entire body trembled like a leaf. Angela reached out and guided her sister to sit down next to her, then wrapped an arm around Nancy's shoulder.

"It's going to be fine," she said, although she didn't have the slightest idea what was happening. A drill . . . no, she didn't think anyone would run a drill now. The disruption would be immense. She could feel the deck thrumming under her feet. Something was clearly wrong. "We'll be fine."

"No, we won't," Nancy whispered.

Angela hugged her sister more tightly, trying not to be scared. Everyone had told her that the cruise was *safe*. Pirates wouldn't dare to attack *Supreme*, right? Maybe there had been an engine failure. Her imagination provided a dozen scenarios, each one more shadowy than the last. She told herself, firmly, not to say them out loud. Nancy was already scared to death.

"I can hear them," Nancy whispered. Another shiver ran through the ship. Angela heard the drive throbbing louder and louder. "Can't you?"

CHAPTER TWENTY

"The enemy ships are altering course," Tidal warned. "I don't think the drones fooled them."

Paul gritted his teeth. It looked as though she was right.

"Hold us steady," he ordered stiffly. "Take us along the edge of the distortion."

He forced himself to think despite his steadily growing alarm. Three pirate ships, any one of which could presumably batter *Supreme* into an air-streaming hulk if it wished. The distortion might hide his ship long enough for the pirates to lose interest and back off, but he doubted it. If they had any idea of the prize awaiting them, and he assumed they did, they'd spend weeks prowling the edge of the distortion, looking for the liner. The ransom for Robert Cavendish alone would be enough to buy a new starship.

"The distortion is growing stronger," Rani warned. A dull vibration ran through the ship as a distortion wave crashed into the hull. "It's reacting to our presence."

Paul swore under his breath. The distortion wasn't a full-blown energy storm, but it was still powerful enough to do serious damage to his ship. They might be crippled if they even brushed against the edge of the distortion, forced to rely on the pirates for rescue. Or the pirates might simply back off and leave them to die. No one would know to come looking for some time. *Supreme* had already been off the main transit lanes when the pirates revealed themselves.

No, they won't leave us alone, he thought. *They'll take the richest prizes and leave the rest of us to die.*

"Hosting confirms that the passengers are all in their quarters," Jeanette said. Her face floated in his display. She looked worried. "They're bombarding the crew with questions."

"Say nothing," Paul ordered. The last thing he needed was panic. He'd have let the passengers continue partying if he hadn't needed to clear the passageways. "Just tell them to remain in their quarters."

"Pirates are altering course again," Tidal reported. "They'll be within weapons range in seventeen minutes."

Paul nodded slowly. The pirates might be reluctant to open fire in hyperspace because a standard warhead could trigger an energy storm. He considered, briefly, trying to trigger an energy storm himself, but *Supreme* wasn't fast enough to escape. A crash-transit might be possible if they used the storm for cover, but it would be chancy. *Supreme* just didn't have the flexibility of a warship.

We should have built her on a battlecruiser hull, he thought. He'd seen the proposals, back during his retraining. Corporate had asked him to comment on them. If nothing else, a battlecruiser hull would look like a *real* battlecruiser. *We might have been able to get the hell out of town.*

"Hold her steady," he ordered.

He felt the tension rising as the enemy ships drew closer. Skirting the edge of the distortion would make it difficult for the pirates to localize *Supreme*. And yet . . . he knew it was just a matter of time. Flying away from the distortion would allow the pirates to run them down, while flying into the distortion would be certain death. Part of him suspected the latter course would be the better option. Corporate wasn't going to ransom his crew. He'd seen the aftermath of enough pirate attacks to know that death might be preferable.

Another quiver ran through the ship. "Captain, the distortion is building in intensity," Tidal said. She sounded perplexed. "I've never seen anything like it before."

Paul glanced at the display just as his ship vibrated again. Hyperspace was twisting oddly, bending in directions the human mind wasn't designed to comprehend. Even his sensors couldn't quite keep track of the phenomenon . . . the distortion twisted and twisted again, waves of gravimetric force spinning out in all directions. The waves weren't powerful enough to pose a threat to his ship, he told himself firmly, but they were still worrying. If nothing else, the feedback might damage the drive nodes.

And if we have a drive failure now, we'll fall right into the distortion, he thought. *And that will be the end.*

He tried to remember if he'd ever heard of anything like this before, but nothing came to mind, not even rumors or tall tales. And yet gravity behaved oddly in hyperspace. The distortion was starting to look like a gravity wave or a black hole. Had they ventured too close to a star's hyperspace shadow? Unlikely. The star chart insisted they were two light-years from the nearest star. Perhaps they'd managed to get lost . . .

"Do a full position check," he ordered. The Commonwealth had established a whole string of beacons scattered through hyperspace. "Get a lock on our position."

"Aye, sir," Tidal said. She worked her console for a long minute. "Position confirmed, sir. I—"

The ship shook again, violently. Tidal cursed. "Captain, the distortion just *tripled* in size," she snapped. "It's expanding rapidly."

Paul bit down the urge to swear too. "Helm, alter course," he snapped. "Get us away from the distortion!"

"Aye, Captain," Rani said.

The pirates are still going to catch us, Paul thought. All three enemy ships were closing in now, skirting the edge of the distortion. The prize was worth any risk. *What do we do now?*

"Ready weapons," he ordered. Perhaps they could force the pirates to back off. They tended to flee if they saw resistance. "Lock tactical sensors on their hulls."

"Aye, sir," Tidal said.

Jeanette coughed. "Captain, we can't outfight them!"

"I know," Paul said sharply. Jeanette wasn't a military officer, but that didn't stop her from being *right*. And yet he knew *precisely* what would happen to his crew if he surrendered. The pirates would rape and kill anyone they couldn't sell for ransom, then loot the giant liner from end to end. "But if it looks like we can put up a fight, we might not have to."

"Weapons range in five minutes," Tidal reported. "Captain, the distortion is *still* expanding."

Paul sucked in his breath. Something was weirdly beautiful about the patterns on the display, even though they kept blurring as his sensors struggled to keep track of what was happening. Order in the chaos . . . his sensor records, if he ever got them home, would fuel the next generation of research into hyperspace . . .

He pushed the thought aside. Better to get the ship home and worry about science later.

"It's coming *after* us," Rani breathed.

"Prepare for crash-transition," Paul snapped. He'd seen energy storms attracted to starships before, like lightning attracted to lightning rods. Even a superdreadnought couldn't take such a battering and live. "Weapons, prepare to unleash a full barrage, timed for two-minute detonation."

"Aye, sir," Lieutenant Thomas Morse said.

"That's *suicide*," Jeanette snapped.

"It's our only hope," Paul said. The distortion was scrambling his sensors, but it wasn't scrambling them enough. He didn't dare assume that the pirates were having a harder time of it. The risk of triggering a violent energy storm had to be balanced with the need to keep the pirates from getting a solid lock on his exit coordinates. "Weapons?"

"Barrage ready," Morse said. "Ready to fire."

"The timing must be absolutely perfect," Paul warned. "We fuck this up, we die."

"Yes, sir," Rani said. The ship trembled again. "Drive nodes powering up now . . ."

"The distortion is expanding again," Tidal said.

Paul stared. The distortion *was* reaching for them, coming right towards his ship. It was impossible . . .

. . . and it was happening.

"Launch missiles," he snapped. "Helm, execute crash-transition on my mark."

"Aye, sir," Rani said.

"It's too late," Tidal said. "Sir, it's . . ."

———

"Hold her," Marie snapped.

Angela struggled to hold her sister still. Nancy was younger and smaller, but she was fighting like a wildcat, screaming and shouting about voices. She'd struck Angela twice and managed to hit Marie with a shoe before the governess caught her legs. Angela would have enjoyed that if it hadn't been so clear that something was horribly amiss. This was no temper tantrum.

"She's frightened," Angela shouted. Panic yammered at the back of her mind. "I don't know what to do!"

Marie let go of Nancy's legs and jumped backward, narrowly avoiding a kick that would have caught her in the face. "I'll get a sedative," she shouted. "Just keep holding her."

She hurried off. Angela glared after her, then held Nancy as tightly as she could, which wasn't easy. Whatever was wrong with Nancy seemed to have given her superhuman strength, allowing her to struggle violently. Her shrieks didn't help. Angela was thoroughly unnerved by the time Marie returned, carrying an injector tab in one hand. It was all she could do to hold Nancy still long enough for the governess to press the tab against her neck and inject the sedative.

"Hold her steady," Marie ordered. "Don't let her go!"

"I don't *dare* let her go," Angela said. Her arm was throbbing. She didn't think Nancy had meant to hit her, but that hardly mattered. "I thought you *couldn't* use sedatives in emergency situations!"

"I can carry her if necessary," Marie snapped. Angela hoped she could. "Hold her!"

Angela clenched her jaw as Nancy resumed her struggles. She had no idea what Marie had given her sister, but it didn't seem to be working. Nancy was *still* awake, still struggling, still screaming about *them* . . .

The ship rocked again. She was no expert, but the drives sounded labored, as if tired. Angela tried to imagine what was going on. Were they under attack? Surely pirates wouldn't be taking potshots at the hull for kicks. She remembered, suddenly, the horror stories she'd heard about girls who'd been kidnapped by pirates. In truth, she didn't want to think that they might be true.

"Let go of me," Nancy screamed. Her face was red. "They're coming!"

Her body convulsed one final time; then she collapsed like a sack of potatoes. Angela had to hold Nancy tightly to keep her from falling to the deck. Marie held a medical scanner against the girl's forehead for a long moment, then scowled as Angela laid her sister on the sofa. It didn't look good.

Angela coughed. "What . . . what did you give her?"

"A standard sedative," Marie said. She sounded worried. She *had* to be worried, if she was actually answering the question. "Most people who take such an injection go to sleep within two minutes."

Angela scowled. "So why didn't Nancy?"

"I don't know," Marie said. She was definitely worried. "Some people have implants or nanites that flush the sedative before it can take effect, but Nancy doesn't." She peered down at the scanner. "There's some unusual brain activity . . . almost as if she was having a waking nightmare. I don't—"

Nancy twitched. Angela stared at her. The girl was bleeding in a dozen places, crimson staining her hands and lips. She'd bit her lips and dug her nails into her palms. Marie fussed over the younger girl for a long moment, tugging her into recovery position. Angela hoped the governess knew what she was doing. God knew Angela had never studied medicine. She cursed herself, again, as another shiver ran through the ship. She was unable to do anything to help her sister.

Angela looked at Marie. "Where are the others?"

"I don't know," she said, sounding oddly annoyed. "Your mother went out with a group of friends, your father was having breakfast with the captain, and—"

Nancy sat bolt upright and shrieked. Angela recoiled in shock. Nancy had been sedated! There was no way she should have been able to move. Angela had used sedatives herself, and they'd always given her at least ten hours of sleep.

"Hold her," Marie shouted. "Don't let her hurt herself!"

Angela couldn't take her eyes off her sister. Nancy was still asleep, her eyes twitching frantically under her eyelids, the girl screaming as though she was having a nightmare . . .

"Call the doctor," Angela demanded as she caught hold of her sister. Whatever was going on outside the ship didn't matter. Nancy was far beyond their help. "We're out of our depth!"

"I've tried," Marie replied. Her voice was detached, calm, and professional. Angela would have been impressed if she hadn't been so terrified. "There was no response."

Angela swallowed, hard. She'd never been anywhere where help couldn't be summoned at once if needed. Even on camping trips, she'd known how to call for help. But now . . . it dawned on her, slowly, that they were alone. God knew what had happened to the other servants, let alone her parents. They were alone . . .

Something *moved* through the air. A small electric shock ran down her spine. She glanced at the room's terminal just in time to see it go dark. Nancy shrieked again, thrashing against her sister. Angela grunted in pain as Nancy slapped her. She tasted blood in her mouth as she bit the inside of her cheek. The lights failed a moment later . . .

. . . and then the shaking *really* started.

———

Paul couldn't believe what he was seeing on the display. The distortion was reaching out for them, almost as though it were a living thing. Space twisted itself into a pretzel, dragging his ship backward into the maw. This must be a black hole, part of his mind insisted, although such an eventuality was impossible. The closest black hole to Tyre was well over two thousand light-years away. No one had ever gone near it . . .

"Crash-transit," he ordered. The move was probably suicide, but it was the only way out. Damn the pirates. He'd just have to hope that they were in the same boat. Maybe they were already running for their lives. "Now!"

"The vortex isn't opening," Rani shouted. On the display, the vortex flashed into existence and then vanished just as quickly. "The energy matrix is disrupted! I can't compensate!"

The display flickered then failed. Paul felt his heart stop, just for a second, before the system rebooted. *That* should have been impossible. The main lighting failed too, plunging the bridge into near-complete darkness. Nearly twenty seconds passed before the dim emergency lighting came online. That too should have been impossible. The emergency systems should have taken over at once.

"Multiple power failures reported, all decks," Tidal said, sounding as though she didn't believe her own words. "A handful of emergency systems are offline. I . . ."

Paul swallowed. *Supreme* had more redundancies built into her power distribution network than anything smaller than a superdreadnought. Even if main power failed, emergency backup systems and power cells waited to jump into action. Losing power completely was damn near impossible. The entire system was designed to survive.

"The main drive field is failing," Rani added. She looked up. Sweat poured down her face, glistening oddly under the lighting. "It . . . the power is draining."

"Divert all power to the drives," Paul ordered. If they *were* caught in a black hole, or something similar, they were dead. There was no way they could outrun its gravity pull. But they had to try. "Get us out of here!"

"The drive field has collapsed," Rani said. She sounded as though she was starting to lose control and panic. "Compensator fields are weakening!"

Supreme shivered, then started to fall into the distortion. Or maybe the distortion was reaching for them. Paul had a sensation, just for a moment, as though they were spinning like a top. His head swam, strange prickly lights appearing at the corners of his eyes and then vanishing back into the semidarkness. Rani screamed, throwing herself back from her console an instant before it exploded. A second console followed a moment later, blowing its operator across the bridge . . .

Paul struggled to stand, to get a medical kit, to do something, anything, to stave off doom for a few more seconds. Consoles *didn't* explode, not outside bad movies. What sort of idiot starship designer would cram explosive packs into a real console?

"Systems failure, Deck Seven," Tidal yelled. Red alerts flashed up on the display. "Engineering reports main power offline. Switching to backups . . ."

Paul barely heard her. The universe seemed to be dimming, the bridge going hazy in front of him. He stood; then his legs buckled, and he fell to his knees. A third explosion shook the bridge . . . something had exploded, but what? He looked up at the display just in time to see the outside universe twisting into madness. There were *things* in the display, things his mind refused to accept . . .

The displays failed a second later. Paul slumped to the deck, suddenly feeling drained. His body felt limp, worthless. Someone was screaming . . . who? Was it him? He didn't know. So hard to think clearly. His mind was sparking, flickers of pain bombarding his thoughts. *Supreme* spun around him, the gravity field twisting slowly out of shape. If the compensators failed, they were dead. He wasn't sure why they still had gravity. If main power had failed, the gravity generators should have failed too . . .

And then the darkness reached out and claimed him.

CHAPTER TWENTY-ONE

Matt was sure he was having a nightmare.

They'd been on the promenade, hadn't they? They'd been making their way back to their emergency stations, when . . . he wasn't quite sure what had happened then. The entire ship had started to shake, the lights had failed, and he'd blacked out . . . or had he? He couldn't comfortably swear to anything. Part of him was still sure he was dreaming.

He heard a moan. His eyes snapped open.

He was lying on the deck, his body so limp and drained—and yet aching dully—that he thought he must be concussed. A sickly yellow-green light poured in through the windows, drenching the entire deck in an eerie radiance. Something was nagging at his mind, something *missing*. What? He forced himself to sit up as he heard the moan again, looking around as quickly as he could. Carla was lying on the deck beside him, blood leaking from her nose and a nasty gash on her cheek. Matt forced himself to rise, despite the lethargy pervading his body, and crawl over to her.

"Carla," he managed. His voice sounded odd. "Can you hear me?"

"Yeah," Carla said. Her voice sounded strange too. "What . . . what happened?"

"Your nose might be broken," Matt said. He helped her to sit up. "I'll call the medics."

He keyed his wristcom. Nothing happened, not even an acknowledgment chirp. Matt tensed, feeling a flicker of alarm. There should have been something, even if the doctors were overloaded with patients who needed immediate treatment. The datanet would have logged the call, if nothing else. He forced himself to look at the wristcom and sucked in his breath when he saw the Power Low message. The battery was at 9 percent.

That shouldn't have happened, he thought, too shocked to think clearly. They'd been threatened with everything from a hefty fine to immediate dismissal for letting their wristcom batteries drop below 20 percent. He'd always made sure to charge his every weekend, even though the power usage was actually minimal. But now his wristcom was practically dead. *That's . . .*

He shook his head. The wristcom should have been able to link to the datanet even if it was on the *last dregs* of its power. The alarm should have been bleeping to warn him to recharge . . . every alarm should be bleeping.

The deck was quiet.

His head spun as he realized what was missing. The omnipresent hum of the drives was gone.

"Check your wristcom," he said, cursing Corporate's paranoia under his breath. Carla's wristcom wouldn't work for him and vice versa. "See if you can call for help."

Something flickered at the corner of his eye. Just for a moment, he was sure there was someone or something behind him. He forced himself to look around. Nothing was there. The deck was as cold and silent as a grave. His fingertips touched the carpeted deck as other implications began to sink in. If the power had failed completely, the life-support systems would be offline too.

"It can't have failed completely," Carla pointed out when he voiced his concern. "We still have gravity."

Matt glanced at her. She was right. If the ship had lost all power, they'd have lost the gravity field too. Still . . .

He forced himself to his feet. The gravity felt . . . odd, as though the generator was slightly out of tune. He hoped that didn't mean it was going to shift without warning. He'd trained in a high-gravity environment, but there were limits. No one would be able to move if the gravity field suddenly got a great deal stronger.

Or worse, he thought as he helped Carla up. Blood stained her tunic from the cut on her cheek, but she seemed otherwise unharmed. *What if the compensators fail?*

They stumbled over to the giant canopy and peered out. The sickly yellow-green light was everywhere. He suddenly grasped that they might no longer be in hyperspace or realspace. Where were they? Hyperspace glowed with light, but this . . . this was wrong. This was . . . just looking at the light made his skin crawl. It was easy to imagine that there were things out there in the light, peering back at him. He thought he could see *something* . . . flecks of light so tiny they were barely visible.

Carla muttered a word under her breath, then knelt down and started hunting through the supply lockers with desperate speed. Matt watched, puzzled, as she retrieved a pair of binoculars and pressed them to her eyes. They were normally used by ship-spotters, if he recalled correctly, who seemed to think that using optical sensors or augmented eyeballs was cheating.

"Shit," Carla said. She lowered the binoculars. Her face was even paler than usual. "Matt . . . what do you see?"

Matt took the binoculars and peered through them. The automated focusing system refused to work, forcing him to set the range manually. His mouth dropped open as the first of the flecks suddenly zoomed into view.

A starship. He was sure it was a starship. And yet he'd never seen anything like it. He couldn't see how it flew. The vessel was . . .

"It looks like a crushed spider," he said. The description was all that came to mind. "It . . ." He nearly dropped the binoculars in shock. "It's *alien*."

"Yeah," Carla said. She sounded as though she was fighting to remain calm. "That is *not* a human ship."

Matt forced himself to look again. Each of the flecks was a starship, drifting within the eerie green light. None appeared to be moving. He wondered, suddenly, if they'd encountered one of the legendary graveyards of space. He'd heard stories; all of them had, though none had ever been verified. They were just . . . tall tales.

He moved the binoculars from ship to ship, taking in their lines. They looked as if they came from a dozen different races . . .

He sat down, hard. This was impossible. There was no such thing as intelligent aliens. Hundreds of years of space exploration hadn't turned up anything more intelligent than a small dog. But he couldn't deny what he was seeing. *Supreme* was surrounded by dozens, perhaps hundreds, of alien starships, all dead. He couldn't see a sign that they had any power at all.

"Crap," he said. There *were* first-contact procedures that had been drilled into his head while he'd been earning his spacer's license, but he'd never expected to use them. It wasn't as if *Supreme* had been planning to explore beyond the Rim. "What . . . what do we do now?"

Carla poked her wristcom. "We report to the captain," she said. "That's our first duty."

Matt swallowed. "What about Angela?"

"The captain might not know those ships are there," Carla said. "What if long-range sensors are down too?" She caught his arm. "Come on," she said. "Let's go."

Matt followed her, privately admitting she was right. They did have a duty to report to the captain, even though normally they'd be expected to use proper channels. But those channels were gone. His wristcom couldn't find a single datanet node within range, bothering him more than he cared to admit. In theory, he should have been able to access a datanode on the other side of the ship. If *all* the datanodes were down, what then?

The captain will think of something, he told himself firmly. Captain VanGundy had been in space longer than Matt had been alive. *We'll get out of this.*

He jumped as he saw another flicker at the corner of his eye. The sensation was like being buzzed by insects in the jungle, yet . . . whenever he turned around, he saw nothing. His scalp itched; he felt unwashed . . . he reminded himself, sharply, that he'd had a shower only a few hours ago. Or perhaps it had been *days* ago . . . who knew how long he'd been unconscious? But . . . if it had been more than a few hours, he'd be hungry . . . right?

Carla opened a hatch and led the way into the passageway. The emergency lighting was working, thankfully, but it was wavering constantly. Matt tried to think about how else they could get light. There should be flashlights in the emergency kits. They should work, shouldn't they? He felt unnerved as he saw yet another flicker and tried to ignore it. He'd seen the emergency systems built into the starship's hull. Nothing short of a major disaster should have been able to knock so many systems offline.

"Shit," Carla said.

Matt followed her gaze. A body was lying on the deck, facedown, the head twisted so badly that its neck was clearly broken. Matt checked for a pulse anyway, just to be sure, then turned the corpse over. An unfamiliar face looked back at him. He felt a moment of relief that the deceased hadn't been anyone he knew, then cursed himself for his thoughts. The dead man, maintenance crew, judging by the uniform, would have had friends and comrades of his own.

"We need to keep moving," Carla said. "We'll come back later."

And we'll be lucky if that's the only dead crewman we find, Matt thought grimly. *We might be the last living people on the ship.*

———

Paul fought his way back to awareness, fighting the mother of all headaches and a roaring sound in his ears that threatened to drag him under. Something was wrong, completely wrong. He took a breath, tasting smoke in the air. Something was *definitely* wrong.

He opened his eyes as he stumbled to his feet. His bridge was a nightmare. The emergency lighting was on, yet blinking and unsteady. Three consoles had exploded, and all but one of the remainder looked to be offline. His crew were fighting their way back too, save for two who were definitely dead. Paul glanced at them—their wounds made it clear that they were beyond salvation—and then stumbled over to his personal console. It was dark.

"Damn it," he muttered as he opened the hidden compartment in his command chair. His fingers felt thick and stubby, useless as they fumbled their way through the emergency section. He could barely pull out the stimulant tab, press it against his bare skin, and push the trigger. "I'll have to . . ."

The drug felt . . . *odd* . . . as it burned through his system, fire tearing into his thoughts. He knew, from countless medical warnings, that he'd have only a few hours before he had to catch some sleep or risk collapse. The stimulant wasn't something he would have taken if he'd seen any other choice. The risk of hallucinations, or worse, was too great as it wore off.

"Captain," Rani managed. She stumbled to her feet. "What . . . what happened?"

"Good question," Paul said. Rani looked a mess, but the sight of her still gave him hope. At least one of his crew was alive, awake, and coherent. "Check the working consoles; then see if you can get a link to Engineering."

"Aye, sir," Rani said.

Something flashed at the corner of Paul's eye. He frowned, then dismissed it as a hallucination. He'd thought they were dead when the distortion swept them up . . . perhaps he *was* dead and in hell. Perhaps they were *all* in hell. He cursed the drug under his breath, unsure if his imagination was working overtime or if the stimulant was causing him to hallucinate already.

He helped Tidal to her feet, then pointed her at the nearest console. There was no time to tend to the guests, let alone the wounded or dead. They had literally no way to see outside the hull. *Anything* could be out there, including one or more of the pirate ships. The distortion could have easily swept them up too. And *Supreme* was blind, effectively defenseless.

"Main power is offline," Rani reported. "We have limited emergency power, but much of the datanet and power distribution network is also offline. Internal communications are down, sir. Short- and long-range sensors are completely offline. The entire network is a mess."

That's supposed to be impossible, Paul thought. *The communications net . . .*

He dropped the thought. It had happened. He had to deal with it.

"Switch wristcoms to direct transmission," he ordered. Corporate preferred to use datanodes, which ensured there would be a record of everything the crew said, but Corporate could go piss up a rope. *Supreme* was in deep shit, perhaps the deepest. "Use it to establish a distributed network."

"Aye, Captain," Rani said. "It may take some time to boot up."

"Better get started," Paul said.

Tidal opened the emergency case and produced a flashlight. It worked, but the light was alarmingly dim. Paul stared at the low glow, feeling an insane urge to start gibbering like an idiot. The flashlights weren't connected to the starship's power net. Whatever had damaged the power grid shouldn't have affected them. And yet it had . . .

"The glow sticks work, sir," Tidal reported. She passed one to Paul, then stuck two more in her belt. "They're about the only things that do."

"Let's hope you're wrong," Paul said.

His thoughts felt as though they were moving through thick molasses. Without power, they were screwed. He'd read novels where starship crews had somehow navigated their way home with old-fashioned sextants, but doing so in real life wouldn't be easy. He wasn't even sure they were back in realspace. If they were drifting through hyperspace, it was only a matter of time before they were sucked into an energy storm and torn to shreds.

And anything could be out there, he thought. *Anything at all.*

"I've started to ping wristcoms," Rani reported. "Got a couple of people reporting in."

"Very good," Paul said. He bottled up his relief. People were alive, but . . . *Supreme* was still in trouble. They had to get a grip on the situation. "See if you can get me a link to Engineering and the secondary bridge."

"Aye, sir," Rani said.

Paul silently reviewed the situation. He had four officers who seemed to be in a reasonable state and five more who didn't seem to be in any shape to help. If he couldn't get a link to Engineering, he'd have to get down there himself, which wasn't going to be easy. The internal hatches would have sealed and locked themselves when he'd sounded the alert. They could be opened without power, but it would be hard to know what was on the far side. If the hull had been breached, his team might walk straight into vacuum.

He tensed as he heard the bridge hatch being opened from the outside. Someone was trying to get in. He glanced at his crew, then hurried over to open the hatch himself. The ship couldn't have depressurized completely. In hindsight, he should have ordered his crew and passengers into spacesuits as soon as the shit hit the fan. A military crew wouldn't have hesitated.

The hatch clicked open, revealing a couple of stewards. Paul blinked in shock. He'd expected engineers or maintenance crew, not stewards. But all stewards were cross-trained, he reminded himself. Beggars could not be choosers.

"Captain," the lead steward said. She sounded as though she was on the verge of a nervous breakdown. "Captain, there are *aliens* out there."

"It's true," the second steward said. "Captain . . ."

Paul looked from one to the other. Aliens? Impossible. A joke. The only spacers who saw aliens were either playing games or drinking too much. Still . . . these two *seemed* in earnest. No one would joke when the entire ship was crippled.

"Explain," he said. Another spark danced at the corner of his eye, just for a second. "What do you mean, *aliens?*"

"We're in a graveyard," the male steward said. His name tag read EVANS. "Captain . . ." He swallowed and started again. "We were on the promenade when . . . when we blacked out," he said. He didn't sound much calmer than his coworker. "When we woke up . . . it isn't hyperspace out there, Captain. It's . . . it's something else. Green light. Greenish-yellow light everywhere. And ships, alien ships."

Paul exchanged glances with Tidal. If they weren't in hyperspace, where were they? Another dimension? Or a part of hyperspace that no one had ever visited? Could they be *inside* the distortion? It had been small, by the standards of hyperspace storms, but easily large enough to contain a thousand starships like *Supreme*. Or . . .

Maybe they are drunk, he thought.

He looked at Rani. "Reroute power to the upper porthole," he ordered. The armored cover had sealed shut the moment they'd sounded the alert. "Open the cover."

"Aye, sir," Rani said. It took her nearly five minutes to set up the power transfer. "Opening it . . . now."

Paul looked up as the hatch opened. Eerie green light poured in.

"Shit," he said. He would have preferred for the stewards to be lying. "Where the hell are we?"

He rubbed his forehead. "We'll deal with it, somehow," he said. He had no idea if he could keep that promise. "I want you stewards to check out the hatches at the bottom of Gold Deck. Do not try to open them unless you have a solid read on the other side."

"Yes, sir."

Paul looked back at the sickly light. Where were they?

And how were they going to get out?

CHAPTER TWENTY-TWO

Angela felt sick.

She swallowed, trying to keep the urge to vomit under control. Her head refused to cooperate. She couldn't tell if she'd been sick or if she was going to be sick or . . . her thoughts ran around and around in circles, taunting her. Her memories were a jumbled mess.

A hand fell on her shoulder. "My Lady," Marie said, "can you hear me?"

Angela opened her eyes. She hadn't realized they were closed. "I . . . yeah," she managed. She felt so rotten that she was pleased to hear the governess's voice. "Where . . . where's Nancy?"

"Lying on the sofa," Marie said. Angela became aware that she was lying on the carpeted deck with no clear memory of how she'd landed there. The lighting was dim and seemed to be growing dimmer. She hoped that was her imagination. "She's not in a good state."

Angela forced herself to sit upright. Her chest heaved. She'd felt bad the first time she'd drunk enough to make her *really* drunk, but this was far worse. Her chest hurt, as if she'd thrown up. She looked down, seeing nothing.

"I hurt," she said. She fought to clear her mind. "What happened?"

"I don't know," Marie said. "The primary and secondary internal communications networks both appear to be down. I've tried to log into the crew network, but it kicked me back out after spewing gibberish into my terminal. We might have taken a massive disrupter attack."

Angela frowned. The governess's words meant nothing to her.

"A disrupter works by damaging exposed electronic devices and suchlike," Marie explained, seeing her charge's confusion. She held up the flashlight in her hand. "Most military gear is hardened against it, but civilian stuff isn't always so well protected. Even the military can have problems. It only takes one exposed datanode to damage the whole network. I thought this ship was hardened, but there are limits." She shook her head. "We may be in some trouble," she added. "I don't know what's on the other side of the hatch."

Angela looked at her. "What do you mean?"

"The hull is over there," Marie said, jabbing her finger towards the master bedroom. "If there's a crack in the hull, say, in the promenade, and the internal hatches have failed, Gold Deck might be in vacuum. If we open the hatch, we die."

"I thought it was impossible to open the hatch into vacuum," Angela said. She was sure she'd read something about that in the safety notes. "The door won't open . . . something like that."

"Normally, yes," Marie agreed. "But now . . . I don't know."

Angela looked at the door. "What happens . . . what happens if we can't get out?"

"We die," Marie said. "Does *that* answer your question?"

"Yeah."

She forced herself to stand. She was *nineteen*. She had at least a century to look forward to, didn't she? She could be assured of perpetual rejuvenation if she wished, ensuring effective immortality. The oldest man on Tyre could recall Earth before humanity's homeworld had been blasted clean of life during the Breakaway Wars. She couldn't perish here, not in a cabin with her sister and her governess. What could she do?

Nancy gasped in her sleep. Angela looked down at her sister, feeling a pang of guilt. Nancy was so *innocent*. God knew Angela hadn't been the kindest sister in the known universe—she'd had problems adjusting to the arrival of a sibling, particularly one who'd been born with unearned fame—but Nancy didn't deserve to die somewhere in the inky darkness of space. Her parents didn't deserve to die . . . hell, *Marie* didn't deserve to die. Finley, on the other hand . . .

Perhaps his stateroom vented into space, she thought vindictively. *Maybe he's dead now.*

"The sedative wasn't perfect," Marie said. She held up the scanner. "And *this* is completely useless. I don't dare give her anything else."

"Fuck," Angela said. "All we can do is wait?"

"It looks that way," Marie said. She frowned. "Can you stay with your sister? I need to check the bedrooms for food and drink."

Angela blinked, then understood. If the ship was crippled and effectively powerless, there would be no water for drinking, let alone washing. Or food. The stasis pods might have failed too. She thought ration bars couldn't decay; they were designed to remain edible for years. But everything else was doomed. Or . . .

"I'll do it," she said. "You stay with Nancy."

Marie tilted her head. "As you wish, My Lady."

Angela headed over to her father's office and tried the door. Locked. She knocked on it out of habit, then remembered that her father had been having breakfast with the captain before all hell broke loose. There was probably a way to break the lock, but she couldn't imagine it. Everything she thought of required tools they didn't have.

The master bedroom was open, but she struggled to force her way in through the suddenly stiff door. An eerie green light greeted her, a pulsing radiance that made her feel sick to her stomach. *That* wasn't hyperspace. It looked as though *Supreme* were trapped at the bottom of the ocean, with light shimmering through water. She hurried over to the window and peered outside, ignoring her stomach's muted rebellion. The sickly light chilled her to the bone. She gazed up and down the ship's hull, but saw nothing. It didn't *look* as though the ship had vented completely, but all the running lights were gone too. *Supreme* looked . . . dead.

She lifted her sight, trying to peer into the greenish-yellow glow. There were . . . *things* . . . out there, no larger than dust specks. She decided they probably weren't important as she tried to spot the source of the light, but found nothing. The radiance came from everywhere and nowhere.

Marie's voice echoed through the half-open door. "Any luck?"

"Not yet," Angela said, remembering herself. Something glinted at the corner of her eye, just for a moment. "I don't think we're in Kansas anymore."

She searched the rest of the cabin as quickly as she could. Her mother's vast collection of clothes, and an exclusive wedding dress that could be only for Angela herself, were completely useless. Angela had to giggle, despite herself. She was surrounded by vast wealth, now worthless. They'd starve to death before they had a chance to sell the dresses, let alone wear them. The thought actually perked her up. Dead or not, she wouldn't be marrying Finley if she couldn't get home.

"I've found my mother's cold-box," she said. The stasis field had failed. Her mother's collection of pricey chocolates was already starting to melt. They wouldn't be very filling, but they would have to do. "It's all I've found."

"Check the servant quarters, if you can get in," Marie called back. "I—" Her voice sharpened. "Someone's trying to get in!"

Angela grabbed the cold-box and hurried back into the antechamber. The outer door was shaking, producing a faint rattling noise that set her teeth on edge. Someone was *definitely* trying to break in, she decided. Help . . . or Finley, trying to track down his intended bride?

She wondered if she should look for a weapon. Marie didn't look alarmed, but that was meaningless. The governess probably didn't know what had happened between her and Finley.

Unless he ratted me out, Angela thought. The door opened slowly. *I . . .*

She smiled. "Matt!"

"Angela," Matt said. "Are you all right?"

Angela ran over and threw her arms around him. "Yeah," she said. It was all she could do to keep from kissing him there and then. "Did you come looking for me?"

"Yes," Matt said. "I—"

"We have to check every last cabin," the other steward said. Her name tag read Carla France. She was a young woman, at least a year older than Angela herself. Her tone was disapproving. "How many people are here?"

"Three," Marie said briskly. She indicated Nancy, still asleep. "She had a fit when the shaking started. She really needs a doctor."

"Right now, we don't have any contact with Sickbay," Carla informed them. She knelt down beside Nancy and checked her vitals. "What did you give her?"

"A sedative," Marie said. "Do you want the full details?"

"It might be better to save them for the doctor," Carla said. "If Nancy isn't in any immediate danger, she'll be low on the list for attention."

Angela swallowed. "But . . . but she needs *help*!"

"So far we've discovered thirty-seven dead bodies," Matt said. He sounded haunted. "And a number of others who require medical attention. Right now, we're trying to catalogue the damage."

"Shit," Angela said. She jabbed a hand towards the far bulkhead. "Where *are* we?"

"I wish I knew," Matt said. Beside him, Carla looked distressed. "We don't have the slightest idea."

"We'll stay here," Marie said. "Good luck."

"Thank you," Carla said. "Come on, Matt."

———

What the fuck, Constable Hamish Singh asked himself, *is that banging sound?*

He rubbed his forehead as he forced himself to sit up. His memories didn't quite make sense, but he forced himself to parse through them anyway. He'd been on duty in the brig, spelling a couple of security guards who'd been called away to deal with a minor crisis. There wasn't much to it, really. He'd sat at their desk and read his eReader, silently bemoaning the lack of time to download more than a handful of books from the planetary datanet. And then . . .

You weren't boozing last night, my lad, he thought. He was fairly sure of it. The days when he'd gone out with the marines and drunk himself into a stupor were long over. God knew he wouldn't have dared to drink on duty. His sergeant would have taken him around the barracks and beaten the shit out of him if he'd had a wee dram to keep himself awake. *You were on guard duty.*

The air felt . . . *wrong*, somehow, as he stumbled through the hatch. His hand dropped to his holster as the banging grew louder, ready to draw his pistol if necessary. The lights were flickering and fading, even though he'd been assured that the brig was on a completely independent power system. God knew it would be stupid if someone managed to cut the power and allowed a prisoner to break out. *Supreme* herself might be an overpriced mess—he would have preferred an MEU—but the brig was surprisingly simple. Escape was effectively impossible.

He cursed as he realized the banging was coming from the lone stasis pod. The power had failed, of course. Roman Bryon was awake. Hamish checked the lock quickly, reassuring himself that it hadn't failed. It wouldn't have, of course. He'd inspected the lock as soon as

Bryon had been shoved into the cell. There was no way to reach its vitals from inside, let alone manipulate them. And Bryon didn't have any tools. The stasis pod crashed open a moment later, allowing the serial killer to sit up. He looked around, blearily. Time hadn't passed for him . . .

Hamish gripped the butt of his pistol. It would be easy to shoot Bryon in the head, then swear blind that the prisoner had been trying to escape. No one was going to waste time arguing over the legalities. Many had suggested that Bryon should simply be executed on Williamson's World without the formality of a trial and extradition. Britannia had provided more than enough proof of the man's crimes.

He didn't look like much, Hamish thought. Roman Bryon was a weedy little man, too small and petty to ever amount to much. He looked like an accountant, the kind of man who would claim to lust for adventure yet never dare to walk away from his life. And yet he'd tortured and killed nine innocent people, perhaps more.

And he'd managed to board ship and escape a manhunt, Hamish reminded himself. Bryon might look harmless, but he was too dangerous to be underestimated. *It was sheer luck we caught him before he started his games on Williamson's World.*

Bryon cleared his throat. "What happened?"

"You will be silent," Hamish said. God, even Bryon's *voice* was weedy. Hamish could barely believe that the small man had killed nine people. But the most vicious bastard in his old platoon had practically been a dwarf. "This ship is in trouble."

"I can help," Bryon said.

"You will be quiet, or you will be gagged," Hamish said. Regulations insisted that no one was to enter a prisoner's cell alone. He was sure he could break Bryon over his knee with one hand but saw no point in taking chances. "For the moment, you will stay in your cell."

Bryon looked back at him evenly. "Is there anything to read?"

"No," Hamish said. Regulations also forbade giving anything to the prisoner without a careful security check. "You get to stay in your cell and meditate on your crimes."

He glanced down at his wristcom, then at his personal terminal. Both were reporting low power, something that baffled him. He'd made sure to have them both charged before he'd boarded the liner. Neither was able to establish a link to the starship's communications network. He and Bryon were possibly the only two survivors on *Supreme*. The brig was meant to be completely isolated.

Anything that gets to us will take out the whole ship, he told himself firmly. *But surely we can't be the last two survivors.*

He forced himself to wait. He'd find out, in time. And if the air started to run thin . . .

Bryon coughed. "What happened?"

"Be quiet," Hamish snapped. He wasn't going to admit ignorance to a serial killer. The really dangerous ones were consummate manipulators. "Keep your mouth shut."

"Or what?" Bryon asked. He sounded amused. "Do you know what they're going to do to me on Britannia?"

"No," Hamish said. "But I look forward to watching."

———

Paul didn't want to leave his bridge, even though they'd made contact with the secondary bridge and Jeanette had resumed her duties as his XO. But he had to see for himself, even if it meant going down to the promenade. He didn't think anyone had lied to him, but . . .

Supreme was a disaster, he discovered. Power surges had destroyed pieces of equipment and killed people, leaving dozens of bodies littering the decks. Half his crew manifest hadn't reported in, suggesting that he was dangerously undermanned. Hopefully most of them were merely out of contact, but they might as well be dead. Some of the recovery crews had lost contact too.

We never planned for ship-wide disaster on this scale, he thought. He'd seen the hulks of a handful of dead ships back during his military service, but none of them had been anything like this. *We assumed that anything this bad would destroy the entire vessel.*

The promenade glowed with an eerie yellow-green light. He picked up the pair of binoculars and pressed them against his eyes, peering out into the shadowy realm. Were they *inside* the distortion? He had no way to tell, but . . . he *thought* he could see an energy storm in the distance. He moved the binoculars from side to side, trying to see if there was a way around the disturbance. But it looked as though there was no way out.

It's like the Gap, he thought, remembering the storms that limited passage into Theocratic Space. *But there's no way through here.*

He focused on the nearest ship and sucked in his breath. The craft wasn't human. Paul had memorized nearly every starship designed and built by humanity, from crude battleships and superdreadnoughts to luxury yachts and cruise liners. They all followed the same basic pattern, even though the civilian craft often had an elegance the military vehicles lacked. But *these* ships were starkly alien, built by creatures he surmised to be far from human. Some of the designs were so alien that his mind refused to accept their existence.

The realization struck him like a punch in the gut. The stewards hadn't lied after all!

And none of the vessels appear to be moving, he thought. *Dead in space.*

Part of him was relieved. He'd reviewed the first-contact protocols, but his ship was in no position to make contact. Come to think of it, he was *supposed* to sneak away and inform higher authorities. He couldn't do that either. He was relieved, in many ways, that the alien ships were dead, but . . . if they couldn't escape the distortion, what did that say about *Supreme*'s chances?

He strode around the promenade, trying to spot the pirate ships. Had *they* come through the distortion too? But there was nothing, save for the brief flashes at the corners of his eyes. He had no idea what they were, but he wasn't the only one seeing them. He'd checked with the bridge crew. *Everyone* was seeing sparks.

His wristcom bleeped. "Captain, we've opened a passageway down to Engineering," Tidal said. "We don't appear to have lost any atmosphere."

"That's something, at least," Paul said. "Inform the chief engineer that I want him to meet me in my office in thirty minutes."

"Aye, Captain," Tidal said.

Paul closed the connection and peered up at the nearest alien ship, which was alarmingly close by interplanetary standards. He was fascinated. Being the first man to meet aliens would ensure his place in the history books, and yet his first duty was to *Supreme* and the personnel under his command. Getting them out was more important than attempting to make contact with inactive starships . . .

And the more he stared out into the eerie light, the more sure he was that something was looking back at him.

You're imagining things, he told himself firmly. *It's the drug.*

But the uneasy sensation refused to go away.

CHAPTER TWENTY-THREE

"We managed to get some sensors back online," Tidal said half an hour later. "As far as we can tell, we're the only living things in this . . . this *graveyard.*"

Paul wasn't reassured. *Aliens!* Their place in the history books would've been assured if they weren't as trapped as any of the alien ships. The graveyard contained at least seventy starships, all seemingly from different races, none of which had succeeded in escaping the trap. *Supreme* was one of the most over-engineered starships in human history—only a superdreadnought had more redundancies built into her hull—and yet she was practically crippled. If any of the alien vessels were alive and hostile, it would be a very short fight.

He looked around the battered conference room, silently assessing his senior crew. Jeanette and Raymond Slater looked tired, while the others were clearly stressed. None of their training had prepared them for *this*. Robert Cavendish, who had somehow inveigled his way into the meeting, looked oddly relaxed. Paul wasn't sure if the CEO truly understood the stakes. He had a nasty feeling that his ultimate boss wasn't used to problems that couldn't be made to go away by a large infusion of cash.

"Dr. Mackey reports that Mr. Garston is dead," Jeanette said. She sounded too tired to feel anything. "His stasis pod lost power and . . . and his medical condition caught up with him."

Paul rubbed his forehead. A disaster, under other circumstances. Now, Garston's death was a minor footnote to a far greater problem. The ship was trapped and crippled. The rest of the crew and passengers could be dead within the week.

"I see," he said finally. "How many have we lost?"

Jeanette glanced at a paper notebook in her hand. "One hundred and seven deaths, two hundred and thirty-six injuries ranging from minor scrapes to broken bones," she said. "Sir . . . there are parts of the ship we haven't managed to reach yet. The numbers could be considerably higher." She winced. "The doctors are doing everything they can, but half the medical tech is offline," she added after a moment. "There's no way we can fix everything until we find a way to bring main power back online."

"Tell them to do their best," Paul said. *That* wasn't going to be easy. Even the third-class passengers were used to prompt, effective medical care. "Is there any way we can bring the stasis pods back online?"

"I wouldn't count on it," Chief Engineer Conrad Roeder said. He sounded frustrated. "Sir, whatever happened to us scrambled far too many control circuits. I wouldn't care to rely on *anything* if it could be avoided."

"That's supposed to be impossible," Jeanette protested.

"Impossible or not, it happened," Roeder said. He shook his head. "We might be able to repower a bone regenerator, sir, but we . . . we couldn't depend on it. I'd hate to risk using something more complex."

"Blast," Paul said. He looked at Jeanette. "Do we have enough medical supplies to handle the wounded?"

Jeanette turned to another page. "Maybe," she said. "Our working assumption, sir, was that anything we couldn't handle onboard could be held in stasis until we reached a planetside hospital. Right now, we should be able to handle *some* of the problems and make the others comfortable, but that won't last. Once we run out of drugs . . . we'll have a lot of people in agony on our hands."

Paul sighed. "See if you can organize some of the passengers into helping with the wounded," he said. It wasn't the best solution, but he saw no alternative. "Mr. Roeder?"

The chief engineer cleared his throat. "We're in deep shit, Captain."

"I noticed," Paul said dryly.

Roeder reached for the console automatically, then stopped himself. "I am confronted by a whole string of problems that don't make sense," he said. "I think . . . I think there's something very odd about this region of space."

Paul narrowed his eyes. "Like what?"

"We are losing power," Roeder reported. "Main power failed the moment we passed through the . . . the *distortion*. At least two of our four fusion cores are beyond repair, while we have been unable to restart the remaining two. And . . . Captain, our emergency power cells are losing power too." He paused. "It doesn't make any *sense*. Captain . . . the high-power cells are losing power at a greater rate than the low-power cells. It's as if something is *feeding* on the cells."

Something gleamed at the corner of Paul's eye. He ignored it. "I think we're going to have to become used to six impossible things before breakfast," he said slowly. "Can we get out of here?"

"I don't think so," Roeder said. He sounded as if he'd already given up. "The vortex generator appears to be intact. The core programming appears to be sound. But it requires a large surge of power to open a vortex, and . . . and the drain, whatever it is, may prevent us from generating the power. I don't even know if we need to reprogram the generator to return to realspace. I've never seen anything like this."

"We don't have a choice," Paul said. He looked at Rani. "Can we leave the graveyard?"

"No, sir," Rani said. "As far as I can tell, the graveyard is hemmed in by hyperspace storms."

"This is a trap," Tidal said. Her voice was unnerved. "Someone *built* this place."

Paul gritted his teeth. "Explain."

"Look at the ships," Tidal said. "They're not drifting randomly. They're lined up, ready for the slaughter. That pattern could *not* have occurred by chance."

"That might be true," Cavendish said. "But anyone who could reformat hyperspace to do *that* wouldn't need to . . . to drag us here."

"That would be impossible," Jeanette said. "Wouldn't it?"

"There are some theories about using a modified vortex generator to alter hyperspace's . . . ah . . . aspects," Roeder said slowly. "The power requirements were so far off the scale that there was no way anyone could *experiment*. It's right up there with the schemes to ignite a gas giant or construct a Dyson Sphere. Theoretically possible, practically impossible."

Paul glanced at him. "Are we actually *in* hyperspace? This isn't a third-dimensional realm?"

"Captain, I honestly don't know," Roeder said. "We can't even *begin* to measure this realm's properties and compare them to what we know of hyperspace. There's no way to be sure of *anything*. I don't even know what will happen when we open a gateway."

"*They* won't let it happen," Tidal said. She waved a hand at the bulkhead. "They brought us here for a reason."

"Calm yourself," Paul ordered. Tidal had been on duty for hours. Normally she would be in bed by now. He yawned, feeling tired himself. The stimulants were wearing off ahead of time. He should be in bed too, before he collapsed completely. "Mr. Roeder . . . how long do we have?"

"It's hard to be certain," Roeder admitted. "I . . ."

"Take your best guess," Paul ordered sharply. Another spark danced at the corner of his eye, just for a second. "How long do we have?"

Roeder glanced down at his notepad. "Assuming the drain doesn't intensify," he said slowly, "we have about ten days before we lose power completely. I'm currently trying to organize my staff to start distributing stored power over the remaining power cells, which may give us some more breathing room, but . . . I can't guarantee that the power drain won't switch to them as well." He paused. "We may be trapped in a lobster pot," he added. "Our struggles may only make our entrapment worse."

Shit, Paul thought.

"If we *can* stockpile enough power to open a gateway, we *might* be able to escape," Roeder said. "But if we try and fail, we'll be dead sooner."

"We'll be dead anyway if we merely conserve power," Slater said.

"True," Paul agreed. "Start making preparations to open a gateway."

Roeder nodded slowly. "Yes, Captain."

Paul kept his face expressionless. Roeder didn't believe escape was possible. *That* wasn't a good sign. Paul had read Roeder's record very carefully before approving his transfer to *Supreme*. The man was a skilled engineer with an extensive record of naval service. If he thought they were doomed, they were probably doomed.

"There's another possibility," Cavendish offered. "We can check the alien ships, see what happened to them."

"Yes, My Lord," Paul said. He smiled, ruefully. Robert Cavendish's rank counted for nothing in the lobster pot. Whatever was out there, if there *was* something out there, wouldn't give a damn about him. "Mr. Slater, put together a team to board the nearest alien vessel."

"Yes, sir," Slater said. "I'll see who I can muster." He leaned forward. "There *is* another matter," he added. "Our unwanted guest."

Paul frowned. "Is he secure?"

"Yes," Slater said. He met Paul's eyes. "I strongly advise his termination."

"You mean *kill* him," Paul said flatly.

"Yes, sir," Slater said. "He's a danger as long as he's alive."

"But he's trapped," Paul said. "Correct?"

"Yes," Slater said. "For the moment."

Paul looked back at him evenly. "For the moment, we have other problems," he said. "Leave him in his cell."

Slater looked irked. "Yes, sir."

"We'll concentrate on getting the hell out of here," Paul said. "We have a plan, as limited as it is. Make sure the guests know it."

"Yes, sir," Jeanette said. She yawned, helplessly. "Food is going to be another hassle, sir."

"Of course," Paul said wearily. They *all* needed a rest. "The stasis pods have all failed, haven't they?"

"Yes, sir," Jeanette said. "I think we need to start distributing food as quickly as possible before it starts to spoil. Ration bars will last longer, of course."

"People will start whining," Slater put in.

Paul rubbed his forehead. *Supreme* carried thousands of tons of expensive foodstuffs, most of which would spoil rapidly outside a stasis pod. God alone knew what would happen if the life support started to fail in the holds. No, he *did* know what would happen. The food would go rotten and start poisoning people. And they were in danger of running out of fresh water too. Did they even have a single working purifier? They had a stockpile of purification tablets, but that would run out sooner rather than later. The ship would soon wind up looking like a refugee camp.

Fuck, he thought. *How the hell are we going to cope with waste disposal?*

He cleared his throat. "We are in an emergency situation," he said. His voice sounded strange in his own ears, as if someone else were speaking through him. "Inform the guests that we cannot provide most of our regular facilities. They . . . they can help, if they have useful skills, or they can sit quietly and wait. The stewards can organize activities for them." His voice hardened. "And if any of them cause trouble," he added, "you are to subdue them as quickly as possible."

"I'll back you up on that," Cavendish said. His lips twitched. "Although it might just mean *both* of us ending up in the shit."

"Thank you, My Lord," Paul said.

He looked down at his wristcom. Half the command functions were still offline, a reminder that his ship was in desperate straits. Normally, he was fairly sure that his crew could contain a riot before it got out of hand. Hatches could be sealed, entire decks isolated . . . now, there was no way to isolate a section without deploying manpower he didn't have to seal the hatches. All automated systems were offline or unreliable.

"I will take full responsibility," he said, looking up. He noticed that Jeanette looked relieved. "Once we return to realspace, we'll proceed to the nearest harbor and make contact with Corporate."

And if we don't return to realspace, a nasty part of his mind reminded him, *it doesn't really matter anyway.*

"Good luck to us all," he said. "Dismissed."

Paul's body felt tired, inhumanly tired. He thought he heard, just for a second, someone whispering in the background. But the voice was too quiet for him to make out the words. He rubbed his ears, fighting down a surge of exhaustion. The drugs were catching up with him. He needed sleep . . . they *all* needed sleep. But there was no way he *could* sleep.

"You won't have to take full responsibility," Cavendish said quietly. "I meant it."

Paul glanced up. He'd zoned out . . . he hadn't even realized that Robert Cavendish had stayed in the compartment. He cursed himself. The drugs were taking their pound of flesh. It probably wouldn't be long before he started seeing things . . . more things. The strange flashes of light had never left him alone.

"Thank you," he managed. "I'm sorry, My Lord."

"I should be apologizing to you," Cavendish said. His voice was reflective. "I wonder . . . were we set up to die?"

Paul gave him a sharp look. "What do you mean?"

Cavendish laughed humorlessly. "The corporation is in deep shit," he said. "We're overextended, Captain. We've been overextended since the war. I practically pimped out my daughter just to put together a deal that *might* save us. And now . . . someone with enough influence could have arranged for our escorts to leave us, perhaps even tipped off the pirates to our planned course."

"The course was random," Paul said. He couldn't believe his ears. "Are you suggesting that someone deliberately intended to get us all killed?"

"It makes sense," Cavendish said. "Captain . . . I didn't dare rock the boat. The risk of exposing our weakness . . . if our investors knew, they'd be bailing out before it was too late, and in doing so, they'd bring on the disaster. But now . . . I was meant to spend the entire trip putting together a plan to put our finances on more solid footing. That won't happen now, will it?"

"We'll get home," Paul said with more confidence than he felt. "Is that why you were unwilling to protest our unwanted guest?"

"There would have been a diplomatic incident," Cavendish said. "Our enemies would have seen us as an easy target without realizing just how weakened we actually are. I might . . . I might have been able to convince them to deny passage to a serial killer, but we might have lost the subsequent lawsuit. The government wouldn't thank us for creating a major incident."

"I suppose not," Paul said. "If *Supreme* never returns home, My Lord, will the insurance company pay out?"

Robert Cavendish laughed, harshly. "It won't be enough to get the corporation out of its hole," he said. "If one of my rivals thinks that killing me and the rest of the guests will solve the problem, he's mistaken. They could lose everything."

Paul wasn't sure how to process what he'd just heard. Cavendish Corporation was *immense*, larger than some stage-four planetary governments. Robert Cavendish controlled more money and power and influence than most of the dukes. And yet if the corporation was dangerously overextended, his power rested on a bluff. No wonder Corporate had been so reluctant to push matters. They didn't dare force someone to push back.

But how could *anyone* have predicted the distortion?

Maybe they intended to let the pirates have us, he thought. He couldn't imagine any way someone could have known what *Supreme* would encounter. *Or maybe they paid the pirates through the nose to have them destroy the ship instead of taking prisoners for ransom.*

"It isn't a problem, for the moment," he said finally. He felt a stab of sympathy for Robert's daughter. He'd met Finley Mackintosh, and he hadn't been impressed. "If we make it back to realspace, My Lord, we can worry about it then."

"Right," Cavendish said. He looked down at the table. "Do we have a hope in hell of escaping this . . . this lobster pot?"

"I think so," Paul said. He wasn't so sure, privately. But he knew he had to sound confident when talking to guests. Thankfully, most of them would assume that a man in uniform knew what he was doing. "We have options."

"True," Cavendish said. "And if we fail, we die?"

"I'm afraid so," Paul said. "This is completely unprecedented."

He considered it for a long moment. He'd heard of starships losing power in hyperspace before, but never anything like the graveyard. Anyone who saw the drifting ships and made it home would have one hell of a story to tell. Maybe someone had . . . they just didn't have any records to prove it.

We should see if anyone's heard such a story, he thought. Commanding officers were supposed to discourage spacers from sharing their tales, although that was a little like trying to hold back the tide. Everyone in space knew someone who knew someone who'd heard of the Lost Planet of Treasure or Missing Planet of Paradise. *Perhaps there's a clue in there somewhere.*

He looked up as Lieutenant Boscobel stepped into the room, looking disgustingly fresh and awake. "Sir," he said, "we have identified a single human starship among the alien ships."

Paul tensed. Something gleamed at the corner of his eye. "Are you sure?"

"Yes, sir," Boscobel said. "It's definitely a human-designed ship."

"Then we'll investigate it first," Paul said. He allowed himself a moment of relief. In theory, reading alien records could be simple; in practice, no one had actually tried. He had no idea if the feat was possible without computer support. "Put it on the top of the list."

"Aye, sir."

"I'll go back to my family," Cavendish said. "Good luck, Captain."

CHAPTER TWENTY-FOUR

"Congratulations on your promotion," Matt said.

"And my first command will be to have you flogged with a rusty chainsaw," Carla said as they carried the heavy box down the darkened corridor. "Or perhaps I should give you all the shit jobs."

"Yes, My Lady," Matt said. "I cower before you, My Lady."

"Perhaps some groveling, later," Carla said. The lights flickered. They both reached for their flashlights before the lighting steadied itself. "It's not how I *wanted* to get promoted."

Matt nodded ruefully. Dominic Falcon had been thrown into a bulkhead hard enough to crack his skull. He might have been saved if he'd been rushed to Sickbay quickly enough, but the stewards had been unable to summon a medical team. Carla was, apparently, the senior survivor. Matt didn't envy her, not really. Rumors were flying everywhere, suggesting that they were doomed. *Supreme* didn't have a hope of escape.

"I'm sure you'll do fine," he said instead.

Carla shot him a piercing glance as they reached the hatch. Someone had jammed the portal open even though it was technically against regulations. Matt didn't blame them. Opening the hatch without power was difficult, even for strong men. The lights flickered again as they stepped through and hurried down to the ballroom. The area resembled one of the refugee camps that had dotted the Commonwealth after the Theocracy destroyed Hebrides. The handful of emergency lights someone had rigged up didn't make the space look any better.

None of these people are used to deprivation, he thought. His nose wrinkled. He could smell the makeshift toilets in the next room. The air filtering system was down too. *They'll be going mad in a hurry.*

He peered around, trying to locate any other stewards or crew in the giant compartment. He found none. The guests were lying on the deck or mingling, talking in hushed voices. A handful of Brethren were standing at the far end of the room, speaking loudly about how *Supreme* had reached the home of their gods. Matt couldn't make out everything they were saying, but the general gist was clear. *Supreme* shouldn't be making any attempt to escape the trap. Instead, they should prepare to welcome their lords and masters.

A hand caught his arm. "My wife's been hurt," a middle-aged man said. Matt recognized him as one of the middle-ranking guests, one of Robert Cavendish's cronies. "Can you get her to Sickbay?"

Matt glanced at Carla, then walked over to check on the wife. She was easily twenty or thirty years younger than her husband, her face marred with a nasty bruise. She'd apparently banged her head into the bulkhead when *Supreme* had run into trouble. She wasn't the only one. Matt had been told not to send anyone to Sickbay unless their injuries were life-threatening.

"Not at the moment, sir," he said after a quick inspection. He was no expert, but he knew enough about medical matters to be fairly sure that the young woman was in no immediate danger. "She'll have to wait for attention."

The man reached out and caught his arm. "She needs attention *now*," he said. "That's not good enough. I paid for this flight and—"

"Medical attention will be provided as soon as possible," Matt said. He gritted his teeth, unsure if he should summon help. Too many guests were taking an undue interest in the discussion. "Right now, sir, our resources are stretched to the limits."

"I'll have your job for this," the man snapped. "Do you understand me?"

"Yes, sir," Matt said.

He turned and walked back towards Carla, bracing himself for the blow to fall. If the man took a swing at him . . . the blow never fell. Matt still felt a shiver running down his exposed back. Someone, he forgot who, had said that civilization was one missed meal away from disintegration. The men and women in the ballroom, gathered together by the stewards, had probably never missed a meal in their lives.

Carla cupped her hands around her mouth and spoke loudly. "We have food here," she said, tapping the box. "Please line up to collect your rations."

Matt opened the box and started to hand out sandwiches. Normally the sandwiches cost about a day's wages. The labels informed anyone who cared to look that they'd been made with the finest organic ingredients without a single vat-grown piece of meat in the batch. Now, with the stasis pods having failed, they were already pushing their sell-by date. The sooner they were eaten, the better.

"I want beer," someone shouted. "Beer!"

"Water," another person added. "I'm thirsty!"

Matt tapped the stunner at his belt as Carla spoke. "Water will be provided," she said. "Please remain calm and—"

"I want a shower," someone shouted. "I'm covered in blood."

"Water is strictly rationed," Carla informed him. "You'll have to wait for it."

If we can, Matt thought. Normally water was cheap. Now . . . he had the feeling that they were going to struggle to keep themselves hydrated. Soon they would be trying to purify the swimming pools. *What happens when we start distilling our own piss?*

He shuddered at the thought. He knew, on an intellectual level, that starships recycled almost *everything*, but he didn't want to think about the implications. No one did.

A voice spoke in his ear, just for a second. He jumped and spun around, but no one was there. Carla gave him a look, then turned back to the older man who was arguing with her. He was demanding water, or booze, and he didn't care about whoever had said he couldn't have it. He was a very important man and . . .

"Sit down, sir," Carla said finally. "There isn't any water yet."

The man glared at her for a long moment, then took his sandwich and stamped off. Matt breathed a sigh of relief. A nasty mood was in the air even though plenty of guests were now eating. It wouldn't take much to start a riot. He would have preferred to lock the passengers in their cabins and feed them one by one, but the captain had other ideas.

And he didn't bother to explain them to me, Matt thought. An orb of light danced past his eyes and vanished again. *No doubt the captain thinks he has good reasons.*

"This is the home of our gods," a voice said. Matt looked up. Brother John was standing there, peering down at him. His monkish cowl gave him a sinister look. "We demand that you let us go to them."

Matt took a breath. "The gods have not spoken to us," he said carefully. He wasn't sure what to say. "This place is a trap."

"There are other ships out there," Brother John informed him. "They too were summoned by the gods."

Shit, Matt thought. *How the hell did he know about the other ships?*

Someone must have told them, his own thoughts answered. Most of the crew knew about the alien ships by now, even though the captain had specifically ordered them *not* to tell the passengers. *Rumors have been flying everywhere.*

"The gods will provide," Brother John said. He took a step forward. "We must go to them in the spirit of submission."

Carla tapped her wristcom, beating out an emergency signal. Matt gripped his stunner. There was no way Brother John could have missed the movement, but he kept coming forward anyway. Matt braced himself, unsure what to do. Brother John was an easy target, but five other Brethren were in the ballroom . . . and plenty of others, all on edge.

"Have you not heard their voices?" Brother John asked. "Can you not hear them calling?"

"Return to your place and sit down," Carla ordered. Matt drew his stunner. "This is not the time—"

"This is *our* time," Brother John said. He reached out and shoved Carla, hard. "Get out of our way."

Matt pulled the trigger. The stunner produced a low hum but nothing else. Matt stared at it in shock, then jumped backward as Brother John threw a punch. He wasn't quick enough to evade the blow. The force of the impact knocked him off his feet and threw him to the deck. He heard someone shout in delight, the deck vibrating as the entire crowd seemed to hurl itself forward. Matt forced himself to crawl backward . . .

"Get down," a new voice thundered. *"I say again, get down!"*

Matt kept moving as the security team raced into the compartment. They wore riot gear, wielding clubs in unison. Their stunners weren't working either, he realized dully. His jaw was throbbing badly, badly enough to make it hard to think. A pair of strong arms caught him and yanked him backward, practically throwing him out through the hatch. More security officers flooded into the section, stunners at the ready. Matt noticed that a number carried chemical weapons.

He rubbed his jaw as he was thrust to the rear. He tasted blood on his tongue.

"Matt," Carla said. "Are you all right?"

"I've been better," he managed. Carla looked uninjured but was clearly shaken. He didn't feel much better himself. "Are *you* all right?"

"My pride took a beating," Carla said. She smiled without humor. "A mortal wound, of course."

"Of course," a new voice said. Matt looked up to see Raymond Slater. He forced himself to stand upright despite the tiredness gripping every part of his body. The security chief outranked both of them. "What happened?"

"Brother John was raving about his *gods* living here, sir," Matt said. "He . . . he attacked us."

He turned to watch as he heard the security team dragging a set of zip-tied prisoners through the hatch. Brother John was bleeding from a nasty wound to the forehead, but his eyes were defiant. Matt fought the urge to take a step backward as the fanatic glared at him. His hands were tied behind his back, yet Matt had no doubt that Brother John was a dangerous man. The other four prisoners looked just as fanatical, save for a man who was already threatening to sue the security team for everything they had.

"Take them to the cells," Slater ordered. "We'll discuss formal charges later."

His hand snapped at the air. Matt stared at him in complete incomprehension, then understood. Slater was seeing the flickers too. They were *all* seeing the flickers. He shivered, wondering what it meant. Nancy Cavendish had talked about hearing voices, hadn't she? Perhaps Brother John wasn't insane after all.

Carla cleared her throat. "What do we do now, sir?"

"Keep feeding the passengers," Slater said. "Unless you think we should seal the hatches and leave them to starve?"

"No, sir," Matt said. Slater looked tired too. "Will your team remain here?"

"For the moment," Slater said. He paused. "Do I misremember, Steward, or do you have an EVA certificate?"

Matt blinked, not seeing the connection. "Yes, sir," he said, surprised. It wasn't exactly *uncommon*. He'd needed to cross-train, and EVA had sounded fun, but he'd never had the opportunity to use his skills. "I have a first-rate civil EVA badge."

"Then report to the shuttlebay at 1700," Slater ordered. "I need EVA-qualified personnel."

Carla looked astonished. "Sir, I thought everyone in security had a full certification . . ."

"Yes," Slater said in a tone that suggested he thought he was talking to a particularly stupid child. "However, I cannot spare more than two or three of my people. They are *also* trained in riot control and emergency medicine."

Carla flushed angrily. "Sir," she said stiffly. "In that case, Matt needs some sleep."

Slater looked Matt up and down, then nodded. "Find yourself a bed and get some kip," he ordered. "I'm sure someone else can help distribute the food."

Matt fought down the urge to tell the security chief just what he thought of him undercutting Carla so blatantly. "Yes, sir," he said. "I'll get some rest now."

"Very good," Slater said.

"And that means actual rest," Carla reminded him. "Go straight back to the wardroom and *sleep*."

"I will," Matt promised. "See you soon."

———

"There's nothing that can be done for your arm right now," Marie said. Her voice was surprisingly compassionate. "I'm going to bind it up for the moment. Don't try to use it." She looked at Angela. "Pass me the bandages."

Angela was too tired to be surprised. Marie . . . a qualified nurse? Angela had certainly never assumed that her governess was qualified to do more than merely supervise her charge's life. But she supposed it made sense. Angela had never gone in for dangerous sports, unlike some of the other aristocratic children she'd known, but she might have changed her mind at any moment. And the prospect of injury on a camping trip could never be eliminated completely.

Not that I would have wanted to take her with me, she thought as she removed the bandage from its packaging. She'd become something of an expert in preparing bandages over the last few hours. Marie had dragged her to Sickbay and put her to work. *She would just have dampened everything.*

"Hold still," Marie said. She took the bandage and wrapped it around the young woman's arm. "Try not to move the arm while the bandage is settling into place."

The woman whimpered, sweat clearly visible on her forehead. Angela shuddered despite herself. She'd seen a handful of war reports, but they'd all been surprisingly cheery about death and injury rates. None had shown the effects of the war on something as fragile as a single human body, let alone hundreds of thousands of innocent victims . . .

She shook her head. She was woolgathering.

"It hurts," the woman managed. She was clenching her uncovered fist. "Can't you . . . can't you give me something for the pain?"

"We don't have any painkiller tabs left," Marie said. "The pain will have to be borne."

She helped the woman to her feet and escorted her out the hatch. Angela watched, feeling cold. Marie had lied. She *knew* Marie had lied. And yet . . . she glanced at Nancy, who was sitting on the chair staring at nothing. Her sister was mumbling to herself. Angela didn't recognize the language.

"Find the next set of bandages," Marie ordered. "We have seven more people to help—"

"You lied to her," Angela said, without thinking. "We have *boxes* of painkiller tabs."

Marie looked pained. "We can't spare them," she said. She jabbed a finger at the bulkhead, indicating the emergency ward beyond. "There are people who we can't save too. They'll die in the next few hours . . ."

"You could help them," Angela protested. "Marie——"

Her governess met her eyes. Angela recoiled. Marie was . . . *different*. She wondered, suddenly, if her governess had always worn a mask. She'd never been scared of Marie—angry, yes; resentful, yes—but scared? She'd never been scared . . . it dawned on her, suddenly, that perhaps she should have been scared all along. What was Marie, really?

She swallowed. She wasn't sure she wanted to know.

"We have a very limited supply of working medical equipment," Marie said. "Our supplies of drugs are *far* lower. The synthesizers are completely offline. We cannot hand out drugs to everyone without running out, nor can we afford to treat everyone who needs to be treated. There are people over there"—she jabbed a finger at the bulkhead again—"who are dying because we cannot give them the treatment they need. We cannot even make their last hours easier."

Angela stared at her. "You're just going to let them die?"

Marie cocked her head. "What would you have us do?"

"Save them," Angela insisted.

"How?" Marie asked. "With what? We are cut off from the outside universe, dependent on our own resources, and those resources are not up to the task. All we can do is let those people die, because the drugs that will ease their last moments will give the others a fighting chance." Her voice hardened. "This is the reality of life for uncounted trillions of people throughout history," she said. Angela took a step backward. "They cannot escape the realities of life, Angela. You can't either, not any longer. Your family name means nothing in . . . in this place. If it was you lying on one of those beds, you'd be left to die too."

"That's not fair," Angela said.

"The *universe* isn't fair," Marie snapped. "You were raised in a protective cocoon. You never saw the harsh reality of life."

"I'm going to marry Finley," Angela protested. She didn't want to marry Finley, but she would. For the family. "That's—"

"Oh, *terrible*," Marie mocked. "Poor little rich girl. Do you want to know what some girls have to do to survive? You are a spoiled little brat."

Angela clenched her fists. "I'm not spoiled!"

"Yes, you are," Marie said. She reached out and tapped Angela's forehead. "How long have I been your governess?"

"A million years," Angela muttered.

"Ten years," Marie corrected. "It only *feels* like a million years. And *spoiled* is a very good word for you." She cleared her throat. "Get the next set of bandages ready. While we've been arguing, people have been dying."

Angela hesitated, then hurried to obey.

CHAPTER TWENTY-FIVE

"We've simplified everything as much as possible," Slater said as he inspected the small group of explorers. "But we cannot afford to rely on any of our navigation aids."

Matt swallowed, hard. He hadn't slept well once he'd returned to his bunk. In truth, he felt as though he hadn't slept at all. He'd awoken four times from nightmares he hadn't been able to remember. Judging from some of the other muttered comments, he wasn't the only one to have an uneasy sleep. Slater didn't look any better.

"Check your suits, then cross-check," Slater said. "Evans, you're paired with me."

"Yes, sir," Matt said. It was the last thing he wanted, but he understood the logic. The remainder of the away team had worked together before. "My suit appears to be in working order."

"Remember to be careful," Slater said. He checked Matt's life-support system, then motioned for Matt to return the favor. "We can't rely on anything."

Matt nodded in agreement. The list of system failures was growing longer by the hour, an endless liturgy of disaster. Some of the failures were annoying—losing the entertainment databases was hardly a major problem, under the circumstances—but others posed a serious threat to the entire crew. Two decks had to be isolated after their local life-support systems had failed completely and refused to be reactivated, no matter what the engineers tried. A second string of such failures would doom the entire ship.

He locked his helmet in place, then tested the radio. It worked, but a hiss of static bothered him. Slater had speculated that something about the local region of space absorbed energy. The team would be leaving a string of relay beacons in their wake as they moved towards the derelict ship, but Matt knew better than to rely on them too. It was growing harder and harder to disbelieve the rumors about an alien trap . . .

Alien ships are out there, he thought as they walked towards the hatch. *Who knows? One of them might still be active.*

The hatch hissed open. Matt braced himself, then stepped into space. The sickly yellow-green radiance washed over him, casting *Supreme* into stark relief. There was no visible source, save perhaps for the sheets of energy in the distance. They were trapped inside a hyperspace bubble, something he'd thought existed only in bad movies. Surely, if there *was* such a bubble, there would be no way out.

He told himself to stop being silly as Slater led them away from *Supreme*. They'd gotten in, somehow. Logically, there had to be a way out too. Alerts flashed up in his suit's HUD as the team moved farther away, warning him of everything from an air leak to total systems failure. He forced himself to remain calm, somehow. The radio hissed, relaying messages from the rest of the team . . . and strange hints of voices that were never quite clear, no matter how hard he tried to pick them out of the background. He couldn't shake the sensation that they were being watched.

The alien graveyard unfolded itself before them as they pressed onwards. A jumbled mass of starships, ranging from simple designs close to humanity's work to designs that made very little sense at all. One looked like a squashed spider, another a giant tear drop; a third, largest of all, favored a bird in flight. They were all covered in sickly green light, making it hard to study the craft closely. He'd seen hundreds of fictional designs in dozens of movies, but something about the alien ships defied him to say they were *human*. The people who'd designed the vessels had different ideas about how the universe worked.

"That might be a hyperspace motivator," Lieutenant Avis Grosskopf said. The muscular security officer sounded nervous. Matt had seen her at work, subduing rowdy passengers. He wouldn't have dared to tangle with her in a bar fight. "Those spider legs might be a way of manipulating space-time to provide propulsion."

"Or maybe whoever built it was a giant spider," Lieutenant Toby Robinson said. "They might have built their ships in their own image."

"Perhaps we're light-years from where we were," Avis said. "There are no aliens within the human sphere, are there?"

"Explored space is tiny," Matt said. He wasn't sure he wanted to take part in the discussion, but talking was better than being alone with his thoughts. "We're a teeny tiny fragment of the galaxy, let alone the universe. *Anything* could be lurking beyond the Rim."

"Watching us," Avis said. "Whoever brought us here could have yanked us millions of light-years from home."

"Stow that chatter," Slater snapped. "We don't know a damn thing about what's actually going on, and until we do, we won't speculate."

Silence fell. Matt was torn between relief and fear. The spacesuit felt cold, cramped . . . he wondered, suddenly, if he was truly alone. He shivered, helplessly. Was someone touching him? Was it just his imagination? The radio buzzed, spitting a string of nonsense words. A moment later, everyone was chattering. They'd all heard the broadcast.

"Remain calm," Slater ordered. "We're moving towards our target now."

Matt braced himself as the ancient starship loomed up in front of them. It was definitely human, he told himself, although he couldn't place the design. The letters on the hull were English: HMMS Gladys.

Offhand, he couldn't recall ever hearing of a ship by that name, although that meant nothing. HMMS . . . His Majesty's Merchant Ship. A Britannic ship, then.

"She's one of the explorer cruisers," Avis said. She sounded calmer, now that they were nearing their destination. "A common design, back in the early days of hyperspace exploration."

Matt thought she was right. *Gladys* was two hundred meters from bow to stern, a long, thin cylinder of a starship with a massive drive section at the rear. Avis chatted happily, telling them facts and figures Matt hadn't particularly wanted to know. *Gladys* and her sisters had been designed for five-year missions into hyperspace, mapping out the first spacelanes and locating planets for human settlement. A number of those ships had gone out and never been seen again . . .

"Evans, we'll go in at the master hatch," Slater ordered. "The rest of you, remain behind."

"Aye, sir," Avis said.

Matt steered his way down towards the hatch, following Slater. Up close, the starship had an air of age that somehow chilled him to the core. The sensation of being watched was growing stronger, nagging at his mind. Slater didn't seem to be bothered as he wrestled with the hatch, but Matt had his doubts. The ancient vessel felt creepy. The hatch opened. The inner hatch was already ajar.

"She's depressurized," Slater said, sounding troubled. "That should be impossible."

"I didn't see any visible damage, sir," Avis said. "Do you want us to come in with you?"

"Not yet," Slater said. "Evans, follow me."

He switched on his helmet flashlight and swam into the ancient ship. Matt followed, shining his light around. *Gladys* appeared to be completely powered down. No lighting, no gravity . . . nothing. His suit told him, just for a moment, that the air was safe to breathe . . . he stared at the reading in disbelief. The hatch was open. The ship could *not* have air.

Something flickered at the corner of his eye. The sensation of being watched was impossible to ignore any longer.

"This way," Slater said. "Follow me."

Matt swam after Slater as he led the way deeper into the derelict. The shadows seemed to move as he watched, drawing back . . . he forced himself to remain calm, somehow. Slater paused in front of an inner hatch, then started to open it. An instant later, a corpse drifted through . . .

"Shit," Matt said. He felt warm liquid trickling down his leg. "Sir, I—"

"It's dead," Slater said dryly. He sounded oddly reassured. "And . . . that's interesting."

Matt frowned as he inspected the body. He'd seen holos of corpses preserved in vacuum before, but . . . the body before him looked dried out, fully desiccated. Matt had the strangest feeling that a single touch would crumble the entire cadaver to dust. It made no sense at all. In the void of space, the corpse should have been frozen solid.

"We've found a body," Slater said, for the benefit of the recorders. "Apparently male . . . no sign of visible genitals . . . appears to be in its early thirties. I can't say for sure, but the rank badges suggest a commander. The body seems to be a husk, nothing more."

"Understood, sir," Avis said.

Slater glanced at Matt. "Come on," he said. "Let's get a move on."

The flashes at the corner of his eye grew stronger as they made their way down to the command deck. Matt glanced from side to side, silently noting the damage. The ship was odd. Some parts appeared to be intact, frozen in time; others appeared to be damaged, although there was no clear cause. But then *Supreme* had been badly damaged when she'd been yanked into the hyperspace distortion. *Gladys* might have been designed for survey work, but *Supreme* might have better protections.

"The hatch is open," Slater said. The radio produced a stream of static. He had to repeat the message twice before Avis replied. "We're going in."

Matt tensed as they moved into the bridge, which was surprisingly intact compared to *Supreme*'s. But bodies were drifting everywhere. One body, a woman, he thought, was strapped into the command chair; others were tied down or drifting through the air. He shone his flashlight around, feeling his stomach heave at the sight before him. The flickering grew stronger once again. It was hard to escape the sense that *Gladys* was a haunted ship.

"The bridge is completely powered down," Slater reported. "I'm checking for a logbook now."

"Check under the command chair, sir," Avis advised. "Some of the early ships required a paper copy as well as datachips."

Slater nodded. "Evans, check the nearby compartments," he ordered. "I'll look here."

Matt pulled himself towards the nearest hatch, which looked as though it had been cut open. The edges were scorched and warped by immense heat. Outside, a handful of corpses drifted in uneasy peace. One held a cutting laser that looked to have come from the past. Matt's lips twitched, despite the situation. It had come from the past. Modern-day cutters were far more efficient.

"Five more dead bodies," he reported. He peered through another hatch into a small cabin. It was too close to the bridge to belong to anyone but the captain, yet . . . it looked tiny. Captains were normally given big cabins, weren't they? But then, *Gladys* was an exploration ship with limited space for her crew. "Sir, there's a handful of books on the desk."

"Bag them up," Slater ordered. "And hurry."

Matt made his way into the cabin, which looked as though someone had ransacked it, tossing pieces of clothing and the captain's personal effects in all directions. They hadn't touched the books, somewhat to his surprise. Three looked to be historical fiction; the fourth was a logbook, and the fifth, a private journal. He opened the logbook and glanced at the text. HMMS GLADYS, LAUNCHED 2119. The last entry in the logbook was dated 2120, less than a year after *Gladys* had departed Earth. He shivered. He'd been told, time and time again, that the people who'd opened up the spacelanes were *heroes*. And yet, they'd been trapped . . .

He put the books in his pouch, then scooped up a number of primitive datachips. There was no way to know what was on them without checking, but he thought it was worth taking them too. Searching the entire ship would take time, time he didn't think they had. He took one last look around the cabin, picking up a picture of a woman in an unfamiliar uniform before leaving. The bridge looked deserted . . .

. . . and then Slater popped up from one of the consoles.

"I've removed the record chips," he said. "We might not be able to read them, but we can try."

"Yes, sir," Matt said. Just for a second, he'd thought that Slater had vanished. *Things* were gleaming at the corner of his eye. "How do you want to proceed?"

Slater's voice was tired, defeated. "We take the logbook and the chips back to the ship and investigate them," he said. "And then . . . we'll have to see what we can do next."

"Yes, sir," Matt said. "Should we take one of the cadavers back for the doctor?"

"If she has time to take a look at it," Slater said. "Put it in a bag before you take it out of the ship."

Matt nodded. He'd hastily brushed up on the alien contact protocols, although none of the writers had envisaged anything like the graveyard. Most of them had assumed an encounter between two starships—one human, one alien—all alone in the dark. Others had assumed the discovery of a primitive alien world. That, at least, had been simple. Contact was strictly forbidden on pain of death. Meeting an alien race at an equal or superior level of tech, on the other hand . . .

They were worried about alien biological matter getting loose, he recalled. *Who knows what might have happened to the drifting bodies?*

He bagged up the nearest corpse, then dragged it back to the airlock. The remainder of the team were waiting outside, exchanging nervous signals. Slater spoke briefly to them, then led them away from *Gladys*. Matt took one last look at the starship before following Slater. How could an entire starship go missing, even from an earlier era, and leave no trace behind? But, then, it had been the dawn of a new age of exploration. Humanity was leaving its native star system and striding out into the galaxy. No one had been willing to count the cost.

The radio crackled time and time again. Matt listened to the voices, but they were never clear, like hearing two people talking behind a wall, their voices muffled. Avis spoke incessantly about what they might have seen on *Gladys*, but Matt tuned her out. The old vessel had been creepy as hell. There was no way he wanted to go back there.

We might have to go back, he thought. *Or inspect one of the alien ships.*

"We'll be going in through the lower hatch," Slater said. "They'll have set up the decontamination facility by now."

"Fuck," Avis said. "Sir, must we—"

"Yes," Slater said. "We don't have a choice."

Matt kept his thoughts to himself as they reached *Supreme*. The cruise liner looked as though she'd been in a battle, her hull scorched and pitted by enemy fire. And yet there was something curiously intelligent about the damage. Sensor blisters and weapons mounts had been disabled or destroyed, but the giant windows had been left completely untouched. He saw no trace of air venting from the ship's hull. Matt wondered if something had wanted to render them helpless yet leave the crew and passengers alive.

He turned to look at the drifting alien ships. Was there some force out there, waiting for them?

"The damage is odd," he said quietly. "Whatever did this was intelligent."

"I'll thank you to keep that speculation to yourself," Slater said. "We don't want a panic."

Matt said nothing as they passed through the hatch and into the airlock, then moved the bags into the next compartment. Hopefully there wouldn't be any danger. He couldn't believe that anything, even a tiny bacterium, could have survived in the vacuum. But if the sensors were unreliable, who knew what might slip onto *Supreme*?

A light danced at the corner of his eye. He shivered.

"Strip down," Slater ordered as they stepped into the second compartment. "Once you're naked, move forward and into the shower."

Avis removed her suit and walked forward. Matt told himself, firmly, to keep his eyes closed when he stepped into the shower. He'd never been through a chemical decontamination—he'd never needed one—but he knew the procedure. It was not going to be pleasant.

Avis yelped as warm liquid cascaded onto her. Matt kept his eyes closed as he inched forward into the shower. The chemical was hot and smelly, hot enough to be thoroughly uncomfortable. His head itched as he kept moving forward, reminding him that the chemical might cost him his hair. He hoped Angela didn't care *that* much for his looks. He grunted in shock as cold water rushed over him, followed by a gust of warm air.

"Come forward," a voice ordered. "You appear to be clean."

"Thank you," Matt managed. "Is it safe to open my eyes?"

"Yes," the voice said.

Matt opened his eyes. He stood in a small quarantine chamber, watched by two nurses. Avis was on the far side of the chamber, climbing into a pair of overalls. Matt took a set for himself and donned the garment, hastily.

"You'll be in here for an hour," one of the nurses said. "If we don't find any reason to be worried, we'll let you go."

"And if we mutate into slime-eating monsters from some unpronounceable world?" Avis asked.

"We'll be sure to feed you lots of slime," the nurse said.

"Oh," Matt said. "Is it *that* dangerous?"

The nurse snorted. "It's unlikely that you could have picked up anything dangerous," she said. "But if we're wrong . . ."

"As if things weren't bad enough already," Matt agreed. The nurses had been assigned to watch them. That, if nothing else, was a clear warning of just how seriously the captain was taking the situation. "We'll wait here and pray."

"A very good idea," the nurse said.

CHAPTER TWENTY-SIX

"No biological hazards, then?"

"Not as far as the doc can tell," Jeanette said firmly. She sounded better after a few hours of sleep. "Joan *was* careful to point out that half her scanners were on the blink. The autopsy may tell us more, sir, but I wouldn't count on it."

Paul nodded. If they saw home again, there was a good chance he'd be put in front of a court-martial board or a formal inquest for gross negligence. The regulations regarding alien biological matter were strict, all the more so for never having been tested. *Gladys* wasn't an alien ship, admittedly, but who knew what the drifting hulk might have picked up over the years? The biological scanners and nanotech repair drones were offline. It was impossible to be *sure*.

Which is a problem, he thought. *We can't be sure there isn't a threat.*

He sat down at his desk and opened the logbook. The object felt *odd* to his touch, as if it was out of place in his office. The book felt as if it belonged to another time and place, which it did, in a sense. Dust fell as he turned the pages, slowly parsing out the handwritten words. It was sheer luck that the UN Survey Regulations had called for a physical logbook as well as computer records.

"Keep an eye on the passengers," he ordered. "I'll read the logbook myself."

"Aye, sir," Jeanette said.

She withdrew silently. Paul rubbed his forehead—a few hours of sleep hadn't made him feel much better—and then read the first entry. HMMS *Gladys* had been launched from the Peter Hamilton Shipyard back in 2119. The handwriting changed twice before settling down into a distinctive hand: Captain Rebecca Hall, Royal Space Navy. Paul ground his teeth in frustration, wishing he could access the historical datacores. There was probably a whole series of books and documentaries about *Gladys* and the other survey ships that had gone out and never returned, but they were beyond his reach.

We'll just have to make do with what we have, he thought as he skimmed through the crumbly pages. *There's no way to access the datacores without wasting power.*

He allowed himself a flicker of admiration for the long-dead captain. Captain Hall had had an eye for detail, apparently, even though she'd written in a chatty manner that felt oddly irreverent to Paul's eyes. She'd outlined everything from an admiral's visit to her ship's first official transit into hyperspace. *Gladys* had been a good ship. Captain Hall had clearly been proud of her. She'd located two life-bearing worlds before setting off to chart out an entirely new region of hyperspace. And then . . .

We detected a hyperspace storm on long-range sensors and attempted to evade contact as much as possible. Unfortunately, the storm appeared to be expanding rapidly, perhaps coming after us. When it caught us, the shock knocked the entire crew out; when we recovered, we found ourselves trapped in a strange region of space. Many of our systems are now nonfunctional. Our

sensors can tell us nothing about local space.
The green light is everywhere. Anything could be
hiding in the light.

Paul sucked in his breath as he read the next set of entries. *Gladys* hadn't been entirely a military ship, but most of her crew were military officers. They hadn't panicked. Instead, they'd run a series of experiments to determine just where they were and to establish the properties of this region of space. Captain Hall had seemed torn between believing they were in an uncharted region of hyperspace and a whole other realm. Paul found that discouraging. Captain Hall and her crew had been far more imaginative when it came to carrying out experiments.

Our engineers believe that we cannot generate
enough power to open a vortex by conventional
means. We have devised a scheme to use the
nukes to generate the power, although this runs
the risk of completely destroying either the vortex generator or the entire ship. The magnetic
bottles cannot be relied upon to contain the blast
long enough to throw us back into normal space.
Too many of our remaining systems are already
failing.

"Shit," Paul muttered. He'd known that the saga of HMMS *Gladys* didn't have a happy ending, but Captain Hall sounded so hopeful. "They didn't find a way out in time."

He closed his eyes for a long moment, then forced himself to read on. The systems failures had continued, each one imperiling the ship still further. Captain Hall ordered her crew into spacesuits, falling back on the most primitive technology at her disposal to keep them alive for a few days longer. It hadn't been enough. Random failures kept mounting up, injuring or killing crewmen. The situation was beyond their comprehension.

> Midshipman Rollins went insane today, scream-
> ing about voices in his ears. He had to be dragged
> off Lieutenant Yeller by Midshipman Perkin and
> Midshipwoman Henri. I was forced to order him
> confined in a vacant cabin. Midshipwoman Yates
> and seven other crew told me, afterwards, that
> they too have been hearing voices. We have
> attempted to record these voices, but they have
> defied our remaining systems.

Paul sucked in his breath. A couple of crewmen had reported hearing voices on *Supreme* . . .

> Four more fights broke out today, seemingly
> about nothing. I ordered senior officers to break
> up the scuffles, but two of them actually joined
> in. The fighting seemed to be nothing more than
> pointless violence. There was no attempt to
> take the bridge, Engineering, or any other vital
> area. By the time the conflict ended, seven crew-
> men were dead, and five more were seriously
> wounded . . .
> . . . I heard the voices myself shortly after-
> wards. No matter what I did, I couldn't make out
> the words. Other crewmen have reported see-
> ing ghosts, or worse. Our sleep is constantly
> disturbed by hellish nightmares. I have ordered
> the doctor to pass out sedatives to anyone who
> asks, but it is a limited solution. Two crewmen

attacked others while seemingly sleepwalking. They have both been confined to quarters . . .

. . . Rollins died today. His last words were about eyes watching him.

Paul trembled. How many *Supreme* crewmen had reported feeling as though they were being watched?

Commander Hernandez attempted to kill me this afternoon, apparently as a diversion. I fought him off, somehow, and knocked him out. But when I reached the bridge, I discovered that a team of crewmen had gone rogue and attacked the nuke assembly, blowing the whole thing into space. I started to organize a recovery team, but the nukes detonated. The blasts seemed oddly dimmed, as if something was draining the power. It didn't matter. We were trapped. The voices are laughing at us . . .

. . . I have lost control of all decks now, save for the command bridge. Half the ship appears to be vented, as far as I can tell. The rest appears to be under mutineer control. I have nine men left under my command, all twitchy as hell. They flinch at shadows, at things lurking in the darkness. Emergency power is failing. I see dead people.

The next few lines were completely illegible. Paul tried to figure them out, then gave it up as impossible. Captain Hall had clearly been on the verge of madness, if she hadn't been mad already. She'd lost control of her ship and her crew. The final entry was stark and utterly hopeless.

> I have put the ship's cores into stasis mode, in hopes that they will one day be recovered. But the voices tell me that we will never be seen again. I hear them laughing, laughing, laughing . . . I cannot escape. None of us can escape. Our doom is upon us. We are in hell. Abandon all hope, all ye who enter here.

Paul started. "Shit."

He forced himself to reread the final set of entries. *Gladys* had degraded rapidly, losing all power within seventeen days. Or so he thought. Captain Hall had been a little sloppy about noting the precise dates and times of her final entries. But Paul found it hard to blame her in her final hours. She'd devised a plan to get her ship and crew out of the nightmare only to see it lost to mutiny and madness. Paul doubted he'd have done much better if he'd been in her place.

I am in her place, he thought numbly.

He forced himself to think, clearly. Something was missing from the logbook, something important. It took him several minutes to place it. Captain Hall hadn't mentioned any alien ships. It was inconceivable that she wouldn't have mentioned them if she'd *seen* the alien craft. And that meant . . . either her sensors had been too badly battered to detect the ships or *Gladys* had been the first vessel to enter the lobster pot. He wasn't sure which one he preferred.

"They had a plan," he said aloud. "But would it have worked?"

He keyed his wristcom. "Commander Haverford, Chief Slater, Mr. Roeder, please report to me at once."

"Aye, Captain," Jeanette said. "I'm on my way."

Paul reread the logbook once again. There was no hope in it, nothing to suggest that *Supreme* had any better chance to escape. And yet there *was* a warning. His crew and passengers were already hearing voices. Would they start going insane?

And if they do, he thought dourly, *what can we do about it?*

"There's little hope in the logbook," he said once his subordinates were assembled. "But Captain Hall *did* have a plan to escape."

Roeder took the logbook and read through the relevant sections. "Their engineers had balls, sir," he said. "I wouldn't care to rig up a bomb-pumped system like this if you paid me."

Jeanette lifted her eyebrows. "It's that dangerous?"

"Yes," Roeder said. "If they lost control, if the magnetic bottle failed, the blast would severely damage a modern warship. There was actually a concept for using bomb-pumped lasers in warships that never got off the ground simply because of the risks. A small failure could lead to a destroyed vessel. Doing this . . ." He shook his head as he passed her the logbook. "They must have been desperate."

"They were," Paul confirmed. "And we're desperate too."

Roeder took a breath. "Yes, sir," he said. "I've inspected the records from *Gladys*. With your permission, Captain, I'd like to dispatch recovery teams to scavenge power cells and whatever else we can find from the hulk. We need power cells, even if they are drained."

"Granted," Paul said. He looked at Jeanette. "Did the doctor's autopsy reveal anything useful?"

"Nothing we wanted to know," Jeanette said. "According to her report, the corpse was apparently . . . well, *desiccated*. It looked to have been dried out completely, utterly drained of energy. The body practically collapsed into dust when touched."

Slater gave her a look. "What can do something like that?"

Jeanette gazed back at him. "Whatever's draining our power cells," she said. "There's something oddly *intelligent* about the . . . the whole thing."

"It might be just a side effect of this region of space," Slater pointed out. "People do have problems when the environment changes sharply . . ."

"Not like this," Jeanette said. She waved her notebook at him. "So far, twenty-two crewmen and seventeen passengers, including Nancy Cavendish, have reported hearing indistinct voices. We're *all* seeing things at the corners of our eyes. Something's out there, Captain."

"There *does* seem to be an intelligence behind the damage we suffered as we fell through the distortion," Roeder said slowly. "The damage wasn't enough to breach the hull. Most of the injuries or deaths came from accidents like people falling into bulkheads. Anyone powerful enough to generate and use a hyperspace storm would have no difficulty ripping us to atoms if that's what they wanted to do."

Paul lethargically shook his head. Unbelievable. Two days ago, he'd known there was no such thing as aliens. None of the tall tales he'd heard were remotely convincing. And now . . . the ships drifting through the graveyard were stark proof that alien life *did* exist beyond the edge of explored space. Perhaps the idea of powerful beings who'd yanked his crew into their domain wasn't completely unbelievable after all.

"If this is true," he said, "where *are* they?"

Jeanette looked uncomfortable. "The Brethren believe that they're waiting for us to come to them," she said. "I caught several of them preaching to the crowd. I think they're winning converts."

Slater snorted. "Captain, with all due respect, I don't think we're dealing with space gods," he said. "Their actions do not suggest any desire for peaceful contact."

A light danced at the corner of Paul's sight. "No, they don't," he agreed. "So where are they?"

He rubbed his eyes, tiredly. Perhaps they were right. Perhaps there *were* hostile aliens lurking somewhere in the greenish light. Or perhaps they were just imagining things, assuming an order to the universe that didn't exist. Hyperspace was a strange place.

"Perhaps they're native to hyperspace," Roeder suggested. "And if that's the case, sir, they might be beyond our ability to perceive them."

"Nonsense," Slater said.

"Imagine you're a crab, living in a rocky pool on the beach," Roeder said. "You're limited to the pool; you don't even know there are *other* pools. And then you clamber onto the beach and see . . . well, you don't know *what* you see. Those giant feet running around, shaking the ground underneath you. You don't know that they're *children*. You think they're monsters if you somehow manage to look up and take in the sight. It's much more likely that you'll be running from them as fast as you can."

Jeanette smiled. "My mother always said they were more scared of me than I was of them."

"You're much bigger than a crab," Roeder pointed out. "How is the little beastie meant to comprehend you? You come from different realms."

"I take your point," Paul said. He frowned. "The lights we've been seeing . . . is that *them*?"

"I don't know," Roeder said. "Captain, this is remarkably unprecedented."

Paul nodded. "We'll continue our plans to escape," he said. "Mr. Roeder, feel free to organize scavenging missions to *Gladys* and any other human ship you discover. I'd prefer not to board an alien ship unless we have no choice."

"It would be a shame not to *look*," Roeder said. "Some of those ships are clearly hundreds of years ahead of us."

And they didn't manage to escape either, Paul thought.

He kept that to himself. "Jeanette, I want you to start organizing the guests into work parties," he said. "Keep them busy, whatever it takes. If there's anyone with medical or military experience, send them to Sickbay or security. Everyone else . . . we have a lot of corridors to clear."

"Yes, sir," Jeanette said. She frowned. "I think we'll run out of work for them to do."

"Then we'll give them busywork," Paul said. "Mr. Slater, I want you to read this logbook carefully, particularly the final sections. We may have similar problems over the next few days. Warn your men to be careful."

"Aye, Captain," Slater said. "I have to warn you that our ability to control the crowd is currently limited. Stunners are offline, it seems. If the guests turn nasty, we might be unable to keep them from doing real damage."

"That leads to my next point," Paul said. "The command deck and engineering sections are to be completely sealed off. *No one* who isn't on the access list is to be allowed to enter, and yes, that includes most of the crew. I don't want anyone to have a chance to sabotage the power cells."

Roeder blinked. "Captain . . . are you saying that someone might want us to *stay* here?"

Paul pointed at the logbook. "Read it," he said. "Some of *Gladys*'s crew wanted to stay here too."

"They must have been mad," Jeanette breathed.

"I think that was the point," Paul said. He yawned. "I think . . . I think that whatever is sapping our power cells is sapping *us* too. Sleep deprivation can do unfortunate things to people after a few days."

"Less than that," Slater said. "How many guests have the actual *experience* of staying up on watch?"

"Very few," Paul said. "We can check the records . . ." He shook his head. The records were inaccessible now. They'd just have to hope.

"We'll keep them working," he said. "Jeanette, make sure they know that they have to work to eat. I want them concentrating on working, not plotting trouble."

"I'm sure that half the lawsuits are already written," Jeanette said. "You do know we have a small army of lawyers on the ship?"

"As long as we're trapped, I have authority to do whatever it takes to keep my passengers and crew alive," Paul said. "If we get home, I dare say the naval attorneys will agree with me."

He sighed, remembering what Robert Cavendish had told him. Corporate was in no state to defend itself, not if a horde of lawyers was battering down their doors. They might win the case, as there was legal precedent that granted commanding officers vast powers in an emergency, only to lose the corporation anyway. They'd probably try to scapegoat Paul for everything . . .

Which won't do them any good, he thought wryly. *It isn't as if I could afford to pay billions in damages. Corporate would still get the bill.*

"And in any case, it doesn't matter," he said. "If we stay here too long, we're dead."

CHAPTER TWENTY-SEVEN

"They're watching us," Nancy said. She stood by the stateroom window, staring out into the eerie green light. "I can hear them."

Angela glowered at her younger sister. Marie had kept the older sibling hopping, forcing her to do everything from unwrapping bandages to cleaning up puke, blood, piss, and shit. Her outfit was completely ruined, and she was aware, all too aware, that she stank like someone who'd just spent the week in a sewer. Not that she'd dared say it to Marie. Now that she'd seen the real person under the mask, she didn't know how she'd ever dared talk back to the governess.

And she sent us back here to rest, she thought. Her body was tired, but she didn't feel like sleeping. And yet she knew they *had* to sleep. *We have to be back in Sickbay in six hours.*

"There's no one out there," she said tartly. She felt a surge of anger and resentment that surprised her. Nancy hadn't been any bloody help at all. She'd sat on the chair and muttered about voices and things in the darkness while Angela had been fighting to keep people alive and well. "Just . . . just shut up."

"They're coming," Nancy said. "I can hear them."

"Shut up or I'll hit you," Angela snapped. She'd never struck her sister, but she'd never been quite so frustrated at her before. *"Shut up."*

Nancy looked at her. "Did Marie manage to unnerve you quite *that* badly?"

Angela glared, torn between relief that the brat was back to normal and a desire to slap her anyway. "What do you mean?"

"Come on," Nancy said. "Did you honestly think that father wouldn't pick someone capable to watch over his teenage daughter?"

"I didn't think at all," Angela muttered. She felt her anger draining away, leaving her feeling numb. "What *is* she?"

"Perhaps she's a genetically engineered killing machine from Sparta," Nancy teased. "Father probably had her grown to supervise you."

Angela made a rude sound. "Do you know how many laws that violates?"

Nancy looked back at her. "Do *you* know how many laws that violates?"

"No," Angela admitted. She was fairly sure it was illegal to grow genetically engineered killing machines, although she wasn't sure just which laws banned the practice and why. Not for the first time, she wished she'd spent more time studying instead of partying. "Father wouldn't do that, would he?"

"He'd do *anything* to protect you," Nancy said. "He favors you, you know."

Angela stared at her. "He does *not!*"

"He does," Nancy said. "Why do you think he keeps letting you get away with everything?"

Angela snorted. She'd always assumed that *Nancy* was the favored child, the *famous* child . . . famous for something beyond her control. Certainly her father had spent more time with Nancy than Angela, although he hadn't spent much time with either girl. She had honestly never considered that Nancy might feel that Angela was their father's favorite. But then, Marie had been right. She *was* a selfish brat.

"I don't know *what* Marie is," she said. "But . . . I'm glad she's on our side."

"That's probably a good attitude," Nancy said.

"Thanks," Angela said. She reached out and gave her sister a hug. "When did *you* become the mature one?"

"*Someone* has to be the mature one," Nancy pointed out. "*You're* not up to the task."

Angela flushed. "Brat."

"I think *you're* the brat," Nancy said. "Marie says so."

"Yeah," Angela said.

She looked down at herself. Her shirt was covered in . . . she didn't want to *think* about what it was covered in, while her trousers were torn in a dozen places. If she'd known what was going to happen, she would have worn something more suitable. But she didn't know if she even *had* something suitable. Most of her clothes were designed for happier climes.

"Fuck it," she said. "I need a shower."

"There's no water," Nancy reminded her. "And the toilet is down the corridor."

Angela shuddered. She'd told herself that she was roughing it when she'd gone camping, but she'd still been surrounded by modern technology. Showers, baths, working toilets . . . she hadn't known how artificial the whole experience had been until she'd found herself *really* roughing it. She was dreading her first trip to the communal toilet. God alone knew how she'd cope, trying to do her business with hundreds of strangers nearby . . .

"I need a shower," she repeated. "Any ideas?"

Nancy shook her head. "You'll be wasting water," she said. "I dare you to explain *that* to Marie. Or Captain VanGundy."

"He works for our father."

"And now you're sounding like a brat again," Nancy countered. "Do you *really* want to be thrown into the brig?"

Angela gave her a surprised look. "We have a brig?"

Nancy winked at her. "You'll be surprised what gets left off the official plans," she said. "I had a lot of fun comparing dad's datapacket to the standard introductory spiel sent to all the guests. Yes, we have a brig. And quite a few other things too." She shrugged. "There *might* be some wipes in the room, if you go look," she said. "But I don't think you can get a shower."

"You stay here," Angela ordered. She was tempted to insist that Nancy accompany her, but that would be too weird. They'd never shared a room, even on the fake camping trips. "I don't want you to go anywhere."

She turned and walked into her bedroom. Boxes lay everywhere, their contents scattered on the deck. Angela felt a moment's dismay—her proud collection of handbags and frocks lay on the ground—which she ruthlessly suppressed. She was going to grow up, damn it. And if that meant learning to do without material things, she'd learn to do without material things. Besides, she told herself as she picked up a particularly pricey handbag, it wasn't as if they'd brought her real happiness. She'd bought half of her stuff only because she'd been competing with the other rich kids.

And they're brats too, she thought. *What will happen to them?*

She dismissed the thought. The room was a mess. It was hard to believe that she'd made love to Matt, then had a nasty fight with Finley, and then . . .

If we don't get home, she thought as she found a pair of slacks and a jumper, *I don't have to marry him.*

She carefully removed her shirt, trying not to breathe. The top was beyond repair . . . not that she'd ever bothered to repair anything in her life. She started to drop it in the washing basket, then caught herself. No point in putting it there, not now. She dug through her drawers until she found a plastic bag and dropped the shirt in there, followed by her bra, trousers, and panties. None were salvageable.

Damn it, she thought.

Someone, probably Marie, had left a box of wipes on her bed. Angela rubbed herself down as best as she could, then splashed perfume liberally over her chest. She could still smell herself, but she hoped she was the only one. But then, she wasn't the only person who hadn't had a shower for the last . . . how long had it been anyway? It felt like *years* since they'd fallen through the distortion and arrived . . . wherever they were.

She bent over the drawers, looking for something to wear under her slacks. Most of her underwear was designed for appearance, not resilience. Once, wearing them had made her feel deliciously naughty. Now, they were useless . . .

A hand touched her bottom. She jumped, stumbling backward. Finley was standing there. His face was so *different*, so animated, that she found it hard to believe it was actually him. There was a nasty cast to his face she didn't like at all.

"You look good," he said. He leered at Angela as she tried to cover herself.

Angela felt a hot flash of rage. "Get out!"

"I'm afraid I'll be coming in," Finley said. He sounded different too. "You and I are getting married."

"Fuck off," Angela said. "How did you get in here anyway?"

She grabbed the nearest dress and held it against her chest. She would have preferred to put it on properly, but that would have meant blinding herself at the worst possible time and giving him a show.

"The door locks aren't working," Finley said. He sounded almost amused, but there was a cruel edge to his voice that worried her. "Annoying *and* dumb. It's a good thing you're pretty, you know. I wouldn't want to marry someone who wasn't pretty."

"I don't want to marry you," Angela snapped. She wanted to take a step backward, to run and throw herself through the hatch, but she didn't dare show weakness. This wasn't the Finley she knew.

His face twisted with rage. "You do realize that you *are* going to marry me? I believe we've already *had* this discussion."

"*You* do realize we're trapped, right?" Angela replied. "If we can't get out, if we can't get home, our marriage is pointless. A farce of a farce of a farce of a—"

"Be quiet," Finley said. He took a step forward. "We are going to get married. Our families *need* us to get married. And that's the end of it."

"We are *not* going to get married," Angela said sharply. She risked a glance at the hatch behind him. Where was Nancy? Was she still staring out into the green light, unaware that Finley had entered the stateroom? Or was she in trouble too? Finley had cronies. One of them might be keeping Nancy under guard while Finley had his fun. "We're *certainly* not going to get married if we don't get out of here."

"It doesn't matter," Finley said. He took another step forward. "You and I are meant to be together."

Angela laughed at him. Finley reached out, yanked the dress from her arms, and threw it right across the cabin. Angela yelped in shock as he grabbed her arm, yanking her forward and then pushing her towards the bed. Her mind churned, unable to quite follow what was happening. He was going to . . .

Her back hit the bed hard. Finley held her down.

"How dare you betray me?" The fury in his voice terrified her. "How *dare* you?"

Fuck you, Angela thought. No matter how she struggled, she couldn't break free. *Let go of me!*

"Lie still," Finley growled.

Angela pulled back her legs and kicked out as hard as she could, striking him in the face, and Finley staggered backward, grunting in pain. Angela forced herself forward, trying to strike between his legs, but he jumped backward. She caught herself as he reached for her again, then rolled over and off the bed as he lunged forward. He caught her a glancing blow as she yanked herself to her feet. Finley was growling, madness clearly visible on his face.

Move, damn it, she told herself. Finley was coming after her, taking off his belt and swinging it madly. *You have to move.*

There was no time to try to open the emergency hatch, not when she wasn't sure it could be opened without power. Instead, she darted around the bed and ran for the other door.

He thinks we won't get out, she thought as she reached her open hatch. Her palm slapped the emergency button, desperately. She didn't know if it was working—the fact that Finley had somehow managed to enter the cabin without permission suggested it wasn't—but there was nothing to lose by trying.

She stopped outside, unsure which way to go. The master bedroom, where Nancy had been, or the hatch?

Finley burst through the door behind her, barreling into Angela and knocking her to the deck.

"Get off," she managed. The impact had knocked the breath out of her lungs. "Finley, get off!"

Finley ignored her. His face was so different that she hesitated to suggest he was human.

Despite feeling sick, she forced herself to breathe. "Finley . . ."

His face was consumed by lust and utter madness, the bruise on his cheek only making him look worse.

Angela drew back her legs and kicked again.

CHAPTER TWENTY-EIGHT

"They're still preaching," Carla said.

Matt nodded as he joined her by the hatch. Brother John and five of his brethren were in the brig, but the remainder were still trying to win converts. The preaching sounded pretty crappy, from what little he could hear, yet the audience was eating it up with spoons. And who could blame them? The Brethren were giving them *hope*.

He peered into the ballroom. "Can't we stop them?"

"I doubt we have the manpower," Carla said. "Getting a few dozen guests to actually *work* isn't easy. They're still gorging themselves on food."

Matt nodded. One upside to the whole crisis was that he'd been able to taste expensive foodstuffs he didn't have a hope of affording on his salary. He'd eaten his way through a dozen different pâtés and bread, then followed them up with jam that apparently cost a month's wages for a single pot. In truth, he hadn't considered any of the dishes to be particularly special. The only thing that gave the food any real significance was the price.

"That won't last," he said. "Some of the food has already spoiled."

Carla made a face. "Never mind that," she said. "What did you see on *Gladys*?"

"A floating tomb," Matt said. He quaked. He hadn't had a chance to catch any rest before he'd been ordered straight back on duty. "I . . ."

His wristcom bleeped, signaling an emergency alert. Matt looked down at it, surprised. He hadn't realized that some of the emergency systems had been rebooted. And then his blood ran cold as he realized where the signal was coming from. Angela's suite. She was in trouble . . .

"Come on," he said. "Hurry!"

He ran down the darkened corridor, one hand gripping the shock-rod at his belt. It wasn't that much more reliable than the stunners, he'd been warned, but he knew from experience that one could still use the device to deliver a nasty blow. And it was all he had. He'd hoped to be issued with a chemical weapon as he did have a firearms certification, but they were apparently being held back for trained security personnel.

The hatch to Angela's stateroom was ajar. As he peered inside, he could hear the sound of someone screaming. Angela was lying on the deck, Finley looming over her. The terror on Angela's face told him immediately that she wanted no part of what was happening. And then Finley looked up at him.

Matt recoiled. This wasn't Finley. Not the Finley who'd threatened his career if he didn't leave Angela alone. *This* Finley looked more like a snarling werewolf preparing to bite its prey. There was no humanity on his face at all, merely unbridled lust and anger. Matt fought down a primal urge to flee as he heard Carla entering behind him, tapping her wristcom to summon help. He knew it might be a long time in coming.

"Get away from her," he snapped, drawing the shockrod and thumbing the switch. It lit up with a sickly yellow color that vanished an instant later as the power cells failed. Matt swore. "Get away from her now."

Finley sprung to his feet and threw himself at Matt. Matt lifted the shockrod, but it was brushed aside as Finley crashed into him, growling like an animal. Matt fell backward, hitting the carpeted deck hard enough to hurt; he struggled, trying to throw Finley off before the aristocrat could choke him to death. He'd never thought of Finley as *strong* before—Matt had assumed his muscles came from a bodyshop—but grappling with him was like grappling with a lion. Finley seemed driven to hurt Matt as much as possible.

"Get off him," Carla bellowed.

She brought her shockrod down on Finley's back, hard. His entire body jerked as the charge ran through him. Matt jerked too, feeling the unpleasant tingle running through his form even though he wasn't the target. But the shock didn't stop Finley. He should have been a twitching wreck, unable to move a muscle; instead, he was still trying to hammer Matt into a pulp. It was all the steward could do to keep dodging his blows.

He doesn't know what he's doing, Matt thought numbly. It was hard to move. Sooner or later, Finley would score a direct hit. *If he knew . . .*

Carla zapped Finley again. The madman's body jerked, but somehow he remained conscious. Matt saw his chance and slammed a fist into Finley's throat, sending him into a choking fit. Carla hauled him off Matt and shoved him to the ground, then sat on his chest and punched his face again and again. The sheer level of hatred on her face shocked Matt to the core. He disliked Finley too, and it was clear the asshole had been trying to rape Angela, but Carla . . . ?

"I think he's stunned," Matt said. "Carla . . ."

His friend looked up. "I think so too," she said without emotion. "Find something to bind his hands."

"There's some duct tape in Marie's cabin," Angela said. She sounded haunted. Her body was covered in bruises. "I'll find it."

Matt watched her go until Carla yanked his arm, hard. "She's nearly been raped," Carla hissed so quietly that Matt could barely hear her. "*Don't* try anything with her. Do you understand me?"

"Yes," Matt said. Sexual assault was unusual in the Commonwealth—it was normally easy to identify the perpetrator and prove what actually had happened—but pirates were fond of raping their unimportant captives. "I—"

"I'll deal with her," Carla said, cutting him off. "You take care of the bastard."

Matt took the duct tape from Angela and used it to secure Finley's hands behind his back, then bind his legs together. He had no idea how Finley had managed to remain conscious after being zapped twice with a shockrod, but it didn't matter. No one could break through several layers of duct tape without more enhancement than a military super-soldier . . .

"Nancy was in the master bedroom," Angela said. Her voice was deadened, completely drained of vigor. "Can you check on her?"

"I'll do that now," Matt said. He didn't want to look at Angela, not now. She deserved some privacy. "Carla, can you take Angela into her bedroom?"

"Of course," Carla said, sounding oddly insulted. "You check on Nancy."

The door to the master bedroom was closed and locked. Matt hoped that Finley had locked it before going after Angela, although he had no way to know for sure. He unlocked the door and stepped inside, holding his shockrod in one hand. Nancy was sitting on the bed, staring out into the luminous, eerie green light. She showed no sign of knowing he was there until he put a hand on her shoulder.

"Matt," she said. She didn't appear to be alarmed. "What happened?"

"Finley tried to attack your sister," Matt said. Had Nancy missed everything? But then, the door had been closed, and the suite was fairly soundproofed. The guests didn't want their servants or children hearing them making love under the stars. "Are you all right?"

Nancy looked up at him. "Is *she* all right?"

"I think so," Matt said. He wasn't entirely sure. "Do you want to see her?"

Nancy didn't answer. "I can *hear* them," she said, nodding towards the windows. Uncanny greenish-yellow light flooded into the room. "They're talking."

Matt felt his blood run cold. "What are they *saying*?"

"I don't know," Nancy said. "But I can hear them."

"You told me you heard voices in hyperspace," Matt said. He wasn't entirely sure he wanted to ask the next question, but he had no choice. "What do you think they are?"

". . . *Things*," Nancy said. "I can hear them, but . . ."

Matt closed his eyes for a long moment. He'd have to bring this to the captain's attention. If the rumors—and the Brethren—were correct, *something* was out there. He couldn't deny that he'd felt watched ever since they'd been dragged through the distortion, or that the sensation had been stronger on *Gladys*. Nancy might be the key to *communicating* with the . . . with the whatever they were.

"I'm sure your sister will be fine," he said, instead. Outside, he could hear the security team arriving . . . finally. Finley would wake up in the brig if there was any space left. "And then I think you need to have a word with the captain."

Nancy looked pensive. "Do you think he'll tell me how to command a starship?"

Matt blinked. "You go to the academy and learn," he said. "You can enter Piker's Peak at sixteen if your grades are high enough."

"I will," Nancy said. She turned to look out the window. "If they ever let us go."

———

"I need to ask some questions," Carla said. "I need you to keep focused."

Angela wished Carla would just shut up. Right now, she wanted . . . she didn't know *what* she wanted. An armed bodyguard, perhaps. Or a team of marines. Or whatever it took to make her feel safe again.

Finley hadn't stolen her maidenhead, but he'd stolen her sense of *security*. The universe was no longer a safe place. She should have realized that *years* ago.

"He was trying to rape you," Carla said. Having it put into words was somehow all the more horrifying. "Did he actually succeed?"

"No," Angela said. Her memories were jumbled, but she was fairly sure Finley hadn't managed to do more than batter her into submission. "He . . . I . . . I fought him."

"Good for you," Carla said, a hint of warmth in her voice. "What happened?"

Angela fought to keep her memories straight. "He came into my room," she said. Her hands began to shake as she remembered the moment he'd touched her. "We argued . . . he threw me to the bed. I managed to escape, but he caught me outside and . . ." She shook her head. "Thank you."

"You've been very lucky," Carla said. "Did you hit the emergency button?"

"Yeah," Angela said.

"That called us here," Carla said. "Good thinking."

Angela smiled despite her shaking hands. "He . . . he was going to *rape* me."

"He's done worse," Carla said. A shadow crossed her face as Angela looked up. "Believe me; he's done worse."

Angela blinked. "What do you mean?"

"He . . . *invited* . . . me into his cabin a few times," Carla said. "It wasn't a pleasant experience."

"Oh," Angela said. She found herself casting around for something to say. "Why didn't you report him?"

Carla made a rude noise. "To who?"

Angela swallowed. "Captain VanGundy?"

"Hah," Carla said. She picked up a pair of trousers and thrust them at Angela. "It may surprise you to know that no one gives a damn about people like me. There are millions of young girls desperate for a job like mine. If I bitch about someone like *him*, guess who Corporate is going to believe." She shrugged, callously. "Being married to *him* would have been a nightmare."

"I didn't know," Angela said.

"It's always the quiet ones," Carla said. "You never know what's hidden behind their masks until it's too late. And the ones who have the money to make their fantasies real . . . he got off on making me hurt. Maybe he would have been nicer to you. I don't know. But you never know what a person is like until you see them without the masks."

"I thought I knew him," Angela said. "I thought I . . ." She shook her head. "The marriage is off," she said firmly. "I don't care any longer."

"Good for you," Carla said. She tossed a jumper at Angela. "Get dressed. I don't know if there's any point in filing a formal report or not, but you'll probably want a word with your father. Or the captain."

Angela felt cold. What if . . . what if her mother and father didn't *listen*? Her marriage had been arranged because the family *needed* Finley's family. What if Father told her to marry him anyway? She found it hard to imagine that he would; the snarling monster Finley had become was not the sort of person who might be of any real use. But it was hard to escape the quiet, nagging doubts. God knew where her mother *was* . . .

"Thanks," she said. She felt unwilling to get dressed. "What . . . why does it happen?"

"Because someone thought he could get away with it," Carla said. She sounded vaguely interested. "Is that really what you wanted to ask?"

Angela looked down at the deck. "Does it get better?"

"I was raped when I was a couple of years younger than you," Carla said. Her voice was quiet. "There was . . . never mind. Suffice it to say that I didn't have a hope of fighting him off. He had his fun and left me lying there. It was all I could do to drag myself up and report it to the police. They caught him a few days later and . . . and, well, he's still in a work camp. Asshole refused the opportunity to be dropped on a penal colony when he had the chance."

Her voice hardened. "I could have sunk into myself. I could have allowed it to dominate the rest of my life. Instead, I threw myself into my studies. I graduated well, got a good job . . . I thought a couple of years on *Supreme* would give me a nice little nest egg. I could put up with assholes like *him* if it meant getting paid enough to retire early."

Angela swallowed. Marie had told her that some girls had to go through hell to earn money, but . . . but she'd never really believed it. Carla had actually *been* raped. And she'd somehow kept going, pushing her way through life. Angela could do it too.

"I won't let him win," she said. She promised herself, silently, that she'd file a report for Carla too. And if her father tried to tell her she should marry Finley anyway, she'd black his eye. "I won't."

"Good," Carla said. She glanced towards the hatch. "Put on your clothes. There are some people outside who want to talk to you."

———

"Well," a wry voice said, "what are *you* in for?"

Finley barely heard it. The roaring in his head was overpowering. Someone was shouting at him, mocking him . . . he had visions of Angela, naked and lovely, then . . . he wasn't sure of anything anymore. All he knew was that he wanted her, that he wanted to make her submit to him . . . like the others. But they hadn't been *real*. They'd do anything as long as he paid them. The voices encouraged him, urging him onwards. He couldn't make out actual words, but no matter. He *knew* what they were saying.

He forced his eyes to open. He was in a cramped room . . . a cell. A prison cell. His hands were bound tightly behind his back. Hot anger flared through him. Didn't they know who he was? How *dare* they leave him in a cell like a common criminal? He looked around, feeling his head starting to pound as the voices grew louder. A robed man was sitting on a bunk looking down at him. Who was he?

"Stop shouting," he said somehow. He felt another surge of pure rage and staggered under the impact. "What are you doing?"

"That is the voice of the gods," the robed man informed him. "They are speaking to you."

"How nice," Finley said. He struggled against his bonds. "Let me go!"

"The gods have a purpose for you, Finley Mackintosh," the robed man said. "You wouldn't be here if they hadn't called you."

The voices rose to a crescendo, then fell back into the background. Finley moaned. It was hard, so hard, to think straight. He wanted Angela, his bride-to-be. He had a right to her . . . didn't he? He'd have to teach her to mind her place, of course, but afterwards . . . she was his. The voices whispered to him, promising the world. He could have whatever he wanted, if he did their bidding.

"I believe you can help me find someone," the robed man added. His expression twisted into something that might charitably be called a smile. "A special young lady."

Angela, Finley thought. He felt another hot flush of anger. Angela was *his*. He wasn't going to share. And then it struck him. *Nancy*.

"You want Nancy," he managed. The Brethren believed their gods lived in hyperspace . . . and Nancy was the first child *born* in hyperspace. Or at least the first one within reach. "Don't you?"

"Of course," the robed man said calmly. The voices started to rise again, growing louder and louder. "Will you help us?"

Finley closed his eyes and surrendered. "Yeah."

"Good," the robed man said. "Be ready. It's only a matter of time before we leave this place."

CHAPTER TWENTY-NINE

"Are you sure this is going to work?"

"No, Captain," Dr. Joan Mackey said. Her eyes were lined with dark circles. Paul didn't think she'd had any sleep since *Supreme* fell through the distortion. "But it's the only option on the table."

Paul nodded sourly. Nancy appeared to have a connection to the aliens . . . or *something*, at least. Joan had suggested hypnosis, reasoning that Nancy might not have any conscious control over the connection. And Paul had had to ask Robert Cavendish for his permission to proceed. And *then* Nancy had refused to undergo the procedure unless her sister was allowed into the room too.

"This looks like something from a bad movie," Slater muttered.

"That's where I got the idea," Joan said. She shot him a venomous look. "Can you think of a better one?"

"That will do," Paul said. He felt tired too. The exhaustion felt chillingly unnatural. "Shall we begin?"

He looked at the chair. Nancy sat there, cloth restraints wrapped around her wrists and ankles. She looked tiny, helpless . . . he felt a stab of guilt for putting her through the procedure, even though he knew he had no choice. Would he have felt better if Nancy had been older, more able to give informed consent? It certainly would have soothed his conscience more.

She refused to allow her father to watch, Paul thought. *Why?*

"The medical telltales aren't working," Joan said. Paul put his worries aside. "Right now, they're insisting that Nancy is a forty-year-old man!"

"I'm twelve," Nancy protested. Beside her, Angela giggled nervously. "I have a birth certificate to prove it."

Joan ignored her. "Angela, I want you to keep a close eye on your sister," she ordered. "If you think something is wrong, let me know at once."

"I will," Angela said.

Paul sucked in his breath as Joan dimmed the lights, then knelt beside Nancy and began the induction. The doctor hadn't been having an easy time of it, not when half her medical tools were either offline or dangerously unreliable. All Joan's normal tricks for monitoring a patient's health were gone, forcing her to rely on guesswork. She had plenty of experience and training, Paul knew, but hardly anyone had been made to work without advanced technology for centuries. Even battlefield medics had more equipment when they deployed to a combat zone.

We'll have to expand our training programs, he thought. Losing so many systems had never really been contemplated, not when there were so many redundancies built into the starship's hull. *And cram more ration bars into storage.*

Joan's soft voice washed over him, threatening to lull him to sleep. Nancy looked fatigued, her chin already nodding towards her chest. Paul couldn't help feeling there was something fundamentally wrong about the whole procedure, even though he *knew* it was safe. Hypnosis had a bad reputation, but it was nothing compared to personality reconditioning or subversion implants.

And Angela had the nerve to joke about Nancy being programmed to cluck like a chicken, Paul thought. He would have felt sorry for the older girl if he hadn't had a hundred different problems to cope with. Angela would have to recover from her ordeal on her own. *Joan was very insistent it didn't work that way.*

He looked at Angela. The older girl looked to be on the verge of nodding off too. Her chin would drift downward, only to snap up a moment later. Paul shot her an encouraging glance, promising himself that he'd have a word with her father later. If they were truly trapped, it might be time for Robert Cavendish to make peace with his daughter before it was too late. Paul had no illusions. *Gladys* hadn't managed to escape, and *Supreme* might suffer the same fate.

"You're going deeper and deeper now," Joan said softly. "You're drifting in a pool of light, listening to the voices. Can you hear the voices?"

"Yes," Nancy breathed.

Paul tensed. Her voice sounded . . . *different.* There was a harder edge to it now, something cutting and foul. The sense of threat was palpable. He touched the butt of his pistol before realizing that he was being silly. Nancy was twelve, small for her age . . . and restrained. But Finley Mackintosh had fought like a wildcat before he'd been subdued. Robert Cavendish had even confirmed that Mackintosh hadn't had any genetic enhancement or military training.

Not that Cavendish's words prove anything, Paul reminded himself. *Finley could easily have hired private trainers and then covered it up afterwards.*

"You can hear the voices," Joan said. "Can you make out their words?"

Nancy's face twisted, baring her teeth. "Hungry."

"Shit," Angela muttered.

Joan shot her a look that said, very clearly, *Be quiet.* Paul tapped his lips firmly, warning the girl to keep her mouth closed. They had to know what they were dealing with, whatever the cost. And if that meant Nancy getting hurt . . . he swallowed, hard. He'd thought he knew how to make the big decisions, but perhaps he didn't have it in him after all.

"Hungry," Nancy said. Her voice was extremely different now, inhuman. Blood dribbled down her chin from where she'd bitten her lip. "We are hungry."

Joan exchanged glances with Paul. "Who is hungry?"

"We are," Nancy said. Her face shifted in the dimmed light. For a terrifying moment, Paul was *sure* she was going to explode in front of them. "You will feed us."

Paul took a breath. Aliens. They were dealing with aliens. He reminded himself, sharply, that their concepts of logic and reason, or morality, might be radically different from humanity's. If these beings were hungry . . . what did they want to eat? He trembled as he remembered the growing power drain, the fatigue that was wearing his crew and passengers down. Were the aliens feeding on his ship and crew?

"I am Captain VanGundy of the Royal Tyre Navy," he said, carefully. None of the first-contact protocols had covered *this* situation. Clearly the planners had experienced a failure of imagination. "To whom am I speaking?"

"We are who we are," Nancy said. Her voice was still inhuman. She turned her head to look at him. "We are hungry."

Paul gritted his teeth. He'd envisaged a peaceful, diplomatic solution. But it sounded as if they couldn't hope to *really* communicate with the aliens.

"You brought us here," he said. "Why?"

"You will feed us," Nancy informed him. Her eyes suddenly seemed darker, as if something else was peering through them. "You will feed us."

"With what?" Paul asked. "What can we feed you?"

"You. Your energy."

Paul cursed under his breath. The aliens wanted . . . energy? First the power cells, then . . . then the ship's crew. No *wonder* every other ship in the graveyard was as dead as the dodo. The aliens had steadily drained them of life until every last spark was gone. He wondered, briefly, if he could leave the Brethren and a few of their converts behind if they wished to stay. He'd prefer to put them all in the brig, just to keep them out of trouble, but he didn't have the manpower to enforce the decision. And they knew it too.

"Where are you?" he asked. Perhaps they could locate the alien base . . . if there *was* an alien base. So far, the only things they'd detected were derelict ships and impassable energy storms. "We could come to you."

Nancy giggled. The sound was chilling. "We are everywhere."

A colorful glimmer danced at the corner of Paul's eye, just for a second. His blood froze as it all fell into place. He wasn't dealing with humanoid aliens; he wasn't even dealing with *matter*-based aliens. The aliens were native to hyperspace, so far beyond his ability to perceive them that all he could see were the tiny flickers. And yet, they were all around him. How could his crew plan an escape when the aliens were watching them?

A thought struck him. "What did you do to Nancy?"

"We touched her," Nancy said. "When the time came, we called to her."

Paul, oddly, found that a little reassuring. It was possible, just *possible*, that the aliens had as little ability to influence the matter universe as humanity had to interfere with *their* universe. Come to think of it, the problem of actually seeing one's enemy might apply to them as well. They could drain the starship's power, perhaps even direct energy storms to cripple the starship, but beyond that, their abilities were limited. There was no sign of alien storm troopers threatening to board *Supreme*.

Careful, he told himself firmly. *You don't know any of that for sure.*

Nancy's body twitched. "We are everywhere," she said. "This is our realm."

"Some of us will stay behind, if you let the rest go," Paul said carefully. The Brethren . . . and that damnable serial killer. He was past caring about making sure the asshole reached Britannia. "We could—"

"You will all come to us," Nancy said. Her body jerked, then twisted violently. "We are everywhere."

Angela looked up. "She's having an attack!"

"She's going into shock," Joan said as Nancy started to struggle against the restraints. The doctor pressed an injector tab against the girl's neck. She should have been out like a light, but Nancy kept fighting desperately. "Captain, she's being drained!"

She was born in hyperspace, Paul thought. *Did they tag her when she was born for future attention?*

"You will all come to us," Nancy growled. Her body convulsed. She threw up violently, then started to choke. "You will all come to us."

She sagged, then collapsed. A foul stench filled the air. Paul realized, to his horror, that she'd voided her bowels too. Flashing lights darted past him. He reached out to swat one of them, only to see it vanish before his fingers made contact. And even if he *had* touched it, part of his mind noted, it wouldn't have made any difference. No one had been able to touch the flickers. They were . . . just *there*.

Joan undid the straps, then moved Nancy to an examination table. "Her heart's beating rapidly, Captain," she said, "but I think she's in no immediate danger. I think they tried to force her body to flush out the sedative, unsuccessfully."

Paul nodded, coldly. He needed to think. They *all* needed to think. And then they had to find a way out of the lobster pot before it was too late.

"When she wakes up . . ." He swallowed and started again. "When she wakes up, make sure she's restrained until we know what we're dealing with," he said. "Is there any way to monitor her brain waves?"

"Not with what we have on hand," Joan said. Her eyes darkened in frustration. People were dying because she lacked the tools to save them. "Engineering *might* be able to put together something a little more primitive, but . . . but I don't know if they have time."

"She's no longer the only one hearing voices anyway," Paul muttered. There had *always* been reports of voices in hyperspace, but no one had ever believed them. Not really. Now . . . now he suspected the voices had been all too real. "Is there anything we can do about that?"

"I don't know," Joan said. "Captain, we have a very limited supply of sedatives. If we hand them out to everyone, we'd run out within hours."

Angela cleared her throat. Paul jumped. He'd practically forgotten she was there.

"What about stimulants?" Angela asked. "You could try to keep people awake instead . . ."

"That would be risky," Joan said. "No matter what you took, you'd start running up against hard limits very quickly. I might be able to keep someone awake for three or four days using civilian-grade pills, but they'd be seeing things by the third day. And without the implants and tools I'd normally use to monitor someone's internal state, I'd be reluctant to risk it."

"And it would come crashing down eventually," Paul added. He'd seen people *die* after taking too many stimulants. Their hearts couldn't take the stress and eventually gave out. Most spacers had nanites to compensate for the stimulants, but even *they* had limits. "After two or three days, you'd fall into sleep, if you were lucky. I've seen it happen during the war."

He wondered, briefly, what would happen if he triggered the self-destruct and blew up the entire ship. Would that spite the aliens, if nothing else? Or would it just give them everything they wanted at once? He frowned as he remembered a note from the recovered logbook. The nukes had detonated, but the detonation had been . . . odd. Had the aliens tried to drain the power even as the nukes exploded?

"Take care of your sister," he told Angela. He looked at Joan. "Keep me informed, please."

"Yes, Captain," Joan said. "I'll let you know when she wakes up."

Paul keyed his wristcom as he walked through the hatch. "Keep working on the salvage operation," he ordered when the bridge responded. "We may have less time than we thought."

A glimmer of light darted past, mocking him. He ignored it. If he was right, the aliens had as much trouble perceiving humans as humans had perceiving them. And if he was wrong, they were dead anyway. He saw no point in fretting about something outside his control.

———

"She's so *small*," Angela said as Joan wiped Nancy down. "Has she grown smaller?"

"Your perceptions of her have changed," Joan said briskly. "That's not exactly uncommon."

Angela scowled. She wished, suddenly, that she'd spent more time with Nancy. Sure, there were seven years between them, but they could still have been friends. And yet, it would have meant social death for both of them. Nancy couldn't take part in adult activities, and Angela would be a laughing stock if she joined childish games and . . .

She shook her head, silently rebuking herself. Nancy was dying . . . they were *all* dying. Her friends, the ones who had seemed so important, were on the other side of the distortion, hundreds of light-years away. They'd thought they were rebelling, but . . . she knew, now, that they'd been childish brats in adult bodies. None of them were prepared for adulthood.

I wouldn't have been so concerned about looking mature if I'd actually been *mature*, Angela thought. She could have spent a lot more time with her sister. She promised herself that she would if they ever made it home. *And I'll work harder too.*

She looked at the doctor. "Can't you give her a proper bath?"

"There's a water shortage," Joan reminded her. "How are *you* feeling?"

Angela shook her head, gently. In truth, she'd forgotten about her aches and pains the moment the session started. Her body had been slow to recover, despite the genetic engineering spliced into her DNA. She told herself, firmly, that it didn't matter. Nancy was in a far worse state.

"I've been better," she said. She wanted a bath too, though she'd settle for a shower. "Take care of her."

She stepped through the door and into the antechamber. Marie would be down there, she knew, helping to tend to the wounded. Angela suspected she should probably go join her governess, but . . . but she didn't know what she wanted to do. It didn't matter anyway, she told herself. If she'd learned one thing over the last few days, it was that the universe was no longer guided by her whims. In truth, it had *never* been so.

Matt was sitting on a chair, half-asleep. He jumped when she touched him.

"Angela," he stammered. "Are you . . . are you all right?"

"No," Angela said, sitting down beside him. "Are *you* all right?"

"That bastard caught me a few nasty blows," Matt said. He shook his head. "And the shockrod didn't help either. I don't know how he shrugged it off."

"He was like a different person," Angela said. She leaned into Matt. After a moment of hesitation, he put an arm around her. "Is that . . . are we all going to go mad here?"

"I don't know," Matt said. He glanced down at his wristcom. "I have to be at the shuttlebay in twenty minutes."

Angela frowned. "What for?"

"We're going to visit one of the alien ships," Matt said. He sounded as though he would be excited if he wasn't so tired. "I'll be glad to be away from *Supreme* for a while."

"I don't blame you," Angela said. She opened her mouth to ask about what Carla had shared, then decided to change the subject. That was *Carla's* story to tell. "Matt . . . what's going to happen to us?"

"I don't know," Matt said. He yawned. "If we can get out of here, we'll be free."

And if not, we'll be dead, Angela thought. *And who cares what happens then?*

She wrapped her arms around him and kissed his lips, as hard as she could. He seemed surprised, but kissed her back with the same intensity. She felt his body shivering against her . . . she expected to feel horror, or fear, but . . . Finley hadn't ruined her. She could touch another man and not be repulsed. And he could touch her too . . .

"Come back," she whispered, putting as much promise into her words as she could. "I want to see you again."

Matt kissed her again. "I will," he promised quietly. "I'll see you soon."

CHAPTER THIRTY

"That is one *eerie* ship," Lieutenant Avis Grosskopf said.

Matt couldn't disagree. The vessel looked like a squashed spider washed with spooky green light. The team was unable to tell which end was the prow and which was the stern, if such concepts had meant anything to the alien designers in the first place. Giant gangly struts—he tried hard not to think of them as *legs*—ran out in all directions, bending and twisting seemingly at random. His head hurt when he looked at them too closely, as if they went in directions the human eye wasn't designed to follow. The thought of *boarding* the alien ship made him want to wet himself in fear. It was powerless, as far as anyone could tell, but . . .

"Remember the procedures," Slater warned. If the security chief was nervous, there was no sign of it in his voice. "Remain in your suits at all times. If you encounter extraterrestrial life, remain calm and alert me . . ."

Matt kept his thoughts to himself as they made their way down towards what *looked* like a command core. The spider's body—he told himself, again, that it wasn't a *real* spider—had to be the command center, didn't it? But then nothing could be taken for granted. He couldn't imagine any merely *human* designer building the spider-craft, then sending it into interstellar space. Something about its appearance resonated with humanity's deepest, darkest fears. He wished, suddenly, that they'd thought to pick another craft. They didn't *have* to inspect the ship closest to *Supreme* first.

Up close, the alien hull looked rugged. He tried hard not to think of it as dried skin. Slater landed neatly on the hull and bent down to inspect it, touching it lightly with his armored hands. Matt followed him, feeling a chill as he realized that the hull felt springy under his feet. He told himself, firmly, that he was imagining the sensation. The aliens couldn't have built a biological starship, could they?

Maybe they could, he thought. Terrifyingly, some of the alien starships were clearly far more advanced than anything humanity had ever launched into space. *We didn't even know that aliens* existed *until we arrived in the graveyard.*

He looked around. A set of something . . . *eyeballs*, perhaps . . . were embedded in the hull, unmoving. He forced himself to inspect them, despite the fear reflex that made him want to throw himself back into space. The eyes looked insectoid. He told himself, once again, that there was nothing to be scared of. There was no reason to think there was anything waiting for them inside the ship but dead aliens. He looked along the hull, noting other eyeballs and protrusions. God alone knew what they were for.

"I think I see a hatch," Slater said. "Come with me."

Matt followed him as they made their way towards a small bump in the hull. Up close, it looked like a trapdoor . . . a well-hidden trapdoor. If it hadn't been slightly ajar, they might never have noticed. His skin crawled as Slater took the edge of the hatch in his hands and lifted it up, revealing another hatch farther inside the ship. It too was ajar.

"They hid the airlock," Avis breathed. "What sort of people *were* they?"

"I remember seeing a trapdoor spider in the zoo," Slater commented, sounding edgy. "It really was a remarkable creature. Its nest was almost completely hidden, almost impossible to spot against the grass. When something small and vulnerable came along, the spider popped out, caught the prey, and dragged it inside the nest."

"Where it was devoured," Lieutenant Robinson muttered. "Does that mean we're walking into a trap?"

"The ship appears to be powerless, and vented," Slater snapped. "There's no reason to believe that something is still alive in here."

Matt said nothing as they made their way towards the inner hatch. The bulkheads looked as though they'd been made from spider webs, although a quick touch convinced him that they were actually solid; the hatch itself looked to have been braided together like a basket, then firmly webbed into place. He couldn't escape the sense that the aliens had *spun* the ship as casually as a tiny spider might craft a web. He wondered, as they forced their way through the hatch, just what advantages the vessels had over human technology. Perhaps the alien ship could repair itself over time.

"Fuck," Slater breathed as he shone his light down the corridor. "Just *look* at it."

"Awesome," Matt agreed.

The craft was . . . *alien*, very alien. He found it hard to wrap his head around what he was seeing. The corridors looked like underground tunnels, lined with solid webbing and . . . and something. Getting a sense of which way was up was challenging, let alone fathoming out a logic to the system. He wondered if the beings had bothered to install gravity generators on their ships. Something about the design reminded him of the early spacecraft and space stations before artificial gravity had been invented. Those designs had never needed to follow the limits of anything built in a gravity field. There had been a randomness about them that no modern starship matched.

"Good thinking," Slater said when Matt shared his ideas. "The aliens might not have needed a gravity field at all."

"They might have used the webbing to propel themselves along," Avis agreed. She sounded calmer now that they were starting to comprehend what they were seeing. "Do you think they actually *looked* like spiders?"

"Humans have lived in weird places too," Robinson offered. He unspooled a length of thread, securing one end to the airlock. "For all we know, the aliens were humanoid too."

Matt followed Slater down the corridor, peering into branching corridors and chambers as they slowly explored the ship. It was impossible to guess the purpose of any of the chambers—one was filled with a frozen jellylike substance, another crammed with something that resembled seeds—and he felt his head start to numb as he took in more and more bizarre sights. There were no bodies, as far as he could tell . . . he wondered, ominously, if they'd all crumbled into dust. He couldn't even begin to guess just how long the alien craft had been trapped in the graveyard. It could have been caught for over a million years.

Hyperspace wears away at hulls, he reminded himself. *The graveyard can't be that old.*

He peered into a compartment and froze. Just for a second, his mind refused to grasp what he was seeing. Something was *clinging* to the webbing on the far side of the compartment, something . . . inhuman. His mind actually had difficulty tracing its lines, even as his heart pounded in his chest, urging him to turn tail and run. The alien . . .

"Sir," he managed. "I think you should take a look at this."

He forced himself to move farther into the compartment. The alien—the alien *body*—didn't move, but it was hard to escape the sensation that it was just preparing to spring. He tapped his recorder, hoping it was working as he captured the scene. He was the first human to set eyes on an alien, albeit a dead one, and yet he wished someone else had the honor. The creature was just too creepy to be real.

Avis was right, he thought numbly. *It is a giant spider.*

He looked closer, despite the crawling sensation at the back of his neck. The alien was roughly the same size as Nancy, covered in brownish fur that looked to be standing on end; it was far larger than any spider he knew to exist, large enough to worry him. The creature had a mass of legs, some broken . . . he swallowed hard as he realized, again, that the spiders had experienced the same problems as *Gladys* when they'd arrived in the graveyard. Its body was covered with eyes, peering in all directions. He couldn't help thinking that it would've been impossible to sneak up on the creature. There was no way to tell which end was its head and which end was its feet, if such expressions had any meaning for the spiders. The being looked capable of moving in all directions without turning.

"Remarkable," Slater breathed.

"That's not quite how I'd put it, sir," Avis said. She sounded as though she was going to be sick. "It's too large. It shouldn't have evolved at all."

"Perhaps it evolved on a low-gravity planet," Matt speculated. "Or maybe it evolved in outer space itself."

"That's not possible," Avis said.

"There are people who *do* live in space without spacesuits," Robinson pointed out.

"But only after extensive genetic enhancements and augmentation," Avis snapped. Her voice hadn't improved. "They're not *born* in space."

Matt nodded. He'd never seen a live space-dweller, but he'd viewed pictures. The modified humans were practically tiny spacecraft in their own right, as if they'd merged themselves with their spacesuits. God knew most of them couldn't live safely within a gravity well. They tended to cluster above gas giants and . . . and do what? He couldn't imagine.

"Bag up the body," Slater ordered. "Avis, wait outside."

Avis did as she was told without protest. Matt found that worrying as he tried to pull the alien away from the webbing. Two legs crumbled into dust at his touch before he figured out how to remove the body safely. The alien seemed to twist as he freed it—just for a second, he had an impression of teeth and claws before it spun away—and he jumped. Somehow the creature still felt alive.

He reached out and touched it gingerly, slowing its spin. The creature's underside—he assumed it was the underside, at least for the moment—had a set of gaping mouths, crammed with pointed teeth and powerful jaws. He wondered what it ate before deciding he didn't want to know. More eyes were clearly visible between the mouths, allowing the alien to inspect its food. How had it managed to see in all directions at once?

"Focus," Slater snapped. "Bag it up!"

Matt carefully wrapped the alien in the bag, then sealed it. The decontaminant team would know what to do, he hoped. There was no way to be *sure* the alien was completely dead, after all. If they were native to space—or even far more experienced with biological technology—they might survive cold vacuum. It sounded like something from a bad movie, and he'd seen two legs disintegrate, but he knew better than to overlook the possibility. They'd just have to pray to God they could handle any threat the aliens presented.

Or at least this set of aliens, he thought. The captain's briefing had made it clear: The graveyard was ruled by aliens who wanted to drain the ship and crew of every last spark of power. *Supreme* had to escape before it was too late. *The spiders should be our allies.*

He left the bag by the airlock, then followed Slater and the others farther into the ship. The mission would be easier, *much* easier, if they'd had more technology with them, but everything they might have been able to use was offline. A properly outfitted survey ship would probably have been able to do a great deal more. Matt suspected that the glory of being the first humans to discover proof of alien life would be tempered by everyone complaining about ham-fisted archaeological research. It wasn't as if any of them actually *knew* what they were doing, was it?

The team discovered two more bodies as they made their way through what he assumed to have been a wardroom, although he knew there was no way to be sure. Both aliens looked to have been beaten to death, their exoskeletons broken and smashed. He glanced around nervously, unsure if they'd killed each other or if there was a *third* being lurking in the shadows. But there was nothing save for omnipresent flickers of light.

"I think this is a command center," Avis said as she peered into yet another compartment. "Take a look at it . . ."

Her voice trailed off as the compartment lit up. Matt jumped, drawing his pistol and glancing around nervously. The bulkheads were glowing, a pearly white light illuminating the giant space. A dozen aliens were visible, bent over pieces of webbing and metal woven cunningly into the deck. He expected them to start moving, but they were all clearly dead. Or biding their time. He held his pistol firmly in one hand as he examined the closest creature.

"Bioluminescent lights," Slater muttered. "These guys were *good.*"

"They weren't *drained,*" Avis said. Her voice was frantic. "Why weren't they drained?"

"Unknown," Slater said. "Perhaps there was something about them that meant they *couldn't* be drained."

"Perhaps they operate on very low power," Matt speculated. He knew there were some plants and animals that were bioluminescent, but he couldn't remember very much about them. "The power drain seems to target large stockpiles of power first."

"Or perhaps this whole ship is a trap," Avis hissed. Matt didn't like the way she was waving her pistol in the air. "They're hunting us right now!"

"Remain calm," Slater ordered. "There's no reason to be alarmed."

Matt carefully removed one of the aliens from its stump. He'd expected to see a console, but instead, he saw a strange mix between a rotting tree and spider's nest. The alien had been directly linked into the ship, he realized slowly. Humans could, in theory, use implants to do the same, but it wasn't favored. There was too great a chance of accidentally causing a real disaster.

And if we relied on our implants to control Supreme, he thought, *we'd all be dead by now.*

"This needs a bigger team with more tech, sir," he said slowly. "I don't understand what I'm looking at."

"Nor do I," Slater said. "The engineers will have to take a look."

Matt suspected the engineers were too busy. A third of them, and a handful of volunteers from among the guests, were busy salvaging as much as they could from *Gladys*, while the remainder were doing *something* with the power cells and the vortex generator. He had no way to know if it was anything more than busywork, but at least it was keeping some of the guests occupied. And maybe the captain had a plan to get them out after all.

He swept his recorder around, making sure to capture as much as he could, then followed the others through a different hatch. The corridors seemed to twist and turn at random, leading down towards the bowels of the ship . . . or were they going up? The craft was so . . . so *alien* . . . that it was easy to believe that someone could get lost within its maze of corridors. Losing the thread would be disastrous.

The lights followed them, throwing the corridor into sharp relief. Matt gritted his teeth, trying not to look too closely. Darkness and shadows were spooky, but . . . something about the light gnawed at him. He found it hard to *look* into the glow. The corridor twisted, then plunged straight down. Matt drifted down, silently relieved that there was no gravity. It was clear, now, that the spiders hadn't needed gravity at all. Judging by their physical form, they'd probably been happier outside a gravity field.

He swallowed, his mouth dry, as he considered the implications. Just how alien *were* the spiders? Were they individuals or one vast hive mind? Was the entire starship a nest? Did they have sex or lay eggs or reproduce in a manner completely beyond his imagination? Or . . . could they even *talk* to humans? It was impossible to imagine those awful mouths shaping human words.

The light grew brighter as he dropped into a large chamber. A single alien was attached to a console, but the remainder of the chamber was empty. It was dominated by four large pods, firmly entangled within the webbing. Warning signals popped up in Matt's HUD, alerting him to strong magnetic fields. Whatever was in the pods, he thought, the creatures definitely hadn't wanted it to get out.

"Antimatter," Slater breathed.

Avis coughed. "Are you *sure*?"

"I think so," Slater said. "What *else* needs magnetic fields for containment?"

"The fields are still operative," Matt said. That didn't make sense. The power drain should have killed them long ago. But then, if the power had failed, the alien ship would have been atomized. "Did they . . . did the flickers leave the fields alone?"

"It looks that way," Slater said. He frowned. "There might be limits to what they can absorb."

Matt glanced at him. "And if we detonated the antimatter pods, we might be able to overfeed them," he said. Maybe the flickers could be overfed to death. "Would that work?"

"I don't know," Slater said. He sounded worried. "First, we have to confirm that the pods really *are* antimatter. And then we have to make sure the fields aren't on the verge of failing anyway."

Matt swallowed. Antimatter was the single most destructive substance known to mankind. It was used for missile warheads, if he recalled correctly, but not much else. If the pods lost containment, the foreign ship would be vaporized, and *Supreme* would be badly damaged, perhaps destroyed. They needed to move the alien vessel *away* before something happened.

"I need to consult with the captain," Slater said. "We'll return to the ship."

"Yes, sir," Matt said. Angela was waiting for him. "And then we'll come back?"

"Not if we can help it," Avis muttered. "The voices are growing louder."

"Ignore them," Slater ordered. "Let's go."

CHAPTER THIRTY-ONE

"So tell me," Marie said. She jabbed a finger at a dead body. "In your *expert* opinion, what killed him?"

Angela didn't quite glare at her governess, but she wanted to. Marie had offered a brief apology for not being there for Angela when the hypnosis session had taken place, then put her to work. Angela would have found the work degrading if she hadn't been glad of the chance to do something mindless. Scrubbing decks, washing the injured, and every other task Marie found for her made it harder to dwell on the past.

She looked down at the body on the examination table. An elderly man, probably in his nineties . . . although she knew better than to take that for granted. There was no sign of any injuries, as far as she could tell. Marie had even cut away the man's shirt and trousers to allow for an easier examination. He had been in good shape, thanks to the bodyshops, she guessed, but he was clearly dead. His expression suggested that his passing hadn't been pleasant.

"I don't know," she said finally. "Poison?"

"Could be," Marie said. She sounded distracted, as though she was concentrating on something else. "But he's not the only one. Seven other bodies were found over the last hour, all without any apparent cause of death."

Angela swallowed. "He looks to have been in pain."

"He does," Marie agreed. "But what actually killed him?"

"I don't know," Angela said.

"Nor do I," Marie agreed. She turned to look at Angela. "Whatever killed him might be coming for the rest of us."

Angela nodded. There were . . . *aliens* . . . out there . . . and they were hungry. Angela had heard the voices too, growing louder with every hour that passed. It was impossible to escape the sense that they were growing stronger too. She didn't want to risk going to sleep, even though she knew she must. Her nightmares wouldn't be pleasant.

The hatch opened. Her father stepped in, looking tired and worn.

"Angela," he said, "can I speak with you for a moment?"

Angela felt a stab of resentment. Her father hadn't spoken to her after Finley had attacked her. He'd been concentrating on Nancy and her *voices*. And yet . . . she rubbed one of her bruises, trying to make him sweat . . . just a little. He deserved to feel shame and guilt for what he'd done to her.

"I suppose," she said, when Marie cleared her throat loudly. "We'll use the next room."

Her father offered no objection. Instead, he opened the hatch and led the way into the tiny compartment. God alone knew what it had been for, back when the universe had made sense, but it was now housing a number of bagged-up corpses. Angela considered, briefly, offering to go to the stateroom instead, yet she *wanted* her father to be uncomfortable, to suffer.

"I won't marry Finley," she said as soon as the hatch was closed. "Never."

Her father nodded. "I don't know what happened to him," he said. "But he clearly can't marry you *now*."

Angela jabbed a finger at him. "Do you know he was abusing some of the stewards *before* we wound up"—she waved a hand at the bulkhead—"here?"

"No," her father said. He sighed. "But, after everything else, it really wouldn't surprise me."

"And yet you were prepared to marry me off to him," Angela said, twisting the knife as hard as she could. Did he have no comforting words to offer? "What *were* you thinking?"

"I was thinking that I could save the family," her father said. He sounded tired, too tired to feel much of anything. "Right now, I don't even know if we'll get out." He shook his head. "Someone back home may have set us up to die out here."

Angela swallowed. "Who?"

"Good question," her father said. "The family has enemies."

"So do some of the other guests," Angela pointed out. "We're not the only ones with enemies."

She smiled, humorlessly. One of the older men on the ship, a braggart she couldn't stand, had chatted for hours about the number of people he'd crushed on his climb to the top. One of his victims might want revenge. Destroying *Supreme* would be a *little* bit excessive, but there were so many rich and powerful people on the cruise liner that it would be hard to establish a motive. Any investigators would presumably focus on her family's enemies first.

"True," her father said. "But does it change the final outcome?"

Angela shook her head. "No."

Her father sighed. "For what it's worth, I am truly sorry," he said. "I believed . . . I believed that you would not have to remain with him, after the corporation had been put on firmer ground."

"I might not have survived," Angela said. She remembered Carla's words and shivered. "I might not have lasted ten years."

Or however long it took, she added silently.

"I wish I'd known," her father admitted.

"And if you had," Angela demanded, "would you have done it anyway?" Her voice rose. "Or would you have betrothed *Nancy* to him, if I'd run away? Or found someone else from our tangled family tree?"

"Your sister is too young to get married," her father snapped. "And do you really think a betrothal would be enough to satisfy *his* family?"

Angela shrugged. It might *just* have been enough, if ironclad guarantees had been made and sealed. But somehow she doubted it would have worked for very long.

"I won't marry him," she said. She hoped her father would get the message. Right now, she didn't much care if she had to live on the streets. "You can use this . . . you can make them uphold their side of the bargain anyway, if it means keeping the scandal buried."

Her father's lips twitched. "You've been thinking about this."

"Yeah," Angela said. "I won't let this get swept under the rug. I'll file a formal complaint when we get back home, unless they agree to exile Finley and ensure no one else has to marry him to save the family."

She met his eyes, daring him to defy her. Carla could be buried under a mountain of lawyers and fabricated complaints if she dared to bring a charge against a person as well connected as Finley, but Angela held a far higher rank. No one could bury her charges, not when *she* was the one making them. There would be a public inquest, followed by the trial of the century. And Finley's family would be crucified by high society, not for allowing him to indulge his tastes—suddenly, some of the more unpleasant rumors she'd heard sounded alarmingly plausible—but for being caught.

And we might not be the only ones in financial trouble, she thought. *This could bring the whole structure crumbling down.*

"I've spoken to his . . . minders," her father said. "We *will* come to an agreement."

"A *satisfactory* agreement," Angela pressed. She'd never dared speak so sharply to her father before, but . . . but this was different. "One that ensures Finley gets tarred and feathered as well as exiled."

"You might have to settle for exile," her father said. "They'll want to bury the scandal, Angela."

"Of course they will," Angela said. "I want him exiled with no hope of return. Dump him on a penal world or somewhere."

Her father gave her a sharp look. "Do you think they'd go for it?"

"I don't care," Angela hissed. "That's my price for keeping my mouth firmly shut!"

"Really?"

Angela took a breath. "He tried to *rape* me, Father," she said. "He would have killed me if he hadn't been stopped. I'm not feeling *forgiving*."

Her father looked down at the deck. "I understand," he said. "And yes, I will use this to claw as many concessions out of his family as I can. But we have to give them some hope that the scandal will be buried, or they'll refuse to cooperate with us."

"And then the family dies," Angela said. "Tell me, is it old age that makes you so detached, *Father*, or is it the simple fact that you spent next to no time with us when we were kids?"

Her father's face flickered with anger. "Is it *youth* that makes you so convinced that the universe can be organized to suit yourself or merely a refusal to face simple facts?"

Angela flushed. "I—"

Her father held up a hand, cutting her off. "We can and we will use this," he said. "But we cannot crush him with all of our might."

"I suppose I'll have to settle for that, then, won't I?" Angela took a breath, forcing herself to step back. "It won't be enough."

"It never is," her father said. "But is your revenge worth the destruction of millions of lives?"

Angela sighed. "No."

"I'm glad to see you're finally growing up," her father said. He gave her a faint smile. "And we might all still die here anyway."

"Maybe," Angela said.

She wondered, suddenly, what he'd say if she decided she wanted to marry *Matt*. She suspected he wouldn't be pleased. Matt was young and healthy, but he hadn't done much with his life. He was suitable as a lover, she supposed, yet he couldn't marry her. What achievements did he bring to the family? What role could he play in their future? Her father would sooner have her married off to Captain VanGundy than a mere steward.

"I'll choose my future husband," she said firmly. "And you won't choose anyone else for me."

Her father nodded, very slowly. "Very well," he said. "But I may send a name or two your way."

"No," Angela said. She sighed. "Where's Mother?"

"She's up with some of her friends, trying to keep them occupied," her father said. "I thought it better not to tell her what happened."

Angela glowered at him, but she had to admit he had a point. Her mother would slip into overprotective mode and insist on following Angela everywhere. Or worse.

"Thanks," she said finally. "You should get her to visit Nancy, when she wakes up."

"I didn't tell her about that either," her father said. "I will, later."

"Is there anyone in this family who tells everyone everything?"

Her father smiled thinly. "We were taught to keep secrets in *my* day," he said. "And what you kept to yourself might prove decisive, if things were different."

"I see," Angela said. "But . . . can I ask you a question?"

"If you must," her father said. "I don't guarantee to answer, of course."

"Of course," Angela echoed. "What *is* Marie?"

"She's your governess," her father said. "Don't you *know* that after ten years?"

Angela shook her head. "I thought I knew her," she said. "And now . . . she's like a different person. What *is* she?"

Her father met her eyes. "Many things," he said. "She was a trained SF operator. She retired before the war. I offered her a *very* long-term contract to serve as your governess."

"Marie was a soldier?"

"One of the best," her father confirmed.

"Impossible," Angela said. She tried to square her image of the fussy governess with a soldier splashing through mud on a foreign world and couldn't. And yet . . . Marie's new personality was far more military. "She . . . she took a job with us?"

"You needed someone special," her father told her. "You were old enough to dress yourself—"

"I should hope so," Angela interrupted. "I could even brush my teeth and wash my face without help!"

"But you did need a great deal of nagging," her father said. "You needed someone who could serve as a bodyguard if necessary, as well as an emergency medical corpsman and a dozen other functions. And also someone who could hide her true nature behind a bland mask. Marie was extremely well qualified for her role. You wouldn't think, if you looked at her, that she holds several records in the SF community. I think only recently she lost the shooting record."

Angela stared at him. "And she gave it up to babysit me?"

"She did raise concerns about your behavior," her father admitted. "There were times when I considered letting her have her way. But . . . I thought it would be better for you to work your way into adulthood yourself."

"Thanks," Angela said dryly. She had no idea how a former Special Forces operative would raise a child, but she doubted she'd enjoy it. Nine-mile forced marches before breakfast, no doubt. And then push-ups at all hours of the day. "I . . . I never thought of her as being *dangerous*."

"She could kick your ass with both hands tied behind her back," her father said. He pointed a finger at her. "If nothing else, understand this: you are a *very* poor judge of character."

"I am not," Angela protested.

Her father ignored her. "That isn't surprising. You were raised in a sheltered environment, perhaps *too* sheltered. You were never in any real danger until now. Everyone you met *knew* who you were. In hindsight, we did you no favors. Perhaps I should have forced you to work harder."

Angela swallowed. "Father . . ."

"If we get out of this . . . this lobster pot, you *will* learn the ropes," her father said. "You never know just what will happen in the future."

"If we get out, I'm going to buy a starship and vanish," Angela said. She wasn't entirely serious. "Perhaps I'll take Marie with me."

"That would be a very good idea," her father said. He turned to the hatch. "And I suggest you stay with her for the time being too. She'll keep you busy."

"I know," Angela said. "It keeps me from thinking."

Her father gave her a pointed look but said nothing. Instead, he pushed the door open and led the way into the next room. Two more bodies, both unmarked, lay on the deck. Marie was bending over one of them, looking worried. It was difficult to believe she'd ever been a soldier.

And then she turned around. Her eyes were hard.

Suddenly Angela believed every word.

———

"Antimatter pods?"

"Yes, sir," Slater said. "I managed to pry loose an engineering team. They confirmed the presence of antimatter."

Paul rubbed his forehead. "Any word on why the magnetic bubbles remained active?"

"Conrad believes that the flickers were careful *not* to drain the bubbles," Slater said. "The antimatter explosion might be too much for them to handle."

"Perhaps," Paul said. He looked down at the latest set of handwritten notes. A string of deaths on *Supreme*, unexplained deaths. And more systems failures, all seemingly random. "Do you think it might kill them?"

"Unknown," Slater said. "Our sensors, such as they are, can't even *perceive* them."

Paul nodded. They had counted over four hundred starships within the distortion, all dead. As far as anyone could tell, the only active vessel was *Supreme* herself. There was no piece of alien technology within detection range, nothing maintaining the energy storms and blocking escape. His ship's power seemed to be leeching away into nothingness. If he hadn't watched Nancy trying to commune with the flickers, he would have thought it something *natural* to this unnatural region of space.

But that means there's nothing to blow up, he thought. *And nothing to fight, even if our weapons were online.*

"Rig up an explosive charge on the alien craft," he ordered. Antimatter was dangerous. The Royal Navy didn't carry antimatter warheads outside wartime, just in case of an accidental detonation. A nuke would damage a ship, if one could be made to detonate inside the vessel, but an antimatter warhead would vaporize it. "And make sure the system is as primitive as possible."

"Yes, sir," Slater said. "I'll see to it personally."

Paul smiled, fighting down a yawn. "Do you believe that anything can be recovered from the alien ship?"

"Beyond a couple more bodies?" Slater asked. "I don't think so. Too much of their tech appears to be organic in nature rather than mechanical. It's just too different from ours for us to comprehend easily. We should probably send missions to the other alien ships, the ones with configurations more like ours. They might be easier to comprehend."

"If we have time," Paul said. He yawned. "Make sure you get some sleep."

"And you," Slater said. "Conrad was looking tired too. Perhaps I should cuff him to the bed."

"It might be a good idea," Paul said. He couldn't risk allowing his engineers to get *too* tired. Their work was delicate enough at the best of times. "Just be sure you have someone watching him."

"Yes, sir," Slater said. "And you too, sir."

"If someone is willing to spot me," Paul said. He sighed. "Good luck."

He watched Slater go, feeling torn. Two days in the distortion and his ship and crew were already coming apart at the seams. *Gladys* had lasted longer, but . . . the flickers might have learned from their experience. *Supreme* might have less time than Paul dared to hope.

The voices buzzed in his ear again. He told them to go away.

They didn't listen.

CHAPTER THIRTY-TWO

"Don't go," Angela said.

Matt sighed. He'd come to her straight after decontamination and debriefing, although he hadn't been sure what to expect. Angela had led him into one of the bedrooms in her stateroom, pinned him to the bed, and made love to him with a terrifying intensity that surprised him. Afterwards, they had drifted off together, holding each other tightly. There had been no nightmares.

"I have to go," he said. He had his duty. "Should I escort you down to Sickbay?"

"Marie said she'd come for me at 1000," Angela said. She glanced at her wristcom automatically, then frowned. "What time is it?"

"Oh-eight-thirty," Matt said. He wiped himself down, then reached for his pants. "You have another hour to sleep, if you want it."

"I don't," Angela said. She swung her long legs over the side of the bed and stood. "Take me to Sickbay now, if you please."

Matt smiled. "Are you going to get dressed first?"

Angela looked down, as if she were surprised by her nakedness. "I suppose I should," she said. "Give me ten minutes."

More like ten hours, Matt thought. She seemed to be a different person now, colder and harder and yet needy. *Or maybe even longer.*

Angela surprised him. She was dressed in a simple tunic and trousers in fifteen minutes. She hadn't bothered to do her face, but she still looked striking. The emergency lighting flickered alarmingly as they headed for the hatch—he touched his belt, just to make sure the flashlight was still there—and walked into the darkened corridor. The passageway felt reassuringly familiar, shadows and all, after the eerie alien ship.

A handful of passengers were scrubbing the decks as the two passed, several more carrying bagged-up bodies to the storage compartments. None of the guests looked particularly happy, Matt noted, but they had to work if they wanted to be fed. The stewards might joke about fending off thousands of lawsuits when they returned home, yet it wouldn't matter if they *didn't* return home. Matt had been told, in confidence, that some of the food was rotting faster than it should. He didn't like the implications at all.

He took Angela's arm as they stepped through a hatch—two security guards stood there, carrying rifles at the ready—and down the companionway into the lower decks. Someone had rigged up additional lighting, but he still took great care as they made their way down to Sickbay. The companionway's emergency lighting was so dim it might well not have been there at all. He had to admit, privately, that the bioluminescent light on the alien vessel was a neat solution. Humanity might want to copy it for future starships, if they ever returned home.

The shadows grew longer as they reached the Sickbay hatch. A line of passengers stood there, waiting for a chance to see the doctor. They weren't complaining, something that worried Matt more than he cared to admit. The guests were wealthy and powerful individuals, men and women who rarely had to wait for anything. And yet, they were just . . . *waiting*. Perhaps they were too stunned by their situation to put up a fight.

Or perhaps they're being drained, he thought. The passengers looked . . . *degraded.* Their clothes were filthy; their bodies smelled.

Only three days had elapsed since *Supreme* passed through the distortion, and her interior looked like a refugee camp. *They might not have the strength to argue with anyone.*

He nodded to the guards on duty, then opened the hatch. Angela followed him in, looking around with interest. Marie was working on an injured man, binding up his arm. Two more wounded sat on the deck, their hands tied behind their backs. Matt guessed they'd been fighting on the lower decks, then arrested by security officers. So many people had been arrested over the last couple of days that the brig had to be overflowing. It was rare to use even two or three of the cells on a normal voyage. No wonder the guards looked worn.

"Angela," Marie said. "You're early."

"I couldn't stay there, not on my own," Angela said.

Marie shot Matt a sharp look. Matt forced himself to look back evenly despite a very primal sensation urging him to run. Marie was . . . *dangerous*. She reminded him of some of his unarmed combat instructors back when he'd joined the corporation. They'd been *very* dangerous men. Marie looked different, but she gave him the same impression of someone it was best not to annoy.

"I escorted her down," he said. "She wasn't alone for a moment."

"Good to hear it," Marie said. Her lips twitched into something that might, charitably, be called a smile. "You'll find ration bars in the next room, and water. Grab something to eat before you go on duty."

"Thanks," Matt said. He glanced at his wristcom. He had ten minutes before he had to be at his post. Carla would kill him if he was late. "I'd better hurry."

Angela followed him into the next room. Matt heard her groan as she saw the pile of ration bars on the table, each one wrapped in a brightly colored packet that couldn't disguise the awfulness within. It was a law of nature, and probably of man too, that ration bars had to be as cheap and disgusting as possible without actually being poisonous. He'd been told that it was to keep people from being dependent on free food," but he suspected the taste had more to do with corporate laziness. It wouldn't be hard to turn the processed glob into something edible.

"They're not that bad," he said unconvincingly. Had Angela ever eaten a ration bar in her life before boarding *Supreme*? He doubted it. "Just cram them down your throat as quickly as possible."

"God help us," Angela muttered.

"You can't buy these things," Matt said, trying to sound enthusiastic. It was true. No one would pay money for a ration bar if there was something else on hand. He unwrapped his bar and took a nibble. The label said it was blueberry, but the food tasted like cardboard. "Just take a sip of water with each bite."

He poured them both a glass as he chewed the bar, trying to work up the nerve to swallow it in one gulp. It didn't taste any better when he took a sip, but at least it made the bar easier to swallow. Angela eyed him as if he'd just swallowed a live insect and then started to eat her own bar. Judging by the way her face twisted, it was hardly haute cuisine. He poured her a second glass of water without being asked, although he knew it was pushing the rationing limits. The captain had announced strict water rationing as soon as they knew there was no way to refill the tanks.

"Disgusting," Angela said. "People *eat* these?"

"If they're desperate," Matt said. The lights flickered again. "And we *are* desperate."

He gave her a quick hug, then hurried out of the room and through the main chamber. Marie watched him as he left, her eyes boring into his back. Matt wondered, absently, just what she was, but he suspected he'd probably never know. Angela might not know either. She seemed to have as little to do with her governess as possible.

"Matt," Carla said when he reached the duty station. "Where *were* you?"

"Angela's bed," Matt said, without thinking. "I—"

"Be careful," she said. "That poor girl has gone through a lot."

"I know," Matt said. "But—"

"So *remember* it," Carla said. She motioned for him to follow her. "And keep one hand on your shockrod."

Matt frowned at her back as she strode down the corridor. The shockrod was largely useless, unless it was used as a club. He would have preferred a pistol, but he hadn't been allowed to carry one off duty. It struck him as an absurd precaution—they were always on duty now, in the lobster pot—but there was no point in arguing. Besides, they didn't have enough pistols to go around.

The air blew hot and cold, chilling him. The life-support systems, or at least their control processors, were clearly on the verge of breaking down. A handful of passengers were scrubbing the decks as they passed, supervised by a couple of crewmen. Matt felt a spark of amusement at watching rich men and women do menial chores, but the tiredness made it hard to feel anything. Others were emptying the swimming pool, filling buckets, and carting the water towards a makeshift purifier. Matt grimaced at the thought of drinking water that had been used for swimming, although he knew it was perfectly safe. The improvements spliced into his genome would keep him from getting ill even if the water hadn't been boiled. But the notion still felt icky.

"We had a fight over food two hours ago," Carla said quietly. "Some people aren't doing their fair share. Others insisted on arguing over what *was* their fair share."

"Joy," Matt said.

A tiny form stepped out of the crowd. "Matt," the little girl said, "is it true you met aliens?"

Matt gaped at Susan, and Maris following her. Rumors had already spread out of control . . . he wondered, absently, why that surprised him. He'd served long enough to know that good stories were always repeated, growing with each retelling. Someone on the lower decks probably believed he'd fought buglike aliens with a flamethrower in one hand and a chainsaw in the other.

He hesitated, unsure what to say. The truth? Or something a little more reassuring?

"We found some dead aliens," he said. He looked Susan up and down. She didn't look to be hungry, thankfully, but her dress was dirty and torn. He made a mental note to suggest that the richer passengers share their wardrobes with the poorer ones. *Supreme* no longer had any laundry services. "They didn't seem to be dangerous."

"Because they're dead!" Susan announced. She waved a hand at the deck. "I've been washing the floors."

"The decks, dear," Maris corrected. She looked at Matt pleadingly. "Is there any hope of getting out of here?"

"Yes," Matt said. "We *do* have a plan."

Maris rubbed her forehead. "I hope you're right," she said. "The voices are growing louder."

Matt opened his mouth to respond, but he heard the sound of a fistfight breaking out down the corridor before he could say a word. "Excuse me," he said. "We have to deal with this."

He drew his shockrod and hurried down the passageway. A fight would be bad enough, but if the brawl sucked in more and more passengers . . . he didn't want to think about it. Better to shut the row down as quickly as possible. Behind him, he heard Carla speaking into her wristcom. Backup would be on the way within seconds.

Matt just hoped they would arrive in time.

———

"There was another fight on C Deck, sir," Jeanette said over the wristcom. "Seven men arrested, all dumped in the makeshift cells."

"Understood," Paul said. He stood just inside Main Engineering, looking at Roeder's collection of giant power cells. "Keep me informed."

"We should space them, Captain," Roeder said. "That's . . . what? The fifth fight in the last few hours?"

Paul was starting to think that spacing the Brethren and a few of the worst offenders might solve at least *some* of his problems. But it would be flat-out murder. There was no real justification for killing them, save perhaps for allowing the rest of the passengers and crew to live. And yet, if his calculations were correct, they'd either make it out in the next two days or die anyway.

He looked up at the closest power cell. "What *is* this thing?"

Roeder beamed. "*Practical* engineering, Captain," he said. "Do you know that, in all my career, I've never had to do anything like this? This is *real* engineering." His smile grew wider. "We tore a dozen power cells out of *Gladys* and transported them over here," he explained. "There's nothing actually *wrong* with them, sir; they're just dead. Once we hooked them up into our power systems, we were able to charge them from our own power cells. Sharing the load a little gives us a chance to muster the power we need to open a vortex without having the power drained completely. It's not safe, but . . ."

Paul frowned. "Just how unsafe is it?"

Roeder hesitated. "Put it this way," he said. "If we'd rigged this up in realspace, we would probably be unceremoniously fired. The power cells themselves appear to be in good order, but the linkages aren't designed to handle such a surge for long without melting. I've actually had to remove about half the safeties to keep the system from breaking down in the middle of the jump. There *is* a very good chance that at least some of the linkages will explode during transit."

"Ouch," Paul said. "Just how bad is it likely to be?"

"Unknown," Roeder said. "Captain, no one's been stupid enough to try this before."

"How very reassuring," Paul said. "What are the odds . . . ?"

He shook his head. It didn't matter. A 10 percent chance of getting out in one piece was worth more than a 100 percent chance of being drained by the flickers. If they were lucky, they'd make it out; if they were unlucky, they'd deny the aliens a source of food . . . until they snatched the next starship that happened to pass too close to their distortion. The entire experience made him wonder what had *really* happened to all those ships that had entered energy storms and never been seen again. No one had any conception that they might have been transported to an alien realm and . . . well . . . eaten.

And when we get out, we'll have to warn everyone, he thought. *But what are the governments going to do about it?*

He dismissed the thought for later. "When can we jump?"

"I've got engineering crews working out the last of the kinks in the system now," Roeder said. He pulled a notebook from his pocket and checked it. "I've decided it would be better to overload the vortex, if only because *they* will try to drain us the moment they notice the power surge. If my calculations are accurate, we should have enough power cells and linkages in place in twelve hours. That should give us the best chance of opening a vortex and escaping." He lowered his voice. "Captain . . . we don't have the slightest idea where we'll pop back into realspace," he added. "We could be . . . *anywhere.*"

Paul nodded. If *Supreme* popped back into realspace at random, there was a very good chance that they'd arrive light-years from the Commonwealth. Given that the flickers had been snatching ships from a large area of space, they might emerge so far from human territory that they wouldn't have a hope of getting back home. And the vortex generator itself might not survive the transit . . .

"We'll deal with that when we come to it," he said. Hyperspace had always been tricky to navigate. Even the UN beacons, now replaced by newer systems, hadn't made travel any easier. "Besides, at least we'd have a chance."

"Yes, sir," Roeder said. He paused. "I've also rigged a nuke on *Spider* . . . ah, the extraterrestrial ship . . . as well as a standard explosive charge. The antimatter will detonate as soon as the magnetic fields are gone. I have a crew pushing her out of position too."

"Good," Paul said. They weren't entirely sure how much antimatter the alien ship was carrying, but he didn't want *Supreme* anywhere near the blast. "Twelve hours, right?"

"Yes, sir," Roeder said. "That *is* how long it will really take, in case you were wondering."

Paul had to laugh. "I've not slept for far too long," he said. "That actually sounds funny."

"Yes, sir," Roeder said gravely. "We were warned not to exaggerate repair times to our commanders at the academy."

"A very good idea," Paul agreed. He took a breath. "Is there anything else you need?"

"Nothing you can get for us, sir," Roeder said. "We've started looking at other ways to generate power, but we haven't found anything the aliens aren't able to . . . ah . . . influence and drain. We haven't even been able to figure out where the power is actually *going*."

"Pity," Paul said. He looked up at the giant power cell. "Is there any way you can stop the drain altogether?"

"We've found nothing, so far," Roeder said. "I don't think the . . . ah . . . spiders came up with anything either. The flickers just didn't want to detonate the antimatter, so they left the magnetic bottles alone. On the other hand, it *is* possible that something very low-powered might be able to last for quite some time. If we had the tools to build something primitive—"

"But we don't," Paul said. He smiled, humorlessly. "A *terrible* oversight."

"Yes, sir," Roeder said.

Paul rubbed his forehead in frustration. If . . . if he'd had the slightest idea what could possibly happen, he would have made sure that *Supreme* was crammed with emergency supplies. Corporate would have to take a good hard look at its protocols in the future, whatever else happened. *Someone* would be liable for the whole mess . . . particularly if Robert Cavendish was correct and *Supreme* had been deliberately exposed to danger. But no one, absolutely no one, could have predicted the flickers.

Our imaginations were far too limited, he thought. *But who would have imagined this?*

His wristcom bleeped. "Captain," Jeanette said, "we've got a major problem."

Paul swore. "I'm on my way."

CHAPTER THIRTY-THREE

"Having trouble sleeping? Hearing voices, perhaps?"

Constable Hamish Singh gritted his teeth. The stimulants on *Supreme* were civilian rather than military, designed for short-term use. Two days of using various booster drugs to keep himself awake and on guard inside a brig already overflowing with unwanted guests had taken a toll. And the voices, buzzing in his ears, weren't helping. It was growing harder to tell what was real and what wasn't.

He forced himself to stand upright, glancing up and down the line of cells. Roman Bryon had been left in his very own cell, although Hamish wasn't sure if that was a curse or a blessing. Serial killers were rarely popular in prison, along with child molesters and outright traitors. Someone forced to share a cell with Bryon likely would have killed him in short order. Hamish knew he shouldn't be quite so pleased at the prospect, but it was tempting. The ship was trapped, and they were probably about to die. Who *cared* if a serial killer was murdered or thrown into space?

"Be silent," he growled. A pity the sleeping gas dispensers were offline. They shouldn't be, he was sure, but the brig's processors were fried. Trying to liberate the gas canisters from the control systems might be dangerous. "Be silent or I'll put you to sleep."

Bryon snorted. Hamish ignored him as best as he could. He should never have accepted the job. It had sounded ideal: two weeks guard duty, then a month of leave on Britannia before taking a ship back home. The bonus was enough to keep his wife and children happy, even though his wife had protested loudly when she'd realized he was going. No doubt she was disappointed that she wouldn't have anyone to nag for two whole months. He loved her dearly—he admitted that much—but she could be a bit much at times.

He glanced at the other two guards, both of whom looked uneasy. They were definitely tired too, twitching at the slightest movement or shimmer in their sights. Hamish didn't like the thought of having two armed, jumpy men right next to him, but he hadn't been given a choice. A trip that should have been simplicity itself—Bryon would have been in stasis for the entire journey—had turned into a nightmare.

I should have gone to those ships, he thought. He'd heard plenty of stories about the alien vessels but hadn't seen them. He was a qualified space-capable marine. And yet he was stuck guarding a man who should be put out of everyone else's misery. *The chance to visit a real alien ship . . .*

The voices grew louder, whispering in his ear. He glowered down at his hands as he fought to silence them, knowing it was a losing battle. The words seemed to come from everywhere and nowhere, echoing through his head, yet he couldn't make out any of the words. He felt as though he was going insane.

He rose and paced the chamber, ignoring the uneasy glance from one of the guards. The cells were sealed. There were no force fields that could fail, no computer-generated codelocks that could be hacked or tricked into unlocking without permission. The only way to open the cells was from the outside . . . and yet . . . and yet . . . a sense of unease grew within him, warning him that the cells weren't safe. He peered into the last cell, eyeing Brother John and his latest convert carefully.

They were trapped. Logic told him they were trapped. Still, he had his doubts.

The voices grew ever louder, egging him on.

"You're *definitely* not in a good state," Bryon called. Hamish spun around. The serial killer was standing against the cell door, staring through the grate. For a hazy moment, the door appeared to be *open* before reality reasserted itself. "Perhaps you should get some rest."

"Perhaps I should beat you to death," Hamish yelled. He was too tired to care about possible consequences any longer. "Or throw you in gen-pop and watch you get knifed in the back."

Bryon leered at him. "There's no gen-pop on this ship, is there?"

Hamish stamped up to the grate, careful to check the door as he approached. It was locked. Of course it was locked. He was tired. His mind was assaulting him with tricks. Bryon's words were scissoring into his skull, poking at weaknesses he hadn't known he had. There was no way anyone could get out of the cell without help. He'd made sure to check the records. Its security had been proved, time and time again.

"No," he growled. "But I could still beat you to death."

Bryon looked back at him, seemingly unintimidated. Hamish felt a surge of hatred that staggered him, an urge to open the cell and just smash Bryon's smirking face into a bloody pulp. It would be easy. So easy . . . his hands were halfway to the lock before he caught himself. Opening the cell wasn't advisable at the best of times, certainly not when he was in a bad state and his backup not in a much better one.

"I'm sure a big strong man like you could think of better things to do to me," Bryon said. He leered. "Do you want to come and try your luck?"

"Shut up," Hamish said. The anger was back, stronger than ever. "Now."

He heard the hatch open and turned, expecting to see another set of prisoners. Instead, a small object flew into the brig and hit the deck with a loud bang. Hamish threw himself down instinctively, one hand grabbing for the pistol at his belt as he landed. He drew it as a set of men rushed into the cell, waving sticks frantically as they moved. The two guards didn't have a chance to draw their weapons before they were overwhelmed.

Hamish lifted his weapon and fired twice, but the men just kept coming. Their eyes were wild, flickering from side to side . . . they were clearly hyped up on something. He'd fought drug-addled fanatics before, during the war, but this was worse. He hit one of the attackers in the head before the pistol was torn from his hands and thrown beyond his reach. A moment later, they were overpowering him, hands hammering down on his body. Hamish kicked out, but the tiredness made it hard to fight back. It was all he could do to curl up into a ball and hope to survive.

The last thing he saw, before the darkness finally reached up and overwhelmed him, was the first of the cells being unlocked.

The prisoners were free.

———

Paul gritted his teeth. "What do you mean . . . we've had a prison break?"

"Someone attacked the brig," Jeanette said. "At least a dozen men. They forced their way into the brig, then beat two of the guards to death. Constable Singh is alive but battered into unconsciousness."

"Someone," Paul repeated. "Who?"

"We don't know," Jeanette said. "All the security monitors—"

"Are offline," Paul finished. Normally, he could track anyone on his ship, wherever they went. Privacy was often an illusion in the modern world. Now . . . the prisoners could go anywhere, and as long as they were careful, they might escape recapture for *days*. Or longer, if they wished. He didn't have the manpower to hunt them down. "Fuck."

He took a breath. "Are *all* the prisoners gone?"

"Yes, sir," Jeanette said. "That's Brother John and his cronies, Finley Mackintosh and some of *his* cronies . . . and Roman Bryon."

"Jesus," Paul said. "I should have spaced the fucker."

A serial killer, loose on his ship . . . like the plot of a clichéd movie.

"Right," he said. "Where's Chief Slater?"

"He's organizing a search party now," Jeanette said. "He thinks he can track them down before they get too far out of hand."

Paul shook his head. Someone *had helped* the bastards to break out of the brig. The problem wasn't limited to a couple of dozen escapees, not now. A mutiny was clearly being plotted, and the Brethren were the obvious suspects. And if the group wanted to stay in the lobster pot, as insane as they sounded, they didn't have much time before *Supreme* made her bid for freedom.

"Hold back on the search parties for now," he ordered. "I want the guard on the bridge, Sickbay, Engineering, and life support doubled. Once that's done, we can start isolating the upper decks and moving the passengers through the bottlenecks while we put the entire ship into lockdown. Hopefully that will be enough to keep the brigands from causing mischief."

He rubbed his forehead. *Supreme* was huge, easily large enough for a few dozen men to hide from security for days. God knew there were a number of decks that had dropped off the grid completely. He just didn't have the manpower to sweep them all properly, not without the sensors. His security teams were outnumbered . . . come to think of it, they might be outgunned too. Bodyguards carried quite a few weapons that could be turned against the ship's crew.

If the bodyguards are turning against us, he thought.

"Aye, Captain," Jeanette said. "Um . . . do you want to tell the passengers anything?"

"We'll have to tell them that the ship is going into lockdown," Paul said. He forced himself to think. Just how well did the Brethren know

Supreme? The staff sections weren't shown on any map that *should* have been available to the guests, but it wouldn't be hard to deduce their rough locations. The concealed hatches weren't *that* concealed. "Make sure you move the children up to Gold Deck ASAP."

"Aye, Captain," Jeanette said.

"I'll be on my way up to the bridge," Paul added. "Inform Mr. Slater that I want to meet him there."

"Aye, Captain."

Paul closed the connection and turned to Roeder. "You heard all of that?"

"Yes, Captain," Roeder said. "It's just like *Gladys*."

"*Gladys* had a military crew," Paul said. "She was far better equipped for the unknown than we are." He shook his head. "Once the security reinforcements arrive, make sure they are deployed to cover your section. And get the power cells charged and ready to go. We *cannot* remain here."

"Understood," Roeder said. "I'll try and shave as much time off the estimate as possible."

Paul closed his eyes for a long chilling moment. The passengers didn't have the training they needed to withstand hunger and sleep deprivation, let alone the voices and the constant sense of being watched. His crew were better prepared, but he was all too aware that they weren't a military crew. It might not be the passengers who cracked up over the next few days. His crew might be on the verge of snapping too. *Gladys*'s crew had gone mad, and they'd been taught to expect the unexpected. *Supreme* was about to come apart at the seams.

He reached down and touched the pistol on his belt. He hadn't fired it in anger since basic training, decades ago. He'd fired missiles and energy weapons from the bridge of his superdreadnought, but he'd never faced an enemy in single combat or led a force of groundpounders into battle. Now . . . now his *ship* was turning into a battleground. He hated to think of just how much trouble even a relatively small group of insurgents could do if they were on the verge of madness. The Brethren wanted *Supreme* to remain in the lobster pot and die. They'd get their wish if they broke into Main Engineering and smashed the power cells and linkages beyond repair.

"Keep your pistol with you," he ordered. "From this moment on, you are authorized to use deadly force."

"Understood, sir," Roeder said. "I won't let you down."

———

"You will die here," Nancy said.

Angela jumped. "Nancy?"

Nancy looked down at the bed. "Did I do it again?"

"Yeah," Angela said. "Can you stop it?"

She sighed in pain. Her sister looked . . . pale and wan, as if she was too tired to sleep. Or perhaps she was unwilling to risk slumber. Angela didn't blame her. The aliens seemed to speak through Nancy whenever they felt like it, turning her body into their puppet. What would they be able to do if she fell asleep?

Which is why she will be restrained, once she tries to sleep, Angela thought. *She won't be allowed to move until she wakes up properly.*

She picked up a bowl and held it up, feeling her stomach rumble in anger. The soup was strictly for Nancy. Angela had been told, in no uncertain terms, that she'd be in deep shit if she took even a drop of the soup. Marie had practically threatened her with grievous bodily harm. Nancy looked as though she didn't want to partake herself but slurped a spoonful anyway. Angela felt relieved. At least her little sister was eating.

"We've fallen far," she mused. "Haven't we?"

Nancy looked up. "What do you mean?"

Angela indicated the bowl. "This is cheap crap meant for patients," she said. "And very *weak* patients at that. Now . . . it's the finest soup in all the land."

"I suppose," Nancy said. Her voice was weak. "Take some, if you want."

"It's all for you," Angela said. "It's crammed with nutrients and stimulants and . . ."—her imagination ran out—"lots of other things that are good for you." She filled a spoon with soup and held it out. "Do I have to feed you like a baby?"

Nancy flushed. "I'm not a baby!"

"You're very young," Angela said. She tried to sound mature. "And you act like it, sometimes."

"I'm twelve," Nancy said. "What's *your* excuse?"

She stuck out her tongue, triumphantly. Angela tried to think of a comeback, but nothing came to mind. Marie and her father had been right. She *had* acted childishly even as she'd grown into an adult. She knew that now, even though she still wanted to deny it. And now . . . there was a good chance she'd die before ever getting the chance to put the lesson into practice.

The hatch opened, saving her from having to concede that her little sister might just have a point. Marie stepped in, a gun in her hand. Angela felt her eyes go wide. She'd never *seen* a gun . . . she hadn't even gone on the hunting and shooting excursions that had fascinated some of the boys in her set.

She told herself not to be silly. Marie was a trained soldier as well as her governess. Of *course* she'd know how to use a gun.

"You're both here," Marie said. "Good."

Angela frowned. "What's happened?"

Marie walked around the room, inspecting the Jefferies tube hatch and the cupboards. "Are you sure you want to know?"

"Yes," Angela said. Whatever it was, it was serious. She was sure of that. "What's happening?"

"There's been a prison break," Marie said. "Finley and a bunch of other undesirables have been broken out of the brig."

An icy hand clutched at Angela's heart. "He's . . . free?"

322

"Yes," Marie said flatly. "You did say you wanted to know."

Angela bit down several words that would probably have got her in real trouble. She *had* wanted to know, hadn't she?

Her throat was suddenly very dry. She swallowed, hard.

"Where . . . where *is* he?"

"Good question," Marie said. "We don't know."

The lights flickered, then dimmed. Angela's heart almost stopped. Finley could be anywhere . . . she felt sick. Was she ever to be free of him? Her hands fluttered, helplessly. He would have killed her if Matt and Carla hadn't arrived. She *knew* it with a sick certainty that could not be denied.

"You will all die here," Nancy intoned.

Angela spun around. Her sister's face looked . . . *different* . . . in the half-light, as if she had rejuvenated her body without rejuvenating her mind. But . . . no, it was worse. Someone, *something*, was wearing her sister's face.

"You fuckers," she snarled. "Why are you doing this?"

Nancy jerked. "It happened again, didn't it?"

Angela felt hot tears prickling at the corner of her eyes. Marie put a hand on her shoulder, reassuringly. After a moment, she leaned into the older woman's touch.

"You'll stay here," Marie said firmly. "This place is heavily guarded."

"Right," Angela said. "Is that going to be enough to stop him?"

"The captain has authorized lethal force," Marie said. She *sounded* confident at least. "And I will be here too."

"You will all die here," Nancy said. "This is our place."

"Oh, shut up!" Angela shouted.

"Don't taunt the aliens," Marie said. "Right now, we have other problems."

Angela gave her a sharp look but said nothing.

CHAPTER THIRTY-FOUR

"You have got to be fucking *kidding* me!"

Matt recoiled as Slater turned his gaze on Carla, but his friend wasn't finished. "You kept a *serial* killer on this ship and you let him *escape*?"

"The brig was attacked," Slater said icily. "Do you, perhaps, think that happens on *every* voyage?"

Carla glowered back at him. "And why is this the first we're hearing of a dangerous maniac on this ship?"

"Because you didn't need to know beforehand," Slater said. He took a breath. "Now, are you going to start acting like an officer, or do I have to confine you to your quarters?"

Matt put a hand on Carla's arm. She shrugged it off.

"We will be moving all the passengers from the lower decks onto the upper levels, specifically Gold and Silver Decks, after we've searched them," Slater said. "We'll put children and their mothers into Gold Deck, then move the menfolk to Silver. I know it will be a squeeze, but we're desperate."

"They won't fit," Carla muttered.

Matt stuck up a hand. "How will we be able to separate . . . *mutineers* from innocent passengers?"

"With great difficulty," Slater said. His eyes narrowed. "We believe the people who attacked the brig were all male, but we don't know for sure. That's why we'll be putting the entire ship into lockdown over the next few hours. We'll be handing out drinking water laced with sedatives."

If they work, Matt thought. He'd heard rumors about sedatives not working properly—or at all. *The captain must have a plan to get us out while the guests are sleeping.*

"Once the decks are in lockdown, we'll start searching parts of the ship," Slater added. "Ideally, we'll be able to seal them into their hiding places and leave them trapped until . . . until this whole situation is restored. If not, we may have to fight."

Matt swallowed. The security team was trained to fight, but the stewards? They barely had real combat training. It had always been assumed that the security teams and onboard systems would be sufficient to deal with any threats. But the latter was offline, and the former was as tired and drained as the rest of them.

"I caution you all to be careful," Slater concluded. "A mistake could get one or more of you killed, or worse. The escapees are very dangerous."

Including Finley, Matt thought. Slater hadn't said anything about taking the escapees alive, had he? Perhaps no one would care if Finley was *accidentally* shot during the fighting. Or the serial killer . . . what genius had thought putting *him* on a ship was a good idea?

"Report to the hatches," Slater said. "Good luck."

Matt looked down at himself. The body armor, which hadn't been designed for him, felt cumbersome. He looked like a fraud. And he felt like one too. He knew better than to think he could put up a fight against a *real* soldier. Beside him, Carla looked even worse. Her outfit had been prepped for someone larger.

"We should dump the armor at some point," he muttered as they made their way to the hatches. It felt like *years* since they'd done a lockdown drill, but his body remembered. The hatches were already closed and sealed, guarded on both sides. "It's hot and icky."

"It might make the difference between life and death," Carla pointed out. She checked her pistol carefully. "Your mortal enemy is on the loose."

"I know," Matt said. "Fuck."

He wondered, briefly, about Angela. She'd been in Sickbay, hadn't she? It was guarded, he told himself firmly. The captain had assigned two entire squads of security officers to guard the compartment. And yet . . . Finley would go for her; Matt was certain. He wanted to run to Angela, to protect her . . .

His wristcom buzzed. "Check in, by the numbers," Slater ordered. His voice was half-hidden behind a wash of static. "Number One?"

"This is Steward Seven," Carla said when their number was called. "Hatch 17-A is closed and sealed."

"Very good," Slater said, followed by a long pause. "We will begin sweeping Gold Deck now."

Matt felt his heart pound in his chest. They'd practiced sweeping the deck before, but they'd never hunted a group of mutineers.

"Check in every five minutes," the dispatcher ordered. "If you do not check in, we'll assume the worst."

"Ouch," Carla grumbled. "This is not going to be fun."

Matt nodded as they reached the first stateroom. The door was firmly closed and sealed. There was no power to the system. He forced the portal open while Carla covered him. Inside, the stateroom was dark and silent. The air was so cold that he felt goosebumps forming inside his jacket, despite the body armor. He clicked on his flashlight and shone it around, half expecting something to jump out of the shadows and attack. But there was nothing.

He peered into the bathroom and froze. A body lay in the bath, unmoving. He shone the light over the corpse, shaking his head in dismay. The young woman—she couldn't be older than twenty—had sat down in the tub and cut her wrists. He found the knife lying on the deck. Suicide, then. Or a murder? He couldn't tell. It would be easy to fake . . .

"I'll call it in," Carla said.

Matt nodded gratefully. They'd been given briefings about how to handle suicide attempts, successful or not, but he had a feeling that normal procedures had been suspended. He glanced into the next two rooms, making sure the stateroom was empty, while Carla reported the body's location. A few days ago, it would have been a disaster. Now it was barely a footnote to *Supreme*'s drawn-out death.

"Maxine Dubois," Carla said quietly. "She was going to university on Britannia. Her family was pretty old money, but . . . she wasn't an entitled brat. I liked her."

"You liked her," Matt repeated. "Did you *talk* to her?"

"A few times," Carla said. She checked the final room as she spoke. "She was very interested in everything. I . . ." She shook her head, keying her wristcom. "Sir, Stateroom 100 is clear," she said as she led the way out of the compartment. "We're sealing the door now."

Matt pushed the door closed and knelt down to open the maintenance hatch and fiddle with the systems inside. It wouldn't be easy to undo his tampering without a clear idea of how the system actually worked. His lips twisted in contempt. Finley probably didn't know how to mix a martini, let alone repair a piece of faulty equipment. He had enough money to replace everything he owned instead of trying to repair it.

But he isn't alone, Matt reminded himself.

"Proceeding to Stateroom 099," Carla reported. "Any news?"

"No," Slater said. "Continue on your current sweep."

"Aye, sir."

"Gold Deck has been swept, sir," Slater reported. "The entire network of staterooms has been sealed."

Paul nodded. It was theoretically possible for a lone man to slip around behind the searchers, but it would be far harder for an entire group. Besides, the hatches were being dogged down and sealed, one by one. Entire sections of the deck had been sealed off. If someone had managed to hide in one of the staterooms and escape detection, they would be trapped until the power came back online or they perished.

"Move the searchers down to Silver," he ordered. "And start bringing the women and children onto Gold."

"Aye, sir," Slater said.

It was going to be a tight fit, Paul knew. The life-support systems were already on their last legs. Putting so many people on Gold Deck might tip the systems over the edge, condemning hundreds of women and children to death.

He turned to look at Jeanette. "Any word from the spider team?"

Jeanette looked over disapprovingly. She'd already made her dislike of the word *spider* clear.

"They've got the ship moving away, as planned," Jeanette said. "She'll be close to one of the other vessels when she blows."

"Let's hope there's antimatter on that ship too," Paul said. There was no way to know. "Recall the team once they've stabilized the ship."

"Aye, sir."

Paul turned back to the makeshift chart. He missed his ship's displays. He even missed the security sensors and telltales, even though he'd always had his doubts about their value. Now *Supreme* was practically terra incognita. Two-thirds of her hull were effectively out of his control, yet he couldn't seal those areas off from the rest of the starship.

And a number of passengers are unaccounted for, he thought numbly. *We can't even do a headcount.*

He looked at the timer. Ten hours, hopefully, before they could try to open a gateway. And then . . .

Get out of the lobster pot first, he told himself firmly. *Worry about the next step afterwards.*

"We've got a fight on Bronze Deck," Slater reported. "Some fathers don't want to leave their children."

Paul didn't blame them. He hadn't told the passengers the *entire* truth; they knew too much already, but clearly *something* was terribly wrong. Rumors would start . . . and spread . . . and grow in the telling until they were unrecognizable. And there was nothing he could do. The poor bastards probably believed that the hull was starting to leak atmosphere.

"Tell them that they don't have a choice," he said stiffly. "The children have to be protected."

He rubbed his forehead. Men were generally more aggressive than women. That was a simple fact, no matter how intellectuals tried to avoid it. Putting so many men so close to the bridge was a risk he was not prepared to take. There was no way to guarantee that the mutineers didn't have friends or allies who hadn't yet revealed themselves. Slipping them sedatives was technically illegal and dangerous as the drugs weren't behaving normally, but Paul had no choice. He'd answer for his orders back home . . .

If we ever do get back home, he thought.

He told that part of himself to shut up. They had a plan. They *would* get out of the lobster pot. And then . . .

I'll worry about that afterwards, he thought again. *There are too many other things to worry about.*

———

"What's going on?"

Matt winced as he saw Maris and Susan Simpson. They both looked terrified as they made their way through the hatch. He didn't think they were used to seeing armed guards on the decks, even now. He'd witnessed armed soldiers on the streets of Tyre during the war, but that had been different. This time, *everyone* was a potential threat.

"We're moving the women and children up to Gold Deck," he said. "Carla will have to pat you down first, just to be sure."

Maris eyed him. "Just to be sure of what?"

Matt opened his mouth to issue a sharp rebuke, then closed it again. Maris was right on the brink of collapse. She was trapped in an alien graveyard—it might as well be hell—and her daughter was trapped too. And the voices were growing louder . . . Matt could hear them, whispering at the back of his mind, mocking him with indecipherable words.

"The security situation has deteriorated," he said. "We're trying to keep you safe."

"By herding us all onto a single deck?" Maris asked. "Is that a good idea?"

"I don't know," Matt said. "But the captain thinks so."

Maris sniffed but made no protest as Carla patted her down quickly. She didn't seem to be carrying anything dangerous, thankfully. Matt had been told that a number of guests had picked up makeshift weapons and complained, loudly, when they were told they couldn't keep them. He didn't blame the passengers, not now. Finley's attack on Angela and a whole string of smaller incidents proved that the starship's society was breaking down. People had been molested, attacked . . .

We're all going mad here, Matt thought as he watched Maris and Susan head up the stairs to Gold Deck. *And if this goes on, we'll all die too.*

Carla nudged him. "We'll have to start sweeping the rest of the ship after this," she pointed out. "Won't *that* be fun?"

"No," Matt said. "I never wanted to be a soldier."

"And no one wanted to wind up here," Carla said. She gave him a completely sweet, completely fake smile. "Just remember, you're fighting for Angela now."

"You're not helping," Matt said.

———

"That's the right section," Engineering Tech Hannah Holliston said. She adjusted her helmet flashlight as she inspected the bulkhead markings, silently thanking all the gods in the known universe that she'd had her brown hair trimmed to the scalp before boarding *Supreme*. Her friends had mocked her, but she'd had the last laugh. Wearing the helmet no one had expected to need was easy. "You got the screwdriver?"

"And a batch of testing tools," Engineering Tech Colin Havelock said. His teeth flashed in the semidarkness as he looked at the hatch. "We should be able to strip the entire section out without problems."

Hannah nodded. She wasn't sure if Conrad Roeder was a genius or simply insane—trying to splice together a power relay network out of scavenged and repurposed components was *asking* for an explosion—but she had to admit that she didn't have any better ideas. The laws of physics, as she understood them, seemed to be breaking down in the lobster pot. She'd conducted a handful of tests as best as she could to determine what laws actually *did* function, but most of the results had been downright erratic. Either the speed of sound and the speed of light were variables in this universe or her testing methodology was flawed. For the sake of her sanity, she hoped it was the latter.

She pulled open the hatch, bracing herself for the darkness within. It should have been lit up with blinking lights, but they were dead. She tested the power-distribution node anyway, making sure it was truly depowered. In theory, no danger should arise when she tried to remove it; in practice, she wasn't so sure she cared to trust the safeties.

Too many systems with multiple redundancies and backups had failed when *Supreme* had fallen into the lobster pot.

"Depowered," she said finally. "Check it."

Havelock leaned forward, pushing his tools against the sensors. "It looks dead," he said. "Do you want to do the honors, or shall I?"

"You're the one with your head in there," Hannah said. She passed him the screwdriver. "Be very careful when you take it out."

"Of course," Havelock said. He paused as he dug into the tiny compartment. "Hey, you know this could be the last day of our lives?"

"And so we should spend it in bed together?" Hannah asked. "Dream on."

Havelock chuckled. It sounded odd in the half-light. "I don't think regulations apply to us any longer," he said. "We're not going to get out of here."

He stepped back, tugging at the power relay. Hannah joined him, pulling at the heavy box until it slid out of its place and came forward. Carefully, very carefully, they lowered it to the deck so they could run an additional set of checks. The device was still usable if it was depowered, but if something else was wrong . . .

"Regulations aren't the point," she said firmly. A flicker danced past her eye as she checked the power relay. "The point is that we have to get out of here."

Havelock closed the hatch with a loud *bang* and latched it in place. "Unless someone comes up with a miracle, we're not going to get out of here," he said. "We should be spending our last few hours entangled instead of—"

"Tell that to the chief," Hannah said. She'd worked hard for her position. She'd earned the respect of her colleagues. She was damned if she was giving up as long as there was the slightest hope of escape. "And after he's beaten you to within an inch of your life, you'll have to go back on duty."

"I hate you," Havelock said, without heat. He walked back to the power relay and bent over the access panel, studying it. "I think—"

He tumbled forward, landing on the deck. Hannah stared in disbelief. A slight man was standing behind him, holding a club in one hand and a knife in the other. He looked *ordinary*, terrifyingly *ordinary*. And the smile on his face chilled Hannah to the bone.

She reached for her wristcom, but he was on her faster than she could blink. He was strong, stronger than she'd realized. Fear gripped her mind as she fell backward, hitting the deck hard enough to knock the wind out of her. His knife pressed against her throat . . .

. . . and the darkness rose up and claimed her.

CHAPTER THIRTY-FIVE

"They are calling to us," Brother John said. "It is our time!"

Finley knelt in the compartment and nodded in time with every word. He didn't know what the compartment had been before they'd arrived in the realm of the gods, and he didn't much care. The rage overpowered him, making it impossible to think. He just knew that he had to fight for the cause. Hundreds of thousands of people were with him, their voices murmuring together . . .

He knew, on some level, that it wasn't right. But he didn't care.

"We will take the ship," Brother John added. "And then we will wait to meet our gods!"

The voices hummed with approval. Finley watched as the Brethren began to pass out weapons, ranging from a handful of guns and knives to clubs and tools. He took a baseball bat and held it up, imagining blood dripping from the wood. Blood *was* dripping from the wood . . . he thought. Or was he hallucinating? He found it hard to care about that too.

The Brethren assembled, moving in silence. Finley recognized a couple of faces, but the others were strangers to him. Servants, perhaps, or merely passengers from the lower decks, the kind of people he would never have deigned to notice. And yet they were united in their cause.

The voices grew louder, urging them to move. Finley started for the hatch, holding his baseball bat at the ready before he quite realized he was moving. Everything felt like a dream or a drunken haze.

"You have your targets," Brother John said. "They will reward us for this."

Finley strode through the doors, visions of blood and slaughter and unspeakable horrors dancing at the back of his mind. He wanted Angela. He wanted to break her. And he wanted to do horrific things to her family and her lover. The voices hummed in his ears, promising him everything as long as he served them faithfully. He no longer knew or cared if he was imagining the voices or if he trusted them to keep their word. All that mattered was that Angela was within his reach.

The darkened corridors seemed nightmarish as the Brethren made their way towards the companionway and access hatches. Finley watched the shadows grow and lengthen, hatches open and close . . . things moving in the darkness before vanishing into nothingness. *Nothing* seemed to quite make sense any longer, as if the very structure of reality itself were breaking down. The darkness should have felt oppressive. And yet he felt as though he were *part* of it. Or perhaps it was part of him.

He reached the companionway and began his climb. *Supreme* was huge, yet most of the ship was unimportant. Brother John had told him that again and again. And the voices agreed, driving him on. They wanted something, desperately. They would reward anyone who served them well. Finley clung to their promise as the companionway shifted beneath his feet, the shadows reaching up to swallow him. He wasn't alarmed, even though he knew, on some level, that he *should* be. It all felt like a dream.

Voices. *Real* voices, ahead of him. For a moment, he hesitated. The human voices were real, and the other voices were not. Weren't they? He clutched the bat tightly, trying to organize his thoughts. And then the voices grew louder, urging him on. The brief moment of resistance faded and was lost. He rounded the corner and came face-to-face with a handful of crewmen. *They* did not belong to the gods.

Screaming, Finley charged.

———

"Four hours," Paul said.

"Yes, sir," Jeanette said. "Unless Conrad manages to pull a miracle out of his ass."

Paul sighed, feeling the tiredness grow stronger. He'd ordered the crew to take stimulants, but he knew that it wouldn't be long before they started seeing things. Or *more* things. A handful of crewmen had already reported hallucinations, everything from the bulkheads caving in to airlock hatches lying open. Whatever the flickers were doing, he had to admit it was effective. His crew wouldn't be in any state to offer further resistance if they didn't manage to escape soon.

"Tell him to do his best," he said, fighting down a yawn. Everything had to be tested . . . but it was growing harder to *care* about testing. "Do we have any updates from Silver Deck?"

"At least a hundred passengers remain unaccounted for," Jeanette said. She consulted her notebook. "The remainder are having an uncomfortable sleep."

Paul wasn't surprised. They'd had to mix the sedatives into water, just to make sure there was enough to go around. The crew had no way to judge dosage, let alone anything else. If they got home, he'd be in deep shit . . . he shook his head. It probably didn't matter. If they got home, Corporate was going to have some problems trying to decide precisely what they'd put on the termination papers. And then the Commonwealth Spaceflight Agency would have the same problem trying to decide what charges to file against him. God knew he'd broken enough regulations governing interstellar spaceflight to ensure he never got a job again.

His lips twitched. After *this* voyage, he never *wanted* a job again.

"Let's hope they stay out of it long enough to go home," he said finally. *Supreme* had done very well, under the circumstances, but she was finally coming apart at the seams. "Or not to feel anything when we die."

"Yes, sir," Jeanette said.

Her wristcom buzzed. "The search parties have cleared D Deck," she said. "Chief Slater has them moving to E Deck now."

"Remind them to make sure that all the hatches are locked down," Paul ordered. "I don't want any of them sneaking up and into the secure area."

"The hatches are already under guard," Jeanette reminded him. "Chief Slater is fairly sure the fugitives went lower into the ship."

Paul knew better than to take that for granted. *Supreme* was just too large to be searched effectively, at least with the manpower he had on hand. If they managed to get home, he'd disembark the passengers and bring in marines to search the ship from top to bottom, or simply evacuate the crew and vent the entire ship. It was a vindictive thought, but he was way past caring. In hindsight, he should have just spaced Roman Bryon and the Brethren along with anyone stupid enough to agree with them.

The voices buzzed in his ear. A flash darted past his eyes. He glared after it, then sat down in the command chair. The consoles were dead— a couple had been cannibalized to replace burned-out components elsewhere on the ship—but the chair still felt like where he belonged. His bridge was a wreck, yet it was *his* bridge. He looked at his command crew, feeling concerned. He had no idea how long they'd hold up. Too many of them had been badly shocked by the whole affair.

He cleared his throat. "Lieutenant Jackson, are you ready to jump us out?"

Rani twitched. She had her back to him, but he could still see her tension. "Yes, sir," she said. "I've programmed the vortex generator for a blind jump. It should get us *somewhere . . .*"

But where? Paul finished silently. *We might end up inside a star or a planet or . . .*

He shook his head. Right now, he'd settle for getting back to real-space. Just being able to restart one of the fusion cores would provide enough power to save what was left of his broken ship. And then . . . the drive system *did* seem to be intact, merely powerless. They might have to spend years in transit at sublight speeds before they reached a populated star system, but they could do it.

You will never get out, the voices whispered. *You are ours.*

Paul started. The voices had been so loud, just for a second, that he thought someone was standing right behind him. But there was no one.

A sense of unease overcame him, a sense that something was wrong . . . *more* wrong. He looked at his crew, wondering just how far they could be trusted. There had been only one recorded mutiny on a Commonwealth starship—HMS *Uncanny*—and Paul had never doubted the loyalty of his crew, but they were trapped in a totally alien environment. The voices might wear them down until they surrendered completely. And then . . .

There was a mutiny on Gladys, he thought. *What might happen here?*

The paranoia was almost overwhelming. Could Jeanette be trusted? She wanted a command for herself, didn't she? Or Slater? Perhaps he'd deliberately allowed the Brethren to escape, putting the entire ship at risk to please his new masters. Or Tidal or Rani or any of the younger officers . . . he reached for his pistol, then stopped himself with an effort. The voices were getting to him too. Their quiet urgings were boring into his very soul.

He *wanted* to gun down his own crew.

Damn them, he thought. *We are all damned.*

Yes, the voices agreed.

He couldn't tell if they were real or if they were coming from his imagination. And yet . . . there was an undertone of gloating malice in the voices that he hoped didn't come from him.

You are all damned.

The sense of wrongness grew stronger. "Jeanette, order Chief Slater to be very careful," Paul said. "I think things are coming to a head."

"Yes, sir," Jeanette said. Her eyes were haunted. Paul couldn't help noticing that her hand kept jerking towards her pistol. "I think so too."

Paul looked down at his wristcom. Three hours, fifty minutes before jump. If they couldn't hold out that long, they were doomed.

You are doomed, the voices agreed. *Doomed.*

———

"Hey," Steward Aziz Flores said. "You know that movie where there's an alien killing machine loose on a starship . . . ?"

"Shut the fuck up," Carla growled.

Matt nodded in agreement. The seven of them were carefully probing E Deck, moving from cabin to cabin and clearing them one by one. Sweat poured down his back, mocking him. He sensed that the temperature was slowly rising even though they were in space. The air-conditioning systems had probably failed as well. And the flickering lights were making them all jumpy.

And the further we go into the ship, the greater the chance of finding the bastards, he thought. His hands felt sweaty too. *Couldn't we just seal off the hatches and vent the lower decks?*

"Captain must be out of his mind," Flores said. "We're naked out here."

"Shut the fuck up," Carla repeated. "You want to be overheard by someone a little more senior?"

Flores laughed. Matt hadn't known Flores very well—he'd been assigned to Bronze Deck before *Supreme* fell into the lobster pot—but he was definitely starting to dislike him. Flores talked and acted like someone several grades above everyone else, even though Carla was the ranking officer. *And* he sounded as though he was becoming increasingly unhinged.

"They're not going to terminate me now," Flores said. "Where would they *put* me?"

"Out an airlock," Carla snapped. "Or maybe just cut your throat and feed your body into the recycling system."

Flores snorted. "We're not going to make it out," he said, waving a hand at the darkened bulkheads. "We're trapped. We should be spending our last hours fucking, not . . . not searching for a bunch of brain-dead religious nuts. Chicks get really desperate when they think they're about to die, you know?"

"They'd have to be to consider doing you," Carla snapped. She sounded as though she was finally reaching her breaking point. "And there *is* a hope of getting out."

"Not much of one," Flores pointed out. He leered at her. "Why don't we do it just now, up against the wall?"

Carla dropped her hand to her pistol. "Because we have orders to search the entire ship," she said. "And because I will shoot you if you take one step towards me."

"That's . . . very exciting," Flores muttered.

Matt's wristcom bleeped. "Team Seven, report!"

Carla keyed her wristcom. "We've just checked E-17 through E-23," she said, shooting a daggered look at Flores. "The cabins were all clear."

"Understood," the dispatcher said. There was a pause. "Proceed to Section ED-12 and search E-24 through E-30. Report every ten minutes."

Matt exchanged a glance with Carla. The dispatcher sounded on edge, even though he was up on Gold Deck, well away from any prospective mutineers. Perhaps Slater was breathing down his neck, Matt reasoned. The longer the mutineers remained uncaught, the greater the chance they'd actually do something to damage the ship. Matt couldn't comprehend how anyone would actually want to damage the ship, but the Brethren wanted to stay in the lobster pot.

Perhaps we should just give them what they want, he thought. *It'll do the bastards good.*

They moved to the hatch and began opening it carefully. Section ED-12 was completely dark. Matt tensed, realizing that the emergency lighting had failed completely. And that meant . . . he gritted his teeth as he drew his flashlight. He couldn't imagine anyone wanting to *stay* in utter darkness, but the Brethren were insane. They might find the darkness just right for them.

Or it's a trap, he thought. He peered into the space, watching the shadows ebb and flow under the light. There was something unnatural about them. *Anything could be waiting in the dark.*

"I can't get the lights on," Carla said. "We'll have to use flashlights."

"Mine's already dimming," Flores said. "We should just seal off the entire section."

Matt looked down at his flashlight. It was dimming too. The shadows seemed to grow longer, as if *something* was lurking within the darkness. He took a step backward, despite himself. His eyes were playing tricks on him. The urge to run was growing overpowering.

"The captain wants the section searched," Carla snapped. "We can't seal it off entirely from the rest of the ship."

"The captain can come do it himself," Flores snapped back. "We don't want to get trapped in the dark . . ."

Matt opened his mouth to back Carla up, even though he suspected Flores had a point, but saw something moving within the darkness. The bulkhead was shifting, flowing . . . he was seeing things. He *had* to be seeing things. And yet . . .

"Get back," Carla shouted. The sound of running footsteps split the air. "Sound the alert!"

The darkness parted, revealing a small group of men charging them. It looked, just for a moment, as though they'd run out of the solid bulkhead. Matt hesitated, unsure if what he was seeing was real, then grabbed for his pistol. It was already too late. One of the oncoming men body-slammed him, knocking Matt backward. He hit the deck, banging his skull against the hard surface. His attacker landed on top of him, drawing back his fist to punch Matt in the face. Matt twisted but couldn't dodge the blow, and he cried out in pain when it landed.

He gasped as he felt a hand pressing against his throat, making it hard to breathe. Strong hands frisked him, removing his pistol, wristcom, and flashlight. The pressure grew stronger, choking him. He could hear the voices growing louder as the world started to dim . . .

. . . and then his attacker pulled back.

Matt recoiled in shock. The attacker no longer *looked* human. His face was twisted into blind rage and hatred. The others didn't look much better . . . he shivered as he realized that the Brethren had picked up converts among the crew. He tilted his head, trying to see what had become of his team. Carla was lying on the ground, pinned down by a heavyset man; the others were either dead or unconscious. Flores was bleeding from a nasty wound to the head, looking as though someone had cracked his skull.

His attacker shoved his wristcom under his nose. "Call your boss," he growled. "Tell him that everything is fine."

Matt swallowed, hard. There *were* emergency codes, drilled into his head during basic training. If he used them, Chief Slater would know that something was up. But if he did, and his captors realized it, he and Carla were dead. Flores was probably already dying if he didn't get medical help, help that was no longer available. He'd doom the rest of the team to death . . .

He took the wristcom. "Chief," he said, "this is Team Aardvark. Everything is peachy; I say again, everything is peachy."

His attacker yanked back the wristcom. Matt barely had a second to react before the man slammed a fist into his chest. He screamed in pain, feeling his entire body convulsing as a second blow fell, then a third. His body felt as though it had been smashed to pulp . . .

The chief knows, he thought through a haze of pain. It was something to cling to, even though he was being beaten to death. *They'll seal the hatches . . .*

"On your feet," the man growled. He pulled Matt up, then grabbed his hands and tied them behind his back. "March."

Matt coughed and spat, sure he was spitting up blood. "What are you . . . ?"

"No questions," the man ordered. "You have work to do."

He stamped his foot on Flores's head. Matt looked away, hastily, as it burst like an eggshell. Beside him, Carla was bleeding from her nose and lips, but at least she was alive.

There's hope, Matt told himself. *We can still get out of here.*

But part of him knew, all too well, that they were on their own.

CHAPTER THIRTY-SIX

"Should you be looking at that?" Angela asked. "I thought there was a biohazard . . ."

Dr. Joan Mackey gave her a sidelong look. "Do you know what that even *means*?"

"I'm not stupid," Angela said. She flushed as Marie snorted. "I know there's a risk of disease spreading from one race to another."

"All of our knowledge is purely theoretical," Joan told her. She jabbed a finger at the alien corpse. "And besides, this poor beastie is pretty damn dead."

Angela shivered. She'd never been scared of insects, but . . . something about the spiderlike alien made her want to reach for a weapon or run screaming into the next room. The thing was so *wrong*, so utterly *alien*, that it seemed almost blurred when she looked at it. Her mind couldn't quite grasp the creature's existence. She could see fragments—brown fur; spidery legs; bulging, misshapen eyes—but the whole eluded her. It seemed to belong to a whole other world.

"You *think* it's dead," she said. She paused. "Is it a *he* or a *she*?"

"No way to tell, yet," Joan said. "There's no obvious sexual organs, although that means nothing. The spiders may have their sexual parts retracted outside congress, or they might lay eggs, or . . . for all we know, this one is a sterile drone. That's not uncommon in the insect kingdom. It also might be completely asexual."

"And you're going to cut into it," Angela said. The doctor was eyeing the corpse with frank curiosity. "Is that wise?"

"This might be the only chance we get to study a genuinely intelligent alien life-form," Joan said. "And besides, if we die here, I'm not going to leave with my curiosity unsatisfied."

Angela exchanged glances with Marie. "Is this safe?"

"Unknown," Marie said. The governess sounded oddly fascinated. "But there are so many *other* things that can kill us here."

"You will not leave alive," Nancy informed them. "I . . ."

Angela turned, wincing. Her sister had bitten her lip again, scarlet trickling down her chin and dripping onto her shirt. Joan and Marie had told Angela, time and time again, they could do nothing for Nancy beyond keeping her restrained and comfortable, but there had to be something. She just couldn't think of any other options. Sedatives would leave Nancy more vulnerable to the aliens than ever before.

"The exoskeleton appears to be detachable," Joan observed. "It's definitely biological in origin, but . . . it may be a form of clothing rather than part of the alien itself. Or they might have harvested it from another creature."

"That sounds *icky*," Nancy said. "That thing killed something to make its *clothes*."

Marie laughed, harshly. "Humans used to shear sheep for clothing," she said. "There was a time when *genuine* fur was all the rage. Even now, a genuine mink coat is worth two or three times the price of a vat-grown coat."

Angela made a face. Wearing clothes . . . it had never crossed her mind that some of her coats had once been part of an animal. She felt a stab of guilt, mixed with irritation. How many *more* of her unspoken assumptions were about to be shattered on the ship of the damned?

"There were protests against the practice," Hamish Singh said from his bed. "I was stationed on Lumpur when protesters managed to convince the Commonwealth to ban animal exports. A large chunk of the planet's economy vanished overnight."

"There would have been riots," Marie said.

Angela glanced at her. "But why?"

Marie looked faintly disgusted. "Think about it," she said. "A stage-two colony world doesn't have much to export. Most of them can't offer anything that buyers can't find on a hundred other worlds. If they were drawing in outside investment by selling animal exports—by raising animals to be slaughtered to *make* the exports—losing that income would have hurt them badly. Of *course* they were pissed at the do-gooders who didn't bother to think about the impact they'd have on ordinary people."

"They were murdering animals," Nancy said. "Right?"

"You don't get to be judgmental when you're on the ropes," Marie said. "And you don't have the luxury of indulging your ethics if your families are on the verge of starvation."

Joan coughed. "Quite a fascinating set of internal organs," she said. "I'd say this creature actually had four stomachs. And I think I've located what *might* be an egg sac. I—" Her wristcom bleeped. "What?"

Marie glanced down at *her* wristcom. "Security alert," she said. Something thumped against the hatch. "All hell's broken loose. The dispatcher is reporting multiple alerts across the uppermost decks."

Angela rocked in fear. Finley was outside the hatch. She had no logical way to know it, but she was *sure* of it. She glanced at Marie, who had drawn her pistol and was holding the weapon at her side, then at Singh. He looked as though he had a pistol under his blankets too.

"What . . ." She swallowed and started again. "What do we do?"

"It depends," Marie said. Her voice was inhumanly calm. "If they haven't managed to liberate any cutting tools, they can bang on that hatch until doomsday and they won't break through. If they have, things become a mite more difficult."

Nancy's face shifted again. "You will not leave this place."

"Angela, get ready to move your sister into the next room," Marie said coolly. Her wristcom was bleeping constantly, seemingly at random. "Doctor, you might want to put your new friend somewhere out of the way."

Joan nodded, placing her tools by the side of the table. "I'll get the specimen into the spare room," she said curtly. She unlocked the trolley and pushed it forward. "Angela, once you've got your sister into the next room, I want you to check on the other patients."

Angela nodded, glad to have something to do. "I will," she said. "Nancy . . ."

Nancy gazed at her. Something else was looking through her eyes. "You will not leave this place."

"Be silent!" Angela roared. Nancy's entire body shook, her fingernails digging hard into her palms. Angela could see blood dripping to the deck. "Just . . . leave my sister alone."

"She belongs to us," Nancy intoned. "Soon, you will all belong to us."

"Get moving," Marie snapped. "The captain is warning that there might be no help on the way."

Angela swallowed. "They have to help us, don't they?" She pushed Nancy's bed into the next room. "Marie?"

"They have to protect the critical parts of the ship first," Marie said. Her voice was so quiet that Angela barely heard her. "We're expendable."

There was a colossal explosion. Angela stumbled, falling forward and landing on the deck. She rolled over just in time to see Nancy's bed hitting the bulkhead on the far side of the compartment. Her sister smiled, just for a moment; then her face fell into shadow again as the aliens reasserted control. Angela felt a surge of hatred as she heard people shouting and screaming, followed by gunshots. Marie was fighting . . .

Angela froze. The noise was growing louder, so loud it overwhelmed the constant whispering in her ears. Somehow she crawled forward to the door. Marie was fighting, her hands and feet moving at terrifying speed. Angela couldn't look away as the governess hacked her way through a dozen fanatics, and for a moment, she thought she'd win, but there were always more. They kept coming until Marie was hammered to the ground, beaten into unconsciousness. Blood poured from far too many wounds when the attackers finally pulled back.

A figure emerged from the mob and strode over. Angela barely had a moment to recognize Finley before he took hold of her shirt and yanked her up into a standing position. His eyes were consumed by madness, a terrifying rage that shook her to her very core. His face . . . he was different, completely different. It was suddenly very easy to believe everything Carla had told her . . . had it really been a couple of days ago? It felt like eons.

"Mine," Finley said. His breath smelled of something foul. "You are mine!"

Angela tried to fight, but he was far too strong. He shoved her against the bulkhead as a trio of robed men entered the compartment, then growled at her to remain still. Angela was too frightened to do anything else. Marie was unconscious, perhaps dead; Singh was wounded, clearly in no state to fight. And the rest of the patients farther into Sickbay were no better off, she knew. The walking wounded, the ones who could still do something useful, had been ordered to leave their sickbeds and get to work.

"Stay there," Finley growled.

Angela watched, numbly, as the newcomers ordered Singh to get up. The constable moved slowly, very slowly. When he stood, there was no sign of his pistol. The fanatics moved in to search him thoroughly, then tied his hands behind his back and moved him over to sit beside

Angela. She wasn't surprised they didn't bother to tie her up. They knew she was no threat.

She shuddered, feeling sick, as the robed men walked into the next room. A moment later, they returned . . . Nancy walking between them as if she didn't have a care in the world. Her face looked normal, but her movements were those of a much older woman. When Angela met her sister's eyes, she saw no trace of humanity. Nancy was gone . . .

I've failed her, she thought, fighting the urge to cry. She barely noticed when the doctor was forced to sit next to her. *I've failed everyone.*

"We beg for your blessings," the robed man said. He knelt before Nancy, his eyes firmly fixed on the deck. "We ask for your reward."

"You will come to us when you deliver the ship," Nancy said. Her voice was different too, as if whatever was controlling her didn't quite know how to use her mouth and throat. "You will all come to us."

"We thank you," the robed man said. He raised his voice. "Bring in the prisoners."

Angela looked up as five men and one woman were shoved into the chamber. Her heart sank as she recognized Matt and Carla, along with four other battered-looking men in various uniforms. Others filed in behind them carrying an assortment of weapons. She couldn't help noticing that some of the newcomers were wearing starship uniforms. The fanatics—and the voices—had been winning converts all over the *Supreme*.

"The doctor will keep them alive," the robed man said. "In time, you will come to us."

Never, Angela thought.

But she could already hear the voices growing louder. The chamber looked *different* somehow, as if it were shifting in ways her mind wasn't designed to comprehend. Nancy looked . . . *alien*, her body changing in ways . . . Angela blinked and everything snapped back to normal. Her heart sank again as she realized what was happening. The aliens that had taken over Nancy were slowly reaching into their minds, twisting their perceptions. Right and wrong would no longer matter, merely servitude to invisible entities. She remembered what Matt had told her of the alien ship and trembled. Finley and his new friends would merely be the last to die.

She looked at Matt, his face bruised. There was a dull horror in his eyes that shocked her to the core. He knew, probably better than she did, just what would happen if the uprising succeeded. *Supreme* would be permanently trapped, crew and guests doomed to madness and death. There was nothing he could do about it either. She forced herself to think, to try to come up with a plan. But there were too many fanatics for her to fight, even if she could work up the nerve.

I'm useless, she thought. *Completely useless.*

Lowering her eyes, she began to cry.

———

Matt gritted his teeth in helpless rage as he saw Angela weep. He knew what Finley would do to her after the Brethren had taken control of the ship, if he bothered to wait that long. He'd heard the horror stories. A pirate might keep Angela alive for ransom, but Finley *wasn't* a pirate. He was a madman.

He'd never been in a real-life hostage situation, but the scenario had been included in emergency drills. And yet much of the advice the stewards had been given was useless. Their captors presumably had no intention of demanding a ransom, let alone making political demands of the government. Their captors had no reason to keep them alive. Finley and the Brethren were dead if *Supreme* ever made it back to real-space, and they knew it. *Their* goal was to keep *Supreme* from leaving, not to take and keep hostages.

Remain calm, do as you're told, watch them, and wait for an opportunity, he reminded himself. Their instructors had warned stewards *against* senseless heroics, although they had admitted that everyone had to make the judgment of when to try to fight—or not—for themselves. *Do not give them a reason to lash out at you.*

He raised his head, carefully. Finley was standing by the bulkhead, eyeing Angela with a terrifying intensity. Matt felt his blood boil. He ruthlessly forced it down. Three of the other Brethren were guarding the hatch while the remainder were searching Sickbay and removing every injector tab they found. Matt hoped they wouldn't find any sedatives. The Brethren might decide it was easier to sedate their captives instead of risking an escape.

And the voices might crawl into our heads if they do sedate us. The voices were echoing through his skull, right on the edge of awareness. *That would be the end.*

He allowed his gaze to drift from face to face as the Brethren marched back out of the compartment. A handful of passengers, a couple of crew . . . Matt saw the fanatical expressions on their faces and shuddered. Was that what awaited him and the other captives if they couldn't hold out?

His instructors had advised him to build a rapport with any captors, to try to show that he was worthy of respect, but he doubted the ploy would work. The fanatics didn't seem concerned about him . . . he hoped that was true. Finley might want him dead, if Finley still had any free will, but the others had no reason to give a damn about him. They were just waiting . . .

"You must move fast," Nancy—no, the thing speaking *through* Nancy—said. She looked like an angel, or a demon. Matt thought he saw light bending around her. "This ship is preparing to depart."

"We will not allow them to take us from you," Brother John said. "This ship will remain here."

Matt gave him an angry stare. Brother John ignored him, ordering his men to join the attack on Gold Deck and the bridge. A dozen arguments ran through Matt's mind, but he knew none would work. Brother John was a fanatic, a man who'd just seen all his beliefs confirmed. Logic

351

and reason wouldn't impress him, nor would appeals to their common humanity. He was planning to sell them out to interdimensional alien monstrosities.

He thinks he's doing the right thing, Matt thought, as Brother John left. *He thinks the aliens are gods. Perhaps I can use that.*

But he was damned if he knew how.

———

Angela was terrified.

Finley could *feel* it. He could sense the terror oozing off her in waves. He'd watched female anticipation turn to fear more times than he could count, enjoying every moment when a woman realized that she was no longer in control of the situation. Still, most of his conquests had lacked power themselves. They'd never had Angela's assurance that her name and family would protect her from harm.

And now that protection is gone, he thought, savoring the moment. The fear in her eyes drew him like a moth to a dancing flame. *She's helpless.*

The voices grew louder, urging him on. Brother John had told him not to kill her, not to kill *anyone*, if it could be avoided, but he could have his fun.

She drew back, unable even to look at him. Finley licked his lips. She didn't know it, but she was advertising her weakness for all to see. The voices danced and sang in his mind, confirming every one of his thoughts. Angela was finally ready for him. It would be glorious. And, afterwards, he'd make her watch as he cut her lover into bloody strips, bleeding him to death. The anticipation was overpowering. He saw no reason to delay any longer.

It was time.

CHAPTER THIRTY-SEVEN

Paul gripped his pistol as more and more bad news flowed into the bridge.

"We've lost contact with all of the search parties," Slater reported. The security chief sounded badly worried. "We've also lost contact with Sickbay and the hatches on Bronze Deck."

"Shit." Paul gritted his teeth as he thought. "If they have control of the hatches, they can presumably get up to Gold Deck and the bridge."

"Yes, sir," Slater said. "They can also get to the women and children." He paused, listening to his wristcom. "Sir, some of the sedated men are also waking up."

"Seal Silver Deck," Paul ordered. He glanced at the timer. Forty minutes to go. "Have they made a move for Engineering?"

"No, sir," Slater said. "We do have a report of them advancing on Life Support."

Paul shook his head. Normally, it would be a significant threat. Someone in control of Life Support could kill everyone on the starship, or sedate them if they released the knockout gas. Now, with the computer network effectively offline, Life Support was on its last legs anyway. Turning it off would create a long-term problem, but *Supreme* would either have made it out or been destroyed by the time the crew ran out of air.

"Seal that compartment; then order the guards to reinforce Engineering," he ordered. "It won't be long before they go for the drives."

"Aye, sir," Slater said. He paused. "And Sickbay?"

Paul gritted his teeth. Dr. Mackey, Angela and Nancy Cavendish . . . and at least twenty patients, none of whom were in any state to be moved. He didn't know what the Brethren would do to them, particularly Nancy, but Sickbay wasn't a priority, not when the ship was struggling to break free of the lobster pot.

"Leave it for the moment, while you concentrate on vital sectors," he ordered. He felt a flush of shame. Abandoning two young girls just didn't feel right to him. "Try to get a patrol down into that section if you have time."

"We can't," Slater said flatly. "We simply don't have the manpower to hold Gold and Silver if we draw guards off to probe that section. Every time we open the hatches, we risk getting something shoved back through—"

Paul held up a hand. "Understood," he said. It had been wishful thinking, and he knew it. "Keep the hatches sealed."

"Yes, sir," Slater said.

"Captain," Rani said, "we have a direct link to Engineering now!"

Paul nodded. Rani's console blinked with lights. His heart leaped, even though he knew the system was still on the verge of collapse. It was a sign, perhaps, that they'd make it out of the trap. He told himself, sharply, not to get too optimistic. He'd known what the Theocracy could and would do to his ship, but the flickers were a completely unknown factor. They might possess other tricks.

He pushed the thought aside. "And the power surge?"

"The drain seems to be picking up," Rani said. She paused. "Captain . . . we may not be able to meet the threshold for opening a vortex. If my calculations are correct—"

"Then ready the nuke on *Spider*," Paul ordered. The aliens *did* seem to go after the largest power surges first. If they were lucky, the drain would concentrate on the antimatter explosion. "I want to detonate it a moment before we flash-wake the drive."

"Aye, Captain," Rani said.

Paul forced himself to sit calmly. The die was cast now. Either they survived long enough to open a vortex and jump out or they died. Either way . . . he checked his pistol as a new set of reports came in. The bastards would get his bridge over his dead body.

Which would probably be fine with them, he thought wryly.

———

"All right, get the next set of linkages into place," Roeder bellowed. "We've got half an hour to get them ready before we go."

He sucked in his breath, feeling the world jerking around him. The stimulant he'd taken had probably been an overdose, particularly when his personal nanites were offline, but he needed to remain awake and aware. If he died afterwards . . . he dismissed the thought as he ordered his crew to work faster. They needed to double or triple the linkages before zero hour, or there was too great a chance that the entire system would melt down when they flash-woke the drive.

His hands shook, despite himself, as he forced the next power cell into place and then checked it carefully. It *should* be fine . . . *Gladys*'s technology and hull hadn't shown any signs of visible decay, had it? The first hyperspace starships had been built with an impressive series of redundancies, but . . . they just hadn't had the technology available to the Commonwealth. *And* there was a very good chance that there might be damage he couldn't detect with his remaining sensors. A hairline crack in a power cell would cause an explosion.

We should be able to handle it, he thought. Three crewmen rushed past him, carrying a power linkage. He watched, nodding in approval, as they slotted it into place. *We've rigged as many circuit breakers into the system as possible.*

He took a step back, wishing he had time to take another stimulant. The voices were dulled, but he could still hear them. Two of his crewmen had gone mad and needed to be tied down while a third had stepped off a balcony and plummeted to his death. Roeder had no idea if it had been suicide or a tragic accident, but either way . . . he looked down at his shaking hands and cursed. His heart was pounding so loudly that he was starting to think it was going to burst.

The hell of it, he admitted as he checked a set of calculations, was that he would have enjoyed the project if the entire ship wasn't depending on him to succeed. Tearing power cells out of a hundred-year-old starship and working them into his own ship's power grid, then tearing out power nodes from his ship and repurposing them for something greater . . . fantastic. It was a piece of improvised engineering that would go down in the history books. And yet, he knew that everything depended on success.

If we succeed, he thought, *it will be listed under the heading of "How Not to Do It." And if we fail, no one will ever know what happened to us.*

His wristcom bleeped. "Sir, they're attacking the main hatch," a voice said. It took Conrad a moment to place Lieutenant Avis Grosskopf. "We're holding them off now."

"Do what you can," Conrad ordered. An engineer appeared in front of him, holding a clipboard. He took it automatically. "We'll—"

He looked up. The bland face looking back at him was instantly recognizable.

And then the knife was thrust into his heart.

"What the fuck are these bastards smoking?" Lieutenant Robinson demanded. "They're just *coming* at us!"

"I don't give a toss," Avis snapped. She put five rounds into another fanatic; two through his head, the rest into his legs. She'd seen too many of the bastards keep moving even after being shot through the head to feel confident that anything less than total dismemberment would keep them down. "Just *kill* the fuckers!"

She cursed under her breath as four more men ran at her. One of them was wearing a starship uniform, but she didn't dare hesitate. If they'd had their stunners . . . she cursed again as she blew the man's head to bloody ruin. They'd lost half their arsenal just because the computer processors were fucked. A pair of plasma cannons would have held the entire section with no risk whatsoever to the guards.

Sure, she told herself. *And if wishes were horses, beggars would ride.*

"They're trying to get to us over the bodies of the dead," she said, tonguing her mouthpiece. Thank God *that* still worked. She would have hated to try to talk into a wristcom while she was still fighting. "We're running out of ammo."

"Understood," Slater said. "Hold as long as you can."

Avis nodded, feeling good for the first time in days. The voices, the flickers, the alien ships . . . she'd found it hard to keep herself going, even though she *was* an experienced military veteran. Nothing she'd seen in the Marine Corps had prepared her for *aliens*. Now . . . now she actually had a physical enemy to fight. The voices seemed to fade as her anger and determination grew stronger. She didn't know if the fanatics were cowards or had merely been overwhelmed by the aliens, but she was *sure* they were traitors. Their surrender risked the entire ship.

Something skidded along the deck and landed far too close to the barricade. She ducked back an instant before it exploded. A makeshift grenade, part of her mind noted. Not powerful enough to damage the barricade but certainly tough enough to cause real problems for the defenders. She wished, again, that she had a suit of armor or even a set of grenades of her own. They just didn't have time to rig them up.

"Two more," Robinson snapped.

Avis kept her head down as the grenades exploded, then glanced up long enough to pick up a stream of fanatics coming at her. She raised her weapon and opened fire, cursing the ammo shortage savagely. In hindsight . . .

She shook her head. What sort of lunatic would expect an all-out war on the decks of a cruise liner?

"They're punching through at Point Stalingrad," her earpiece chirped. "Fall back!"

"Understood," Avis said. The bastards would have to get through the next set of hatches before they did anything else. It would slow them down, a little. "I—"

"Emergency," the dispatcher said. "Get to the main compartment now!"

———

Conrad felt the knife stab into him. The pain . . . the pain felt dulled. His head felt dulled too, his thoughts starting to slow. It took him a long chilling moment to realize that the stimulants were keeping him alive, just for the moment. And, perhaps, the knife remaining in the wound . . . Bryon was staring down at him, insanity dancing within his eyes. Conrad couldn't muster the strength to do anything but stare back. His entire body felt weak, as if it no longer belonged to him. Flickers of light danced at the corners of his eyes as his legs started to buckle. He could no longer stand.

"You will all die here," Bryon whispered. Conrad couldn't tell if it was the aliens or the serial killer speaking for himself. No doubt the prospect of taking thousands of people to the grave was attractive to a man like him. "You will all die."

Fuck you, Conrad thought. The asshole was wearing an engineering uniform. How had he found an engineering uniform? Somehow, it no longer seemed important. *I . . .*

He stumbled to his knees as Bryon removed the knife, turning to lash out at the closest crewman. Conrad hit the hard deck as his crew started to shout, then charge the serial killer; Bryon sliced four of them before his head simply exploded. Conrad needed several seconds to comprehend that the serial killer had been shot. Blood drifted everywhere, mocking him. He was dying and . . .

Someone slapped a medical pack against his chest. Conrad could have told them not to bother . . . he would have told them, if he could have mustered the energy. Normally, a medical pack would ensure that he had a reasonable chance to survive. Now the power was failing, and the pack was unlikely to work.

Get the ship out, he thought. Or said. He wasn't sure. *Get moving, you . . .*

———

Avis closed her eyes, just for a moment, as Chief Roeder died. She'd liked him, the couple of times they'd met. He'd deserved better. They'd all deserved better. Now . . .

She glanced at the engineering crew. "Get back to work," she snapped. "We don't have much time."

Gritting her teeth, she ran back to the hatch, tonguing her mouthpiece on the way. "Sir, Chief Roeder is dead," she reported. "Bryon killed him. He's dead now too. No apparent damage to Main Engineering."

"Understood," Slater said. "Hold the section as long as possible."

Avis exchanged looks with Robinson as the next set of reports came in through the command net. They *had* managed to fall back, but now . . . the enemy was breaking through the hatches. There was nowhere else to go. They had to hold, or die. And die, perhaps. Their deaths would buy time, but would it be enough?

"If we get out of this alive," she muttered, "I'm going to go into something safer. Naked lion taming, perhaps."

"Or bungee jumping without a rope," Robinson agreed. "Or food tasting in King Putt's Court."

Avis had to smile as they took up their positions. She'd thought she'd seen enough of serious combat. Getting a job with the Cavendish Corporation had seemed like a good way to keep her toe in the water without either remaining in the Marine Corps or joining a mercenary group. She certainly hadn't expected anything more dangerous than bar fights and lovers' quarrels . . . besides, the drunkards on *Supreme* would wet their pants if they walked into a marine bar during happy hour. Now . . . now she was taking part in a last stand that no one would ever know about . . .

"They're striking at all four hatches," Robinson said. "We're in trouble."

Avis nodded. No resupply, no backup . . . unless the other guys got down to Main Engineering in time. A nightmare. They were *very* short on ammunition. She shot Robinson a sidelong glance. They were on their own, for all intents and purposes. The engineers couldn't put up a real fight.

"It's been fun," she said. She stuck out a hand. "I hope you enjoyed it as much as I did."

"Yeah," Robinson said. He shook her hand. "I did."

A moment later, the hatch exploded inwards.

"Main Engineering reports that they're on track to get everything finished in time," Jeanette said. "But Conrad's death . . ."

Paul nodded harshly. Engineering *needed* someone who could not only supervise but fix problems as they popped up before they turned into disasters. Roman Bryon—damn the man!—might just have killed them all. Roeder's staff were good, but they didn't have his vast experience.

"Keep focused," he snapped. "Do we have main power?"

"Twenty minutes," Jeanette said.

"All control systems are online," Rani reported. "But I don't know how long they'll hold out."

"As long as they last long enough to get us out of here," Paul said. He rubbed his forehead. "Security report?"

"They're pushing into Gold Deck," Slater said. "I don't know how they made those damned grenades, sir, but they smashed through one of our barricades and hit the hatch before we could get reinforcements in place. Half of them look like fucking zombies."

"Order the women and children to retreat," Paul said. "And concentrate on guarding the access route to the bridge."

He glanced at his wristcom. Nineteen minutes . . .

"Rani," he said quietly, "if they start to break through the bridge hatch, activate the vortex generator . . ."

Rani turned to stare at him. "Sir?"

"You heard me," Paul said. *Supreme*'s command-and-control network was already shot to hell. There was no time to set up a system to trigger the vortex generator from Main Engineering, let alone the secondary bridge. Something that could have been done with the press of a button, once upon a time, was now an impossible task. "If there's a chance of them taking the bridge, we'll leap."

". . . Aye, sir," Rani said.

Paul watched as she turned back to her console. He understood her concerns, better perhaps than she suspected. The moment they triggered the power surge, the flickers would start to drain it. And if it fell below the threshold for opening a vortex, they were dead. There would be no further hope of escape.

But we won't have hope if a bunch of fanatics storm the bridge and get us killed, he told himself. *We have to take the risk or die.*

"Main Engineering reports that the defenses are holding, for the moment," Slater reported. "The reinforcements will be there in five minutes."

"Thank God," Paul said. He glanced at his wristcom. Ten minutes to go. "I—"

An alarm sounded. "They've broken through the lower hatches," Slater said, checking his wristcom. "They'll be on the bridge in two minutes."

"Shit," Paul muttered. He drew his pistol. "We'll make our stand here." He looked at Rani. "You know what to do."

"Yes, sir," Rani said. "The command set is already programmed into the system."

Paul sucked in a breath. Did they have enough time? All their planning was based on guesswork . . . and something that couldn't even be called *that*. There were too many unknowns . . .

"Send a signal to *Spider*," he ordered. "The charge is to be detonated in two minutes."

He braced himself. The system was as simple as his engineers could make it. He hoped, prayed, that it couldn't be disabled. The flickers hadn't shown any real ability to manipulate matter, had they? And yet, there were the weird reports from some of the search parties on the lower decks. They'd reported seeing entire decks twisting out of shape . . .

They were seeing things, he told himself. *We are all seeing things.*

"Punch the vortex as soon as the charge detonates," he ordered. "We won't have much time."

"Aye, sir."

CHAPTER THIRTY-EIGHT

Angela watched, feeling cold, as Finley stepped towards her. She couldn't move. Her legs refused to obey her. Her eyes flickered from side to side, seeking a help she knew wasn't coming. Matt and Constable Singh and their friends were tied up, Nancy off in her own little world, Marie lying on the deck, bleeding to death. Angela was half-convinced her governess was already dead, yet another person who had died to save her from herself . . .

Finley loomed over her. His eyes caught and held her gaze. She couldn't believe, now, that she'd ever thought of him as a colorless milksop. He'd hidden his true nature well, but now . . . free of all consequences, the real Finley could emerge. Or maybe the voices had driven him to madness. She could hear them at the back of her mind as he reached out, yanked her to her feet, and shoved her back against the bulkhead. She still couldn't make out their words.

"Let go of her," Matt pleaded. "Please . . ."

"Take me instead," Carla said. Angela gaped at her. "I can—"

Finley hit her, hard. She fell to the side and lay still.

"Watch," Finley growled. His voice sounded animalistic, all traces of humanity gone. "She is mine."

Angela's arms felt heavy. She couldn't raise them, even to defend herself. The voices howled in her head, mocking her. She had to fight to keep her legs from buckling, to keep from collapsing in front of him. Finley couldn't see her weaken any further . . . she knew it didn't matter. He already knew that she was no match for him.

Think, she screamed at herself.

She wanted to lift her leg and knee him in the groin, but her legs refused to move. She was too *scared* to move, too convinced that whatever she did would bring her only more pain. Finley was going to kill her; she *knew* he was going to kill her, but she couldn't muster the energy to resist. The voices grew louder and louder, drowning out her thoughts. She staggered as they hammered against what remained of her sanity, inviting her to surrender. She knew, now, why so many people had just given in. The assault was overpowering. She had to bite her lip to keep from collapsing entirely.

"Take off your clothes," Finley ordered, his face consumed with an unholy lust. "Do it slowly."

Angela shuddered. He was going to rape her in front of her little sister . . . she opened her mouth to appeal to him, but she knew it would be useless. Finley was insane . . . or gone, replaced by a monster. And Nancy was staring up at the ceiling, mumbling to herself as the lights flickered constantly.

A dull throbbing echoed through the deck . . .

"I said undress," Finley growled. "Now."

Think, Angela told herself. Her hands went to her shirt, despite herself. What was one meant to *do* if one was taken prisoner by a maniac? It wasn't something she'd ever been taught . . . her thoughts ran round and round in circles, mocking her. *There has to be a way out.*

A thought struck her. It wasn't much, but . . .

"Not here," she said. She nodded to Singh's bed. "On the bed."

Finley's mouth dropped open in an inhuman expression. "And do you think it will be better there?"

"Nancy won't see," Angela said. She didn't know if Nancy was seeing *anything*—there was a vacant look in her sister's eyes that chilled her to the bone—but it was a reasonable request. "Please. I'll do anything as long as Nancy doesn't have to watch."

———

Finley smirked, the expression growing wider and wider as he drank in her fear and submission. The voices had been *right*. Angela was offering herself to him, offering to surrender . . . for a price. And it pleased him. He reached out and tugged her forward, then pushed her towards the bed. Nancy didn't have to watch; she belonged to the voices anyway, but Matt would have no choice. He'd watch as his lover surrendered completely . . . a fitting last memory. Finley was going to kill the bastard as soon as he had his fun.

He watched, admiring Angela as she stumbled over to the bed, her hands running under the pillows. He was going to enjoy himself with her, using pain and pleasure until she knew no will but his. And then he was going to kill her . . .

"Get your trousers down," he ordered. He couldn't wait any longer. "Stay in that position; just get your trousers down."

Angela turned, a gun in her hand.

Finley gaped at it. The shock was enough to drive some of the cobwebs out of his mind. A gun . . . where had she found a gun?

Terror froze him, just for a second. His prey wasn't meant to be able to fight back! She was his . . . the voices screamed at him, ordering him forward. But it was too late.

———

Matt watched, torn between relief and astonishment, as Angela pointed the gun at Finley and pulled the trigger. The gun fired, time and time again, the sound echoing in the confined chamber. Finley staggered, his hands going to his chest, but somehow remained on his feet. Blood dripped down to the deck, yet . . . somehow . . . he kept going. Angela's eyes were wide with horror as the gun clicked dry.

"Up," Singh snapped.

Matt forced himself to his feet and hurled himself at Finley's legs. The man staggered, then fell on the deck. Matt fell also, grunting as he hit the hard surface. His ears were ringing . . . Angela was screaming. The voices were screaming too. Sickbay suddenly seemed a vast and unknowable *alien* place. The shadows changing . . .

Finley convulsed once, then lay still. Matt forced himself to roll over, tugging helplessly at his bonds. Finley wasn't moving, but that meant nothing. The man had taken one hell of a beating earlier and just kept coming. And yet Angela had put five or six bullets in Finley's chest. The shock alone should have killed him.

"Matt," Angela said. She wrapped her shaking arms around him. "I . . ."

"It's all right," Matt said. He wished he could hug her back. "It's all right."

"You need to untie us," Singh said. "Quickly."

Angela flushed. "I killed him," she said as she untied Matt. "Didn't I?"

Matt hesitated, then carefully checked Finley's pulse. Gone. The wound in his chest certainly didn't *look* survivable. A low quiver ran through the hull, and he smiled, despite himself. The drives were powering up. It wouldn't be long before *Supreme* tried to jump out.

"He's definitely dead," Singh said once he was untied. He gave Carla a quick once-over. "She's knocked out, but alive. She should recover."

He gave Angela a warm smile. "Well done, miss."

"Thank you," Angela said. She took hold of Matt's arm and held it tightly. "I . . ."

Singh gave them a reproving look, then tapped his wristcom meaningfully. "You'd better report to your CO, lad," he said. "I'll check the door."

Angela looked down at the pistol. "Do you have more . . . more bullets?"

"I have a spare clip," Singh said. He took the pistol and hunted through his jacket until he found the bullets. "But I don't know how much use they will be."

Matt nodded and keyed his wristcom. "Captain, this is Evans in Sickbay," he said. "We killed our guard and broke free. I don't know what's happened to the others."

"Attacking the bridge," a voice said. The signal was so bad that Matt didn't realize who was speaking at first. Normally, he would *never* have spoken to the captain without going through several intermediate layers first. "Can you do something to get them off our backs?"

"We can try," Singh said into his own wristcom. He checked his pistol. "Doctor, are there any other weapons here?"

"No," Joan said. Angela untied her, quickly. "You might be able to recover weapons from the guards outside, but . . . I don't know how much difference it will make."

"None," Nancy said. She turned to face them as another quiver ran through the hull. "Your escape plan is futile. We have your ship now."

Matt swallowed. Nancy seemed . . . *larger* somehow, as if she were slipping into dimensions he couldn't even begin to perceive. Her eyes were inky pools of darkness. Blood leaked from her mouth and palms, dripping downward and splashing on the deck, but she didn't seem to care. She stood as though she were a much older woman, gazing down at them from a great height. His eyes had problems even *looking* at her.

"You enjoy it," Angela said. She clung to Matt desperately. "You like making us suffer."

"You exist to feed us," Nancy said. "You are ours."

"We're not yours yet," Matt snarled.

"You don't understand," Nancy, or the thing speaking through Nancy, said. "You are already ours. You feed us."

Matt gritted his teeth. The tiredness pervading them all . . . the flickers were draining them, inch by inch. He understood, now, why they'd driven so many people to madness. The dementia created more energy for their consumption . . . or, perhaps, it made it easier to harvest the passengers. They . . .

"Angela, I have to go to the bridge," he said. He wasn't sure what he and Singh could do, but they'd think of something. They'd *have* to think of something. "Can you stay here with the doctor and Nancy?"

"It is futile," Nancy informed them as Singh left the compartment and headed farther into Sickbay. "You may as well stay where you are."

"Humans don't give up," Matt snapped.

Nancy said nothing.

Angela squeezed his arm. "You'll come back, right?"

"I will," Matt promised. Singh returned, carrying a pair of small canisters under his arm. "Whatever it takes, I'll come back."

He gave her one last hug, then hurried out the door. A dozen bodies were lying on the deck, including a couple of people he recognized. He wondered, as he searched them for potential weapons, which side they'd been on. The battle for *Supreme* was practically a civil war, with friends on both sides of the divide. He hoped, prayed, that the fanatics returned to normal once *Supreme* was out of the lobster pot.

"When I get back," he muttered, "I'm going to apply for a post on a prison barge."

Singh surprised him by laughing. "It would be safer, wouldn't it?"

He picked up a pistol from one of the bodies and passed it to Matt. "Not much ammunition," he said. "Didn't your corporate masters anticipate a mass uprising?"

"It wasn't on the training syllabus," Matt said. He'd thought *Supreme* could handle any internal trouble, hopefully without the majority of the passengers ever realizing that something had happened. But he'd been wrong. "A terrible oversight."

"Quite." Singh started towards the companionway. "We'd better hurry. I don't know how much time we have."

Matt nodded, following him up to Gold Deck. The interior of the ship had been devastated: the bulkheads were charred and pocketed by bullet marks; bodies lay everywhere, unconscious or dead. Some had been savagely mutilated; others looked as though they'd killed themselves . . . he wondered if they'd gone to their deaths hoping to spite the aliens one last time. Perhaps the aliens didn't eat souls . . .

And perhaps they do, Matt thought. Hadn't someone once speculated that souls were nothing more than an energy pattern, imprinted on the universe by intelligent life? He couldn't recall the details. *They might consume even our souls before letting our bodies drift within the graveyard forever.*

Singh caught his arm as they reached Gold Deck. "They cannot be allowed to get onto the bridge," he hissed. The sound of shooting and cutters echoed down the corridor. "We *have* to stop them."

"I know," Matt said. He tightened his grip on the pistol, slipping off the safety. "We'll hit them from the rear—"

"There's two of us and . . . how many of them?" Singh made a rude sound. He passed Matt one of the canisters. "We need a plan. This is what we're going to do . . ."

———

Brother John could only dimly remember just where and when he'd converted and become one of the Brethren of the Holy Voice. He felt as though he'd *always* believed in the gods, even though he knew, intellectually, that he'd been an unbeliever before he'd heard the voices for the first time. In truth, he could barely remember any details of his former life . . . or anything that had happened before *Supreme* fell through the distortion and emerged in the realm of the gods.

He allowed himself a smile of pure joy as the resistance collapsed, allowing the Brethren to rush towards the final hatch. The bridge waited beyond, manned by unbelievers who would try to yank them all out of the godly realm if they were given half a chance. John could not understand any longer why they were trying to fight. Did they not realize that they were on the verge of joining the gods? Their mortal bodies would soon be gone, but their souls would live on.

The voices sang in his head, promising everything he had ever wanted and more. He could hear them, even though he couldn't make out the words. And yet he knew what they were saying. They were answering questions he hadn't known he had, quelling doubts he had never allowed himself to face. The Brethren had been right. No one could deny, now, that they'd been right all along. The mockery they'd faced on a dozen worlds no longer tore at his soul. They'd been right, and everyone else had been wrong.

Soon, he promised the voices. The bridge hatch was tough, but cutting through it would be just a matter of time. *Soon.*

Something clattered behind him. He turned just in time to see a canister, a second canister, flying through the air and striking one of his men a fearsome blow. The victim shrugged it off, of course—the gods had granted them all the strength they needed to defeat their enemies—but it was still painful. And the canisters were hissing . . .

. . . and then a third object rattled through the air and hit the ground. There was a spark . . .

———

Matt had taken cover, but he still felt the wave of heat from the explosion. Super-compressed oxygen, pure oxygen—the blast had been strikingly powerful. He remembered the safety lectures he'd received and shivered. Singh had been trying to spark an explosion, something Matt had been warned not to do. But there hadn't been any choice.

The fire might have caused the cutters to explode too, he thought. *It would have been very hot indeed.*

"Now," Singh snapped, "move!"

He jumped out of cover and ran towards the hatch. Bodies lay everywhere, some clearly dead; others were moaning in pain as they tried to roll over and suppress the fire. Matt recoiled at the stench of burning flesh, trying hard not to gag as Singh moved from fanatic to fanatic. A handful of them were immediately put out of their misery. They'd been so badly burned that recovery was unlikely, at least without prompt medical care. He forced himself to look away as Singh crushed a skull, eyeing what remained of the bulkheads. They'd been scorched by the heat, paint dripping down onto the deck. The metal behind the paint looked blackened as well.

They'll probably try to take it out of my salary, he thought numbly. He stumbled, leaning against the bulkhead. His entire body felt tired, as though he could no longer go on. *Or make me clean up the mess myself.*

"There'll be others on the way," Singh warned. "Get ready to face them."

Matt barely heard him. Fatigue dominated his universe now. He slumped, landing on the deck with no clear memory of how he'd gotten there. The pistol clattered to the deck beside him. He was too tired to think, too tired to care . . . he *knew*, deep inside, that he was being drained, but it was impossible to feel any concern.

"Get up," Singh ordered. He kicked Matt in the leg, hard enough to jerk him awake. "We might have to make a last stand."

"Fuck you," Matt managed. He reached for the pistol. His vision was darkening, making it harder to see. The voices were growing louder and louder. "I . . ."

"Your girlfriend is going to be fucked if you don't," Singh snapped. "Get up!"

Matt forced himself to kneel, then stand as he heard the sound of running footsteps. The rest of the fanatics were on their way. If they'd brought more cutting tools, the bridge would fall . . . if they didn't manage to hold them off. He stumbled into cover, bracing himself for one last stand. Definitely the last. The pistol suddenly felt too heavy to lift . . .

He gritted his teeth, biting his cheek to keep from collapsing. The pain didn't keep him focused for long. He held the pistol at the ready, bracing himself. One way or the other, it would all be over soon.

I'm sorry, he thought. *But this is the end.*

CHAPTER THIRTY-NINE

"Charge detonated, sir," Tidal said.

Paul turned to Rani. "Hit it!"

"Flash-waking the drive now," Rani said. Her voice rose as a quiver ran through the giant ship. "Overriding automated safeties . . . power surge in ten seconds."

"The antimatter explosion is already draining," Tidal said. *Supreme* shuddered again, violently. "They're switching their attention back to us."

"Flash the drive," Paul ordered sharply. The aliens knew what they were doing. Even if they hadn't caught on earlier, they'd sense the vortex forming. If he didn't react quickly, they were doomed. "Open the vortex!"

"Aye, sir," Rani said. "Vortex in five . . . four . . ."

Supreme shook, again and again. Paul gritted his teeth. The sensors were almost completely offline. What remained wasn't enough to tell him if *Supreme* had been struck by the shockwave, or if the vortex was spinning out of control, or if the aliens were doing something to prevent them from escaping. He'd hoped to have observation teams in position along the promenade, but that plan had gone out the airlock. He honestly wasn't sure just how many crewmembers remained alive.

The gravity field twisted, just for a second. "Vortex opening," Rani snapped. *Supreme* lurched as if she'd been slapped by an angry god. "Power drain increasing . . . vortex destabilizing!"

"Take us forward," Paul ordered. They'd configured the vortex to produce a gravity well, but it was clear that the field wasn't strong enough to yank *Supreme* into the maelstrom. "Trigger all maneuvering jets!"

"Aye, Captain," Rani said. The ship bucked again. "Gravity field is failing . . ."

"Strap in," Paul said. If the compensators failed too, they were dead. There would be no hope of survival. "Take us into the vortex."

Supreme quaked. He looked up just in time to see lightning flickering over the overhead porthole. The edge of the vortex looked odd, as if it were unable to focus properly. Light, sickly green light, was bending out of shape, turning into long fingers . . . he told himself, firmly, that he was seeing things.

Jeanette swore. "Emergency alerts, decks . . ."

"Leave it," Paul ordered. The hull was creaking loudly, strange sounds echoing through the ship. He had the sudden impression that *Supreme* was about to be caught between an irresistible force and an immovable object. He'd never heard of a starship bent out of shape, let alone shattered, by gravitational force, but there was always a first time. "Concentrate on getting out."

"The vortex is failing," Rani reported. Paul could hear a hint of panic in her words. "I can't hold it!"

"Shunt all remaining power to the vortex generator," Paul ordered. "Take us through!"

His stomach clenched as *Supreme* plunged into the vortex. They were going . . . going somewhere. He dry-retched helplessly, silently praying that Rani would remain unaffected until they reached the other side of the vortex. His wristcom bleeped, a babble of voices reporting blown power linkages and expended power cells. He ignored them, even as the shaking grew stronger and stronger. They would either make it out or die in the lobster pot . . .

And then the hand of God reached out and slapped his ship.

———

"Hang on to something," Joan screamed. "Hurry."

Angela barely heard her over the creaking running through the entire ship. The noise was deafening, terrifying her. And yet, it wasn't what *truly* terrified her. She was staring at Nancy. Her sister looked . . .

"You will not escape," Nancy said. "You will . . ."

The girl threw back her head and started to scream, then crumbled onto the deck. Angela crawled forward, ignoring Joan's warnings, and wrapped her arms around her trembling sister. Nancy struggled frantically, but there was no strength in her body. She suddenly felt thin, helpless.

"It'll be all right," Angela said, although she had no idea if that was true. "I've got you."

She forced herself to keep hold of Nancy as her wails grew louder. The racket was terrifying, the shrieks blurring together into a single discordant howl. The shaking was growing worse . . . she thought she saw the bulkheads start to cave in on them before they stopped. Her head was spinning . . . she was no longer sure if there was a banging noise echoing through the ship or if her head was pounding like a drum. The gravity seemed to be changing rapidly, shifting upward and downward at random. She prayed, desperately, that it would end soon, for all of their sakes.

I'm sorry, she thought. She wasn't sure, in truth, what she was apologizing for. Did the universe hate her? Or had it set out to teach her a lesson? Or had she merely been in the wrong place at the wrong time, a victim of random chance? Cold logic told her that the latter was the most likely explanation, but she didn't really believe it. *I'm so sorry.*

The shaking grew worse and worse. The remaining lights snapped off, leaving them in utter darkness. Angela held Nancy tightly, wondering what had happened to their parents. Where *were* they? They should be with their daughters, shouldn't they? But . . . she swallowed hard, cursing herself. She wanted to go back to her birth and start again. She knew that was impossible . . .

And then, something changed.

———

Matt held on for dear life as the fanatics charged, screaming their incoherent battle cry. He lifted his pistol, promising himself that he would make every shot count, though he could barely hold the gun steady. The tiredness . . . and the shaking . . . made it impossible to aim . . .

And then the fanatics tumbled forward and hit the deck, like puppets whose strings had been cut. Matt stared in disbelief, exchanging a quick glance with Singh. The constable looked equally surprised, and suspicious, as the fanatics started to scream and whimper like children. The overwhelming sense of *threat* was gone . . .

. . . and so too were the voices.

———

Paul jerked up in his command chair as the universe seemed to shatter around him, then reform. He felt as though a weight had been lifted from his shoulders, as though a pane of dirty glass that had been blurring his view was gone. And the voices . . . the voices were gone.

"Flash-wake Fusion One and Three," he ordered. The other two fusion cores would require careful inspection before he risked trying to reactivate them. He wasn't too sure about the first set of cores, but without power they were doomed anyway. "Bring sensors online as soon as you can."

"Aye, Captain," Rani said.

Paul looked up. Darkness greeted him, darkness broken by pinpricks of light. He smiled in utter joy and relief. They were back in realspace . . . *somewhere* in realspace. And that meant . . . they were safe. He had no idea where they were—*that* would have to wait until they booted up the navigation computers—but at least they were out of the lobster pot. He felt . . . *alive.*

"Fusion One is warming up now," Tidal reported.

Jeanette looked up from her wristcom. "I'm getting reports from all decks," she said. "The . . . ah . . . mutineers have collapsed. I've got security teams trying to take advantage of it now to secure them."

Paul rubbed his forehead. Sorting out the good from the bad was going to be a nightmare. It was a point of law that no one could be held accountable for anything they did if they'd been mind-controlled, but . . . how did one determine what counted as mind control? The flickers hadn't used subversion implants or forced conditioning. They'd seduced people who were already tired, already prone to making mistakes. God alone knew what the courts would make of the incident.

"The vortex went . . . *odd*, at the end," Rani said. "I—"

Alarms howled. Paul jumped. "Report!"

"Shit," Rani said.

"I said *report*," Paul snapped. "What's happening?"

"Captain, we're heading right for a planet," Rani said. "We'll hit the upper atmosphere in five minutes!"

Paul blanched. There was no way that could be random chance. The flickers had managed to get one last kick in after all. He had no idea how they'd done it, but they'd done it . . . if that was a Commonwealth world, *Supreme* was about to be blown out of space. They wouldn't have a choice. Something the size of a cruise liner hitting a planet at speed would slaughter millions of innocent people.

"Reverse the drives," he snapped. *Supreme* might *just* have a chance. "Get us into a stable orbit!"

"I can't," Rani said. "The drive control system is fucked! We're going down!"

"Trigger the emergency beacon," Paul ordered. He glared at his console. Half the sensors were still offline. He didn't have the slightest idea if anything was out there. And if the planet was heavily defended, he doubted the defenders had any time to organize a rescue mission. They'd open fire before it was too late to save their world. "And ramp up the antigravity systems."

"Sir . . . half the antigravity pods are down," Tidal yelled. "I'm trying to boot them up now!"

"Do it," Paul snapped. "We're about to hit a planet!"

He forced himself to think. *Supreme* might make it down to the planet's surface reasonably intact. There would be no hope of getting the hulk back into space, of course, but he was past caring. And if they didn't . . . he cursed the flickers, savagely. Their parting gesture had been one of utter contempt for matter-based life.

The display brightened, updating rapidly as more and more systems came online. Paul silently thanked God for the multiple redundancies built into the ship, even though they'd been utterly useless in the lobster pot. Now, with power flowing into the distribution network again, the datanet was hastily reconfiguring itself to reroute around failed or cannibalized components. It would have given him hope, if he hadn't been all too aware that they were heading straight for the ground. If there was a city underneath, they were going to kill millions of innocent people.

No one has blown us out of space, he thought as *Supreme* hit the upper edge of the atmosphere. The shock nearly threw him out of his command chair. *The planet might be uninhabited.*

"Going down, sir," Rani said. "We're slowing our fall . . ."

Paul nodded. *Supreme* was just too large to hover like an aircar. The best they could do was slow their fall enough to prevent a major impact. He briefly considered triggering the self-destruct, but it was already too late. An explosion in the upper atmosphere would be very bad for the planet . . .

"Impact in thirty seconds," Rani reported. "All systems are straining . . ."

"Reroute all power to the antigravity pods," Paul ordered. The creaking grew louder, sending shivers down his spine. *Supreme* was tough, but her hull had taken a beating. "And I mean everything."

"Aye, sir," Rani said. "We're going down!"

Paul glanced at Jeanette. "Alert the passengers," he ordered. "Tell them to take up brace positions."

"Aye, sir," Jeanette said. "If they'll listen . . ."

"Do it," Paul said. Most of the passengers probably hadn't bothered to read the safety procedures. The instructions had initially been very short until Corporate's lawyers had gotten their hands on the text and insisted on major revisions. Now the instructions were multiple pages long and used ten words where one would do. "And then brace yourself."

"Aye, Captain," Jeanette said.

———

Matt forced himself to remain steady as the entire ship shook violently, the bulkheads shaking like a shuttle passing through particularly bad turbulence. He didn't know what it meant, let alone how to deal with it. Were they being sucked back into hell? Or had they run into another problem? He checked the fanatics one by one, confiscating their weapons. It looked as though they were no longer dangerous, but he took care anyway. He wouldn't turn his back on anyone for a long time.

"You might want to see this," Singh said. He was standing by the hatch, peering down the corridor towards the promenade. "Look!"

Matt walked up to him . . . and stared. Just for a second, his mind refused to accept what he was seeing. The giant windows should have shown the inky darkness of space . . . or the sickly light of the lobster pot. Instead . . . he saw blue sky and white clouds, rushing by at terrifying speed. The ship bucked and twisted again, shaking violently . . .

We're going to crash, Matt thought in horror. *We've come out in a planetary atmosphere!*

"Brace yourself," he snapped. The gravity field was twisting below his feet, growing stronger . . . they had to be about to hit the ground. "Get ready for—"

The deck came up and hit him. Matt found himself lying on the hard surface, unable to move. For a chilling moment, he thought he'd been paralyzed. A terrible crashing noise echoed through the air, pieces of debris hitting the ground. And then, somehow, he managed to force himself to stand and peer down at the windows. They were gone. Warm air was drifting into the ship.

He swallowed hard. He had no idea where they were, but . . . there might be something dangerous in the air. Or . . . he was breathing it. There was no point in worrying any longer. The windows might have looked fragile, but he knew how strong they were. If they'd broken, chances were that the entire ship was open to the atmosphere. They were already breathing the alien air.

"Shit," Singh said quietly.

Matt forced himself to walk down to the promenade. The deck was covered in pieces of transparent metal, just waiting for him to stumble. He picked his way between them as he walked up to what had once been a window. Careful to keep his distance from the jagged edges, he looked out onto a whole new world. *Supreme* had come down hard. Hundreds, perhaps thousands of tree trunks lay shattered on the ground. Beyond them, in the distance, he could see blue mountains rising into the sky.

"No sign of life," Singh said. Matt hadn't even heard the man following him. "No helicopters, no aircars . . ."

Matt looked at him. "Where *are* we?"

"God knows," Singh grunted. "But we might want to get used to it. We might be staying here a long time."

"Fuck," Matt said. A thought struck him. "Angela!"

He turned and ran back into the ship.

———

Angela picked herself off the deck, carefully. Nancy was lying next to her, tired and wan. Joan was bending over Marie, injecting her with some kind of stimulant. Some of the medical equipment seemed to be coming back online, lights flickering on darkened consoles as they rebooted. Carla groaned loudly as she sat upright. She didn't look pleased.

"All of the equipment will need to be tested," Joan said. The doctor seemed pissed. "I don't know how much can be trusted after . . . after *everything.*"

Carla nodded. "What happened?"

"I don't know," Joan said. "But the gravity feels odd."

Angela agreed. The gravity field felt a little heavier than she recalled. Or maybe she was just imagining it. She'd been outside a gravity field only a couple of times, both for zero-g sex. Everywhere else, the gravity field had been one-g.

The hatch opened. Matt hurried into the compartment.

"Angela," he said. "Are you all right?"

"She's fine," Carla said as Matt swept Angela into a hug. "What happened?"

"We crashed," Matt said.

Angela's mouth fell open. "We *crashed?*"

"You have got to be kidding me," Carla said. She rubbed her head. "I'm having a hallucination, right?"

"No," Matt said. "We're on a whole new world."

"Fuck," Carla said.

Angela looked up at Matt. "Where? I mean . . . where are we?"

"I don't have the slightest idea," Matt said. "But I can tell you that it's definitely not a stage-two or above colony world. None of *them* could have missed us passing through their atmosphere and crashing on their planet."

"Lucky they didn't kill us on sight," Carla offered. She stood, peering down at Finley's corpse. "You think we'll ever get home?"

"I don't know," Matt said.

"They did it," Nancy said.

Angela looked down at her sister. Nancy was awake.

Matt loosened his grip on her. "What do you mean?"

"I was aware of them," Nancy said. "I . . . they were *big*, so big I couldn't really grasp them. But I could feel them. They were angry that we would dare to escape, that we would succeed. They did something . . ." She shook her head. "I don't remember anything else."

Matt frowned. "We might have to consider it later," he said. "Right now . . . we have too many other problems."

"I should say so," Joan said. "Matt, report to the captain or whoever's in charge up there; Carla, go with him if you feel up to it. Angela, you and Nancy can help me get the rest of the equipment online. We'll have a lot of customers in a hurry."

"Understood," Matt said. He gave Angela a kiss on the forehead. "I'll see you later."

Angela smiled at him. "We could be anywhere, couldn't we?"

"We could be thousands of light-years from home," Matt agreed. "We might never see Tyre again."

"Go," Joan ordered.

Angela watched him leave, feeling conflicted. If she never went back to Tyre, she would never have to run the risk, again, of being married off to serve the family. She could build a new life somewhere else. But being on an alien world . . . who knew *what* would happen to them? She doubted survival would be easy. *Supreme* had become a battered wreck long before she crashed on their new home.

I'll just have to wait and see, she decided. *I have work to do.*

CHAPTER FORTY

"The insurance company isn't going to pay out on this," Robert Cavendish said. He sounded oddly amused despite the situation. "What a fucking mess."

Paul couldn't disagree. Two days after *Supreme* had crash-landed, his remaining crew and passengers had started to build a settlement. It wasn't much—he would have sold his soul for a colonist-carrier with all the tools and prefabricated buildings—but it was a start. *Supreme* was largely intact, yet her innards were a mess. There was no way they could live permanently in her hull, not for more than a year or two.

He looked down as the shuttle flew over the settlement. He'd ordered vessels to survey what they could of the alien world, but they'd found no trace of human life, or intelligent life in general. They were alone, as far as they could tell. And they still didn't have the slightest idea where they were. The civilians might cling to hope of rescue, but the spacers knew it wasn't going to happen. None of the stars Paul's sensors had noted before they'd crashed into the upper atmosphere matched any recorded in the database. That suggested, at the very least, that they were on the far side of the galaxy. They could, in fact, be a great deal farther away.

"I don't think we're going to see an insurance company ever again," he mused. "Or the Commonwealth."

Cavendish smiled. "It won't be that bad."

Paul gave him a sharp look. "Really?"

"I spent much of my life battling to shore up a corporate structure that was constantly on the verge of collapse," Cavendish said. "It was driving me insane. Balancing all those competing agendas, telling everyone that everything was fine and there was no reason to panic . . . I was sick of it, yet unable to leave. None of my potential replacements had the talent necessary to make the company hum.

"And now"—he waved a hand towards the settlement below—"I have a chance to start afresh and build something completely new."

"Really," Paul repeated dryly. He wanted to slap the older man . . . he *could* slap the older man. "Do you have any idea how bad it's going to be?" He let out a long breath. "Our survival gear is based on the assumption that any trouble we encountered would be in space," he said. "Most of our remaining tech is built to last, but not forever. We'll have to harvest crops from this world to survive . . . and we'll be screwed if we can't find anything to eat. Survival here, *My Lord*, means rediscovering skills most of us have never bothered to study. It's going to be a nightmare."

"It won't be easy," Cavendish agreed.

"No, it won't." Paul said. "And you do realize that your title means nothing here? None of the titles mean anything. You're no longer the man who gave up a dukedom to run a corporation. You're one old man of limited value to the community."

"I knew that the moment I realized we wouldn't be going home," Cavendish said tartly. "And I have no intention of forgetting it."

Paul silently gave him points for honesty. At least he'd recognized the truth. Others hadn't been so understanding. His men had already had to break up several fights between first-class and third-class passengers when the former hadn't been able to adjust to their new circumstances.

Losing all their servants, particularly when their servants had the talents necessary to survive on a whole new world, hadn't helped. But then it had been only two days. Perhaps they'd get better.

Sure, he told himself. Keeping the former fanatics working might prevent them from brooding on their submission to the aliens, but it wasn't easy. *And perhaps pigs will fly.*

"Very good," Paul said. He doubted Cavendish would last long. He had a great deal of genetic engineering spliced into his DNA, but he'd never had to do physical labor for a living. "Try to make sure the others don't forget it either."

"Yes," Cavendish said. He paused. "What do you think they *were*?"

Paul shrugged. Nancy Cavendish had insisted that the flickers had deliberately aimed *Supreme* at a planet, although it was just as likely they'd been trying to hurl the starship into a sun. Stars and planets *did* cast shadows into hyperspace, but if the flickers couldn't see into realspace, they might not have been able to tell the difference. He suspected, in the end, that it didn't matter. There was no way *Supreme* would ever fly again.

"I don't know," he said. He'd interviewed a number of people who'd been overwhelmed by the voices. They'd all agreed that the ever-increasing whispers had promised them whatever they wanted, but . . . they weren't sure if the voices had been real or if they'd heard what they wanted to hear. "I think they were *different*. Aliens so different to us that they didn't comprehend that we were intelligent, actualized beings."

"They taunted us, in the end," Cavendish said slowly. "I think they knew what we were. They just didn't care."

"Perhaps," Paul said. "Or perhaps we *thought* they were taunting us." He shook his head. "We were on the ship of the damned, weren't we?"

"Someone set us up," Cavendish agreed. He smiled rather thinly. "I don't think it matters any longer, Captain."

Paul nodded. The Commonwealth would realize, eventually, that *Supreme* and her passengers were missing. And then . . .

"It doesn't matter," he said as the shuttle came in to land. "We'll never know what happened back home once they realized we were gone. *This* world is our home now."

"And we'd better get to work taming it," Cavendish said. "It should be fun."

Paul sighed. He knew it wouldn't be remotely fun.

———

"All right," Matt called. "Start shoveling in the dirt now."

He picked up his shovel and tossed a hunk of dirt into the mass grave. The work party followed suit, a handful giving him nasty stares when they thought he wasn't looking. He'd already had to squash two attempted mutinies when a few former first-class passengers, some of whom had been Finley's cronies, had tried to argue that they were too good to do physical labor. Given that they were next to useless for anything else, Matt was convinced they were lucky they were getting fed at all.

"Not too bad," Carla muttered. "But keep going."

Matt nodded as the grave filled, the bodies being steadily buried under a pile of earth. The funeral had been basic—Captain VanGundy had said a few words—and he couldn't help feeling bad about it, even though he knew the survivors had no choice. They just didn't have the *time* to dig an individual grave for each body. He knew there were passengers who didn't like it—he didn't like it—but their feelings didn't matter. The cold imperatives of survival were all that mattered.

They can come to pray at the graveside, he thought morbidly. Finley's body was down there, somewhere. *Or leave flowers for all the dead.*

"Very good," he said when the grave was finally covered. "Go back to the kitchen and collect some food."

He watched as the workers hurried off, the former first-class passengers in the lead. They'd grab some food, then go back to work chopping up wood or drawing water from the nearby rivers. They weren't very good at it, yet it was all they could do . . . at least until they received some proper training in basic survival techniques. Matt had heard that the captain was drawing up a training schedule, but it would take some time to get everyone on the rota. Until then . . .

Carla nudged him. "Are you going to speak to Angela?"

Matt looked back at her. "Do you think I should?"

"If you want to pop the question, then yes," Carla said sardonically. "Not that *I* consider her to be much of a catch, of course . . ."

"She's trying," Matt defended her. "The doc said she was very useful."

"She's also completely untrained," Carla said. She sighed. "But she will probably pair up with someone else if you don't ask her."

Matt swallowed. "You're right," he said. "I'll go now."

Carla slapped his back. "I'm always right," she said. "And the sooner you realize that, the better."

"You're not always right," Matt said. "You're sometimes *left*."

He winked at her, then hurried towards *Supreme*. The giant ship loomed over him, casting the entire settlement into shadow. There was something profoundly *odd* about looking at her, even though she was half-buried in the soil. *Supreme* didn't belong on the ground, and everyone knew it. Matt pushed aside his feelings as he stepped through the airlock and navigated his way up to Sickbay.

At least the corridors are clearer now, he thought as he walked through the hatch. *The work parties did some good there.*

Angela was standing just inside Sickbay, speaking quietly to Susan as Joan ran a bone regenerator over her mother's arm. The little girl seemed to have adapted well to her new situation, Matt noted, although the young were always adaptable. He'd seen too many spoiled brats—each one only a few years older than Susan—screaming that they shouldn't have to work or they should have extra food. He hoped Susan wouldn't go that way.

"Thank you," Maris said when Joan had finished. "I feel better now."

"Don't put too much weight on that arm for a day or two," Joan said. She glanced at Matt. "Are you here for a reason, Mr. Evans?"

"Yes," Matt said. "Can I talk to Angela?"

Joan's lips thinned. "It is close enough to her break," she said. "Very well. But come back quickly."

"Thank you," Matt said. "Angela, can we go into the next room?"

"Sure."

Matt took a moment to study her as they walked into the private chamber. Angela looked as lovely as ever, but she seemed to have grown up over the last few days. Her eyes were haunted, even though she hadn't surrendered to the aliens. He couldn't help thinking that she wasn't in a good state . . . and yet, she was forcing herself to carry on anyway. There were other girls who'd been in first-class who weren't carrying on, as far as he could tell. *They* hadn't realized, yet, that there would be no going home.

"Angela," he said. He took a breath. Why was it suddenly so hard to talk? "I . . . will you marry me?"

Angela gave him a long look. "I . . ." She gazed down at the deck for a long moment. When she looked up, she was smiling. "If you'll have me, I'll have you," she said. "But . . . you do know you'll be marrying my family?"

Matt looked back at her. "Does that matter any longer?"

———

Angela honestly didn't know what to say. Her father seemed cheerful enough about winding up stranded on an uninhabited planet, while her mother had lapsed into a funk and refused to talk to anyone. But *she* wasn't sure how to deal with being stranded. On one hand, she *was* free of society and the social obligations that came with it; on the other hand, she was trapped in a vastly different world. The entire universe had turned upside down. Part of the reason she'd thrown herself into working for the doctor was because she knew she had no survival skills, nothing that made her valuable for building a settlement . . .

And yet Matt wasn't asking her for anything but herself.

They *couldn't* have gotten married on Tyre. She knew that, beyond a shadow of a doubt. But here . . . maybe they *could*. And maybe it would be *better* for her to marry into the new aristocracy. Girls like her, and boys like Finley's surviving cronies, were suddenly on the bottom, while their servants and the crew were on the top. No one cared who had been what on Tyre. All that mattered was what skills they had.

The irony gnawed at her even as she opened her mouth to give an answer. She'd escaped one marriage for the good of the family, only to fall right into a second . . . *also* for the good of the family. But it was also for her own good. She liked Matt, even loved him. She'd never expected the attraction to last—all the stories she'd heard about cruise-liner romances had ended with a parting and the lovers never seeing each other again—but they were stuck together now. There was no way they could go back to their separate lives . . .

And that, more than anything else, decided her.

"I will," she said. They were trapped on an unsettled world. They might as well make the most of it. "I *will* marry you."

And she leaned forward and kissed him.

───

Nancy was young, but she was no fool.

She'd spoken to dozens of people who'd been affected by the flickers, who'd heard the voices, ever since *Supreme* had crashed on the isolated world. Many of them—most of them—had chosen to believe that they'd imagined everything, that the combination of the alien realm, starvation, and panic had driven them temporarily insane. They blamed

Brother John and his fellows for leading them into a desperate fight to keep *Supreme* from escaping the alien realm . . .

Nancy knew better.

The experience had a vague dreamlike quality, but she knew it had been real. The voices had been real. The sense of being surrounded by something much greater than herself had been real. And when they'd spoken through her, she'd sensed . . . something . . . that could have swatted her like a bug if it had truly understood her. The flickers had been so *different* that she couldn't parse their thoughts.

But they were hungry.

She was in realspace now, but she could still hear them. They were hungry . . .

. . . and waiting, waiting for the next starship to enter their realm.